"YOU PLAN TO HOLD ME CAPTIVE?"

Count Vahnti released Rayna's wrists abruptly and ran the end of his thumb along the curve of her defiant jaw. "Not quite. The word *captive* denotes a temporary state, and I assure you, there is nothing temporary about your situation."

The thought of being held in bondage to him was more than she could bear. "If not a captive, what am I then?"

"My possession," he said in a matter-of-fact voice.

Disbelief and anger warred in her expression. "Slavery is illegal!"

He grinned down at her, a dark wolfish smile that displayed even, white teeth. "We don't use terms like slavery in Dominion society. Forfeiture is a much better word. In case you were unaware, the assassination or attempted murder of a clan lord is a treasonable offense under Dominion law. If caught, the assassin's life is forfeit . . . bound forever to the clan or lord he injured."

His thumb brushed over her trembling mouth. "The moment you raised a weapon to me, you became my possession. . . . I own you, Rayna Syn, body and soul."

Other *Love Spell* books by Jan Zimlich:
NOT QUITE PARADISE

HEART'S Prey

JAN ZIMLICH

LOVE SPELL BOOKS   NEW YORK CITY

For Louis and Ryan, the men in my life.
And
The Deep South Writers Salon:
Rebecca Barrett, Carolyn Haines, Renee Paul,
Stephanie Rogers, and Susan Tanner.
True friends all.

LOVE SPELL®

September 1998

Published by

Dorchester Publishing Co., Inc.
276 Fifth Avenue
New York, NY 10001

ISBN 0-505-52277-2

The name "Love Spell" and its logo are trademarks of Dorchester Publishing Co., Inc.

Printed in the United States of America.

HEART'S Prey

Chapter One

Nirvanna's sun slipped beneath the horizon, and a clear, true night snuggled down across the fertile Lakota plain. The sky, peaceful and dusky gray just a moment before, turned a dense, empty black. The night thickened, a darkness so still and complete that time itself seemed to pause. Twin moons rose in graceful tandem, slender crescents that brushed the low hills and endless sea of prairie grass with pools of silver. Then a myriad of stars blazed to sudden, violent life, a dense wash of golden light that heralded the rise of the galactic core.

The old man lifted his head and stared at the distant heavens, awed, as always, by the terrible beauty of Nirvanna's night sky. Around his stooped frame, the tall prairie grass rippled and swayed, the soft sighing sound like a gentle surf rolling onto a nearby shore.

His ancient eyes narrowed, straining to see in the darkness, but his ears, old though they were, could still hear the spirits' voices. The grass and wind and stars were whispering, reminding him that it was nearly time.

The signs and portents were there, had been for more years than he cared to remember. His gnarled fingers tightened around his wooden staff. A great change was coming, riding the night wind. He could feel its coming in the marrow of his bones. His beloved world, the peaceful coexistence with the spirits and nature that his people had always known, was about to end.

Javan Syn, last shaman of Nirvanna's seven human tribes, bowed his head, gray hair rippling about his bent shoulders. He prayed to the gods that his sacrifice would be accepted, begged for guidance and wisdom and strength. Strength most of all. He would need an abundance of that in the approaching hours.

A tiny night creature stirred in the thick, reedlike grass, round, iridescent eyes peering up at him curiously. The furry creature edged closer, unafraid.

"Go," Javan whispered. "Save yourself. Hide until sunrise."

As the gi scampered away, Javan cast one final look at the endless vista of sky and grass, then walked slowly down the crest of the hill, back to the sprawling village cradled in the valley below.

A hundred warriors waited at the base of the narrow footpath, cinders from their torches drifting on the chilly wind like a swarm of flameflies. Their eyes followed the shaman's every footfall and searched his time-worn face anxiously.

Javan kept walking, and the milling throng of warriors parted reverently to allow him passage through their midst. No one spoke; no one asked the question uppermost in their minds. The tears coursing down the shaman's wizened cheeks were answer enough.

The warriors fell into step behind him, moving slowly toward a hazy circle of firelight glittering on the far side of the valley. Flames from a thousand ceremonial fires danced and weaved in the darkness, creating the circular effect. As they walked, shadows played across the coarse mud walls and low thatched roofs of countless village huts, the unpretentious homes of the twenty-thousand-strong Lakota tribe.

The drums began their rhythmic pounding as the warriors approached the circle of light, the throbbing sound reverberating over the valley floor like the echo of distant thunder.

Javan's people were waiting, huddled shoulder to shoulder around the warmth of the fires, a quiet, endless ocean of unmoving humanity.

As he walked to a dais at the center of the circle, Javan steeled his heart and soul against what was to come. The drumming stopped, and silence reigned once again. Even the children were quiet, the collective tension hushing their whines and wails far better than a mother's admonishing words.

He climbed the log staircase with slow, deliberate steps, each footfall sounding loud and hollow in the stillness of the night. Destiny awaited, in the small, supple form of his beloved granddaughter.

Arms outstretched to embrace Nirvanna's night, Rayna Syn knelt motionless atop the dais, eyes closed, knees and legs nestled in the thick white fur of a snowbear hide. Firelight danced across her fragile features, and the wind lifted a long cascade of russet hair, curling its length about shoulders too slender to bear the fate of an entire world.

"Daughter of my daughter," the old shaman whispered, tears burning hot and bright in his cloudy eyes. "Heart of my heart."

Rayna sucked in a sharp breath, her mind gradually withdrawing from the Inner World; then her lids drifted open to reveal eyes of luminous green. "Grandfather," she said in a low, throaty voice. "What news do you bring?"

He could feel the preternatural heat of her emerald gaze, the power and strength hidden in the depths of those guileless eyes. "The portents are unchanged." Javan offered a hand to help her rise. "The time of the prophecy is at hand."

She clasped his gnarled fingers and rose to her feet with the grace and rippling ease of a forest cat. The dark silk of her loincloth fluttered in a freshening breeze, and the diagonal bands of black painted across her face and chest and arms glistened wetly in the haze of firelight. She touched the carved hilt of the knife strapped at her waist, reassuring herself for the hundredth time that the cold length of steel was where it should be. Her gaze held her grandfather's, and the edges of her full mouth curled in a confident smile. "I am prepared. The demon lord shall meet his end tonight."

9

Jan Zimlich

The old shaman pulled her against his chest and embraced her lightly, mindful of the tribe's watching eyes. To do more, as his heart demanded, would display his fear for all to see. He had to be strong, for all their sakes. "May the gods go with you, child." His withered fingers closed about her hand once again, clasping her flesh to his with a strength that belied his years.

Together they faced the sea of anxious faces standing before them, young and old, warriors and women with babes in arms, all waiting silently for their shaman to speak.

"People of the Lakota tribe," Javan began, his powerful voice echoing on the chill night wind. "The evil times foretold by my father, and his father before him, have finally come. For a thousand years our people have lived upon this land . . . nurtured it, protected it, and been nurtured in return. We have indeed been blessed."

He was silent for a moment, struggling against a wave of sadness more powerful than any he had ever known. When he finally spoke again, his voice was raw, ragged with emotion. "But now the unthinkable has occurred, and all that we have, all that is sacred to us, could soon be lost." Grief crept over his sun-weathered features. "The serpent has come to cast us out of paradise. This demon's spawn lusts for Nirvanna's bounty and has ordered that we leave the plains, our homes . . . uproot our children and begin new lives in a strange land half a world away."

A sound akin to a moan flowed through the crowd. Near the dais, an old crone, her face a maze of wrinkles, keened in an anguished voice.

Javan bowed his head in despair. "The spirits have told me that it is useless to fight any longer, that we are no match for the serpent's evil magic. Our brothers the Pawnee, the Cherokee, the Kansans, and the Texans have already been defeated by the serpent and his minions, and their tribes are now scattered to the four winds."

In the shocked silence that followed the terrifying news, the shaman suddenly lifted his head, his ancient gaze sweeping across the blackened sky, searching for what his senses told him was there. Beyond the low hills, a glimmer of light moved like a silent wraith across Nirvanna's heavens, then another and another, a tiny cluster of manmade stars arcing downward toward the Nirvannan plains.

Rayna followed her grandfather's gaze and shivered. "The serpent has come," she whispered.

Others stared at the strange formation of stars streaking through the night. The keening grew louder, more wrenching, as the sound spread to a thousand lips.

"Take heart!" Javan told them, shouting to be heard over the crescendo of noise. "Remember the prophecy! We will gather our belongings and leave the valley tonight! We will be like the mist. The serpent cannot force us to leave our land if we can't be found! Go now! Prepare yourselves!"

The crowd began to move, slowly at first, then with more urgency, hurrying to their huts to retrieve the bundles of food and clothing they had prepared for the long journey north.

The stars were still falling, pinpoints of light raining from the distant heavens. No, not stars, or meteors, or any cosmic creation, Javan reminded himself. These were something infinitely worse. His fingers trembled as he pulled a small leather pouch from his tunic and pressed it into Rayna's hand. "A gift, child, to protect you."

Rayna stared at the bit of string and black leather cupped in her palm, the same amulet her grandfather had worn on his neck for as long as she could remember. Her emerald eyes moved to his weathered face. "Grandfather, this is yours. I can't take it."

"Take it, Rayna." He lifted a bony hand and moved his palm in a slow half circle around her head and shoulders. "Along with my blessing."

She smiled and slipped the leather cord over her head. The amulet slid downward, where it came to rest nestled between her bare breasts. "Thank you," Rayna said raggedly. "I'll wear it always."

"Cunning and strength, child." He touched her cheek with a fingertip one last time. "Cunning and strength."

She met his gaze for a long moment, knowing she might never see him again. "I love you, Grandfather." Then she slipped down the steps and was gone, her sinewy legs carrying her into the night. Rayna raced onward, the orange glow of campfires and the faces of her people flashing past her as she ran. But no one spoke to her or tried to stop her. They knew where she was going and why.

Her footsteps quickened, swift and silent, tawny hair billowing behind her like the voluminous folds of a ceremonial cape. The village faded in the distance, visible only by the haze of countless fires.

Rayna plunged headlong into the vast sea of prairie grass, darting unerringly between the tall golden stalks. She sprinted up a hillside, a sense of anticipation pulsing through her blood. This was the moment, the night she had spent a lifetime preparing for.

I will not fail, Rayna told herself, repeating it over and over again as she ran toward her fate. Chest heaving, she paused at the crest of a hill to catch her breath. Around her, the thick grass swayed and shifted in a fitful wind. The moons had reached their apogee, two milky crescents poised at midsky before beginning their slow descent. Time was short.

Her breathing steadied and her lids slowly closed. Tension faded from her features as she allowed her mind to drift on Nirvanna's currents. A chant no louder than a whisper escaped her lips, the sound of her quiet murmuring lost in the wind and grass. Then she touched a fist to her forehead and reached out with her mind.

As always, the massive wolfens were the first to answer her call, panting and whining in joy as they padded toward her through the grass. Rayna lifted an arm to shoulder level, greeting the first three beasts with a swift scratch between their upright ears. Tongues lolling from enormous maws, the yellow-furred wolfens whined happily, long rows of needlelike fangs gleaming whitely in the moonlight.

''Good boys,'' Rayna whispered as several more padded out of the shadows.

The grass rustled as other night creatures began answering her call, near-elk and grasscats, as well as scores of tiny newts and gi.

The animals waited, mewling, chirping, and growling, knowing eyes fixed on the human who had summoned them.

"We have work to do," Rayna said quietly. "Dangerous work."

Chapter Two

An explosion of sound rent Nirvanna's night, a thundering, ground-trembling roar that shattered the quiet peace of the Lakota plain. Plumes of steam and flame gouted from a hundred landing thrusters as an immense black starship bled momentum and settled onto Nirvanna's shuddering earth.

"Honor guard!"

A hatchway dilated open and a long metal gangway slid soundlessly to the ground.

"Take your positions!"

Battle armor gleaming dully in the moonlight, a squadron of soldiers marched into view, forming two long lines leading out from the ship's metallic hull.

A tall, black-clad figure moved into a pool of light spilling from the hatchway, steam curling about his dark form like a wispy fog.

"Ten-hut!" the commanding officer shouted.

Visored eyes cutting to the gangway, the honor guard snapped to attention, right arms striking their hearts in the clan salute.

Count Daxton Vahnti, hereditary ruler of Hellfire, Arkanon, the Logo colonies, and a score of lesser worlds in the Dominion, warlord of the ever-powerful Vahnti clan, acknowledged the salute with a single nod. He paused in the hatchway for a moment, cold, pale eyes surveying Nirvanna's unfamiliar terrain, then strode briskly down the gangway to the ground below.

An officer broke ranks with the honor guard and quick-stepped forward. He stopped and clicked his heels, his head dropping forward in a formal bow. It was an archaic gesture from another time, another world. "Welcome to Nirvanna, Count Vahnti."

The stern-visaged count arched an ebony brow. "An impressive display of protocol, Commander. It would seem that your months on this godforsaken world have improved your manners considerably."

"You did call me an ill-mannered boor the last time we met." Armor creaked as the officer lifted his shoulders in a shrug. "I hoped to prove you wrong."

A faint smile touched the corners of Vahnti's firm mouth. "No chance of that. You'll always be an ill-mannered boor, Haywood."

Haywood March, military commander of the Vahnti troops, slipped the visored helmet from his balding head and grinned. "Good to see you, too, Dax."

The smile Vahnti gave him in return was genuine but restrained, one befitting a warlord in front of his troops. Haywood had been in his family's employ for over a score of years, an old and trusted retainer whose counsel had been sorely missed in the past six months. "Now that you've proved me wrong, let's dispense with the formalities and get to the business at hand." His piercing blue eyes met and held the soldier's. "Word travels, Haywood. I hear you've run into a bit of a problem."

Haywood blew out a noisy breath and dismissed the honor guard with a wave of his hand. He'd hoped to have a little time before the talk turned to the colonists. In fact, he'd hoped the count wouldn't come to Nirvanna at all, much less arrive in the midst of a rebellion. But that wasn't Vahnti's style. Haywood sighed. "It hasn't gone well," he admitted.

The corners of Vahnti's mouth tightened, and his lips settled into a flat, grim line. "A full-scale war with my own subjects wasn't exactly what I had in mind when I agreed to your plan to relocate the colonists to another continent."

"It wasn't what I had in mind, either," Haywood said ruefully.

14

There was a bellowing roar behind them as a huge ore ship landed on a nearby hill. Overhead, a second mining ship lumbered past, exhaust from its engines lighting the sky as it banked toward the south.

Vahnti scowled but said nothing. His clan's reserves of platinum and beryllium had fallen to dangerously low levels months ago, a shortfall that would prove disastrous if it wasn't righted soon. They needed the Nirvannan ores desperately, but sporadic fighting had reduced mining activities on the planet to almost nothing in the past few weeks.

He touched Haywood's arm and led him toward a dense thicket of grass near the landing field, out of earshot of his troops and any interested spies. "What happened, Haywood? The relocation and mining operations were supposed to be well under way by now."

"It's the damnable colonists." Haywood shook his head in frustration, a frown shadowing his square-jawed face. "I've never seen the like, Dax. They're primitives living out some sort of old-Earth fantasy. The tribes were given the word months ago, but thousands of them simply refuse to leave the plains. They say we're desecrating sacred ground with our mining, and that they're justified in using whatever force is necessary to stop us and protect their way of life." A trace of wonder shone in the soldier's dark eyes. "They've actually attacked us with spears and arrows, Dax. Stone Age weapons against troops armed with pulse rifles and laser cannon!"

The count eyed him curiously. "You almost sound as if you admire them, Haywood."

"Admire their actions?" He shook his head slowly. "They're fools to stand against us. But I must admit I admire their tenacity. There's a certain nobility in refusing to relinquish their land against such overwhelming odds."

Vahnti's hooded blue eyes sharpened and turned cold. "*Their* land? I own this world, Commander. This star system has been part of my family's holdings for over two thousand years, and those people you seem to admire so much have lived upon our world at our sufferance. They were temporary guests here, nothing more. This continent was never theirs to take or defend!"

A long breath rattled up from Haywood's chest and seemed to stick in his throat for a moment; then he expelled it in a raspy sigh. "I know the clan history, Dax, and I agree with your assessment wholeheartedly. It's just that the last months have been difficult, to say the least, dealing as we have with thousands of fanatics bent on committing suicide. But the end is in sight now. The last of the seven tribes is on the run, and I hope to take their rabble-rousing shaman into custody by dawn tomorrow."

"Shaman?" Vahnti had heard the word before, but couldn't remember what it meant.

"The Nirvannans' spiritual leader. My spies tell me he's been manipulating events behind the scenes. He's just an old man, nearly a hundred years old from what I've heard, but the colonists respect him and listen to him. They even believe he has some sort of magical, mystical power."

Dax Vahnti snorted in disbelief. Now he remembered the ancient term. It was from a text on Earth history he'd read as a boy. "He's a medicine man."

"A what?"

"Never mind. It's not important. Just take the shaman into protective custody before he stirs up any more trouble." For a fraction of time, the cool veneer of detached nobility slid from Vahnti's features, replaced by a troubled frown. The relocation plan had been designed to prevent bloodshed, not create it. Perhaps a wiser course would have been to come clean with the colonists, elicit their cooperation instead of their animosity, but the fewer who knew the truth, the better for all concerned. If word leaked before his clan was ready . . .

The count's frown vanished abruptly, and his face resettled into dispassionate lines. It was too late to change direction now. "Order the troops to use as little force as possible, but to get the job done. The relocation must be completed within the next few weeks without fail. The first of the harvesting ships will be here in a little over a month, and word will spread soon after that. I want those colonists to be far from the open plains when the other clans get wind of what we've been up to."

"Thy will be done, oh great lord and master."

The count's eyes turned colder than usual, but a hint of amusement glinted in their pale depths. "As I said, you'll always be an ill-mannered boor."

Haywood laughed, greatly relieved that the count's dark mood had lifted just a bit. "A little food and a few goblets of Logo wine should put you in a better frame of mind. But first I have a surprise for you." He signaled a waiting soldier. "How about a quick ride before we dine?"

A spark of interest flared in the count's solemn face. "A ride?"

The soldier sprinted off, returning a moment later with two mammoth horses in tow. Dax smiled. They were krulls, actually, the towering, three-toed beasts that passed for horses in this part of the galaxy. Close enough. True horses were a rarity. "Gladly. It's been weeks since I breathed unfiltered air."

"I thought as much." With the help of a young soldier, Haywood heaved himself atop the smaller of the furry beasts, saving the larger, more nervous one for Dax. Of the two of them, Dax was by far the more accomplished rider, experience gained from the stable of real horses he kept at Drakken Castle.

"I must say I'm surprised, Haywood. Riding has never been high on your list of favorite pastimes."

"Krullback is the best way to get around on the plains." The soldier adjusted his stirrups. "The grass has grown so high in some areas that you can barely see the sky."

Dax easily mounted the ten-foot beast and took the reins. "Where to?" The krull flattened its ears in response to his weight and skittered around in a nervous circle.

"Across that line of low hills." Haywood pointed south. "Our troops are moving into position. They're scheduled to enter the shaman's village before daybreak."

"Good. I'd like to see the operation firsthand. And I want to meet the old man who's caused us so much trouble."

"I wouldn't be surprised if the shaman wanted to meet you, too," Haywood said. "Word is, he even has a new name for you. My spies have heard the natives whispering it among themselves."

"Oh?" A brittle smile crossed the count's chiseled features. The Nirvannans had been calling him the demon lord for years. "And what is that?"

"He calls you 'the serpent.' "

The count wasn't the least bit amused. His gaze turned a freezing, glacial blue, and a forbidding scowl settled over his face. He was the serpent come to cast the righteous out of paradise.

"Ya!" Dax slapped the reins against his mount's huge neck. The krull grunted and lumbered toward the hills at a swift trot, forcing Haywood to follow suit.

They rode into the reedlike grass side by side, a contingent of mounted bodyguards following at a slower pace. As the minutes passed, and they rode deeper into the sea of grass, Dax began to understand what Haywood had meant. If not for the krull's great height, he would barely be able to see through the stalks to Nirvanna's darkened sky.

His grim mood gradually lifting, Dax stared at the star-strewn heavens, enjoying the view, the feel of the krull's sin-ewy muscles rippling beneath his thighs. He dug his heels into the krull's sides and forced the animal to increase its speed. Haywood and his mount soon fell behind, lost in the shadows and towering grass.

The terrain rushed by, long tendrils of grass whipping about his legs and arms. Ebony hair streaming behind him, Dax urged the krull to even greater speed, exhilarated by the sense of freedom and release afforded by the ride.

A blur of gold suddenly leaped across the krull's path. The skittish beast screamed and reared in fear, its bony hooves striking at empty air. Dax struggled to keep his seat, his thighs and arms straining to control the panicked beast. There was a low, feral growl to his right; then something large and heavy slammed into the krull's withers. The krull squealed and top-pled sideways, its massive body careening downward at a heart-stopping speed. Dax threw himself in the opposite direction. Better to face the unknown creature lurking in the grass than be crushed to death by three tons of thrashing krull flesh.

As he rolled to a stop amidst a jumble of trampled grass, a

tiny creature with glowing eyes sank its teeth into the back of his hand. Dax gave the creature a fleeting glance, then ignored it. A beast that small was the least of his worries now. The krull had clambered upright and galloped away, and with it his only avenue of escape. His heartbeat drummed in his ears as he climbed to his feet and peered into the shifting shadows, trying to gauge the amount of danger he was in.

The grass came alive with snarls and eyes, and an army of animals charged from the darkness. A huge flash of gold sprang through the air and slammed into his chest, the impact squeezing the air from his lungs and knocking them both to the ground. The beast leaped atop him, its curved fangs only inches above his face. As a swarm of smaller creatures descended on him, nipping at his legs and arms, Dax locked his hands about the golden beast's throat to fend off the deadly teeth.

"Dax!"

He could hear Haywood and the bodyguards shouting and crashing through the grass, but couldn't tell how far away they were. Knife-sharp teeth tore through the armor protecting his torso, and his world narrowed to the fangs and luminous yellow eyes of the beast poised above him. A spasm of pain ripped through his left shoulder but he continued to fight, his muscles screaming in agony as he struggled to hold the creature at bay.

There were shouts around him, bursts of green light from a dozen pulse rifles. Animals squealed in pain and rushed off into the night. The creature crouched above him growled, a rumbling, furious sound. Saliva dripped onto his face as its fangs snapped at his throat. More green light lanced the darkness, sizzling the air just inches above his head. Then the beast yelped and went limp, collapsing atop his chest.

Dax remained utterly still, more concerned now by the soldiers' panicked firing than the fangs of any beast. Seconds passed, punctuated by animal yelps and flashes of green. There were scuttling, scurrying sounds in the grass around him but they were fading into the distance.

"Cease fire!" Dax yelled into the darkness. "They're retreating!"

He pushed the limp carcass from his chest and rolled onto his hands and knees, crawled a few feet, then collapsed back onto the ground, trying to gather his wits and breath. A sudden jab of pain made him glance at his hand. The incessant little creature with the glowing eyes was still chewing on the back of his hand, and doing a good job of it, too. Dax jerked the animal free and tossed it into the grass. It squeaked and scampered away.

Light from a dozen hand torches daggered through the shadows, the beams cutting back and forth across the grass and dark. "Dax!" Haywood yelled, his voice raspy with fear. He crashed through a curtain of grass into the little clearing created by the animals' rampage and came to an abrupt stop.

The Vahnti count managed to pull himself up on his elbows. "A little worse for wear, but I'm still here."

For a split second, Haywood simply stared around him in disbelief. There were animal carcasses strewn everywhere. "By the gods, what happened here?" He rushed to Dax's side and moved a hand torch over the count's body, searching for wounds.

"You tell me." Dax sucked in a ragged breath and shook his head. "A pack of animals just rushed out of the grass and attacked." He winced as a wave of pain stabbed through his shoulder. "One of the larger beasts managed to rip through my armor. It hurts, but it's nothing the meds can't fix."

The light moved, shining on Dax's shoulder and the blood-soaked ground beside him. The hand torch stilled, as well as Haywood's rugged face. "Since when do animals carry knives?" he said quietly.

"What?"

Haywood picked up the bloody, double-edged knife and examined it under the light. The hilt was ornate, with a delicate filigree etched into the gleaming silver. The design was unusual, one he'd never seen before, but he would stake his career that it had been wrought by native hands. He glanced at the enveloping darkness warily. Someone out there wanted the Vahnti warlord dead.

Dax stared at the knife in confusion. His attackers had all

been four-legged, a snarling mass of fur and teeth and claws. "That's impossible."

Soldiers were moving around the clearing, examining the dead and injured animals. "Commander March!" one of them yelled. "Come have a look at this."

Overhead, a scad-about flew into view, landing lights blinking in a steady rhythm as the pilot hovered in preparation to land. Several combat ships streaked past, searchlights turning the night to day as they scanned for signs of Count Vahnti's attackers.

Dax climbed to his feet before Haywood had a chance to object. "Wait for the evac shuttle, Dax. The meds will be here in a moment."

He waved a hand in a curt gesture of dismissal. "Later. I want to see what that soldier found." Still a bit unsteady, Dax walked unaided to where the soldier was standing, light from the hand torch he held illuminating a pale, still form crumpled on the ground. The Vahnti count's brows lifted in amazement. It was a woman, a girl really, no older than seventeen or eighteen if he was any judge. Small and reed-thin, she was curled on her side amidst the trampled grass, a shower of thick, coppery curls fanning over her slender frame. Feathers were twined in her hair, as well as several strings of colorful beads.

Haywood threw him a questioning look. "A pack of animals, you said?" He frowned and spoke into his wristcom, ordering the combat ships to expand the search.

Dax continued to stare at the girl, his brows threatening to vanish beneath a dark shock of tousled hair. Her chest and back and arms were painted with wide bands of black that met in strange diagonal lines. Across her face the stripes were horizontal, the widest one painted masklike across her eyes. Even her lids were blackened, giving the eerie impression that she had no eyes. She was naked, too, or nearly so, her only clothing a scrap of black material tied around the delicate curve of her waist. "I never saw her," Dax whispered, unable to tear his eyes from the sight of her full, young breasts.

"Must have been hit when my men started firing," Haywood said, glad that the mystery had been solved. The native girl must have been hiding in the grass, and while Dax was busy trying to fend off the crazed animals, she had thrown the knife to rid Nirvanna of the evil "serpent." It was even possible that she'd drugged the animals as well, made them rampage by administering some exotic chemical. A ridiculously simple plan, one that had come frighteningly close to success.

The girl moaned, no more than a low exhalation of breath, but for some reason Dax was profoundly relieved to hear that ragged sound. She was alive—injured, obviously, but very much alive.

A young leftenant, his face invisible beneath his helmet's glassy visor, came to full attention. "Commander March, sir, the brigade commander reports that the native village is completely deserted, and that no other hostiles have been spotted within five square miles. As for the animals, those that weren't killed outright have fled, save for a few too badly injured to run."

"Round up the survivors double-quick," March ordered. "I want those maddened beasts taken back to Count Vahnti's ship for a full biochemical scan. For all we know they might be diseased. And order a full-scale scan of this section of the continent. There were at least twenty thousand natives in that valley. Those damnable people couldn't have vanished into thin air."

As the leftenant rushed off, Haywood turned his attention back to the girl and found Dax bending over her, staring curiously into her slack face. "Dax, not so close. She may be faking. These natives are a cunning lot, and the best guerrilla fighters I've ever seen."

"Not cunning enough to fake a laser burn this size." His hand moved down her leg, strong fingers probing gently at the circle of charred flesh marring the outside of a perfect thigh. "She needs the meds more than I do."

His pale eyes were drawn back to her face again, lingering briefly on the soft curve of her painted breasts. Something fierce and primitive stirred in his blood. There was a look of wildness about her that intrigued him, an elemental air of savagery and danger that harkened back to humankind's earliest days. He trailed a fingertip across the smooth plane of her cheek, running it down the horizontal stripes. Would that air of savagery be there without the paint? Would the eyes trapped beneath those blackened lids reveal an untamed spirit that matched her feral form?

Dax wasn't certain. And in that instant he realized that he wanted to know, wanted to wash the layers of paint and barbarity away to discover what was hidden beneath. "So very beautiful," he murmured under his breath.

Haywood sighed and shook his head. He'd seen that heated look in Dax's eyes far too often not to know what it signified. "And so very dangerous."

"Yes, that, too." The hue of his eyes turned a hot, smoky blue, and his lips curled in a dangerous smile. "Have the meds tend her; then take her to my ship. I leave for Hellfire in the morning."

"Don't risk yourself like this, Dax, not on a whim. The girl is a prisoner, an assassin who came close to taking your life tonight." A knot of dread formed in Haywood's chest. She'd already tried to kill him once and would surely try again. "I took a blood-oath to serve the Vahnti Warlord. Your word is law, but I'm also duty-bound to protect you—even against yourself."

"Fine," Dax said tersely, "if you feel compelled to protect me from myself, by all means do so. But you'll have to accompany me to Hellfire to do it. I leave at first light, and the girl goes with me." The tension faded from his face and voice. Haywood was only doing his job. He was also the only being in the universe Dax considered a friend. "Besides, you've spent far too long on this accursed world. It's time you returned to civilization."

There was a tone of finality in his voice that told Haywood the subject was closed to further discussion. Still, he continued to press. "Dax, please reconsider. The girl is dangerous."

The Vahnti warlord smiled thinly. "There's an old Earth saying I heard once: 'Hold your friends close, and your enemies closer still.' "

Chapter Three

Rayna awakened by slow degrees. Breath was moving in and out of her lungs, a low, raspy sound no louder than a sigh. She flexed a finger experimentally, then another, aware in a dull sort of way of a burning, itching throb in her upper thigh. But where there was breath and movement and sound, there was life. She moved a hand, and something soft and cool slid beneath her palm. Softer than a snowbear's pelt, more luxurious than anything she had ever felt. Strange sensations. Alien.

A rush of fear crawled up her spine, and she willed her body to remain utterly still. *Think,* Rayna told herself; *pretend unconsciousness until you remember where you are.* Her senses came alive, heightened by the surge of fear. The air smelled different, fresh and clean but strangely bland, lacking the thick, sweet scents of grass and soil. A haze of light burned behind her closed lids, but it wasn't the brilliant white created by Nirvanna's sun, or the flickering shadows made by a campfire. Artificial, then, and that frightened her even more.

There was another scent in the air, too, pleasant and tantalizingly familiar. She sniffed delicately, careful not to move. It was a heady, masculine scent that hinted of leather and sweat and something else, something indefinable that plucked at a thread of memory. . . .

Rayna gasped and bolted upright, her heartbeat thundering in her ears. Her panicked gaze swept back and forth across the strange white room and sparse furnishings, then stilled abruptly. A dark, deathly chill crept through her veins.

He was there. Watching her through those hooded, serpent eyes. Tears of rage and frustration threatened to spill down her cheeks. She had failed her world, her people, doomed them all. The demon lord still lived.

Across the well-appointed cabin, the Vahnti count folded his arms across his chest and watched a series of conflicting emotions chase across the girl's arresting face. First pain, then a wild surge of grief and rage. He smiled slowly, intrigued. She was obviously furious that he was still alive.

Enjoying the view, Dax leaned forward and rested his elbows on the arms of a deep, plush chair swathed in Arkanon silk. His pale gaze darkened as he watched the woman sitting in his bed, the lower half of her lithe body hidden beneath a pile of pillows and stark white satin. Without the hideous black stripes, she was even more magnificent than he had envisioned. Her well-scrubbed skin was smooth and bronze, burnished to a rosy glow by a lifetime spent beneath Nirvanna's sun. Tawny hair streamed down her chest and arms in a curly cascade that shifted when she breathed. Her eyes were the largest surprise, though, a sight well worth the hours he'd spent waiting for her to waken from a drug-induced sleep. They were a deep, rich green, a brilliant, jewel-toned hue that glittered with an eerie inner flame.

No doubt about it: he was going to enjoy this hunt immensely. She was an enchanting contrast to the droll, pampered beauty of the women he had known, the stultifying legion of well-bred ladies who were part and parcel of the Dominion Court. He knew them well, and had played their boring little games of capture and conquest until he'd grown weary of it all. He had always been cast in the role of hunter, and they the terrified prey. The only problem was that they had never run very fast or far at all.

This time would be different. The girl's savage vitality enthralled him. Even the air around her seemed supercharged, crackling with a current of tension and danger that made him feel alive for the first time in a number of years. If she pleased him, he might even keep her when he was finished.

His heart rate quickened at the prospect of the coming days. "I'm glad to see you've rejoined the world of the living."

Rayna tensed and offered up a silent prayer. His voice was deep and hoarse, roughened by some dark emotion she'd never heard before. Like the low growl of a wolfen at the instant it charged its prey. She watched him warily but didn't speak.

25

"Sorry to disappoint you by remaining alive." He ran the tip of a finger across his mouth, the nail gliding over lips that were generous but firm. "You should have planned your attack more carefully. The timing and location were truly inspired, but your method lacked the finesse of a master assassin."

She stared into those pale blue eyes, unable to free herself from his hypnotic gaze. So pale and so very, very cold. She retreated slightly, edging backward in the opulent bed until her shoulders brushed against the smoothness of a wall. Her eyes cut left, then right, but there was no place to flee, nowhere to hide from the demon lord's wrath. Instinctively, she lifted a hand to her throat, but the amulet Javan had given her was gone, and with it any hope of protection from the retribution he would surely inflict. She'd always known the price of failure would be the serpent's terrible wrath, swift and deadly vengeance for daring to spill his noble blood.

Her chin lifted in defiance. Let him do his worst. Death would be a welcome release.

"Tell me your name, girl." Dax allowed his gaze to roam downward, from her face to a tantalizing glimpse of flesh visible beneath the long mantle of hair.

Rayna refused to answer. Though her chin rose another fraction, she inched the satiny sheet upward to cover her bare chest. The heated look he was giving her was disquieting in the extreme.

"Are you mute, girl?" A scowl settled over his face, and his voice dropped dangerously low. "Speak up, or suffer the consequences."

Rayna's lips thinned in disdain. "Do what you will. Your threats mean nothing to me, Vahnti demon!"

She'd spat his name like some vile curse, and Dax supposed it was in many quarters, but no one had ever dared such in his presence before. He folded his hands in front of him, tapered fingers moving up then down from the base of his nose to his lips. A faint, gratified smile touched the corners of his mouth. This hunt was going to be more of a challenge than he had anticipated. "Since you're aware of who I am, I think it's safe to assume that your attack upon me was no accident."

Rayna stared at him incredulously. "The only accident was that you survived."

"I see." She had a wonderful voice, rich and melodious. His steepled fingers moved in unison again. "If I may be so rude as to ask, why do you want me dead?"

Her incredulity turned to astonishment. "Must the Vahnti demon lord ask such a question? After you sent your soldiers and digging machines to plunder my world? You try to force my people from the land that has been their home for a thousand years, and you wonder why we seek your death?"

A single muscle twitched along Dax's jaw, the only visible sign that the girl's angry words had struck a nerve. Though she had spoken the truth, it was only the truth as she knew it. And sometimes truth was simply a matter of perspective. "Does everyone in your tribe feel the same way you do?"

"Yes," she said venomously, green fire glittering in her slanted eyes.

"Your shaman, too?"

"Yes!"

"I see. Then I suppose it was the shaman who ordered the attempt on my life. He is your tribe's leader, after all, so it must have been him."

Rayna's eyes narrowed, but she willed her expression to remain calm. She would not allow him to cast blame on Javan for her actions. "No one ordered me. I was chosen by the spirits, as foretold in Nirvannan prophecy."

Dax snorted. *Spirits, indeed.* He relaxed his fingers and shifted forward. "Spirits or not, the ultimate responsibility for your actions rests with the person who motivated you, and in your case I believe it was your shaman. Under Dominion law, you are both equally culpable for the attempt on my life."

Rayna went pale. "Javan had nothing to do with this."

The Vahnti count shrugged indifferently. "We'll see soon enough. I've already ordered that he be taken into custody. When he is, he'll be put on trial for treason and attempted murder. The truth will come out then."

"No!" Rayna shouted, and launched herself from the bed in a blinding burst of speed and fury.

Dax leaped from the chair to defend himself, and she was

27

on him a split second later, a hellish vision of nails and fists and flying hair. An elbow slammed into his sternum, and fingernails raked at his cheek.

"Put me on trial and leave Javan be!" she raged, determined to save her grandfather from the demon lord's wrath, even if it meant she had to die.

Her hair swung toward him, and Dax siezed the opportunity, twining steely fingers around the silky mass. Undaunted, she continued to fight, delivering a fierce kick to his abdomen that sent him stumbling backward into the wing chair. The chair toppled sideways and Dax lost his balance, momentum sending them both in the opposite direction. Their legs tangled and they went down hard, landing in a jumbled heap of limbs and hair.

He spit a tangled curl from his mouth and rolled sideways, pinning her beneath him with the weight of his body. She thrashed and squirmed to free herself, but her wild contortions only served to press their bodies even closer together.

Lungs heaving, Rayna glared into the dark face poised just inches above her own. A tremor of shock coursed down her spine. There was a smile twisting across his lips, a smile that was so smug and calculating that the sight of it took her breath away. Anger and humiliation suffused her cheeks with red. "I am responsible, Vahnti pig!" she said between clenched teeth. "Leave Javan alone! He's done nothing to harm you!"

A tremor of desire coursed through his body. His smile, smug and calculating just a moment before, turned bold and sensual. The girl literally despised him, loathed him with a passion so hot and fierce that he could almost feel the heat of it rising from her flesh. And that made him want her all the more.

"A bargain, then," Dax said slowly. "Because you wish it, I'll let the old shaman, this Javan, live. You, too, if you behave yourself. I'll even consider letting Javan go free, but you have to give me something in return."

Dread knotted in her chest and throat. There was a smoldering gleam in his crystalline eyes. She knew what the demon lord wanted, but she would rather die than suffer his touch. "What do you want from me?" she whispered hoarsely.

A triumphant look stole across his face. "Your name, girl
. . . just tell me your name."

She blinked and stared up at him, thoroughly bewildered.
Had he threatened Javan simply to force her into revealing her
name? If so, then he was far more devious than she had ever
imagined. And infinitely more dangerous. She had to find a
way to escape, to flee back to the hills and warn her grandfather. For now, though, she had no choice but to submit. "My
name is Rayna," she said in a small voice. "Rayna Syn."

"Rayna . . ." He rolled the name around his tongue, experimenting with the combination of sounds it made. His grip on
her arms loosened, but only slightly, and he eased his weight
from her chest, again just the barest of movements. "Well,
Rayna, what should I do with you?"

"You should let me go back to my people," she said
tightly, a sliver of hope building inside her. "You did promise
to let me live."

"True." Her chest was heaving beneath him, quick little
birdlike movements that revealed her fear. Not for the first
time, he was all too aware of her nakedness, the curtain of her
hair and the dark silk of his tunic the only barriers standing
between them. "But I never said that I would let you go," he
told her in a husky whisper.

Rayna stiffened. "You plan to hold me captive?"

He released her wrists abruptly and ran the end of his thumb
along the curve of her defiant jaw. "Not quite. The word 'captive' denotes a temporary state, and I assure you, there is nothing temporary about your situation."

The thought of being held in bondage to him was more than
she could bear. "If not a captive, what am I then?"

"My possession," he said in a matter-of-fact voice.

Disbelief and anger warred in her expression. "Slavery is
illegal!"

He grinned down at her, a dark, wolfish smile that displayed
even, white teeth. "We don't use terms like slavery in Dominion society. 'Forfeiture' is a much better word. In case you
were unaware, the assassination or attempted murder of a clan
lord is a treasonable offense under Dominion law. If caught,

the assassin's life is forfeit . . . bound forever to the clan or lord he injured.''

A dank chill seeped into her bones. The price of failure was far steeper than she had ever imagined.

His thumb brushed over her trembling mouth. ''The moment you raised a weapon to me, you became my possession. . . . I own you, Rayna Syn, body and soul.''

Rayna glared at him from beneath her lashes, just as she'd done for the past few hours. Her mind ranged over an infinite number of ways to kill him, all of them painfully unpleasant. But she had to plan carefully, bide her time until she caught him unaware. She couldn't afford any more mistakes. This time she'd rip his evil heart out, then escape through the door when his servants came back to remove the remains of his meal.

Her eyes narrowed even more, catlike and dangerous, as she watched him devour a tempting assortment of meats and unfamiliar vegetables artfully arrayed on his golden plate. *Enjoy it, you arrogant bastard. This meal will be your last.*

Dax watched the girl watching him, all too aware of the murderous gleam in those slitted eyes. He and the girl were separated by only a few short feet, across the rounded width of his dining table, but it might as well have been the distance of a light-year. Her body was tense and rigid, the muscles in her arms taut beneath thin green sleeves of diaphanous silk. For better or worse, the rest of her body was hidden from view. The robe had been his idea, not hers, and had resulted in a lengthy clash of wills and strength. He'd won, of course. But it was a dubious victory at best. Although tantalizing, the sight of her naked body had become far too distracting and had inspired a great amount of prurient interest on his part. Premature interest. The color of the robe was a good choice, though. It matched her eyes perfectly.

He chewed on a mouthful of banji steak, savoring the rich, spicy taste, then took a sip of wine from an antique goblet, his finger moving over the delicate crystal stem. Her plate still lay untouched, despite his order to eat. Dax shrugged inwardly. When she got hungry enough, she'd eat.

Gold struck gold as his fork scraped against the oval platter. The venom in her eyes had increased to a lethal level. He smiled slowly. She was staring at the serrated edge of the knife lying at his elbow. "If you're harboring thoughts of murder in that savage little heart of yours, think again. Even if you did succeed, there's nowhere to run. You'd be signing your own death warrant—and maybe Javan's as well. You seem to care about the old man; why put his life at risk?"

Her hand closed around the handle of a golden spoon, the only utensil he'd allowed on her side of the table. Rage shimmered in her eyes like emerald flame. "I *will* kill you, Vahnti. Maybe not today or tomorrow, but rest assured, I will!"

Dax leaned back in his chair and steepled lean fingers in front of his chest. The movement was casual, almost leisurely, but the muscles in his broad shoulders coiled in response to the girl's hostility. "Let's be perfectly clear on the subject, shall we? You are now my possession, and therefore I demand certain behavior from you, such as not trying to assassinate me each time my back is turned. You may threaten me verbally whenever you feel the urge, but only in private, and you will *never* raise your hand to me again."

A frown rippled across his brow. "If you do, I assure you, you *will* regret it. Javan is not the only colonist on Nirvanna. How many others are there? A hundred thousand? It would be a simple matter to have them all deported. Nirvanna is my world, after all. I can do what I want."

The fire in her eyes banked to angry embers, and her grip on the spoon loosened. He truly was a demon, one who possessed the power and will to act on his threats.

"Do we understand each other now?"

"Perfectly," she said, and gave him a baleful glare.

"Good." Though the fire in her eyes had been damped somewhat, the hostility remained, tempered with a bit more caution. Dax smiled inwardly. The girl possessed an inner strength he'd rarely seen, and a fiery temperament to match. "Now, then, on to other matters. As my possession you are also expected to keep yourself clean and appropriately attired at all times. No more paint or bird feathers. Your appearance

31

and demeanor are reflections upon me and my station. Is that clear?''

"Perfectly," she said again. Her glare turned diamond-hard. There were a thousand things she could do to annoy him, and she would think of them all.

Dax surveyed her from beneath lowered brows. The coming weeks were going to be interesting, to say the least. "Since I can't watch you every moment, I plan to grant you a small measure of mobility. You'll be able to move about freely—within set boundaries—but only as long as you don't abuse my hospitality, or my generosity."

Hope kindled in her eyes and face. If she could move about, she could escape. Javan and the tribe had fled northward to hide. If she moved fast, she could rejoin them within days, plan her vengeance from the safety of the tribe's hidden caves.

Her veiled expression didn't pass unnoticed. He shook his head slowly. "Don't ever try it, Rayna. Don't even think it." He rose from the chair with the fluid grace inherent in his powerful frame, then strode toward a control panel recessed in the wall. He smiled and touched a button. On the opposite side of the room, a rectangular section of wall began curving away, revealing an immense viewing window conccaled beneath.

Starlight streamed through the transparency, a chaotic blend of golds and reds and blues spattered against an ebony backdrop.

Rayna gasped and leaped to her feet. She stared out the window in shock, numbed by an emotion as black and cold as the endless darkness beyond. The stars streaming past the transparency weren't the familiar denizens of Nirvanna's night skies. She'd been a fool, ignorant enough to think that he was holding her prisoner on Nirvanna, just a few short miles from the safety of the grass and hills. All along she'd been on his ship, a ship streaking through the vast emptiness of space at unimaginable speeds, each second taking her farther away from everything she knew.

"As I said, you have nowhere to run," Dax said gruffly.

Tears burned in the corners of her eyes. *Too late. Too late for anything.*

Chapter Four

Rayna stood motionless by the viewport, a dense maze of stars glinting like jewels inside her shadowy reflection. She had been standing there for hours, staring across that star-drenched sea, an endless sea of darkness so black and deep that at times she thought it would swallow her whole. Against such a backdrop, she felt small and insignificant, a lonely bit of flotsam drifting across the cosmic night.

She pressed a palm against the thick transparency, feeling a hint of the numbing cold of space through her fingertips. So cold, like his eyes. She squeezed her lids shut and closed her heart to the aching grief and loneliness. The past was gone, stripped away in a single moment. All she had left were memories.

The cause of her pain had left hours before, sealed her alone inside the stark white room with its window to the universe. At least she'd been left in solitude to deal with her emotions. Time had drained her of tears, and she would shed no more. Her shoulders stiffened, grew rigid with resolve. Never again would she display such weakness in front of him.

Cunning and strength, her grandfather had said, and she drew a measure of comfort from the remembered words. She could still defeat the demon lord at his own game, make him rue the day he had claimed her as his possession. Her life was forfeit anyway, so what did it matter if she died trying?

She smiled grimly at her reflection in the glass. She had seen the way he looked at her, the heat smoldering in those pale eyes, and knew the look for what it was. Underneath that cold veneer of arrogance and nobility, he was just a man, one who'd sorely underestimated her intelligence and abilities, as well as her resolve. Her smile turned calculating. With time, careful planning, and endless patience on her part, that mistake would lead to his downfall. In the meantime, she would strive to make his noble life a living hell. And since owning things seemed to mean so much to him, the destruction of a few of his "possessions" would be a good place to start.

She turned from the viewing window and walked to a far corner of the room, where long tiers of recessed shelves stretched up the curving bulkhead to the high ceiling. The lowest tier was carefully sealed in glass and held a treasure trove of ancient books, their covers old and faded by the passage of centuries. Rayna sucked in a breath, both exhilarated and angered by the sight of such costly museum pieces in the demon lord's quarters. The titles of such rare books as *Brave New World, The Adventures of Huckleberry Finn,* and the more recent classic, *Ribbon of Stars,* stared at her from the brittle spines. Higher up, the shelves contained a diverse assortment of small art objects, all meticulously displayed and arranged. There were ornate vases and pottery figurines, even a small marble sculpture she recognized from history texts as having been carved by a famous artist of old Earth.

"Disgusting," Rayna muttered under her breath. That any one person, much less the Vahnti warlord, should own such a collection of priceless artifacts was obscene. The very idea nauseated her, and made her want to kill him all the more. Treasures such as these belonged to all of humanity.

With a frustrated sigh, she turned her back on the shelves and the valuables they held. No matter how much she hated him, she couldn't find it within herself to destroy such objects. Doing so would be an obscenity on a par with his owning them.

She walked around in a slow circle, contemplating her surroundings, then unceremoniously tipped the silk-covered wing chair to the floor, wishing she had a knife to slice the costly material to shreds. Next she overturned the wooden dining table and another chair, gratified by the thumps they made as they collided with the carpeted floor. The odious bed fashioned in the shape of a fat half moon was her next target. She ripped the satiny coverings and pillows off and threw them in a jumble on the floor, then stomped and kicked and tore at the soft material to vent a portion of her pent-up rage. A satin pillow sailed into the viewing window; another came dangerously close to the upper tier of the shelves. Throwing his things about was an impotent gesture, but one that made her feel a great deal better.

"Evil worm!" she muttered. The last of the pillows hit the bulkhead. She just wished it was his arrogant face slamming into the wall.

A chime sounded somewhere in the room. Rayna ended her tirade and looked around, wondering where the sound had come from and what it signified.

The doors slid open soundlessly, and Haywood March surveyed the destruction in Dax's quarters through narrowed eyes. "My, haven't you been a busy girl?"

Rayna wheeled around and flinched in surprise when she found herself face-to-face with a great hulk of a man with a balding pate and dark almond eyes. A guilty flush crept up her cheekbones. She'd been expecting the demon lord to discover the results of her wrath, not some stranger.

Haywood glanced around the disheveled room and raised a brow, noting in the back of his mind that Dax's collection of antiques had escaped her tantrum unscathed, and that simple fact told him much about her background. This was no illiterate savage. She understood the intrinsic value of such objects and had acted accordingly. He studied her more carefully than he had the night they found her, catching glimpses of her heart-shaped face beneath a shining tangle of waist-length hair. Strange green eyes were peering up at him through that sheath of coppery hair, eyes that glittered with an innate intelligence far beyond her years. Haywood's graying brows drew downward in a troubled frown. Without the distraction of paint and feathers, it was abundantly clear why she had piqued Dax's interest. But Haywood had the uncomfortable feeling that there was far more to the girl than her breathtaking looks. Granted, she was a delectable morsel, enough to heat the blood of any man, even the Vahnti count's, but a bite of this particular morsel might well prove fatal.

Rayna met his rude stare with one of her own. He was clad in the dark body armor of a Vahnti soldier, a single red stripe and star etched onto each shoulder. An officer, then, one who had risen to the level of command. "Who are you?" Rayna demanded, growing uneasy under his probing stare.

Haywood's head dipped forward in a mock halfbow. There had been an imperious tone in her voice that both amused and annoyed him. "Haywood March, military commander of the Vahnti troops."

Her mouth curled in distaste. "Yes, I've heard about *you*." She brushed the hair from her face and lifted her chin. "You're the puppet who gave the serpent's ultimatum to my . . . to the shaman." She had to be careful. If they discovered she was Javan's granddaughter, they would use the knowledge against him. "It was you who commanded the soldiers that fought against my brothers, your orders that drove my people from their homes and tribal lands."

Haywood's hands bunched into fists, the gold rings he was carrying biting into his palms. He didn't need this slip of a girl to remind him that he'd failed to resolve the troubles on Nirvanna. "We didn't start the bloodshed. Your people managed that feat on their own."

"What did you expect?" she snapped. "That we would just leave our land without a whimper? Not fight to protect our way of life? No one has the right to order us to leave, or to plunder a planet of its natural wealth!"

His square-jawed face reddened. "Nirvanna belongs to Count Vahnti, girl. It's his to do with as he wills."

"By what right does any one man claim ownership of an entire world?" she demanded.

"By right of birth. The Vahnti clan is the most powerful in the Dominion, and he is the clan warlord, by blood and by law."

"The law is unjust, and the foul stuff running through his veins is the black blood of a demon!" Rayna snorted and gave the soldier a disgusted look. "Why would you serve such a beast? Has he made a slave of you, too?"

"Watch your tongue." His eyes darkened with anger. "I serve Count Vahnti and the clan because it pleases me, just as my father and his father did before me." Haywood bit back his next words. Why was he arguing with her? "I will not discuss this subject any further," he said in an impatient voice, wondering anew what Dax could possibly see in this she-cat. "Do not speak of it to me again."

He tilted his head and eyed her steadily. If she could enrage him so in such a short time, what would she do to others? "A word of warning . . . if you value your life, keep such thoughts to yourself in the future. Everyone aboard this ship, and all who serve the Vahntis, do so of their own free will. Many are loyal to the point of obsession and would gladly slit your lovely throat if they heard you slander the count's good name." He leaned toward her, threatening her with his bulk and eyes. "Some would like to see you dead because of what you did, so be very careful. Mind what you say and do, because they'll be watching your every move." His gravelly voice dropped even lower. "I'll be watching, too. The count's safety is my responsibility. If you so much as harm another hair on his head . . ."

Rayna forced herself not to show any emotion, even though a chill had raced up her spine. If he'd spoken truth, she would find no allies here, or anywhere else in the serpent's domain. How had a man as loathsome as the demon lord inspired such unswerving loyalty? It was a perplexing question, almost a paradox, and one she was determined to find the answer to.

"All right, I won't speak of it again," Rayna said calmly, her outward display of tranquillity only skin-deep. "But only if you answer a question." She studied the soldier intently, as if she could find her answer somewhere within his muscular frame. Though his face was lined and hardened by decades of soldiering, and the years had stolen most of his hair, there was a strange softness about his eyes and mouth that hinted of a youthful, gentle nature.

"Only if your question doesn't involve Nirvanna."

"It doesn't."

"Then ask."

She paused for a moment, then drew in a breath. She had to find out if what the demon lord had told her was true. "Am I truly the serpent's possession? He says I am under the laws of forfeiture."

Haywood managed to conceal his astonishment, but only barely. Gods, what was Dax up to? The right of forfeiture hadn't been practiced in hundreds of years, and then only rarely. "If the Vahnti warlord has claimed you, then you are indeed his possession," he told her smoothly. What else could he say?

"For life?"

"That's the law."

"I see." The color faded from her face, and her eyes grew dull, devoid of any animation.

Haywood felt a stab of guilt in response to her vacant expression. Assassin or not, she was still hardly more than a child, and the look on that youthful face was a terrible thing to behold. And he was about to make matters worse.

He sighed heavily. "I didn't come here to do battle with you. The count sent me."

She glanced up.

Haywood lifted his hands palm up and displayed the large golden rings for her to see.

"What are those?" She didn't like the looks of them or the way he was acting.

"Sensor cuffs. The count has ordered that you wear them."

"Why?"

"They have locators imbedded in them, tracking devices that will home in on your location if you stray too far from Count Vahnti."

She glared at the demeaning things, hating what they signified. But if wearing them afforded her even a small measure of freedom . . . "Does that mean I can move about freely?"

"If you wear the cuffs, yes."

Rayna held out her arms and grimaced as he locked them around her wrists. She stared down at the slender golden bands, deciding they looked more like matching bracelets than some sort of technological devices.

"Count Vahnti ordered that they be made especially for you. He wanted them to look more like ornaments than security cuffs."

Her mouth curved downward in a grimace. *Ornaments for his ornament.* "How thoughtful of him." Her voice was brittle, edged with a layer of sarcasm. "I'll remember to thank him when next I see him."

Haywood cleared his throat noisily. "I'll release the door lock when I leave. You're free to wander about if you wish." He dipped his head, then turned on his heel and left.

The door slid shut behind him, and Rayna rushed toward it, certain that he had sealed her inside. But when she came within a few feet, sensors detected her presence and the doorway slid open automatically. She stepped to the line where the plush carpet gave way to bare metal and peered into the corridor beyond. No alarms sounded; no soldiers shouted warnings. She shook her head in astonishment. The demon lord had actually kept his word.

Rayna wandered down yet another of the tubelike corridors, growing more disoriented with each step she took. Hours had passed since she had left her cell, but she had no idea how many. Her sense of direction had deserted her, as well as her perception of time. Each of the curving metal corridors was much like the next, winding around in a complex pattern that seemed to double back on itself.

A squad of soldiers rounded a curve, followed by a group of technicians dressed in jumpsuits of Vahnti black. Rayna pressed herself flat against a bulkhead as they marched past.

She considered asking one of them for directions, then discarded the idea. What was the point? She would only end up back in her cell again, and she wanted to delay that moment as long as possible.

Rayna sighed and started walking, wondering how long it would be before the demon lord came in search of her. She rounded a section of curving wall and froze. *Not long at all.*

He was lounging against the bulkhead, arms folded across his chest, the heel of one boot propped casually on the gray wall. He gave her a knowing grin, an evil twisting of his lips that told her he'd been expecting her. As if he'd known exactly where she was and had simply lain in wait.

She glanced down at the bracelets encircling her wrists and her expression soured. He'd known exactly where she was at every moment, most likely since the very second she'd left her cell.

"Pretty, aren't they?" Dax gestured toward the cuffs.

"You said I was to have a measure of freedom."

He pushed away from the wall and lifted his arms in an exaggerated shrug. "You do. But I'm not a fool. There's no telling what sort of mischief you might create if I don't keep a careful eye on your whereabouts . . . and I plan to keep a careful eye on you for a long, long time."

Rayna felt a sudden chill, as if a dark wind had blown through her soul. For a short while she'd been able to cast aside thoughts of her future, but the sight of him had brought home the cold reality of her situation once again.

"Don't look so glum," Dax said, and gave her a happy smile. "Captivity does have its rewards. Just think of all the time we'll be spending together. We're going to become very close, you and I."

Hatred smoldered in her exotic eyes. "I can hardly wait."

Dax laughed and grabbed her by the elbow, propelling her down the wide corridor at his side. "Come along. We're dining in the officers' mess tonight instead of my quarters." He glanced covertly at her rigid profile. "Oddly enough, there was some sort of storm in my cabin. The wind did quite a bit of damage, I'm told. You wouldn't happen to know anything about it, would you?"

She didn't answer. What purpose would it serve? They both knew she had done it and why. She tried to pull free, but his grasp only tightened, his lean fingers digging deeper into her skin. His grip wasn't brutal, just incessant, and where her flesh met his, her skin felt scorched, heated by his touch.

They reached a juncture where the corridor curved, then fed into a larger tube. Dax moved into the wider of the two, pulling her along with him. A group of soldiers trundled past, their arms lifting in the stiff-armed Vahnti salute as they marched by the head of their clan.

One of the soldiers threw Rayna a daggerlike glare, a malevolent look that declared his feelings for her in no uncertain terms. Rayna stiffened in response.

Dax saw the soldier's hostile look and tightened his grip on her arm even more. Loyalty was a double-edged sword at times. "Your reputation precedes you, Rayna. It might be best

40

if you didn't wander about alone for a while, at least until my security guards' tempers cool a bit.''

Another knot of soldiers moved past. The cold stares of several burned holes in Rayna's face. How many soldiers were aboard the ship? A hundred? A thousand?

"I don't think they like you very much," Dax said lightly. "It's understandable, though. Their sole duty is to protect me from my enemies, and you nearly succeeded in killing their charge.''

So many guards. Their very presence spoke volumes about the man they were duty-bound to defend. She wasn't alone in her hatred for the Vahnti warlord. The Dominion must be rife with his foes, potential allies all. "You must have quite a few enemies," Rayna muttered, and stole a quick look at the chiseled planes of his hawkish profile.

"A few," Dax said in an offhand tone. "Border wars, trade disputes." He paused and looked her full in the face. "I even have to deal with an occasional malcontent every now and then." His eyes burned into hers. "But those who battle with me never do so again. I like to win, you see." His thumb began moving in a languid circle across her arm, the emerald silk of her sleeve rasping and sliding sensuously beneath his finger. "Failure leaves a foul taste in my mouth, Rayna, one I just can't abide.''

The flesh along her arm came alive beneath his touch, a hot prickle of sensation that sent a flush of red across her cheeks. She was conscious of his presence in a way she'd never felt with any male, acutely aware of the feel of his finger moving round and round on her arm, the smooth lines of his full mouth, the coiled strength clearly visible in his broad shoulders and lanky frame.

Dax saw the glaze of desire wash through her eyes and smiled inwardly, pleased with himself. The hunt had begun in earnest. He widened the slow circle across her arm, gently caressing her pliant flesh with the tip of his finger.

A glint of amusement flashed in his pale eyes, and Rayna suddenly understood. Her cheeks flamed crimson. He *knew!* She jerked her arm free and took a step back. The evil worm knew exactly what path her senses had taken! "Vahnti dung

41

pig!'' she said angrily, and stalked off down the corridor.

Dax shoved his hands inside the pockets of his dark breeches and sauntered after her, humming softly beneath his breath.

Chapter Five

Dinner was an abysmal affair, an endless series of toasts and testimonials praising the virtues of the notorious Vahnti clan, as well as their evil demon lord. Rayna stared straight ahead, her mind focused on nothing and everything. The drone of voices faded, along with the dreary dining hall, but she didn't need to see or hear to sense the powerful essence of the man seated at her side. Daxton Vahnti was like a malevolent shadow, a darkling force whose mere presence could hold weaker souls in thrall.

The dining hall would have been unpleasant even without the demon lord filling the seat beside her. Other than a single plaque bearing the Vahnti crest of a serpent twined around an upright sword, there were no decorations of any kind, nothing to relieve the sterile gray metal of the walls and floor. Long rows of hardwood tables and stiff-backed chairs were spaced across the room, all occupied by an assortment of stone-faced soldiers. A few cast lethal glances at her every now and again, but for the most part they avoided any overt contact with her eyes, as if to do so would contaminate them in some way. All wore the same wooden expression, their rigidity a perfect match for the rock-hard chairs. Even so, Rayna had the uncomfortable feeling that without her presence, those stony faces might have softened a bit and the meal taken on a jovial air.

To her eternal relief, the last of the soldiers finally ended his litany of lies, lifted his glass in salute of the Vahntis, then sat back down to finish his meal. She hoped the ordeal would soon end. If not she might suffocate from the weight of the untruths lingering over the room.

The plate in front of her was still piled high with meats and chilled fruit, but she made no move to eat, allowing herself only an occasional sip of the sweet blue wine. She'd sooner starve than feed from the serpent's table. How could she anyway, sandwiched as she was between him and a glowering Haywood March? The soldier obviously didn't relish her presence, and she felt the same way.

Daxton Vahnti was another matter altogether. Rayna glared at him from the corner of her eye. His chair was pressed close to hers, so close his hand, boot, and knee kept brushing down the length of her leg. It hadn't taken her long to realize that his movements were no accident at all.

She stiffened as his palm grazed her thigh again. "Worm," she whispered furiously, and leaned toward Haywood March, trying to put as much distance as possible between her and Vahnti's wandering hand.

Dax grinned slowly, the even whiteness of his smile dazzling against olive skin. He continued to feign interest in the battle tale Leftenant Robichau was telling, but his interest really lay in the girl trapped beside him. He brushed his elbow against a rounded breast, stoking the flames of her anger a little more.

Haywood shifted sideways and stared curiously at Dax over the top of the girl's russet head. The girl herself had moved so far in his direction that she was practically in his lap. As for Dax, although he was deep in conversation with the officers seated on the opposite side of the table, there was a watchful fixity about his face that Haywood found disconcerting, as if the total force of his mental energy were concentrated on achieving a single goal.

A worried frown angled across the soldier's brow. The preoccupied look on Dax's face didn't bode well for clan business, not well at all. It foretold of missed briefings, forgotten appointments, and a host of other duties left untended. It was a temporary aberration, he was sure, since the reclusive warlord was far too diligent to allow any female to distract him for long. Haywood sighed. He just wished that someone other than the murderous little she-cat had inspired that obsessive look.

"Dax," Haywood said, leaning to his right to give the squirming girl more room. He had to rest his elbows on the table and shift forward in order to see Dax's face. "We need to talk."

"Hmm?" Dax made himself focus on Haywood's gravelly voice.

"I said we need to talk."

"So talk." He downed half a glass of Logo wine and slouched back in his chair, forcing Haywood to lean back as well.

Haywood pinched his lips together in a single line. "Dr. Bahleigh would like to see you right away."

"About what?" He ran the toe of his boot across her ankle, eliciting an angry glare.

"About the animals, for one thing."

Dax frowned and downed the rest of his wine. A servant refilled his glass as soon as he placed it on the table. "What of them?"

"He didn't find a trace of chemicals or drugs in the animals, so he wants to examine the girl to see if he can find anything in her blood scan that might account for their behavior."

"Fine."

"He needs to do it before any more time has passed. Tonight if possible. You want me to take her to the lab?"

Rayna's emerald gaze flicked back and forth between the men on either side of her. The words *lab* and *blood scan* had set her teeth on edge.

"No, I'll take her myself." Dax twirled the stem of the glass between his fingers and gave her a heated glance. Gods, how he wanted her, more than any woman he'd known in years. But he had to be careful, rein in his runaway lust before he lost his reason and took her too soon. He drained his glass of the sparkling blue liquid and placed the goblet on the table upside down, signaling that he'd had his fill. The longer the hunt lasted, the sweeter his victory would be. "The walk might clear my head."

Haywood snorted. *Cool him off, more likely.*

44

Emboldened by the wine and the rush of heat surging through his blood, Dax allowed his hand to stray under the table again. His palm explored the soft line of her inner thigh, then slowly inched upward.

Rayna bolted from the chair, her face and eyes blazing with rage. "Get your hands off me, you loathsome worm! You've been pawing me ever since we sat down and I'll take no more of your abuse!"

A shocked, angry silence descended over the dining hall. A dozen officers leaped to their feet, hands moving swiftly for the weapons strapped at their waists. The barrels of several pulse guns gleamed dully in the harsh white light.

"Don't ever touch me again!" Rayna shouted. She snatched a fork from the table and waved it threateningly.

Dax sucked in a breath and held it there. The girl had no idea how close to death she was. If she so much as touched him, the security officers would kill her where she stood, and he wouldn't be able to stop them. He raised an arm slowly and motioned with a curt wave of his hand that all was well.

The tension ebbed but not completely. Several guns were still pointed at Rayna's midsection.

Dax eased himself from the chair and grinned, a lazy, artificial smile designed to lay their fears to rest. "Haywood," he drawled in a mock-bleary voice, "you really should watch where you put your hands."

The accusation elicited several chuckles, then a burst of laughter and howls. The remainder of the pulse guns vanished back inside leather holsters.

Haywood reddened and glanced at Dax, silently acknowledging the diversion for what it was. He would have to take a barrage of ribbing, but no one truly believed that he had caused the uproar. They knew whose hands had enraged the girl, and most likely reveled in the knowledge that their warlord would be so bold as to fondle a would-be assassin. They were also well aware that if the Vahnti count chose to let the girl's outburst pass unpunished, it was not within their realm to object. He obviously had other plans for the girl who'd humiliated them, private plans she didn't much relish, and that was a revenge far sweeter than any the security force could inflict.

A steely hand clamped around Rayna's forearm, and the fork clattered to the floor. "You little fool!" Dax hissed in her ear. "You almost got yourself killed!"

Indignation flared in her eyes and voice. "Why? Because the demon lord put his vile hands on me, and I dared to object?"

His grip tightened even more. "We're leaving, and I want no argument." He jerked hard on her arm.

To the delight of the watching soldiers, Dax stalked to the doorway and into the corridor beyond, dragging the reluctant woman behind him. Shouts and ribald catcalls trailed in their wake.

The door slid shut, and Dax shoved her against the corridor wall. He pinned her with his body, his lanky frame pressed tight to hers. Their eyes met, his cold and pale with fury, hers dark with sudden fear.

"Don't ever do that again, Rayna," he said in a hoarse, uneven voice. A pulse beat at his temple in tempo with his angry breathing. "You have no right to object to anything I say or do." Regardless of the cause, she had humiliated him before the soldiers of his clan, and they were the lifeblood of the Vahnti empire. To save her life he'd had to act the besotted fool, diminishing himself, however slightly, in their collective eyes. And without respect, the warlord was nothing but flesh and bone.

His mouth set in a flat, dangerous line. "I can touch you whenever . . . and wherever I want." To drive his point home, Dax thrust himself against her and gave his lust free rein. His hands roamed over her body with savage abandon, lean fingers cruelly exploring the swell of her breasts, then moving lower, dipping below her abdomen every now and again just to remind her that he could.

Rayna stood stock-still, too stunned to draw a single breath. A technician ambled down the corridor, gaping in wide-eyed astonishment at the sight of the warlord engaged in such an intimate act. He averted his gaze and hurried past. Rayna squeezed her lids shut and choked back a flood of embarrassed tears. She wanted to cry, to scream her rage at the universe for dealing her such a fate. But in the end she just stood there, numb and trembling, suffering the indignity of his touch because she had no other choice.

Dax pulled away abruptly. For a long moment he just stared at the girl's fear-blanched face, chiding himself for going too far. He'd almost lost complete control, come within a hairbreadth of taking her in a public corridor.

"Come along," he announced gruffly. He squared his shoulders and swept a dark lock of sweat-dampened hair from his face, then straightened the front of his black tunic. "I promised Commander March that I would take you to the med lab."

Her lids slowly opened, a thick haze of unshed tears glistening in her eyes. The heat and fury had faded from his gaze, and his darkly handsome face had resettled into dispassionate lines. No hint of emotion played across those chiseled features. He was the jaded warlord once again, stiffly proud and ever arrogant, his power and noble lineage revealed in the cut of his fine clothes, the arrogant set of his broad shoulders. She gave him a cold stare, one measured in intensity, not time. The demon lord felt no shame or guilt for what he had done. And if truth were known, his black heart was probably incapable of such emotions. Feelings were burdens carried by lesser men.

Chittering nervously, the small creature backed away from the bowl of dried vegetables, its round, luminous eyes glowing with suspicion.

"I know you're hungry," Lett Bahleigh told the gi quietly. "Come on. Take a bite. I promise not to dissect you." He pushed the bowl closer and lifted his hand palm up for the animal to sniff.

The furry gi arched its neck forward. "That's it, just a little bit more." Lett pulled his hand back and the gi followed. It inched across the examining table and began nibbling the dried food.

The doctor sat back on his stool and peered at the gi with a critical eye. It was a fascinating creature, small and luxuriously soft, with strange yellow eyes and a mercurial temperament. At times the gi was endearingly gentle, and at others downright vicious, as the bites on his hand would firmly attest.

There was a growl behind him, a low rumble coming from the huge metal cages lining a wall on the far side of the lab. Lett glanced over his shoulder and shivered. There was no ambiguity about the nature of the other specimens collected on Nirvanna. The golden-haired wolfens were predators through and through. Fierce and intimidating, the giant wolfens were a good five feet high at the shoulder, with double-rowed fangs and hooked claws long enough to rip out the throat of a grown man.

One of the wolfens growled again, then bared its gleaming fangs in a hideous death's-head grin.

Lett shook his head, wondering how Daxton Vahnti had managed to survive an attack by these creatures. "You are a lucky man, Count Vahnti," he muttered under his breath.

"So I've been told."

The doctor flinched and swung the stool around, startled to find that he wasn't alone. His dark eyes widened. Daxton Vahnti was standing casually in the doorway, one shoulder propped against the metal frame. The wolfens growled and charged the bars of their cages.

"Count Vahnti . . ." Lett jumped to his feet and made a miserable attempt at a formal bow, smoothing his rumpled lab coat as he rose. The nervous gi leaped from the table and scuttled into a corner. "Forgive my appearance, sir. I wasn't expecting any visitors this late, especially not you."

Dax lifted a hand in dismissal. "I should be the one to apologize, Doctor. The officers' end-of-cruise dinner lasted longer than I expected." He folded his arms and stared around the cluttered research lab. Young Bahleigh was nervously watching his every move, but didn't seem inclined to speak, as if Dax's presence in the lab had rendered him mute.

"Commander March said you wanted to see me," Dax prodded. His eyes were drawn to the huge beasts caged along the opposite wall. Fangs bared, the wolfens stared back as if they recognized him. Had it been only four days since he'd fought off those giant maws? It seemed longer somehow.

"Something about a blood scan on the Nirvannan girl?"

"Oh." Lett shook himself mentally and broke contact with that overpowering gaze. "Right." He picked up a datapad from the top of the table and began scanning his notes. "I've run every test on the animals that I can think of, and come up negative at every turn. There was nothing unnatural in their blood or tissue. About the only thing left is to start looking for a natural cause instead."

Dax lowered his brows in a puzzled frown. "A natural cause?"

Bahleigh shrugged, straight blond hair falling in his eyes. "Not much is known about Nirvanna's indigenous life-forms, Count. It's possible that you stumbled into some sort of natural phenomenon . . . like maybe a climatic change that caused the animals to hunt in a pack that wasn't species specific, or a group migration of some kind." He pursed his lips and shook his head. "It's also possible that the scent or pheremones of a human might have triggered some kind of violent, instinctual response. I just don't know."

Dax peered intently at the younger man. "My scent, you think?"

"Maybe . . ." Lett drew in a nervous breath. It was well known that Count Valinti dealt solely in hard facts and was quick to anger when presented with speculation. "But I think it more likely that the girl was the cause, and I'll need your permission to study her to see if I'm right." He rushed to present his case before Dax had a chance to object. "As I said, we don't know much about Nirvanna. The planet has been held in trust by your family for over two thousand years, kept in its natural state to protect its resources for later use. The colonists were granted permission to settle there solely because they promised to establish an anachronistic society free of technology and leave the planet untouched."

"So?" There was a note of impatience in his voice. Dax knew Nirvanna's history far better than anyone. Still, there was a point here somewhere. Bahleigh's research skills and his penchant for delving into scientific mysteries were well known within the clan. "What does that have to do with the girl?"

"There've been rumors about Nirvanna within the scientific community for years, Count Vahnti, but no one has ever been allowed the opportunity to make detailed studies. Strange tales about spontaneous cures, native mysticism, and preternatural abilities."

Dax blew out a noisy breath. Somehow he'd known the spirits would enter into this again. "Come on, Doctor," he scoffed, "you're a man of science, not some medieval Earther who believes that trolls live under his bed."

The doctor's thin face and oval eyes came alive with a boyish sense of wonder and excitement. "The universe is far stranger than we ever imagined, Count. Those colonists have been living there for a thousand years, with very little contact with the rest of the galaxy. We know little about them other than the fact that they based their way of life on some obscure Earth tribal culture. As a scientist, I feel it's my duty to try to discover if there's any truth to those tales."

"And you think the girl might be the key?"

Bahleigh lifted his shoulders in a half shrug. "She's here, and she's Nirvannan." He raised his hands imploringly. "This may be my only chance, Count. Her culture might not even exist twelve months from now. Nirvanna itself might be unrecognizable."

Dax's face darkened. Had he detected a trace of censure in the doctor's tone? Or was it just a twinge from his own conscience? He'd suffered more than his share of those lately. "I'll consider your request, Doctor. For now, just do your blood scan and be done with it." He glanced over his shoulder to make sure Rayna was still waiting for him. She was wandering around the deserted ship's hospital, touching and examining the banks of medical equipment. She turned, and Dax beckoned her into the lab.

Rayna approached the open doorway with no small amount of trepidation, fearing a repeat of what had happened earlier. She eased past him warily.

Dr. Bahleigh stood motionless beside the examining table and stared at the girl, mesmerized by the wild look of untamed beauty about her slim form and glittering green eyes. A rumor making its way around the ship was that the count had made a forfeiture claim on her life. If so, Lett could see why.

The wolfens howled, a piercing, mournful crescendo of sound that began on a low note, then drifted upward to an anguished, high-pitched conclusion. They lunged and clawed at the confining bars.

Rayna's eyes swung toward the sound, and a radiant smile transformed her face. The wolfens howled again, but it was a different sound this time, one that managed to convey their joy. Rayna let out a happy cry and ran to greet them.

"Rayna!" Dax grabbed at her sleeve and missed.

Overjoyed, Rayna ran to the cages and stuck her hands through the thick steel bars. The wolfens whined and whimpered as she reached up and began scratching the tops of their heads.

An uncertain frown rippled over Dax's face. Clearly the girl was not in need of rescue. The wolfens' great tongues were lolling about happily, one even slipping through the bars to lick her face. The small brown creature the doctor had been feeding darted from a corner and leaped onto her shoulder, squeaking and chittering as it wound itself around her neck.

Dax exchanged a puzzled glance with the doctor. "About that request you made," Dax said slowly. "We reach Hellfire in the morning. Begin your research then, Doctor. You have my permission, as well as my support."

Chapter Six

The endless darkness of space gave way to blinding blue as the Vahnti warlord's shuttle plunged inside Hellfire's atmosphere, arrowing downward through a bright morning sky. Far below, Rayna could see a thin veil of white clouds scudding along the wide curve of the horizon, a dizzying sight that brought the sour, sick taste of bile to her mouth. The sensation of falling grew as the jagged black peaks of a hundred mountains suddenly loomed through the mantle of clouds, swelling in size with each second that passed. Rayna closed her eyes and clenched the armpads of the chair with white-knuckled hands.

Dax keyed a command into the shuttle's navigation console and stole a glance at the girl strapped into the copilot's chair beside him. He frowned in alarm. Her skin was clammy white, and her face was set in tight, rigid lines. "Open your eyes, Rayna," he said sharply. "Keep them focused straight ahead."

"I can't," she whispered in a weak voice.

"Do it right now before you make a mess of my control board." Her skin had taken on a sickly greenish cast. "Just look straight ahead and take slow, deep breaths." He pulled the nose of the shuttle up and dumped speed, easing off on his angle of descent. For the first time he questioned the wisdom of seating her in the control pit of the sleek little craft. He should have locked her in the luggage bay as Haywood suggested. It wouldn't matter if she got sick back there.

Her lids fluttered open. For once she did as he ordered and stared straight ahead. Much to her relief, the sensation of falling began to fade, and her rebellious stomach quieted. She took a great, cleansing breath and relaxed the muscles in her hands.

Dax gave her a sideways, cynical smile. She wasn't the first to suffer from the effects of his piloting, and probably wouldn't be the last. Some had accused him of being reckless, a thrill-seeker intent on ending his life in a blinding plasma explosion. Truth was, flying fast and hard brought him intense pleasure, a momentary escape from the constraints placed on the life of the clan warlord. "Feeling better?" he asked, a hint of amusement edging his deep voice.

"Yes." Rayna scowled at him, then turned her attention back to the vista of white clouds and dark mountains rushing past the viewport.

The shuttle plunged inside a deep, winding valley, and Hellfire's scorched landscape spread beneath them, a nightmarish vision of blackened soil and brooding monoliths of rock. Atop the jagged valley walls, steam and dark red magma plumed from the cones of countless volcanos, the only trace of color in the lifeless terrain.

Rayna shivered. "Hellfire" was an appropriate name.

The shuttle angled up, climbing over the crater of an active volcano, then dipped below the ridge again, streaking across a flat, dry sea of volcanic ash and dust. A web of deep chasms crisscrossed the baked terrain, the ground rising and falling along spidery, uneven lines gouged by countless earthquakes.

The sight caused Rayna's hopes to plummet. Even if she did manage to escape, where would she go? There were no forests here, no fields of prairie grass or ripening maize. The only life at all was an occasional stunted tree, and they looked more like desperate skeletons than living things. Even worse, now that she knew the wolfens and the gi had been taken prisoner, she needed to formulate a plan that included them, too. They were here because of her, unwitting victims whose only crime had been to answer her call. But even if she was successful, how would the four of them survive on this empty, lifeless world?

She was trapped, like an insect frozen in amber. "Why would anyone choose to live in such a place?" she whispered, more to herself than to him.

Dax banked the shuttle onto a more northwesterly course and began the slow process of deceleration. It wasn't hard to guess what she was thinking. Most first-time visitors to Hellfire spoke in that same hushed tone of horror and disbelief. "Intimidating, isn't it?"

She glanced at him sharply. "That's not the word I would use."

The smile Dax gave her in return was almost cheerful. "Maybe not, but it's the truth. Hellfire is a natural fortress. In over two thousand years, no invasion force has ever been foolhardy enough to attempt a landing here."

Her hopes dwindled to nothing. She would never escape him, never see Nirvanna or Javan again.

As the shuttle streaked northward into Hellfire's polar region, the landscape shifted slightly, the dark volcanic ash interspersed with barren patches of rocky tundra. In the distance, mountains still daggered skyward, the obsidian peaks ringed by clouds and steam, but their numbers were fewer, their hulking shapes less threatening. Fields of silvery grass appeared, then an occasional bush or tree, not the skeletal things she'd seen earlier. Soon they were flying over a dense forest of oranges, browns and brilliant greens, a vivid canopy of leaves that stretched to the northern horizon. Narrow rivers snaked and slithered through the thick foliage, the first hint of water that Rayna had seen.

Hellfire was alive after all.

And then she saw it, a massive, towering citadel of black volcanic glass set against the deepening blue of Hellfire's sky. The smooth walls of polished black stone soared upward for perhaps a thousand feet in a profusion of sharp angles, rounded arches, and steepled towers that dwarfed the surrounding forest and dazzled the eye.

A gasp of surprise escaped her lips. Nothing she had ever heard or read had prepared her for the sight of Drakken Castle. The demon lord's keep was breathtakingly beautiful, a sprawling, graceful edifice of mirrorlike stone that glinted like some great dark jewel beneath Hellfire's sun.

Dax glanced at her covertly and smiled, pleased by her reaction. In this day and age, few appreciated Drakken Castle's stark beauty and neo-Gothic lines. Even some among his own clan and family viewed the thousand-year-old castle as an archaic, outdated monstrosity that should be razed in favor of a more modern design.

A tight frown settled over his face. His cousin Caccia had been pushing for demolition for years now, whining and complaining about the outmoded castle ever since he'd become warlord. But her endless complaints had fallen on deaf ears. As long as he lived, Drakken Castle would remain.

He brought the shuttle lower to give Rayna a better view, skimming the tops of needlelike spires gracing the mile-wide roofline and battlements. On a flat section of roof between two turrets, beacons flashed around a circular landing pad guarded by a squad of soldiers standing at attention. The shuttle hovered for a moment, then settled gently onto the pad reserved for his use.

As the whine of the engines faded, Dax touched a control

to open the air lock, then unfastened his harness and rose. He turned to Rayna, who was regarding him with a look of uncertainty mixed with blatant fear. "We're home, dear," he said with a mocking smile, and bent to unstrap her from the seat.

Bright sunlight slanted through the open hatchway. Rayna reluctantly took the hand he offered and climbed to her feet, following a step behind as he led her down the shuttle's ramp. To her surprise, a cool rush of wind touched her cheeks and twined long strands of hair about her shoulders. She'd expected Hellfire's climate to live up to its name.

The soldiers saluted and clicked their heels. "Welcome home, Count Vahnti," a young guard captain said. His reddish eyebrows lifted slightly when he saw the girl standing shyly behind the warlord. "We're glad to have you back, sir."

Dax smiled thinly, aware of the curious glances cast Rayna's way. The first order of business was to make certain their curiosity didn't turn into something else when word of the assassination attempt arrived. "Thank you, Captain Remi. It's good to be back." He pulled Rayna forward. Now was as good a time as any to deal with the problem. "Captain, please advise the Drakken security force that Miss Syn is here under my protection. She is to have free run of the keep and grounds unless her safety is at issue. Any assault or insult upon her shall be considered a personal affront to me. Is that understood?"

The captain's curiosity turned to bewilderment. No one would dare mistreat a castle visitor. "Yes, sir, very clear."

"Good." Dax grinned. They would find out soon enough. Haywood and the remainder of the security force were scheduled to arrive within the hour. "Anything I should know about before I retire to my quarters?"

The soldier squared his shoulders and grimaced, a pained expression stealing over his broad face. "Yes, sir . . . young Lord Dunstan is in the great hall awaiting your arrival."

Dax's face darkened, and his eyes widened incredulously. *Petwitt Dunstan?* He muttered a choice curse under his breath. The Dunstan and Vahnti clans had been at odds for centuries, bitter rivals clashing over everything from trade routes to asteroid mineral rights. Even more so since old Alfred Dunstan, the Dunstan warlord, had picked that oaf Petwitt from his conniving brood to be his successor.

"The castle shields were dropped to allow a Dunstan entry!" Dax suddenly shouted, causing Rayna to flinch away. "On whose authority?"

Remi swallowed nervously. "He asked for and received permission from Lady Caccia, sir. He told her it was a matter of the gravest importance to both clans."

Dax glowered. A Dunstan inside Drakken's walls. *Invited,* no less. He was going to throttle Caccia. His cousin had gone too far this time. She'd allowed a Dunstan entry inside the shield wall just to needle him, her way of letting him know that she would do as she pleased, when she pleased, no matter the political ramifications to the clan or its warlord. Caccia couldn't care less what Dunstan wanted, and most likely hadn't even deigned to find out.

"Just how long has Dunstan been here?" Dax said in a growl, a muscle working angrily along his jaw.

"His ship arrived at first light."

"And he knew I was due to arrive?" Dax's eyes narrowed. The guard captain paled. "Yes, sir, he did."

Rayna's heart skipped a beat, and she had to force herself to suppress a surge of hope. Whoever this Dunstan was, he was an enemy of the Vahntis, and that made him a potential ally.

"I want a full-scale security scan of every star system within a hundred light-years of here immediately," Dax ordered. "Those bastards have a spy beacon hidden somewhere, and I want it found!"

"Yes, Count Vahnti, right away."

Dax half pulled, half dragged Rayna toward a triangular archway set in the polished stone. "Damn it all!" he muttered under his breath, and led her inside the battlement to a lifttube imbedded in a stone buttress. Still muttering, he pulled her into the clear tube and jabbed the controls with the heel of his hand.

Rayna's stomach lurched as the tube began descending at a sickening rate. She closed her eyes and took a deep breath, the sensation of falling almost as strong as it had been in the shuttle. The sensation stopped abruptly, and she heaved a relieved sigh.

The tube door popped open and the Vahnti count stalked into a wide corridor carpeted in a rich lapis blue. Rayna stared around in wonder. Delicate brocade chairs and costly hardwood tables were scattered along the ebony walls, the chairs covered in the same deep blue as the thick carpet. The arched ceiling had been cut of the same dark glassy stone as the exterior, rising several stories into triangular peaks at intervals along the corridor's enormous length.

They passed door after immense door, the lustrous wood etched with a series of ornate carvings that she longed to study at leisure. But the demon lord kept dragging her along. If not for the fact that his hand was attached to her arm, he probably would have forgotten that she was there at all.

Dax threw open a set of double doors and pulled Rayna inside a palatial sitting room, the sharp clack of his boot heels striking polished stone echoing in the cavernous silence.

Rayna drew in a startled breath and glanced around in astonishment. The high walls and tiled floor had been made from the same black stone as the rest of the castle, but the resemblance ended there. A domed ceiling rose a full ten stories above her, the curving structure adorned with frescoes depicting pastoral scenes of old Earth painted in jewel-toned hues against a creamy backdrop. Perpendicular windows lining the length of one wall reached upward toward the dome like thin fingers clawing for the sky. Sunlight streamed through the faceted stained glass, throwing bright prisms of red and white light across the ebony walls and floor.

Overwhelmed, she continued to gape at her lavish surroundings, nonplussed by the sheer opulence of the Vahntis' everyday lives. She had heard wild tales of their extravagance, but would have never believed the rumors if she hadn't seen it with her own eyes.

"Caccia!" Dax bellowed, his voice reverberating in the cavelike silence. He came to an abrupt stop and released Rayna's hand. "Where the hell are you?"

Finally free, Rayna crept toward the nearest of the narrow

windows, putting as much distance between herself and the serpent as she could. The dark look on his face boded ill for this Caccia person.

A door slammed somewhere and a tiny figure appeared at the far end of the sprawling room. The steady *click-click* of heels beat across the endless expanse of stone.

His mouth fixed in a hard, angry line, Dax folded his arms across his chest and watched his cousin approach through narrowed eyes.

Caccia Vahnti quickened her footsteps, rushing toward him in a billowing flurry of dark hair and crimson silk. "Dax, darling!" she said breathlessly. "I'm so glad you're back!" She gave him a bright, sweet smile, then brushed cold lips against his cheek. "What's it been? Six months?"

"Three," Dax said tightly.

"Only three? Oh, dear me." She pulled away from him and flicked an imaginary bit of lint from the front of her scarlet robe. "You know I've never had any sense of time at all." She lifted one shoulder in a delicate half shrug. "It's good to have you back all the same."

"I'm sure." His mouth hardened even more. Caccia couldn't care less whether he came back or not as long as she had access to the family funds. "I hear we have a visitor, cousin, and that you ordered the castle shields lowered to allow his ship entry."

"Petwitt?" The cant to her almond eyes grew more pronounced. "He's such a boor, but he was so incessant, Dax, I just couldn't refuse him." A sly, pouty look passed over her oval face. "You're not angry with me, are you, darling?"

"Of course not," he said through gritted teeth. "All you did was lower the castle defenses to allow a *Dunstan* entry inside the clan fortress. Why should I be mad?"

For a split second, the pouty look turned sullen; then her mouth dipped in a penitent frown. "Oh, Dax, I'm so sorry." Tears trembled at the base of her dark lashes. "I just didn't think!"

Dax sighed and shook his head. It had taken him years to realize just how vain, cold, and brutally manipulative Caccia could be. Men were her private play things, to be used and abused at will, especially the corps of noble fools who strutted about the Dominion Court. Even members of the castle's security force fell victim on occasion. Fortunately, her younger brother Carlo hadn't been cut from that same cold mold.

"Spare me the tears, Caccia, as well as the 'poor dim-witted me' routine. We grew up together, remember? I've been immune for quite a few years now."

She blinked the tears away and tucked a perfect black curl into place beneath the high coronet perched atop her head. Dax could be such an ogre at times.

"You endangered the lives of everyone here, Caccia . . . everyone on Hellfire." He pinned her with his eyes. "Not to mention your own precious skin."

"Oh, spare me the lecture, Dax." Sighing, she threw up her hands and glared back. "I was just trying to breathe a little life into Drakken's musty walls. Petwitt's harmless enough, and his father is a doddering old fool. It's you who's obsessed with this silly rivalry, not the Dunstans!"

"Alfred Dunstan is nobody's fool," he said in a lethal voice. "Neither is Petwitt. And you'd best remember that."

Caccia sniffed and straightened her shoulders, then tilted her head to a haughty angle. She was deciding on a suitable retort when she caught a glimmer of movement out of the corner of her eye. Her jet brows feathered upward in surprise. A girl dressed in a simple green robe was standing quietly beside a window, her slender figure all but veiled by a haze of sunlight. She was a pretty little thing, even though she was unfashionably thin. The high cheekbones, fine, straight nose, and exotic green eyes all merged together in a waifish package framed by a chaotic tangle of tawny hair. Caccia puckered her mouth in distaste. Someone needed to have a talk with her about that hair.

Realization suddenly dawned, and she glanced at her cousin in astonishment. Dax, the brooding introvert who prized his solitude and riding to the hounds above all else, had brought a woman home? To Drakken? Gods, what was the galaxy coming to? "Why Dax, you should have told me that you'd brought one of your hunting trophies home." A sly glint of mischief flashed in her dark eyes. "Where do you plan to mount this one? In your quarters?"

His mouth flattened, and his eyes turned a paler shade of blue. "She's not a trophy," he snapped, an angry flush riding up his sun-ruddied cheeks.

"Oh?" A smile of victory curled the edges of her mouth. She didn't know why, but she'd definitely hit a nerve. "Then what is she? Just a little something to keep your bed warm this winter?"

"What I do with my property is my concern, Caccia. Mind your own business." He beckoned Rayna with a wave of his hand. "Come along. I have business to tend to." He wasn't about to leave her alone with the castle's resident viper this soon.

Property? Caccia had to struggle to mask her surprise. Had she heard that right?

Rayna stared at the two of them and considered her options. She could stay where she was and force another confrontation, one that might possibly end in her being left alone with the dark-haired woman who was studying her with those sly, burning eyes. Or she could do as the demon lord ordered and accompany him. Not much of a choice. She walked toward the Vahnti warlord warily. Better the demon that she knew.

Sunlight danced across the gold bands encircling the girl's wrists. A slow, understanding smile spread across Caccia's pale face. Dax was full of surprises today. "Will your 'guest' be staying with us for a while, cousin?"

His eyes cut sharply in her direction. "I said it was none of your concern."

"Where are your manners, Dax? You can at least tell me the child's name, can't you?"

"Her name is Rayna . . . Rayna Syn."

Caccia stepped forward and gave her a patronizing smile. "Rayna . . . what a pretty name." Those strange green eyes were watching her with an intensity Caccia found unnerving. "Where are you from, child?" There was something unnatural about her eyes, something preternaturally bright that shimmered in their fiery depths.

"Nirvanna," Rayna said in a whisper, both awed and leery

of the older woman's striking looks and audacious manner.

Caccia's brows climbed. Nirvanna was in the middle of no-where, hundreds of light-years from civilization. Strange eyes or not, the girl was nothing but a lowly colonist, just some pitiful little waif Dax had plucked from a miserable existence to warm his bed. She shook her head slowly. There was no accounting for taste.

Still smiling, she reached out and grabbed the girl's arm, holding her wrist aloft. "Why, what beautiful bracelets, Rayna! Wherever did you get them?"

"That's enough." Dax's voice had dropped to a low, dangerous growl. He snatched Rayna's hand from her and clasped it tightly. "I'll warn you once, Caccia, and only once . . . interfere with my life at your own peril." With that, he tucked Rayna's arm firmly beneath his and stalked across the stone floor toward a doorway at the far end of the room. Their footsteps rang in the sudden silence.

"Where are you going?" she called after them.

"To air out the castle," Dax shouted back, his voice echoing across the glassy walls. "Drakken reeks with Petwitt's stench."

Caccia watched them go, a slow, speculative smile playing at the corners of her mouth. And to think, just the day before she'd been living in dread of another boring winter spent at Drakken Castle. How things could change in the course of a single day.

Chapter Seven

The sheer size and magnitude of the castle's great hall took Rayna's breath away. It wasn't a hall at all, or even a room, for that matter. It was a magical place that words failed to describe. The dark trunks of hundreds of trees jutted from beneath the black stone floor, soaring toward a haze of milky sunlight filtering through a crystal ceiling a thousand feet above. A wild profusion of dense green foliage filled the narrow spaces between the tree trunks and spilled across a maze of footpaths angling outward like the spokes of a wheel from the center of the hall.

Rayna craned her neck to gaze upward, mesmerized by the sight of a flock of exotic birds winging their way from treetop to treetop. Everywhere she looked there was a cacophony of color and sound. Multihued birds cawed and chirped from secret branches beneath the thick canopy of leaves. Vines laden with heavy pastel blooms climbed the tree trunks and slithered through the dense tropical foliage. And somewhere off in the distance she could hear the cool rush of cascading water, as if there were a waterfall hidden nearby.

"Beautiful, isn't it?" Dax said in a contented tone. He watched in silence as a large bird dappled in shades of yellow and blue arced overhead, spiraling upward toward the atrium ceiling. "It took me years to create the effect, but I think it was well worth the effort."

She turned and stared at the demon lord in mute wonder. A man such as him had created this enchanted place? Was that possible? She lifted a skeptical brow. Only someone with a soul and a true reverence for nature's blessings could have done this, and the Vahnti warlord possessed neither.

"Feel free to wander about in here whenever you wish, but not today." Caccia might be lurking somewhere. But that wasn't the only reason. Beneath that sometimes fierce exterior, Rayna was still an innocent, inexperienced in the ways and lifestyle of Dominion nobility. It was far too soon just to let her go where she wanted. And in truth, he was actually enjoying showing her around the castle he called home for most of the year. "Like it or not, you'll be spending most of today with me."

"I can hardly wait," Rayna said, her mouth curling in disgust.

Grinning, he took her hand and led her down a footpath that angled toward the heart of the atrium.

A turquoise parrot swooped down from a tree limb and

landed atop Rayna's shoulder. Cawing excitedly, the bird arched its neck and peered into her face.

Rayna tugged free of his hand and stroked the parrot's soft feathers, smiling in delight. "Oh, you're so beautiful!" she murmured to the bird, which squawked and flapped its wings in response.

Other birds fluttered down from the trees, landing gently around her feet. Dax watched in fascination, a puzzled frown slanting across his forehead. Their round black eyes were staring up at her with an air of anticipation, as if the birds were waiting for her to speak. His frown deepened. *How strange. First the wolfens aboard the ship, now this. Could Dr. Bahleigh's theory be correct?* It was an intriguing thought, one that served to deepen his infatuation with her even more.

His pulse quickened as he watched her. She was cooing happily to the birds, her exotic face wreathed in a joyful smile. "You should smile more often, Rayna," he said huskily.

At the sound of his deep voice, the birds took to the air in a flutter of wings and sound. She glanced up at him, her joyous grin vanishing as quickly as the birds. When she spoke, her voice carried a brittle edge of hatred and contempt. "I haven't had much to smile about lately."

Their eyes locked for a frozen second. "No, I suppose not," he said finally, then turned on his heel and stalked down the footpath. Dax tried to focus his thoughts on the man waiting for him at the base of the waterfall. Instead he found himself listening in vain for the sound of her footsteps on the pathway behind him.

Frowning, Rayna watched him march stiffly down a long footpath and disappear into the leafy bowels of a thick stand of blooming foliage. For a split second, an emotion akin to regret had seemed to shadow his cold eyes, but surely that had been her imagination. Remorse was an unknown word to a Dominion warlord.

She stared at the distant ceiling once again, watching as a flock of birds dipped and weaved their way among the treetops. The soft sounds of nature settled around her, the quiet coos and quick rustles of birds and fleet-footed animals, and somewhere near, she could still hear the tantalizing rush of water cascading over rock. Drawn by the sound of the water, she moved down a footpath, though she was careful to choose a different one than the demon lord had taken.

Leaves rustled in the bloom-laden vines, and a covey of scarlet birds suddenly took to the air, singing in sharp, sweet voices as they circled high above her head. Smiling to herself, Rayna closed her eyes and lifted a hand to her forehead. At least she had friends now.

The crimson birds fluttered toward the atrium floor, landing in unison on the ground around her. The turquoise parrot dove from a tree limb and landed atop her shoulder in a flurry of caws and drifting feathers. Several dark-furred creatures darted from a burrow inside a tree trunk, their tiny claws making scratching sounds on the pathway as they crept toward the human who had called.

A hundred pairs of eyes watched her expectantly.

Petwitt Dunstan shifted his bulk in the spindly little chair and scowled at his surroundings, his fingers tapping an impatient beat on the narrow chair arm. He'd been cooling his heels for two hours now, ever since Caccia had deserted him, left him to stew alone in this putrid indoor jungle until the lord of the manor deigned to see him. The servants hadn't even bothered to offer him refreshment, not even a light repast. Insulting, that was what it was. Insulting and unforgivable, a breach of protocol the likes of which he'd never seen. How dare they treat the Dunstan heir in such a way?

His scowl darkened, and the tempo of his fingers increased. He was hungry, tired, and his throat was as parched as Hellfire's volcanic deserts. Even worse, his formal robe was positively damp from the moisture in the air, sticking to his skin in the most awkward places. He glared at the dripping greenery, at the cascade of water rushing down the atrium wall, and shook his head in utter disbelief. Why would anyone build such a hideous place inside his keep?

A spot of white moisture splattered on the tiles beside his chair. Petwitt wrinkled his nose. *Bird poo. How disgusting.* He'd heard that Daxton Vahnti was an eccentric, but this was going too far. This was deranged. A veritable army of creatures was roaming free about the hall, dropping their smelly cargoes wherever they pleased, creeping around beneath all that greenery. Sly little beasts he'd caught spying on him more than once in the last two hours. Petwitt sniffed disdainfully and shook his head again, wondering idly if the Vahntis had a history of breeding among themselves.

The thud of boot heels striking stone sounded somewhere in the distance. Petwitt glanced up expectantly and breathed a sigh of relief when Daxton Vahnti strode into view. At least now his ordeal would soon end. He climbed to his feet gracefully and inclined his head. "Count Vahnti. Good of you to see me on such short notice."

"Dunstan . . ." Dax peered at him suspiciously. In height, Petwitt was almost on a par with him, but was heavier by fifty pounds or so. He had a powerfully built body that was slowly being ruined by rich food and an endless thirst for wine. Each time Dax had seen him in the past few years, which was only at the opening of the court season, he'd added a few more pounds to his aristocratic frame. Pretty soon his fashionably pale face would run to elegant fat. "Needless to say, I was surprised to hear you were waiting to see me."

Petwitt met his appraising stare measure for measure. Daxton Vahnti still had that dark-edged look of a ruffian about him that Petwitt had found so distasteful in the past, the same arrogant look that had gained him entry to many a noblewoman's bed. "Undoubtedly," he said in his most urbane voice. Women were such perverse creatures.

Dax folded his arms and waited.

"My father sends you his greetings and felicitations."

"How kind." Dax eyed him steadily. "How is Lord Alfred these days?"

Petwitt straightened the sleeve of his voluminous blue robe, then smoothed his well-trimmed beard with a tapered hand. He sighed audibly. "Troubled."

"Oh?" He cast a fleeting glance at the deserted pathway angling through the trees. Rayna had yet to make an appearance. "Troubled in what way?" Dax waved him toward a small grouping of wing-back chairs clustered near a pool at the base of the waterfall.

Dunstan bent to retrieve a gilt-edged briefcase, then pursed his lips and followed reluctantly. The air near the waterfall was thick with moisture, a cloying dampness that would completely wilt his carefully chosen clothes. He sat in the chair Daxton indicated, trying hard to veil his impatience.

A servant appeared from nowhere and offered him a heavy gold goblet filled with amber liquid. Petwitt reached for the icy goblet and gave the gray-haired woman a covert glare. Where had she been during his hours-long wait? He took a tiny sip, hiding his grimace behind the rim. Tea. Such a barbaric, low-class drink, but he should have expected such from the Vahntis. Upstarts were upstarts, regardless of their wealth or supposed lineage.

"Thank you, Vannata," Dax told her. The woman nodded and vanished into the forest. "You were saying, Petwitt?" Dax prodded.

"Father is deeply troubled by the growing discord between our clans, and has sent me to offer a proposal."

Dax downed the rest of his tea and set the goblet atop a low table made of glass and Arkanon bamboo. "What sort of proposal?" he said in an offhand tone.

"An alliance."

Startled, Dax almost laughed aloud, but stopped himself short when he saw that Petwitt was actually serious. At least he seemed to be, on the surface. Looks could be deceiving, though, especially where the Dunstans were concerned. "Do go on, Petwitt." He kept his expression carefully bland. "I'm listening." What was Alfred up to this time?

Petwitt placed the fishskin briefcase on his lap and withdrew a thick sheaf of legal documents bearing the ornate Dunstan seal. "This is the instrument through which we hope to end the acrimony and form a lasting alliance between our clans." His dark eyes stilled, and the suggestion of a smile hovered around the corners of his overly ample mouth. "Simply put, what my father proposes is a marriage, Count Vahnti, a permanent joining of the Vahnti and Dunstan clans." With a dramatic flourish, he handed the sheaf of parchment to Dax. "A marriage between the Dunstan heir . . . and Lady Caccia."

Dax's bland expression evaporated, and he arched a disbelieving brow. Surely he hadn't heard that right. "You . . . and Caccia?" He wasn't quite certain which was more ludicrous— the thought of an alliance with the Dunstans, or the prospect of marriage between those two. "You can't be serious."

"Indeed I am." Petwitt stiffened and lifted his chin. "Lady Caccia would make an eminently suitable mate."

"*Caccia?*" Dax's laughter echoed through the atrium. And Petwitt? They'd probably devour their young.

"I fail to see what you find so amusing, Count Vahnti," Dunstan said in an outraged tone. "Your cousin Caccia is a very desirable woman."

"Oh, of that I have no doubt." Dax wiped at his eyes with the sleeve of his tunic and forced all trace of amusement from his face. An endless succession of lovers would testify to Caccia's desirability. "Forgive my outburst, Lord Dunstan; it's just that your offer was so . . . unexpected." *Unbelievable* was more like it.

Petwitt dipped his head in mute acceptance of the apology, though inwardly he was seething. Vahnti had actually *laughed* at him. He waved a bejeweled hand toward the stack of parchment Dax was holding. "May we get down to business?"

"Please do." His face expressionless, Dax made himself concentrate on the matter at hand. If he didn't, he would likely dissolve into another fit of laughter, and this time Dunstan wasn't likely to shrug off the insult.

"I believe you will find the terms of the marriage contract to be mutually beneficial," Petwitt went on in a cool voice, careful to mask his rage. "The usual economic and trade considerations have been incorporated into the contract, with each clan's monetary outlay matched so that the net result will be an equal exchange of funds and property. In part C of the contract, beginning on page one hundred and fifty-seven, legal solutions to all trade matters currently in contention between our clans are addressed on a tit-for-tat basis. A concession from you on one matter will merit an equal compromise from us on another."

"I see," Dax said mildly. He thumbed through the thick stack of parchment resting in his hands, scanning the endless pages of monotonous legalese as he did. Two hundred and ninety-one pages in all. Quite a contract. And knowing the Dunstans, there was a trap or pitfall lurking in every paragraph. Did the Dunstans think him a complete fool?

A thought suddenly occurred to him, one that he hadn't considered before. Dax frowned. Was it possible that Caccia actually wanted to marry this lout? She had allowed him entry through Drakken's shields, after all, and did seem quite eager for the clans to set their acrimony aside. And marriage to the Dunstan heir would afford her far more prestige than she would ever receive as the cousin of the Vahnti warlord.

He peered at Petwitt intently. "Have you broached the subject of marriage with Caccia?"

For a fraction of a second, Petwitt looked bewildered; then his mask of urbane composure slid back into place. "Whatever for?" he queried. "The proposal and negotiations are interclan business. Only the outcome concerns her."

So Caccia didn't know. Dax pursed his lips to keep himself from smiling. "You don't know Caccia very well, do you, Petwitt? Or me for that matter. She does exactly what she pleases, regardless of the repercussions. If she wants to marry you she will; if not she will tell you so in no uncertain terms." He sighed heavily. "Perhaps I've been overly indulgent with her since the deaths of my parents and hers, but it's far too late to change that now."

Petwitt gave him an incredulous look. "You are her liege lord, are you not? She has no choice but to marry me if you so order."

"Like I said," Dax told him, and this time he did smile, "you really don't know me very well. I won't force Caccia into a political marriage merely to advance clan interests. The final decision must rest with her."

Petwitt's eyes darkened but his cool expression remained unchanged. Daxton Vahnti truly was an eccentric. The idea of him giving Caccia a choice in the matter was outrageous in the extreme. "The Lady Caccia is an exceedingly intelligent woman. She will see the inherent wisdom in a match between us and respond accordingly."

"Possibly." Dax shrugged. "Then again . . ." His gaze drifted to the vacant pathway once again. Where was Rayna?

He shouldn't have left her to her own devices. It was far too soon.

Petwitt cleared his throat to regain the Vahnti count's attention. What was wrong with the blasted man? Daxton had seemed preoccupied ever since he'd arrived. Time was passing, and he wanted to be on his way before the humidity did permanent damage to his attire. "My dear Count, might I be so bold as to ask how *you* look upon the proposed match?"

He shifted his gaze back to Petwitt. If he said what he really thought, an affronted Petwitt would storm out of Drakken Castle in an outraged huff. The troubles with the Dunstans were bad enough without feeding more fuel to the fires. He had to buy time, time enough to formulate a careful response that would leave Alfred and Petwitt's dignity intact. Otherwise, there'd be hell to pay, both now and in the future.

"Tell your father that I promise to broach the subject with Lady Caccia. Then I and my advisers will give the contract the ... consideration it so richly deserves." He moved a thumb over the thick stack of heavy parchment. "But you must understand, a proposal of this magnitude will take time to consider."

"When might we expect a final answer?"

"A month or so, three at the most."

Petwitt inclined his head and forced himself to contain his glee. *Perfect timing.* "That is acceptable to us."

Business concluded, they stood abruptly. Petwitt retrieved his briefcase and dipped his head in a polite bow, though it galled him to do so. "Thank you for your hospitality, Count Vahnti. Father and I both hope that this historic meeting will mark the beginning of a new and lasting friendship between our clans."

"Oh, I'm sure it will." The necessary lie left a sour taste on Dax's tongue.

Petwitt turned to leave but stopped short when he spotted a young girl standing as still as a statue amidst a tangle of greenery near the pathway. A bird of some kind was perched on her shoulder, twittering and moving about in a flurry of turquoise feathers. A shower of coppery hair fell past her waist, and pleading eyes the deep green of Malcon's seas seemed to

stare right through him, as if she were silently begging him to
. . . what?

For the barest of seconds Petwitt wasn't quite certain the
nymph was real; then her eyes slowly blinked and her head
turned in Vahnti's direction. The bird took wing, spiraling upward toward the atrium ceiling, but the girl remained where
she was, poised like some graceful animal who'd caught the
scent of danger on the wind.

"What an enchanting creature," Petwitt said breathlessly.
Was she some minor member of the Vahnti household he'd
never met? A servant girl? His dark gaze narrowing in appreciation, he turned toward Vahnti, his mouth thinning as well
when he saw the hungry look in Daxton's pale eyes. Now he
understood why Vahnti had seemed so preoccupied. Petwitt
smiled inwardly. The files his clan kept on the Vahnti warlord
had never mentioned that he liked his women quite so young.
Valuable information, that, maybe something they could use
against him in the future. Magnificent though she was, the girl
didn't look as if she'd reached the age of consent. And bed-
ding a minor was considered a breach of ethics under Dominion law. Possibly even a crime if the situation warranted legal
action.

A sly, self-satisfied smile teased the corners of Petwitt's
mouth. The Vahnti warlord might just have an Achilles' heel
after all. He coughed lightly to break the heated stare the two
were exchanging. "Count Vahnti, might I beg the favor of an
introduction?"

Dax blinked and swung his gaze toward Petwitt, adding a
measure of calm into his expression that he didn't feel. He'd
been greatly relieved when Rayna appeared, but the mere sight
of her standing amid the vines and greenery had also released
a flood of desire within him that he found hard to contain. His
pale eyes hardened, grew cold with anger and confusion. Was
he a slave to his loins? She was just a girl, intriguing and
beautiful, yes, but just a girl nonetheless. What was it about
her that made him ache with such burning need?

"Rayna, come here for a moment," he said more harshly
than he'd intended. He was angry at himself, and at Petwitt
for forcing an introduction. But refusing such an innocuous

request would be a breach of protocol he could ill afford.

Petwitt arched a brow but said nothing. Curious. Not exactly the tone of voice one would use to entice a lover.

She stepped onto the pathway and walked toward them reluctantly, a sullen expression creeping over her face. The solitude and peace of the last half hour had ended abruptly when she'd wandered through a wall of foliage and found the demon lord and his guest standing in a clearing at the base of the waterfall. Why had she come in this direction? Why had she been foolish enough to follow the sound of rushing water? She might have been able to elude him for a while longer if she'd been more careful. Her emerald gaze flickered downward to the thin gold bands around her wrists. As long as she wore them, she would never be able to elude him, not for a single minute.

She stopped and stared at the Vahnti warlord coldly. She was tired of him ordering her about like some wayward child or pet.

"Lord Dunstan, this is Rayna Syn . . . a guest of Drakken Castle," he said tightly.

"Enchanted to make your acquaintance, my dear." Petwitt clasped her fingers to his and brushed his lips across the top of her hand.

Rayna pulled her hand free and suppressed a grimace. His lips were as cold as the serpent's eyes.

"How long have you been a guest here?" Petwitt prodded. The arctic glare she'd given Vahnti was food for thought. Was it possible that she was a reluctant guest?

"Since today," Rayna said quietly, searching the stranger's bearded face with her eyes. There was obviously no love lost between the serpent and this Lord Dunstan. Was he a potential ally?

"Ah, and where exactly is your homeworld?"

Her chin lifted. "Nirvanna. I am a member of the Lakota tribe . . . at least I was until the warlord's ships and soldiers came to plunder our world."

"How interesting." Petwitt gave Daxton a sidelong glance. Dunstan spies had told them months ago that the Vahntis were finally planning to harvest Nirvanna's resources, but it was nice to have firsthand confirmation. "Isn't Nirvanna that barbaric little Vahnti world where the colonists live like uncivilized savages?"

"We are not savages," Rayna said in a brittle voice. She'd thought this man to be a potential ally, but she'd obviously been wrong. "We choose to live the way we do, to live our lives free of the stench of your so-called civilization."

"Really? Whatever would possess you to leave such an idyllic lifestyle behind?"

Dax's face darkened. Dunstan was purposefully goading Rayna in hopes that she'd make some sort of revelation. "I have a busy schedule today, Petwitt."

"Quite right. I must be on my way, too." Petwitt smiled unctuously. He'd pushed as far as Vahnti would allow. But no matter. "We'll have to continue our discussion at another time, Miss Syn." His spies would soon discover the truth of the girl's status at the castle.

Chapter Eight

Shades of pink and fiery gold tinged Hellfire's deepening sky as the massive sun plunged beneath a ridge of mountains crouched along the horizon. Rayna pressed her forehead against a pane of glass and watched the fading daylight ebb into night. Behind her, the demon lord's vast library was bathed in gray shadows, the endless rows of leather-bound tomes the only witnesses to her despair.

For the first time since that morning, when she'd lost herself in the jungle-like great hall, she was alone. Alone for a few precious moments until Daxton Vahnti beckoned her again.

Rayna sighed and fastened her pensive gaze on the horizon once more. Tomorrow, perhaps, her future wouldn't look quite so bleak. She couldn't let go of her hope, couldn't give the Vahnti demon lord the satisfaction of defeating her spirit. She was his captive, his property, in name only. If she was patient and vigilant, a way to escape would eventually present itself. A spirit couldn't be held in bondage forever.

In the far distance, steam ringed the faceted cones of several volcanos, cruel reminders of what she would face if she did escape. Her expression hardened. But escape she would. She was an adept trained by the most powerful shaman who'd ever walked the plains of Nirvanna. Somehow she would find a way.

Until then she would bide her time. Observe, prepare, and carefully plan. She studied the line of mountains, committing to memory the shape of the terrain. The first step would be to learn everything she could about her surroundings, the movements of troops and people, and the Vahntis as well. Her new-found friends in the atrium had shared what information they could, but their knowledge was limited by the fact that they were captives, too.

Worklights flared to life in the sprawling courtyard ten stories beneath the bank of windows. Rayna peered downward, watching as a transport ship landed in the darkness and began disgorging a steady stream of troops and cargo. She smiled in relief as a beam of light glinted off the metal bars of several cages being unloaded from the belly of the ship. The wolfens were finally here, as well as the gi.

"We'll find a way," she told them quietly. "I promise."

"A way to what?" a soft voice asked.

Startled, Rayna flinched and whirled around. In the far corner, a young man was seated in an overstuffed chair, his slight form all but veiled by the deepening shadows. He'd been so still and silent she hadn't known he was there. "I'm sorry. I didn't know anyone else was here. Count Vahnti told me to wait here until he returned." She turned toward the doorway, embarrassed and angry with herself that she'd been so preoccupied that she'd failed to notice the stranger's presence.

"Please, don't leave on my account," he said gently. "I come here every day to watch the sunset."

Rayna paused. There was something poignant about his voice, a soft note of kindness and understanding that could only come from the soul.

Jan Zimlich

"I was glad for the company, even if you didn't know I was here." There was a ripple of movement within the chair. "Truth is, I've enjoyed watching you almost as much as that glorious sunset." His eyes drifted closed, as if he were savoring a pleasant memory. "I'd like to paint you sometime, standing just as you were in front of the windows, the sun and glass throwing highlights through your hair." His currant black eyes suddenly reopened. "Yes, I think I'd like that."

She stared back at him curiously, noting his dark good looks, the thin, elegant hands holding a well-worn book against his chest. She was about the same age and build as he was, but on a male his slight frame looked fragile somehow, as if a quickening wind might blow him away. "Who are you?"

He placed the book on the arm of his chair, then climbed to his feet and bent at the waist in a formal bow. "I'm Carlo Vahnti, Dax's cousin. And who might you be?"

She stared back in shock. The demon lord's cousin? The familial resemblance ended with the dark hair and skin. "My name is Rayna Syn."

He walked toward the bank of windows, his movements slow and graceful. "You're the girl my sister Caccia spoke about."

That announcement stunned her even more. In temperament, Carlo Vahnti and his sister seemed to be as dissimilar as day and night. "She's your *sister?*" Rayna said, then immediately wanted to bite back the words.

Carlo chuckled, his dark eyes shining with a hint of amusement. "Don't worry. You haven't offended me. Nature can indeed be perverse at times. And frankly, you're not the first to react that way." He folded his hands behind his back and sighed, long and deep. "Caccia just can't help herself, I suppose."

"And your cousin?" She watched his youthful face intently. "Can he not help himself either?"

"Daxton?" Carlo barely shrugged one shoulder. "Dax is like the elements, a force of nature, if you will." For long seconds, he gazed out the window as Hellfire's sky turned a deep purple-black. "Indomitable, unchangeable. Like gravity or the passage of time."

In the distance, bright streams of red veined the mountains huddled along the horizon. A faraway look crept through Carlo's velvety eyes. "Did you know that there are over ten thousand active volcanoes on Hellfire?"

"No, I didn't know that." The odd shift in conversation sent a chill up Rayna's spine.

"Strange, isn't it? You'd think with so many the atmosphere would be choked completely with volcanic dust. But it isn't." A bewildered frown moved across his boyish face. "I've never understood why that is. Wind patterns maybe."

She stared with him at the enveloping darkness, at the fingers of lava staining the horizon. "I hadn't thought about it, but it does seem strange."

Carlo sighed, an anguished sound filled with emotion; then his train of thought shifted once again. "Like the quakes. They come and they go, but the animals always seem to know. I do, too, every once in a while. The center of my forehead will ache, as if nature is trying to warn me, tell me something. . . ." He frowned again and touched his brow. "Doesn't make sense."

There was pain in his voice now, emanating from a source she couldn't fathom. But she sensed no madness, no well of insanity feeding this fragile young man, only an aching loneliness that equaled her own. This kind and gentle soul lived in a universe of his own making, a distant, dreamy place divorced from reality. And with that realization came the sure knowledge that she liked Carlo Vahnti, regardless of who or what he was.

"I really would like to paint you," he said suddenly, his face and voice no longer shadowed with pain. "With your permission, of course."

She touched his forearm, an impulsive gesture on her part, but one designed to put him at ease. "I'd like that." Carlo Vahnti made her feel as if her opinion mattered, unlike his cousin, who neither sought nor needed her permission for anything. "Anytime you want."

75

"It might take a while." He averted his eyes. "I tend to get distracted at times."

Rayna smiled. "It doesn't matter. Time is all I have at the moment."

He clasped her hand with a gentleness born of uncertainty. "Let's go."

She stared at him in confusion. "To paint my picture?"

"No, not that." He led her toward the doorway. "To dinner."

"But Count Vahnti told me to wait here for him."

He pulled her into the central corridor. "Don't worry about Daxton. He'll find you."

The bracelet on her right hand brushed against his wrist, a brutal reminder of just who and what she was. "I suppose he will," Rayna said with a resigned sigh, and allowed Carlo to lead her down the endless hallway.

After a long walk down the deserted corridor, Carlo paused in front of a set of carved doors. "Ready?" he asked in a whisper.

Rayna nodded.

He gripped her hand tighter, as if he were drawing on her strength instead of the other way around, then pushed the doors open and stepped inside the family dining room.

A dark wooden table stretched from one end of the room to the other, the polished surface burnished to a high gleam by age and endless care. Blue and cream rugs in an Oriental design covered the obsidian floor, colors carried through in the delicate china placed along the table. Rayna gazed in wonder at the immense chandelier suspended above the table, the soft white light glinting and shifting behind thousands of crystal prisms.

"Sit here, Rayna, beside me." Carlo beckoned. He pulled a high-backed chair from beneath the far side of the table and waved her toward it.

Rayna took her seat apprehensively, uncertain if she should be there at all. She was a prisoner in Drakken Castle, not an honored guest invited to dine with the family. Besides, she would rather eat alone in some dank cell than suffer another meal with Daxton Vahnti. "I don't think I should be here, Carlo," she said in a hushed voice.

"Nonsense. You have to eat, don't you?"

Her gaze moved to the end of the room. A ten-foot section of wall was covered by a black-and-gold shield bearing the Vahnti crest of a serpent coiled around the length of a sword. She shuddered inwardly. The crest was his emblem, symbolic of everything she hated. "I'm not very hungry."

The door clicked open and Caccia Vahnti swept inside, the crimson robe she'd worn that morning replaced by a floor-length gown of deep blue velvet.

Caccia's eyes widened when she saw Carlo, then narrowed to tiny slits when she noticed the girl seated next to him. This day was full of surprises. It had been close to a year since Carlo last dined with the family, ordering that his food be brought to his rooms instead. She hated to think the crude little colonist might be the reason for his sudden spurt of sociability.

"Oh, dear me, are you lost, Rayna?" she said archly. "*Prisoners* are fed on the basement level, eleven stories down." It hadn't taken her long to discover the little savage's true situation. A lingering kiss in a darkened corridor and Captain Remi had been more than willing to bare his soul. And she would wheedle more out of him later when she paid a private visit to his rooms. "Carlo, would you be so good as to show her to the nearest lift-tube?"

Rayna reddened and started to rise, but Carlo belayed her with a hand.

"I want her here, Caccia," he told her firmly. "I'm going to paint her." His gaze became unfocused, drifting to the doorway behind his sister. "It's going to be such a wonderful painting, filled with light and symbolism."

"Really, Carlo!" Caccia snapped. "Have you lost your wits completely? Where's your sense of decorum? She's a prisoner, as well as a commoner. Rumor has it that Daxton has even placed a forfeiture claim on the girl. She tried to murder our darling Dax, for heaven's sake! Stabbed him right through his armor!"

He turned to Rayna in confusion. "Is that true, Rayna?"

Her back stiffened, and she met his gaze defiantly. She

Jan Zimlich

wasn't ashamed of what she'd done. "Yes, it's true, Carlo."

"More symbolism," Carlo said softly. "I think I'll paint you with a knife cradled in an outstretched hand."

Rage swept across Caccia's face. "Get out," she demanded, glaring at Rayna through narrowed eyes. "Or I'll have the guards throw you out." Her wrath shifted back to her brother. "As for you, you mindless dimwit, I forbid you to paint her! I forbid you ever to speak to her again. And just to be sure you obey me, I'm going to have the servants throw out your paints and canvases immediately!"

The hand gripping Rayna's arm began to tremble with emotion.

Rayna cast a sidelong glance at Carlo's pale, beatific face and gently pulled free of his grasp. How could a brother and sister be so different? "I think I should go now, Carlo. If I stay I might be tempted to stab your sister, too."

"Stay where you are, Rayna," a deep voice growled.

Her gaze snapped up. Daxton Vahnti was standing in the doorway, his dark features mottled with fury.

He strode into the room and paused, Haywood March close on his heels. "No one has the right to order you from my table except me." ·

Caccia swung toward her cousin in a rustling flurry of velvet and crinolines. Her rouged mouth tightened. "Dax, you can't be serious! It's unseemly!"

"Shut up, Caccia. I told you not to interfere in my life. If you don't wish to eat with Rayna, you may take your meals in your rooms." He kept his voice even, but it took all of his control. "And I never want to hear you speak in that manner to your brother again. He doesn't need your permission to paint or talk to a guest in his home. Carlo is free to do what he wishes, when he wishes. Is that clear enough for you?"

She glared at him from beneath her lashes but said no more. Still scowling, Caccia settled into a chair opposite Rayna. She wouldn't give them the satisfaction of leaving the table in disgrace.

Haywood March cleared his throat and took a seat across from Carlo. Though it troubled him greatly to be present during family disputes, he was happy that Dax had finally decided to take his shrewish cousin firmly in hand.

Dax eased into his chair at the head of the table and studied Rayna out of the corner of his eye. She was obviously ill at ease but didn't look any the worse for wear after the encounter with Caccia. In fact, there was a predatory gleam in those bright green eyes, as if she were contemplating the slow removal of one of Caccia's organs. He pursed his lips thoughtfully. She'd acquitted herself quite well in the confrontation. Perhaps tomorrow he could let her have free rein of the castle and grounds. She would need more clothes, though, and soon. The green robe he'd had made was beginning to look a little rumpled.

His pale gaze moved to Carlo, who was whispering something in Rayna's ear. The sight gave him pause, but he wasn't overly concerned. Anyone who drew Carlo from the solitude of his rooms, even for a single night, was a positive influence. Even if it was Rayna.

"It's good to see you, Carlo," Dax said with an affectionate smile. "I hope you'll make a habit of dining with us more often. I've missed your company."

Carlo gave him a boyish grin, looking for all the world like the bright and mischievous five-year-old that Dax had taken under his wing when their parents were killed. Dax sighed inwardly. So much had changed since then. Carlo especially.

"I'm glad to see you, too, boy," Haywood told Carlo. "It's been quite a while."

For the life of him, Carlo couldn't remember exactly why he'd stopped taking his meals with them. "I'll take my meals here when I can, but I'm going to be very busy in the next few months. I've decided to paint again."

"That's wonderful," Dax said sincerely. Carlo had drifted further away since he'd stopped painting, as though art was the only thing that had kept him grounded in reality.

"I'm going to paint Rayna."

"Fine," Dax said with an offhand shrug. Silently he thanked fate for intervening on the boy's behalf. His art might bring him back to life. "I look forward to seeing the finished work."

Caccia snorted beneath her breath.

Puzzled, Rayna cast the demon lord a sidelong glance. Until this moment she hadn't thought he possessed an ounce of compassion, but his feelings for Carlo were evident in his gentle tone and the concerned looks he threw the boy's way every now and again. An aberration? She stared at him more closely. His pale eyes were hooded, unreadable, yet she knew he was watching every movement at the table, surveying them all with a relentless intensity veiled by that facade of detachment.

A stream of servants bustled into the room, carrying huge golden platters piled high with an assortment of foods. An elderly woman wearing a severe gray robe and an equally severe expression snapped her fingers and directed the servants where to place the platters.

A server dressed in the black-and-gold livery of the Vahntis heaped copious amounts of steaming vegetables and meats atop Rayna's plate. Her stomach rumbled as the scent of maize roasted with sweet basil touched her nostrils. She stared down at her plate hungrily, knowing her vow to never eat from the serpent's table had been for naught. It had been days since she'd last eaten, a state her body was beginning to protest in no uncertain terms. She would eat his food, and she'd enjoy every bite.

"Vannata," Caccia snapped, and puckered her mouth in distaste. "You know I don't like the color of steamed rockbeans. It annoys me. Take this plate away and bring me a new one."

"Of course, Lady Caccia." Her shoulders stiffening, Vannata removed the offending plate and swiftly replaced it with another.

Dax's jaw tightened. Caccia's arrogance and increasing demands had thrown the entire household into turmoil. And in the past three months her expenditures of family funds had risen to outrageous proportions. His jaw tightened even more. The temptation to sign the Dunstans' contract increased each time Caccia opened her mouth.

Carlo picked at the savory fare, while Haywood attacked the contents of his plate with obvious relish. The only sounds to break the awkward silence were the steady clicks of forks striking the fine bone china.

Dax leaned back in his chair and turned his attention to Rayna, watching in amusement as she began devouring a serving of maize. He smiled in satisfaction. One less battle to fight. "I see you've ended your hunger strike, Rayna."

She responded with a hostile look.

"That's a pity," Caccia said nastily, and stabbed at a slice of roasted emul. "I wouldn't have thought such rich fare would agree with someone accustomed to a diet of roots and berries. What do you Nirvannans do at mealtime? Grub around in the dirt until you find something vaguely edible?"

The look Rayna threw her way was even more hostile than the one she'd given Dax. "We cooperate with nature . . . we don't exploit it as your people do." Her chin lifted disdainfully. "Judging by your pasty complexion and the amount of animal flesh piled on your plate, you could stand to eat a few roots and berries yourself."

Haywood coughed to hide his bark of laughter, while Carlo simply stared in amazement, both thrilled and terrified that someone had dared to speak to his sister in such a way.

Caccia leaned forward and dropped her voice to a contemptuous whisper. "My complexion is fashionably pale, I'll have you know, and I take great pains to keep it that way. But then, what would an illiterate savage know about court fashion?"

"Enough to know that you and your highborn kind are nothing but arrogant parasites, despite your fancy finery."

"Why, you disgusting little slut! How dare you speak to me that way!"

"Careful, Caccia," Dax warned in an amused voice. Rayna had given as good as she got. Even so, it was time to end the war of words before it escalated into blows. "Behave yourself or I might find myself tempted to put a pen to that contract."

Caccia's dark brows lowered, and her angry gaze focused on her cousin. "Contract? What are you talking about, Dax?"

Dax smiled slowly. Petwitt might have unwittingly given him the means to keep Caccia in line. "You really should have taken the time to find out why Petwitt wanted to see me."

A sense of foreboding settled in the pit of Caccia's stomach. She didn't like Dax's tone of voice, or his silky smile. "Whatever do you mean?"

"The Dunstans have proposed a merger of sorts." His smile widened. "A marriage between you and Petwitt."

"Marriage?" Caccia's mouth opened and closed, then fell open again, as though she were having difficulty forming intelligible words. A flush crept up her neck to her face, edging upward like a scarlet tide cresting across a pale shore. Petwitt was vain, overbearing, and callous, a cold and manipulative man despised by men and women alike among Dominion nobility. How could Dax even entertain the notion that she might marry him? They had nothing at all in common. "Why, I wouldn't marry that obnoxious oaf if he were the last man in the galaxy!"

Dax took a sip of wine and peered at her over the rim of his glass. The split second of terror he'd seen in her eyes told him that she did indeed fear the prospect of a marriage to Petwitt. "I must admit the proposal caught me off guard, too, but the idea does have merit. I told Petwitt that I needed time to study the contract, and that I would give him and Lord Alfred my final answer in a couple of months. But it is food for thought, wouldn't you say?" He smiled and let his voice trail off, both a threat and an overt warning.

Caccia's body went still, and her eyes turned cold and opaque. "You wouldn't dare."

Rayna's gaze shifted from one to the other. The tension in the air was dark and palpable, like a malevolent cloud poised above them. Her appetite fled, and she laid her fork down with an audible clack. She gave the demon lord a piercing glare, and wasn't surprised to see a glint of pleasure lighting his hooded eyes.

"Don't be so sure," Dax said, and smiled coldly. "Marrying you off to Petwitt would solve several problems at once, both political and financial. Our trade conflicts with the Dunstans would end, and Petwitt would assume responsibility for your expenditures, though I doubt the Dunstans would be as generous and patient with you as I have been." He lowered his voice several notches. "And I'm quite sure the household staff would breathe a bit easier without your constant haranguing.''

The flush on her face and neck turned bloodred. ''You can't force me!''

''As Petwitt so aptly put it, I am your liege lord. If I order you to do so, you have no choice.''

Carlo glanced up from his plate and stared around vacantly. ''Are you getting married, Caccia?''

She flung her plate over Carlo's head, where it slammed into an antique sideboard and shattered into a hundred fragments. Part of her dinner oozed down a leg of the sideboard. Caccia leaped to her feet, glared malignantly at Dax, then burst into tears and fled the dining room. Her wails echoed down the corridor for endless seconds.

Rayna gaped at the open doorway in shock, then looked around the table. Though a silence fraught with tension had descended over the room, the demon lord, Carlo, and Haywood March had continued with their meal as if nothing at all had occurred. Behind her, the quiet servants were meticulously cleaning the mess from the sideboard and floor, going about their duties with smooth precision. She shuddered inwardly. They were all mad—cruel, uncaring people without a shred of human feeling.

Haywood cleared his throat noisily. ''That went well, I think.''

Dax downed the remains of his wine and chuckled low in his throat. ''The next few months might even be pleasant. The threat of Petwitt hanging over Caccia's head might be enough to keep her in line for a while.''

''I doubt it,'' Haywood said with a snort. ''A fleet of battle cruisers wouldn't be enough to keep that girl in line.''

Carlo pushed his plate aside. ''Is Caccia really getting married, Dax?''

''Maybe, maybe not.'' Carlo was too honest for his own good. If he told the boy that he had no intention of agreeing to the Dunstans' proposal, Carlo might repeat it, and his hold over Caccia would slip away. Dax's mouth softened into a smile. ''You just concentrate on your painting and let me deal with Caccia.''

"I will." Carlo's gaze wandered to Rayna's delicate profile. He saw a hint of fragility there, as well as anger and a wellspring of hidden strength. And something else, something almost mystical about her eyes, as if she could see beyond the bounds of this world into infinity. That was the look he decided to capture. "Will you sit for me tomorrow, Rayna? Just an hour or two?"

"Of course." Her eyes cut right, to the watching demon lord, daring him to object. She would do anything to be free of him, even for an hour.

Dax shrugged. "She can sit for you whenever you like, Carlo, but you'll have to share her with Dr. Bahleigh." His eyes caught and held Rayna's. "He has plans for her, too."

An emotion akin to dread danced along Rayna's spine. What did he mean by that? Bahleigh was the long-faced doctor who'd been holding the wolfens prisoner.

Haywood stood and nodded to Vannata and the line of servers waiting to clear the table. "Good meal, as always, Vannata."

Vannata dipped her head in acknowledgment. "Thank you, Commander." She exchanged a meaningful look with Haywood March, then glided soundlessly to Dax's side. "My lord, I have taken the liberty of preparing a suite of rooms on level fourteen for your . . . guest. I'm sure she'll be quite comfortable there."

Dax's gaze shifted from a tense Vannata to Haywood's unreadable face. He smiled to himself. *A conspiracy, and a rather thin one at that.* The top level of Drakken Castle was his, a good thirty stories above the suite Vannata had chosen. "That won't be necessary, Vannata." He grinned at Haywood. "Rayna will be staying in my rooms for the foreseeable future."

Dread skittered along Rayna's spine again.

"Oh, and Vannata," Dax said quietly. "Would you be so kind as to have the tailors make some clothes for Rayna? Whatever you think necessary."

"Of course, Count Vahnti."

Haywood sighed. It had been worth a try. He gave Rayna a final warning glance and turned to Dax. Though the girl had behaved fairly well today, he still didn't trust her alone with Dax. "The troop review is scheduled for ten tomorrow morning." He opened his mouth to say something else, then shut it again. It would do no good to object.

"Good." Dax lifted a brow. Haywood was still worried and uncertain about leaving him alone with Rayna. "Night, old friend. See you then."

"Come along, Carlo," Haywood prodded. "I'll walk you to the lift-tube." After that he'd have a little chat with the guards stationed on Dax's floor.

Carlo smiled and climbed from his chair, accompanying Haywood without a backward glance.

The servers made short work of clearing the table, bade their warlord good night, and vanished soundlessly through a doorway hidden in the scrollwork along the far wall.

To her dismay, Rayna found herself alone with the demon lord. She avoided his probing gaze and squirmed restlessly in her chair. What torment awaited her now?

Dax ran a thumb around the rim of his wineglass, enjoying her discomfiture. "Ready for bed, dear? I know it's early yet, but I'm weary from the trip."

Her face reddened and her eyes snapped around. She'd had more than enough of his arrogance for one day. "You may be able to force your cousin into a loveless marriage, but you cannot force me to sleep in your bed," Rayna said furiously. "I'd sooner be strangled to death by a sand-snake than awaken next to you!"

The hint of a smile played around the corners of his mouth. "Never make assumptions." His smile widened. "Sleeping might not be what I had in mind."

Her eyes darkened to a smoldering green. "I would sooner die!"

"That's not what I had in mind, either."

Chapter Nine

A soft haze of silver had replaced the deep purple-black of Hellfire's night, bathing the demon lord's sprawling bedroom suite in shades of milky gray. Shadows stretched and lengthened, fingers of inky darkness that crept and pooled along the wide expanse of richly woven rugs scattered about the cold stone floor.

Rayna lay in the predawn darkness and continued her vigil, listening to the slow, even sound of the demon lord's breathing across the width of his enormous bed. He'd been sleeping deeply for hours now, a contented sleep, no doubt, while she in turn lay awake, nervously awaiting an attack on her maidenhood that had never come.

Above her, the dark wood bedposts soared toward a domed ceiling decorated with hunting scenes painted in deep masculine greens against an ivory background. The paintings were grotesque, stilted renderings of hunting dogs baying after some pathetic creature, while noblemen astride huge Earth horses closed in for the kill. Living, breathing creatures being slaughtered for sport. What sort of man would enjoy such a thing? What sort of man would place such nightmarish scenes above his bed?

She raged at the demon lord silently, longing to free herself and creep from the bed, but worried that if she moved he might awaken and do what she feared. Her hopes that she would be placed in a cell far from him had been for naught. The worm had won the battle over where she'd sleep by ripping a cord from the draperies and tying her arms to the post.

But his victory had come at a price. She smiled grimly in the shadowy darkness. An armoire and an antique chest had been overturned in the skirmish, and the plush velvet draperies were lying in a useless heap near the tall bank of windows.

She pulled on the satin cord binding her wrists and glared at his sleeping form. After he had bound her to the bedpost and ripped off her overrobe, she'd closed her eyes and gritted her teeth, fully expecting him to do his worst. Instead, much to her amazement, he had simply shrugged off his clothes, rolled to the other side of the bed, and promptly fallen asleep.

A curious frown softened her glare. She was bound, utterly defenseless, helpless to stop whatever depravity he had in mind. So why hadn't he taken her? His ice blue eyes had been dark with desire as he ripped away her one and only robe. What had stopped him? It certainly wasn't his conscience, or any sense of morality, because the demon lord possessed neither of those.

Her frown deepened. Daxton Vahnti was truly an enigma, a cold and powerful man who callously ruled entire worlds and the fates of millions with a steely hand. A man who was capable of forcing one cousin into a loveless marriage while exhibiting a measure of kindness to another. Stranger still, why had he taken such an obvious interest in her? She was his captive, wasn't she? An enemy who'd done her best to murder him, and made no attempt to hide her desire to try again. So why was she here, forced to sleep in his bed, eat at his table? Why go to the trouble of ordering clothes made for her?

It didn't make sense, any of it.

She studied him as he slept, her gaze roving curiously over the strong line of his jaw and aquiline nose, his angular chin with its small, clefted hollow, the firm yet ample mouth that lent an air of sensuality to the mystery surrounding him. His aristocratic features were framed by a thick sheath of jet hair that streamed down to brush his pillow and the tops of lean, well-muscled shoulders. When he was awake, long, sooty lashes and straight black brows served only to accentuate his dark looks and glacial eyes, eyes so pale and hypnotically bright that at times she found herself unable to free herself from his cryptic gaze.

He moved slightly, and the soft pile of bedcoverings slipped to his waist, revealing a smooth expanse of olive skin. As she stared down the corded length of his torso, Rayna felt her pulse quicken in response. He was extraordinarily handsome, she admitted to herself, so much so that if the circumstances were different, she might even be attracted to him. Any woman would be, noble and commoner alike. It was more than his looks, though. There was something quite compelling about Daxton Vahnti, a sense that deep beneath that cold, brooding surface lay a furnace of emotions that would singe anyone foolish enough to stoke its fires.

As her gaze roamed back to his face, she was startled to find those veiled blue eyes regarding her with a watchful intensity she found disquieting. Her heartbeat drummed in her ears as she stared back at him. How long had he been awake?

For a moment Dax didn't move, didn't breathe. He simply absorbed the sure knowledge that he had awakened in the dawn light to find those exotic green eyes wandering over his body in a manner that was anything but maidenly. It wasn't a fantasy dredged from his imagination. She'd been exploring him with her eyes. And the knowledge that he and he alone had been witness to the first glimmer of desire flaring to life within this woman-child was like a sweet draft of heady wine heating his veins.

Time hung suspended, the seconds frozen into a beguiling memory Dax knew he would take out and savor again and again. The first pale slivers of sunlight were slanting through the curtainless windows, dappling her russet hair and lithe body with traces of silver. Her lips were parted slightly, trembling at the corners, and her jewel green eyes were dark with a confused mix of anger, curiosity, and embarrassment. With her arms bound above her head, the lush outline of her breasts was made more visible beneath the thin white undergown, the peaks of rosy nipples taut and erect as they strained against the filmy material.

His hand seemed to move of its own accord. Slowly, gently, he traced the hollow between her breasts with the tips of his fingers, then eased the thin undergown downward to explore the delicate curves that lay beneath.

Rayna trembled but didn't flinch away. His eyes burned into hers, holding her as tightly as the cord binding her wrists. And where his fingertips touched, her flesh felt scorched, as though the skin itself had come alive. His touch was surprisingly gentle, tender in a way that she had never expected, evoking a languid heat deep within her body that sent shivers of pleasure skittering along her spine.

Too soon, Dax chided himself, but the ache in his loins kept telling him otherwise. Her body had gone utterly still, rigid with anticipation and uncertainty. A pulse was beating along the base of her throat, quick and thready, and her eyes had turned a dark, sensuous green. The ache within him became insistent, demanding. He moved toward her unconsciously, unable to resist the subtle aura of innocence and raw sexuality she wore like a second skin.

A shudder passed through his body as his mouth closed around the crested peak of one breast. A soft gasp of surprise escaped her throat, but she didn't pull away. Dax reveled in that throaty sound, the taste and feel of her pliant flesh beneath his lips.

Rayna lost herself in the moment, in the wild surge of pleasure pulsing through her blood. She arched against his questing tongue, driven by an urge she didn't understand, yet was powerless to resist. She moaned softly. It was his lips, his fingers that her treacherous body was responding to. Daxton Vahnti, the darkling lord who was bent on destroying her people's culture and way of life. She tossed her head from side to side, a silent battle raging between her body and mind. *Forgive me, Grandfather.* Tears glistened in the corners of her eyes, but she didn't allow them to fall. *My heart and flesh are no longer one.*

Dax cupped her other breast within his palm and stroked her gently. He had felt her rise against his mouth and knew that he had won. He could take her now if he wanted, just kindle the flames of her newborn desire a little more and be through with her once and for all. Coupling with her here and now would bring him the release his body so desperately craved. But once the deed was finally done his interest in her would begin to wane, just as it had so many times before, with so many other women.

He pulled away abruptly, and quelled the fires raging within him by sheer force of will. His gaze moved back to her heart-shaped face. The look of passion was gone. Instead, her catlike eyes burned hot and bright with unshed tears, and her cheeks were flushed with shame and humiliation.

"Not yet, my pet." Dax sighed deeply, then rose on his elbows and tugged the undergown back into place. "Much as I'd like to, I think I'll wait."

The glare she gave him was laced with venom. What was his game? He knew full well the effect his touch had had on her flesh. Was this some new, more insidious form of torture? For a few short moments she had actually craved the feel of the demon lord's lips and fingers against her naked skin. Shame reddened her cheeks even more. She had betrayed her tribe, her people.

"I hate you," she whispered bitterly.

He lifted a dark brow and traced the outline of her jaw with the back of a finger. "You have a strange way of expressing it." His thumb grazed over the curve of her chin. "Very strange indeed."

"Filthy dung worm!" She jerked her head sideways, away from the tapered finger brushing across her face. "Give me a knife and I'll express my hatred in a way even you can't mistake!"

A haze of sunlight struck the faceted windows and spilled across the bedroom, setting her russet hair aflame with tawny highlights. Her mercurial eyes glittered with green fire. For a split second Dax regretted his decision to wait. She looked so beautiful lying there, beautiful and dangerous. He picked up a curly tendril of hair and looped it about his fingers, marveling at its silky texture. "Sorry to disappoint you, pet, but I have a busy day planned. No time for you to remove any of my vital organs." He dropped the lock of hair and began working at the knot binding her wrists.

There was a discreet rap on the bedroom door.

"Come." He pulled on a section of the knot and her left hand slipped free.

A rectangle of light spilled through the doorway as Vannata glided into the room. Head bowed respectfully, she placed the bundle she was carrying across the back of a velvet wing chair, then turned to face the bed. "I've brought the clothing you ordered, my lord. The tailors worked all night to finish several outfits, but it will be the end of the week before the rest are completed."

"Excellent." Dax freed Rayna's other arm and tossed the drapery cord to the floor. Pillowing his arms behind his neck, he slouched against the carved headboard, unmindful of his state of undress or Vannata's disapproving stare. "Tell the tailors thank-you, and have a hundred credits added to each of their pay chits as a reward."

Rayna flexed her stiff and achy arms, then quickly pulled the bedcoverings up to her neck. If possible, she would have crawled inside the downy mattress and disappeared. The stone-faced old woman was staring at her as if she'd just overturned a moldy rock and discovered something loathsome hidden beneath.

"Yes, my lord." Vannata turned and left as silently as she had come.

Dax climbed from the bed and stretched, the muscles in his shoulders rippling as he moved. "Up, Rayna." He walked to the wing chair and rummaged through the pile of clothing that Vannata left, finally selecting a light blue robe made of Arkanon silk, a pair of matching slippers, and several frothy underthings. "No one lies abed in Drakken Castle past dawn." He snorted to himself. No one except his cousin Caccia. "Get dressed." He dumped the clothing onto the bed. "These will do quite nicely for today."

His toes sank into a plush rug as he walked to the overturned armoire and extracted fresh clothes for himself, no mean feat considering the chaotic state the armoire and drawers were in.

Rayna squeezed her eyes shut as he tromped about the room without a stitch of clothing. In the course of her life she'd seen the naked bodies of many a Lakota warrior, and many had seen her in various stages of undress. But this was different somehow. Frightening. She kept her lids firmly closed, more concerned by her traitorous body's reaction to his nakedness than the sight itself.

He tugged on a fresh pair of breeches and his black leather riding boots, then fastened the top of his uniform tunic and cast a quick glance Rayna's way. An impatient scowl passed across his face. She was still in the bed, eyes tightly closed, the covers drawn up past her chin. Last night she had refused to take off her robe, and the torn heap of green material lying on the floor had been the result. Now she was refusing to dress. When would she learn to do what he asked?

His scowl darkened. "I assure you, Rayna, if I'm forced to dress you, it will not be a pleasant experience." The corners of his mouth curled in a mocking half smile. "Then again, I might decide to keep you just as you are, minus that under-gown, of course."

Her lids flew open. She glared at the clothing he'd tossed on the bed, then cautiously peered at him. Relief flooded her face. At least he was clothed now, clad in the dark garb of a Vahnti soldier, the gold sword and serpent emblazoned on the front of his tunic. But even that hated uniform was better than nothing at all.

"Well?" he demanded. "What's it to be? I don't have all day to dither about while you decide whether to come willingly or not."

Her expression hardened. Was every word that spilled from his mouth a pronouncement of some kind? His every utterance a command? "You said I was to have free rein of the castle today. Why must I go with you?"

Dax sighed, long and loud. He wasn't used to explaining himself. To anyone. He gave instructions, issued edicts, and people obeyed. So why did she have to question him at every turn, carp on his every word? It was annoying in the extreme. But then, he'd brought the annoyance on himself by his insistence on bringing her to Drakken. His own obstinacy and lust had created the situation, so he'd have to deal with the inconvenience as best he could.

For the space of a single heartbeat he toyed with the notion of sending her away, but he didn't much relish that thought at all. She was annoying, yes, but her very presence stimulated him in ways he'd never felt before. As if the air around her burned white-hot with some mysterious electrical charge, and he was a hapless flamefly drawn to that unnatural light. His impatience faded. He wanted her here, and an occasional annoyance was a small price to pay to keep her by his side.

"I thought you would want to go with me," he explained in an even voice. "I'm meeting Dr. Bahleigh at the kennels." His ice blue eyes imprisoned hers. "Your creatures are there."

Rayna grabbed the clothes.

Autumn leaves curled and drifted on a quickening breeze, pinpoints of orange and green set against an azure sky. A thick stand of white-barked trees came alive with the cries and squawks of Hellfire's creatures, a hungry chattering that seemed to reverberate across the valley floor. In the distance, a long chain of volcanoes burned like dark glass beneath a newborn sun. Closer by, insects droned through the coarse yellow grass, flitting to and fro in their quest of a late-blooming wildflower.

Rayna took a deep, cleansing breath and drank in the quiet beauty of Hellfire's morning. The scents and sounds of nature rode the autumn wind like wood smoke from a Lakota campfire. But it was hard to reconcile these sights and smells with the scorched emptiness she'd seen from the air. Hellfire was more alive than she had ever imagined.

Dax paused and glanced back. "Hurry along, Rayna. You can wander about later if you wish, but not now."

"I'm coming," she said with a sigh. Though she longed to kick off the ill-fitting slippers and run barefoot through the stubbly grass, she hurried to catch up. The wolfens were waiting, as well as the gi.

The ground leveled out, and a series of long stone buildings loomed ahead. Fencing made from the white-barked trees and volcanic stone surrounded the area, enclosing the low-slung buildings and neat squares of well-manicured grass inside. Rayna paused a moment and sniffed curiously. The scent of animals was strong in the air, a pleasant blend of fur and leather that she'd never smelled before.

"What sort of creatures do you keep here?" Rayna asked. The scent was completely alien, as was the purpose for the high fencing.

Dax stared at her in surprise, then unlatched the gate to a walkway running between two paddocks and held it open as she walked through. How could she know? When humanity had moved to the stars, most of their heritage had been left behind. "Don't they teach anything about Earth history on Nirvanna?"

The scorn in his voice caused Rayna's eyes to narrow. "Of course they do. We're not illiterate. We have books, as well as the Rememberers, tribesmen who pass knowledge verbally from one generation to the next. Nirvannans reject the concept and tools of technology, not knowledge itself."

"They don't teach you enough, obviously," Dax scoffed. He'd been right to disrupt the Nirvannans' lifestyle. They were too isolated, their culture too backward for this day and age. "Well, here's a part of your heritage that you've never seen." He lifted two fingers to his mouth and whistled loudly.

There was an answering call inside the nearest building, a high-pitched animal sound that prickled the hairs along Rayna's arms. A huge black beast charged out of a doorway and into the paddock, thundering across the manicured grass in a blinding burst of power and speed.

Rayna stared at the towering beast in awe. As it ran, sunlight played across powerful muscles and glistened like ebony fire over its glossy hide. "A horse . . ." she said softly.

Dax whistled again and the horse reared in response, then skittered to a trembling stop on the opposite side of the fence. He pulled a ripe plum-apple from his pocket and fed it to the skittish animal. "His name is Blackfire."

"The name seems appropriate somehow," she commented quietly. As far back as she could remember, Rayna had heard the tales told over Lakota campfires, listened wide-eyed as the tribe's Rememberers spoke in reverent tones of the integral part these creatures had once played in her culture. But nothing she'd ever heard did these creatures justice. They were truly magnificent, in every sense of the word. "He's beautiful."

"Touch him if you want," Dax offered. He was pleased by her reaction, by the look of awe and wonder playing across her upturned features. "But be careful. The foul-tempered brute bites on occasion." Dax tensed, ready to pull her from harm's way at the slightest provocation from Drakken's prize stud.

She lifted a hesitant hand and stroked the creature's velvety muzzle with trembling fingers.

At her touch, the horse quieted, its quivering muscles relaxing into fluid lines. Rayna closed her eyes for a moment, and the horse moved closer, its massive head only inches from her face. The dark, soulful eyes stared at her raptly.

Dax arched a brow and frowned curiously. Blackfire's usual demeanor was anything but mild. He possessed an unpleasant disposition that was legendary among the stablehands, so much so that most of the workers refused to go near him at all. But now, with the diminutive girl standing before him, the spirited horse was simply nickering softly and nuzzling her cheek, as though he and Rayna were engaged in some sort of private rapport. Dax's frown grew more pronounced. Curious, indeed, something he'd have to be sure to mention to Dr. Bahleigh.

Rayna reopened her eyes, a slow, happy smile playing across her lips. She leaned forward and whispered a few words into the horse's great ear. The animal nuzzled her once more, then turned and broke into an excited run, ebony mane and tail streaming in the morning wind.

Her smile faded as she watched the horse thunder about within the confines of the fencing. She glanced at the demon lord, a trace of anger shadowing her eyes. The sight of the fencing had set her teeth on edge. "I didn't know there were any horses within a thousand light-years of the Dominion. How did you manage such a feat?"

He failed to notice the emotion lighting her eyes, or the hint of anger edging her voice. "My ancestors brought them along when my family migrated," Dax told her. He was proud of his family for what they had managed to achieve. It had been an amazing, remarkable feat to transplant horses halfway across the galaxy, one that others had tried and failed. "There are a few other horses scattered here and there within the Dominion, but they're all direct offspring of the original Vahnti stock. My clan owns and controls the only studs."

Her emerald gaze narrowed. Did he have to own and control everything in his miserable life? The horses were nothing more than possessions to him, like the collection of Earth artifacts she'd seen aboard his ship. "Your clan has no right to keep those creatures penned within fences and walls," she said indignantly. "They need to run free as nature intended."

The Vahnti count's face darkened, and his anger simmered to a sudden, violent boil. Who was she to chastise him? "Run free? Without the protection of those fences and walls, without the nurture and constant care given by my clan for a hundred generations, there would be no horses at all!"

"Possibly. But by your intervention, you've upset the harmony of nature. The horses must be allowed to live or die as nature wills."

He snorted in disbelief. "Your naïveté amazes me, girl. Nature, indeed! Look around you." He waved a hand, a dramatic flourish that encompassed the entire planet. "Look at the grass, the fields and forests, the castle, the very clothes you're wearing right now. Everything you see here was created by my family."

Rayna's gaze followed his outstretched hand. Fields of grain rippled and swayed in a light, shifting wind. Trees heavy with sap and ripening fruit filled the morning air with a tantalizing scent. Nature's bounty, not the Vahntis'. "You can use your technology to reshape, remold, or imitate to your heart's content. But in the end, only nature can create."

A cold mask of rage settled over his aristocratic features, and his eyes burned like hot blue diamonds. "My family forged a dynasty out of Hellfire's wastelands, then went on to bring nature to heel on dozens of other worlds! We made those worlds fit for human habitation, then invited colonists like your ancestors to share in the prosperity we created, refugees who've repaid our generosity by trying to lay claim to what we willingly shared!" He took a deep, shuddering breath to force his anger under some semblance of control. Why did the girl have the ability to enrage him so? His hands bunched into fists at his sides, fingers clenching and unclenching in tandem with his accelerated heartbeat. "You Nirvannans have sucked from the Vahnti teat long enough."

Rayna steeled her spine against his anger, but deep inside she was trembling. The demon lord's wrath was a terrible thing to behold. She gazed at him steadily, but it took every ounce of will she possessed. "We have never taken anything from you or your clan, Vahnti demon, never asked for anything except to be left alone. Nirvanna provides all that we need."

A muscle along his jaw tensed. The fact that she had spoken the truth only enraged him even more. "Nirvanna, and everything on it, belongs to me. If I want I can deport every single colonist and *create* an entirely new culture." His pale eyes narrowed. "Or I can strip the planet clean of every blessed ounce of minerals and leave it a rocky hulk if I choose. It's mine to do with as I will."

Her lips flattened and turned white with anger. He didn't understand, was too obstinate and myopic to see that any development on Nirvanna was an abomination, a knife thrust into nature's very heart. "Nirvanna was never yours or your clan's . . . and neither are the horses."

He stared at her for a moment, fury etched in every line of his face; then he spun on his heel and stalked up the walkway between the paddocks. No one had ever dared criticize him in such a manner. Not even Haywood would be so bold! And he would argue with a rock if it suited his mood. Just who did she think she was?

Grumbling beneath his breath, Dax continued toward the kennels. As he walked, the tension in his face began to ebb, and a small, incredulous smile touched the corners of his mouth. She'd actually had the temerity to call into question his clan's right to own Nirvanna, when there wouldn't even *be* a Nirvanna if it weren't for the Vahntis. The girl was absolutely maddening!

He paused for a moment at the door to the kennels, his smile turning dark and sensual. Maddening, and oh, so desirable. He shook his head in disbelief. Perversely, the more she infuriated him, the more he wanted her.

"I'm so sorry," Rayna whispered to the wolfens. The larger of the shaggy beasts whined and licked her cheek through the bars of the cage. "It's my fault you're imprisoned in this hideous place." She glanced surreptitiously at the rumpled young man who was watching her from the far side of the pen, his clothes and long blond hair in complete disarray: Lett Bahleigh, the sad-faced doctor she'd met aboard the demon lord's ship. He'd been watching her for the past few minutes, ever since she'd followed the wolfens' scent and discovered the pen. Undoubtedly, the demon lord had sent him to spy on her.

She lowered her voice even more, so low it was hardly more than a sigh. "I promise that I'll get you both out of here." Her eyes narrowed as she surveyed the spacious pen and high steel bars. There was plenty of room inside, as well as a sturdy shelter for the wolfens to escape the chilly wind, but a cage was a cage, no matter the name. She sighed and scratched the wolfen behind the ears. "I'll get you out of here somehow."

Lett Bahleigh moved toward the front of the pen, careful not to step too close to the bars. One poor fool had already made that mistake, and lost a piece of himself as a result. The young boy was sporting a brand new cyberhand, the latest model available on such short notice, but it was still artificial, and would never work as well as the original.

A wolfen growled, fangs gleaming like wet bones in the morning light. Lett froze, the hair on the back of his neck standing on end. Those golden eyes were watching him, tracking his every move. He cleared his throat nervously. "Ah, excuse me, Miss Syn?"

Rayna turned slowly. "Yes?"

"Do you remember me?" Lett pushed self-consciously at a hank of hair that had fallen in his eyes and tried to stop his hands from shaking. The girl was just so beautiful he found it hard to breathe in her presence. "I'm Dr. Bahleigh. We met aboard Count Vahnti's ship."

"I remember you."

"I'm sorry to intrude, but, well, you see, Count Vahnti has given me permission to study you and your . . . pets."

Rayna stared at him suspiciously. "Why?"

"I want to learn about your culture . . . about Nirvanna. Your people have been isolated for so long that we know next to nothing about you."

Her gaze sharpened, and her expression turned scornful. "What does it matter? If your demon lord has his way, a year from now there will be no such thing as Nirvannan culture. There might not even be a Nirvanna.''

Lett shifted from foot to foot, eyeing her nervously. "It matters to me,'' he said quietly. His cheeks reddened, and he dropped his gaze, staring at the toes of his boots for long seconds. "Even though your way of life might no longer exist, the *memory* of your culture deserves to live on, even if it's only through computer texts. With your cooperation, I can work to preserve your people's history, record their myths and beliefs for posterity.''

He lifted his gaze suddenly, a quick flash of emotion lighting his dark eyes. "A thousand years of history shouldn't be lost, not on the whim of a single man.''

She studied him curiously as she pondered his words. For the space of a single heartbeat, his face and voice had seemed to darken with barely suppressed anger. Could it be that she had found a potential ally? "What would you want to know?''

"Everything,'' Lett said in an earnest voice.

One of the wolfens licked at her hand. Rayna stroked its muzzle absently. "If I told you what you wanted to know, Doctor, would you be willing to do something for me in return?''

He swallowed hard and forced himself to meet those bright green eyes. He was treading on dangerous ground here. The girl was a captive, property claimed by the Vahnti warlord. She had no right to ask anything of him, and he no right to enter into any sort of bargain with her. "That would depend on the favor asked,'' he said anxiously.

"Your warlord, or someone else, took something from me the night I was captured. . . . I want it back.''

Lett blinked in surprise. He'd fully expected her to ask him for aid in escaping, or some other request beyond his ability to fulfill. "What was it?''

Her fingers moved unconsciously to her throat. "An amulet I was wearing on my neck. A small black pouch hanging on a bit of leather cord. It's very important to me.''

"I was on board the count's ship the night you were captured, Miss Syn. I was one of the meds who examined you and tended your leg wound. But I saw no amulet, nothing even remotely matching the description you gave.''

"Then it was removed before then . . . or lost." A shadow of pain moved across her eyes.

"Perhaps Count Vahnti has it," Lett offered, hoping to lift her spirits. "You could ask him."

She gave him a piercing look. "Are you aware of my position here, Doctor?" Her tone was more bitter and angry than she had intended.

Lett's face reddened in embarrassment. By now, everyone within Drakken's walls had heard. "I've heard tales—"

"Then surely you understand why I'm asking you, not him. I don't want to ask anything of Count Vahnti. I don't want to be beholden to him in any way." The amulet was extremely important to her, a link with Javan and Nirvanna she was unwilling to relinquish, but it was less important than what its return would represent. The retrieval itself was a test, a means to discover how far Lett Bahleigh would go to help her in exchange for the information he seemed to want so desperately. If he found and returned the amulet, he might not be averse to doing more. "Count Vahnti might even destroy it if he discovered that it meant something to me. In truth, I might be asking you to go on a fool's errand. He might have destroyed it already.''

Lett frowned as he considered her request. What she wanted him to do seemed innocuous enough. Utterly harmless, in fact. Chances were that the amulet had already been disposed of, so what difference would it make if he actually agreed? In return he would get her cooperation and gain her trust. "I'll do my best to find it for you."

Rayna smiled slowly. "That's all I ask." *For now,* she added to herself. "Thank you, Doctor."

Chapter Ten

"Go ahead." Alfred Dunstan grinned at the terrified girl, a brutal flash of perfect white teeth that appeared almost luminescent in the milky light. "I'm feeling somewhat magnanimous tonight." Above, Malcon's trio of tiny moons cast odd-shaped, chaotic shadows across the water and deserted beach, pale swaths of quicksilver that moved and crisscrossed as the moons slowly aligned themselves in a vague triangular pattern. "Run if you can, but you can't get away from me."

The girl stared at him for an uncertain second, then tried to flee, but after three quick steps she came to an abrupt stop, her feet mired ankle-deep in the mudlike sand. She turned back to Alfred Dunstan and fell to her knees, young eyes wide with fear, resignation, and the subtle glaze of rising passion.

"You see?" Alfred said huskily. Thick vines clawed to the surface of the sand and twined snakelike about her legs. "I told you that you couldn't escape me."

She dipped her head in silent acknowledgment. "Do with me what you will, my lord," she whispered. Her voice was like music, soft and sweet and melodiously clear. "I live to serve you . . . to attend your every need." She prostrated herself before him and kissed the tops of his feet, slender fingers clutching at the hem of his flowing robe.

Alfred Dunstan twisted his hands through her ebony hair and jerked her head upward, forcing her to meet his lust-filled eyes. She was absolutely perfect, a devastating blend of youthful fear and come-hither seduction. In fact, everything was perfect. Behind her, a cluster of palm trees shifted and sighed in an artificial wind, and a plethora of stars filled the virtual sky. He could even see and hear the sea cresting onto the sandy shore. The only thing wrong was the colors. The palms were a deep purple-blue, and the sea was a strange orange-red. Something was wrong there.

"Take off your clothes, slave," the Dunstan warlord ordered. "I want to see your body . . . judge for myself whether or not you're worthy to tend my needs."

"Yes, my lord." Her diaphanous robe drifted to the sand. *"Father."*

Her fingers slipped beneath his underrobe and slid up his legs, talonlike nails teasing vertical shivers up the length of his calves, the fleshy expanse of his thighs.

"I'm yours, my lord." The nails moved higher, sliding over his skin in just the right places, with the precise amount of pressure he desired. The pleasure was exquisite, moving every so often past the borderline into outright pain.

"Father?"

Alfred grimaced and kicked the girl away from him. Petwitt always had such miserable timing. "Can't it wait, Petwitt? I'm a little busy here." The girl crawled back to him and started slavering over his feet again.

"We need to talk."

Alfred sighed. "Very well."

"Shall I put on a headset and come in?"

"No, no." The last thing he needed was for Petwitt to be privy to his favorite fantasy. Besides, his desire had begun to ebb the moment he'd heard the vexing sound of his son's voice. "I'll be out in a moment." He stared down at the girl longingly, sighed once more, then switched off his headset.

The beach and odd-colored palm trees vanished abruptly, as well as the simulacrum girl, fading into the technological nothingness from which they'd been created. The real world reformed around him with a suddenness Alfred always found quite jarring. He blinked to focus his eyes and thoughts. He was back within the walls of Dunstan Keep, inside his spacious office again, slouched in the high-backed chair behind his desk. He ripped the neural stimulators from his temples and tossed the headgear atop the ornate desk carved from a single slab of lapis. "This had better be important, Petwitt." He should never have given his cloddish son the override codes to the privacy lock on his office. "You interrupted me at a most inopportune moment."

"Sorry, Father." Petwitt's lips twitched upward in a sarcastic smile, but the movement was lost behind his neatly trimmed beard. He'd rather enjoyed catching his father unawares, being a silent voyeur for long minutes while the Dunstan warlord indulged himself with a sexual fantasy. Besides, Alfred was spending far too much time with his virtual playthings, so much so that Petwitt had begun to wonder if his father was losing touch with the real universe. "You said to report to you the moment we received a transmission from our spies on Hellfire."

Alfred leaned back in the thronelike chair and regarded his firstborn son through hooded eyes. "So I did." He would have to watch his wording next time. Petwitt had an annoying habit of taking his statements literally. "And?" Alfred prodded.

"My suspicions have been confirmed." Petwitt gazed down at his father across the width of the desk. There were no other chairs in Alfred's private office and never had been, forcing any visitors, even family, to stand before the warlord like supplicants who'd come to beg a favor from a king seated upon his throne. "It appears that the Vahnti count is quite obsessed with the girl I met at Drakken Castle. The operatives' reports were filled with references to her, and Vahnti's obvious preoccupation with her."

A calculating look stole across the Dunstan warlord's corpulent face. "Excellent." He laced his fingers over the folds of his stomach and smiled, his dark eyes bright with glee. "What's the Nirvannan girl's name again?"

"Rayna . . . Rayna Syn."

"Ah, yes, that's right. Any information on her yet?"

The suggestion of a smile hovered around the edges of Petwitt's mouth. He had saved the most tantalizing bits of information for last. "Rumor has it that the girl tried to assassinate Count Vahnti when he made his inspection tour of Nirvanna a few weeks ago . . . and from all accounts very nearly succeeded."

Alfred leaned forward suddenly, the ornate gilded chair

creaking in protest as he shifted his massive bulk. He stared at his son incredulously. "She what?"

"Reports are still sketchy as to what happened exactly, but firsthand accounts suggest that she drugged some indigenous wild beasts and set them upon the count as he rode in the open on Nirvanna. In the melee that followed she also managed to stab the blackguard in the shoulder, just inches from his heart. Unfortunately, the damnable man survived." Petwitt smiled openly, enjoying his father's look of stunned disbelief. "Haywood March and the Vahnti security force are said to be up in arms over the entire affair."

"Incredible." Alfred stared vacantly at the jewel-toned mural adorning a length of wall behind Petwitt. Wood nymphs and angelic-faced cherubs in various states of undress frolicked through a forest inhabited by a bevy of satyrs bent on pleasuring themselves. He sighed and shook his head. If only the girl had been successful. From the sound of it, she had come very, very close, far closer than any assassin had ever managed before. "And you're sure this is the same girl you met—the one our spies report Vahnti to be obsessed with?"

"Exactly the same. The descriptions fit perfectly."

The Dunstan warlord shook his head again, his amazement growing even more. "Our dear friend Daxton must have taken complete leave of his senses."

"There's more, Father. . . . It's rumored that the Vahnti count has taken her into his own bed, even though she's vowed to try to kill him again. He's also stated openly to members of his clan that he has placed a forfeiture claim against the girl's life, and that he intends to keep her as long as she continues to hold his interest."

Alfred laughed aloud, a harsh, brittle sound edged with venom. "Let's pray that the fool's interest holds long enough for the girl to keep her vow . . . or for us to set our plans into motion. If he's distracted, it will make things all the easier."

"So far Vahnti hasn't shown the slightest indication that he intends to rid himself of her. In fact, the operatives report that if anything, he's growing more enamored of her by the day."

"Daxton has always enjoyed a good challenge," Alfred said absently. In that trait, he and the Vahnti warlord were very much alike. "And you say she's quite beautiful?"

"Breathtaking. The sort of unenhanced natural beauty one rarely sees in this day and age. I must admit that even I found myself attracted to her, despite her youth and uncivilized background." Petwitt closed his eyes a moment, remembering how she'd looked standing in that horrid atrium, surrounded by pastel flowers and brightly colored birds. "There's something almost ethereal about her I find hard to describe."

Alfred arched a bushy brow. Any female who could make such a profound impact on his dispassionate son—much less Daxton Vahnti—must truly be a sight to behold. He stared at the mural again, at the dark-haired wood nymph he'd used as a mental model for his latest virtual companion. Youthful and uncivilized, Petwitt had said, with remarkable green eyes and thick coppery hair that flowed past her waist. He wetted his lips. "How old did you say the girl was?"

"Seventeen, no more than eighteen."

"Perfect." A wash of desire glazed Alfred's slitted eyes. "The count has all but handed us his head on a platter." If Alfred moved carefully, the girl could be made into a formidable weapon against Daxton Vahnti, and once Vahnti had been dealt with, she could be put to other, better uses within the thick steel walls of Dunstan Keep. "Advise the legal department to file a formal grievance with the Dominion High Council. I want Daxton Vahnti brought up on two separate charges . . . contributing to the moral corruption of a female below the legal age of consent, as well as illegal use of arcane forfeiture laws to enslave that same minor female."

Petwitt smiled grimly. Alfred had taken his suggestion about bringing Vahnti up on charges and made the idea his own. "Another plot within a plot, Father?"

"The best kind." Alfred climbed to his feet slowly, straining to pull his girth from the chair. "If nothing else, Vahnti will be so distracted by having to defend himself against the charges that he won't even realize what we're doing until it's already done." He felt his half-gravity boots switch on and his body grow lighter, instantly easing the strain on feet too small and narrow to support his tremendous weight.

"And the Lady Caccia?"

Alfred flashed his son an impatient look. At times Petwitt failed to grasp the subtleties of a finely woven plot, a shortcoming that occasionally caused the Dunstan warlord to regret anointing Petwitt his heir. Unfortunately, his firstborn was still the best of the lot. "The Nirvannan girl's part in this doesn't alter our basic goal. By spring you'll have wed and bred the esteemed Lady Caccia, and we'll have complete control over the Vahnti holdings." He gave his son a predatory smile. "All things come to those with the patience to wait, my boy, and our family has waited a very long time."

The Dunstan warlord eased around the desk to signal that the interview was at an end, his floor-length robe and half-gravity boots making it seem as if he were gliding across the room on a thin cushion of air. "If there's nothing else, I have work to do. You may see yourself out."

"There is one more thing, Father." Petwitt arched his left eyebrow, an habitual gesture he'd picked up from his father years before. "The meds asked me to speak to you. It seems that they have diagnosed your current wife as terminal, and need your permission to replace several vital organs with implants before further deterioration of her condition occurs."

"How tragic." Alfred shrugged slightly and glided toward the wall mural. "I hadn't heard." His voice contained just the right amount of surprise. "What seems to be ailing the poor woman?"

"The meds have been unable to diagnose the cause, I'm afraid." Petwitt eyed his father carefully. Wife number four was about to meet the same untimely end as wives one through three, whose numbers included his own dearly departed mother. "Do you give your permission for the implant procedure?"

Alfred stared at the mural, carefully studying a tawny-haired wood nymph half-hidden behind a tree. He wondered idly if Rayna Syn resembled the nymph. "No, I don't think so. The woman has grown quite tiresome in the past few years, and implants are just so terribly expensive these days."

Petwitt straightened the cuffs of his bloodred robe, then inclined his head in admiration of the neat and untraceable fashion in which his father had finally extracted his revenge. "As

you wish, Father. I'll inform the meds.'' The Dunstan warlord's current wife had only herself to blame for her terminal
predicament. The fool woman had been caught in a compro-
mising situation by a minor servant who owed his fealty to
Lord Alfred. Worse still, her partner in the commission of the
intimate crime had been Petwitt's younger half-brother, Marcus, whose whereabouts were, and had been, a complete mystery since the day they'd been discovered four years before.
Marcus had either been banished from worlds controlled by
the family, or his bones were moldering in a very deep grave.
Whatever his unfortunate brother's fate, there was now one
less sibling Petwitt would have to contend with when he assumed his rightful place as head of the clan.

The heir to Clan Dunstan smiled inwardly, gratified by how
well things had turned out. Marcus had been such an utter
dunce, a self-righteous intellectual whose penchant for tasting
forbidden fruit had been easily exploited. All it had taken was
a word here, a little encouragement there, and Marcus had
fallen headlong into the intricate trap Petwitt had laid for him.
Plots within plots, his father was fond of preaching, webs so
tight and thickly woven that the victim couldn't see the forest
for the abundance of trees.

Petwitt strolled toward the office door. Too bad he could
never tell his father just how well he'd learned that lesson. He
would have been very proud.

Scowling impatiently, Dax stalked down Drakken's wide
central corridor shoulder to shoulder with Haywood March,
the clack of their boots on the polished stone echoing off the
walls. A flock of harried, exasperated aides hurried in their
wake, nervously darting this way and that as they tried to keep
pace and gain their warlord's ear.

"The Lyseene clan's trade ambassador will arrive in less
than one hour, Count Vahnti!'' Dax's appointment secretary
shouted over another aide. "You're to take your midday meal
with him in the atrium. The agenda for today's negotiation
session is limited to the import concessions they're willing to
grant in exchange for the right to buy ores from the Nirvannan
system in bulk quantities.''

Dax increased his pace. "Put him off," he barked over his shoulder. To hell with the Lyseene ambassador. Since the day he'd first taken Rayna down to the stables, almost every waking hour had been filled by clan business, so much so that he'd begun to think it might be a conspiracy hatched to keep him away from her. It had been over a week since he'd had time to spend more than a stolen hour with her, and that had been over a hasty dinner squeezed between appointments. When he was finally able to make his way to the castle's top floor each evening, frazzled and exhausted, she was already abed, curled in an uncommunicative little ball as far from his side of the mattress as she could get. Feigning sleep, no doubt. And when he awakened at dawn, she had already managed to slip, ghostlike, from his rooms.

"Count Vahnti!" another aide shouted above the others. "Cost overruns on the squadron of patrol ships being built at the clan shipyards have exceeded ten percent. The project manager needs your approval to continue the work."

"He has it," Dax told him, his scowl darkening. She'd been spending more time with Carlo and Lett Bahleigh than with him. He'd seen her with each of them on more than one occasion from a distance. Laughing together, talking in quiet, contented tones.

Haywood glanced sideways and blew out a worried breath. Dax was headed for an explosion. He could see it in his eyes, the rigid way he was carrying himself. In the past few weeks the Vahnti warlord had grown ever more weary of the constant nagging from countless aides, the endless clamoring for his attention, and he had begun rebelling at the demands placed on his time by his title. So far, his rebellion was an inward thing, visible only to those who knew Dax well. But it wouldn't be long before his frustration took an overt form. Just as Haywood had feared, clan business had begun to take a distant backseat to Dax's infatuation with Rayna Syn.

"Count Vahnti," the protocol officer said breathlessly. "You need to approve the final seating arrangements for the hunt banquet by the end of the day."

"Take it up with Vannata."

"Grain production on Beta Seven has fallen by three percent. Field techs need a shipment of—"

Dax ground to a sudden halt and spun around, narrowly avoiding a collision with several startled aides. "Enough!" he bellowed, the sound reverberating down the length of the corridor. "I've had more than enough of your incessant carping for one day!" He glared at the nervous aides, who'd frozen in place like a small herd of startled near-elk. "Whatever the problems are, solve them yourselves, and leave me be until I instruct you otherwise!"

His mouth settling into a hard, thin line, Dax pivoted and marched down the corridor, the sharp *click-clack* of his boot heels the only sound to break the stunned silence he left behind.

Haywood gave the slack-mouthed aides a penetrating look, his eyes sliding over each of them in turn. "You heard what the man said," he told them finally. "Get to work and earn your pay chits. Count Vahnti will be unavailable for a while."

The aides took flight like a covey of birds with a hunter close on their tails. Shaking his head, Haywood watched them scurry away, then turned and quick-marched down the triangular hallway to catch up with Dax.

He caught sight of him again inside the vast domed chamber that served as the castle's formal entrance. "Wait up, Dax!" Haywood hurried across the shiny mosaic floor, the black and gold tiles carefully arrayed in the shape of an immense Vahnti crest.

His back still rigid, Dax paused and waited for Haywood while a liveried footman hurriedly swung open the castle's immense double doors to allow them egress.

Haywood threw him a curious look but said nothing as they strode through the doors and walked down a long flight of stone steps made of Hellfire's abundant basalt. A stablehand was waiting near the base of the steps, trying hard to control the count's skittish black stallion. The saddled horse was dancing around in half circles, fighting to free himself from the nervous young boy who had a death grip on the reins.

The Vahnti military commander glanced at the chronometer imbedded in the face of his wristcom, his expression souring

109

as he did. It was just after ten. According to the castle security force, Rayna and Lett Bahleigh went for a long walk in the woods south of the stables around ten each morning, a routine they'd fallen into during the weeks since Rayna's arrival at Drakken.

"Going for a ride in the woods, Dax?" Haywood said softly.

Dax's eyes turned cold and flint-hard. "What if I am? I'm entitled, aren't I?" The hue of his gaze deepened to a glacial blue. "Or has my military commander taken it upon himself to tell me what I can and cannot do?"

Haywood ground his teeth together in frustration. Dax had been infatuated with women before, but his obsessions had always been short-lived, lasting no more than a few weeks or so. This one had already lasted longer than any other, and there was still no end in sight. Haywood was even beginning to suspect that the roots of his interest in the girl might go far deeper than a simple infatuation, and that thought terrified him all the more. "Dax, please, if you want the damn girl just take her and be done with it. Don't do this to yourself. She's not going to relent and come to you willingly like the others. It's not a game to her. The girl would sooner carve out your liver and feed it to those wolfens then ever spread her legs for the Vahnti 'serpent.' You'd probably be dead already if your aides and the security force weren't keeping such a tight watch on you."

A muscle along Dax's jaw tightened, and his brows pulled downward in a furious frown. His suspicions turned to certainty. Haywood had been doing far more than keeping a tight watch on him. "You've been manipulating my schedule, haven't you, Haywood? Conspiring with my aides to keep me buried beneath a mountain of trivial duties so I won't have time to spend alone with her."

Haywood stiffened and met his gaze head-on. "If I hadn't, you wouldn't have gotten a minute's worth of work done these past three weeks, or worse . . . the clan might be weeping over your dead bones." It was time for total truth between them, even if it meant provoking the warlord's wrath. "You're obsessed with her, Dax, and for the life of me, I can't figure out why. I've even begun to think that you might actually have feelings for her.''

"Feelings?" For a fragment of a second, no more time than it took for a heart to beat then beat again, the Vahnti count stared at him in silent wonder. *Feelings?* The very notion was too unexpected, too incredible to give any credence. He shook his head, slowly at first, then more vehemently as Haywood's insinuation began to rankle him. Rayna was just his prisoner, a pleasant diversion he planned to use and discard. A shadow moved across his features. Wasn't she? "That's ridiculous."

There'd been a moment's hesitation in Dax's face and voice, a glimmer of uncertainty that Haywood found hard to dismiss. He stared at the Vahnti count for a long moment, weighing his words before he spoke. "Then I guess it must be a simple matter of ego. You just can't stomach the knowledge that a pretty little colonist isn't bedazzled by your wealth and lineage, and seems immune to your well-known charms. Is that it, Dax? Are you keeping her near because you just can't come to grips with the fact that she doesn't want you?"

Dax's face darkened ominously; then he drew a noisy breath to calm himself, and the rage began to ebb. It was Haywood's duty to confront and chastise the head of the clan when the situation warranted such an action. Besides, Haywood had only spoken aloud the very same thoughts that had been gnawing at him for a number of days. For some unfathomable reason, he'd been utterly obsessed with Rayna since he first saw her nearly naked body amidst the carnage on Nirvanna. Just the sight of her was enough to make him burn with a lust so deep and all-pervasive that it threatened to ignite his soul. But as much as he wanted her, he couldn't just take her, not unwillingly, at least. He wanted her to come to him, to reach out to him with eager arms, set him aflame with a passion that equaled his own.

Instead she loathed the very sight of him, a state of affairs that appeared permanent, and the game of hunter and hunted he'd so eagerly anticipated lost its luster when the hunted refused to take on the role of willing prey. The chase would mean nothing if at the end he found only a hollow victory and Rayna's bitter tears.

He straightened his back and the formal uniform jacket he'd worn to meet with the Lyseene ambassador, unconsciously smoothing the heavy black fabric. Had his ego truly grown so enormous that he couldn't abide the thought that a woman didn't want him? Was his motivation as simple and ignoble as that?

Sunlight glinted off the thick golden braid hanging from his jacket's epaulets. Dax closed his eyes a moment and sighed raggedly. Since the days when he was a gangly adolescent, Dominion women had flocked to him, flaunted perfect, bioengineered bodies before him in ceaseless bids to gain the Vahnti warlord's undying attention. They would smile and simper, flutter long lashes, then hastily spread their sculpted legs in hopes of permanently laying claim to his heart and wealth. The same boring scenario had been played out over and over until he'd finally lost interest and sought to enliven his life by turning the tables and pretending to hunt them instead. Still, no female had ever come close to refusing him, even those who'd instinctively grasped the unspoken rules to his game of catch-me-if-you-can and played hard to get.

Dax opened his eyes again and stared absently at the distant copse of white-barked trees where Rayna was sure to be. Haywood was right. This was no game to her. Deep down she might be mildly attracted to him, but any fledgling desire she harbored for him was damped by her overwhelming hatred of him and his entire clan. She loathed him with a ferocity that bordered on fanaticism, and would surely try to kill him again if given the chance.

A grim, self-deprecating smile crept over his lips. "Has my ego really grown so immense?" Dax asked, half in jest, half out of genuine concern.

Haywood blew out the breath he'd been holding and acknowledged the lessening of tension with a relieved smile. Perhaps now Dax was ready to admit the futility of trying to outwait the girl. "Enormously so, I'm afraid. Especially where women are concerned."

Dax saw a veiled look of worry pass over his friend's weathered face and knew that Haywood had far more to say. But he wasn't going to lecture him any more today. Eventually he would because they both knew he had to. "I'll take what you said under advisement, old friend, in the spirit in which it was intended."

The soldier nodded slowly. "Good enough."

Dax moved down the steps and gathered the horse's reins, freeing the much relieved stableboy from his nerve-racking duty. "Let's strike a bargain," Dax said as the boy hurried away. "Cease hatching conspiracies against me, and I promise to resolve the situation by the end of the hunt." His voice sharpened, grew steel-edged with determination. "One way or another it will be over by then." He climbed into the saddle, the horse skittering sideways as he did.

Haywood grinned broadly, the first genuine smile that had touched his lips since that night on Nirvanna. "Deal," he agreed, his bleak mood already beginning to lift.

"Until then, I intend to spend as much time with her as I wish. Without any interference from you, my aides, or the security force." A glum expression spread across the planes of his face. Several hundred guests would soon descend on Drakken Castle for the annual hunt, noble-born visitors who required an outrageous amount of personal attention lest their prickly egos be bruised in some way. The demands on his time would be just as great as they'd been in the past three weeks. How was he to finish things with Rayna if he was hip-deep in visitors?

Frowning, Dax pulled smoothly on the reins, and Blackfire wheeled around in response, hooves scrabbling for purchase on the gravel pathway.

Haywood watched the horse and rider thunder off toward the south. Just six more days and Drakken would be rid of Rayna Syn once and for all. He'd sleep a lot easier then. So would the security force.

Wind sifted through the dense stand of trees, a forest of pale monoliths clawing toward a sky made thick and hazy blue by a coating of volcanic dust. The stark white trunks, bleeding with dark sap, soared upward for a hundred feet or so, then suddenly gave way to heavy, conical roofs made of yellow and crimson leaves. Rayna's thoughts drifted as she stared at the treetops, watching as a flurry of leaves rained down on the small clearing in a storm of startling color.

It was so peaceful here. The thick, heady musk of living things drifted on the morning air. She could smell the tree sap and sweet-scented flowers, the brightly plumed birds and shy, ground-dwelling mammals. Occasionally she caught a faint whiff of other creatures, too, larger and not so shy. Predator smells, more malevolent than anything she'd ever experienced before. Fortunately, those traces came from a great distance away. She glanced over her shoulder, toward the open end of the bowl-shaped clearing. The barren vista of Hellfire's tundra and volcanic mountains was visible through a wide breech cut through the densely packed trees. Not far away, a faint layer of gold seemed to shimmer slightly in the morning sun. Her mouth tightened. Drakken Castle's shield wall, a thin barrier of directed energy that kept enemies of the Vahntis safely out—and her trapped inside.

Lett Bahleigh leaned forward and watched a flicker of dark emotion play over Rayna's exotic face. They were sitting in a field of wildflowers, the reedlike stalks swaying gently in a fitful breeze. The multihued flowers had opened their petals wide to catch the last traces of moisture in the morning air, the pistils releasing bits of cottony seed that drifted like snowfall on currents of wind.

Unconsciously, Lett lifted a hand to brush away a bit of seed fluff clinging to a lock of her hair, but his fingers stopped just shy of their destination. His hand bunched into a tight fist and fell back to his knee. No matter how much he longed to, he had no right to touch her, even to entertain the wild notions that had crossed his mind more than once in the past three weeks. Rayna was strictly off-limits. He could interview her to his heart's content, research her people's history as much as he wished, even try to deepen the platonic friendship that had developed between them. But that was where it ended. To attempt more would invite certain disaster. She belonged to Count Vahnti, a man who'd made it clear to any and all that she was his possession.

He sighed and clicked on the recorder, placing the palm-size device on the ground between them. "Are you ready to go on, Rayna? Our time's almost up for today."

Rayna heard the distant voice but didn't understand the words. She was drifting. Her body was still sitting cross-legged amidst a field of flowers, but her mind had moved on to the Inner World, the place deep inside her where the voices of the spirits whispered, and her thoughts were free to roam the endless plains of her soul. For a timeless second she was one with nature. She was a tree, the dark sap of her lifeblood spilling down her white-barked body. Her spirit soared upward, spiraling against a thin blue sky in the shape of a bird. She glanced down at the small clearing, and her bird eyes saw a tiny Lett Bahleigh sitting amidst the swaying flowers.

"Rayna?" Lett said worriedly. He'd seen her face take on that same faraway look several times in the past few weeks, as if she'd suddenly departed this world and moved into a dreamlike existence he couldn't reach. A chill ran up his spine, but he still had the presence of mind to move the recorder closer, the scientist in him determined to fathom the unfathomable. Each time he'd witnessed her trancelike states he'd become ever more certain that Nirvannan mysticism wasn't a myth at all. "Answer me, Rayna." His anxiety grew. This trance had lasted longer than the others. Far too long. "Are you all right?"

Her body slumped slightly, the muscles relaxing as she slid inside her skin once again. She blinked several times and gradually focused on the doctor's anxious features. "Did you say something?"

Lett expelled a shaky breath. She was back from wherever she had gone, staring at him as though nothing at all had occurred. "Where were you, Rayna?" His voice was pitched high, sharpened by a blend of anxiety and fear. "One moment you were beginning to tell me the story of the three wolfens, and the next you just sort of drifted away."

An absent, dreamy smile stole across her lips. For a few precious moments, she'd been free. "I was here, Lett. . . . I never left."

"I don't believe you," Lett said in as firm a voice as he could muster, then lifted his hands imploringly. "How can I

115

hope to understand your people if you won't tell me the truth?''

She stared at him a moment, her thoughts ranging back through the weeks to the day she'd first struck a bargain with Lett Bahleigh. Their relationship had changed since then, the result of long hours spent together and growing familiarity. She had planned to use him unmercifully, but instead Lett had offered her a tenuous friendship much like the one she shared with the gentle Carlo. Each morning they spent several hours sitting in the clearing, Lett and his tiny recorder silent as she traced the history of her people from present-day Nirvanna back to ancient Earth. He never judged, never offered his own opinions, only interrupting to guide the path her words took on rare occasions. Her sessions with Lett, and the time she spent sitting for Carlo's painting, had become the high points of her life. They had both gifted her with far more than they received in return. She owed Lett the truth, but could the scientist in him accept a truth that ran counter to every concept he held dear?

"I'll finish the story tomorrow, Lett." She smiled at him softly. "And someday, when I think you're ready to listen, I'll tell you about my grandfather.''

"Your grandfather?" Lett frowned curiously. "What about him?''

"Not today." She glanced at the hazy sky. Hellfire's sun was climbing toward its zenith. "Carlo's probably wondering where I am.''

She started to rise but Lett belayed her with a touch on the hand. He pulled in a quick breath to steady himself. "Wait . . . I have something for you." He lowered his eyes, unable to meet her probing gaze, and reached inside his tunic with a trembling hand. "It's a gift . . . from me to you." He placed the amulet in her palm and closed her fingers around it.

Stunned, Rayna stared down at her clenched hand, the familiar leather string hanging between her fingers. She squeezed the amulet tighter, tears of joy clouding her eyes. "Lett . . ." She had never expected him to find it, never expected him to truly look. "Where did you find it?''

He gave her a tremulous smile, her joyful reaction to the

amulet's return well worth the fear of discovery he'd suffered during his search. Once he'd narrowed the search to only one possibility, he'd spent many a night stealing through the castle's shadows, trying to find the best way to slip undetected past the security fields and guards to retrieve it. "I think it's best that you don't know where I found it, Rayna. Just accept the amulet's return at face value, and know that giving it back to its rightful owner has brought me great happiness."

Pulling the small black pouch free of her fingers, he slipped the leather cord over her head, and allowed the amulet to settle of its own accord into the hollow between her breasts. "You must be careful, though," Lett instructed her. "Keep it out of sight beneath your clothing. If Count Vahnti were to see it . . ."

The warning was unnecessary. Rayna quickly tucked the pouch inside the bodice of her robe, arranging the silky fabric to make sure the amulet was completely hidden. "I promise." His words and tone had told her much. Lett had taken far more risks to retrieve the amulet than she had ever envisioned. "I owe you a debt I cannot ever hope to repay."

Lett shook his head and smiled. "You owe me nothing, Rayna. But I will hold you to your promise to tell me about your grandfather." He forced himself to meet those piercing eyes. "And I would like very much to know what the amulet means." Curiosity had driven him to study the interior of the small leather pouch, but the significance of its contents eluded him. A tiny bit of bone and an animal claw, a silvery pebble, a small amount of dark soil, and what appeared to be a grainy powder made from pulverized grass.

"The amulet is a focus, Lett, an object used to draw the threads of nature's energy into the wearer."

He gave her a dubious look. "You mean it's supposed to be magical in some way?"

Her eyes glittered, fiery green stones that seemed to catch and hold all trace of sunlight. "It *is* magic." She placed the palm of her hand flat against her chest, feeling the pulse of heat emanating from the amulet's core in response to her touch. "White magic."

A tingle of fear and uncertainty ran along the base of Lett's neck. No matter how implausible the notion sounded to him, it was obvious that Rayna truly believed that the amulet held some type of mystical power. Her belief in it was fierce and abiding, a shining, heartfelt faith in the unseen written clearly on her youthful face.

Rayna saw the sudden look of concern move over his face and sought to allay his fears. She touched his arm, his shoulder, her hand finally coming to rest against the smoothness of his cheek. "White magic is just a name, Lett, a term Nirvannans use to define what there are no words to describe. The magic, if that's what you wish to call it, lies within each of us, within every living thing in the universe. We are each connected to something far greater, a spiritual union that flows to the edges of the universe and beyond." Her voice fell to an impassioned whisper. "To understand my people, you must reach beyond the borders of science. You must look into your soul and acknowledge that this thread of universal oneness might actually exist."

Lett stared back at her for long seconds, mesmerized by her words and those hypnotic green eyes. He didn't really believe such a thing actually existed, but there was something quite compelling about the very possibility. He shook his head and switched off the recorder. "You'd best go. Carlo will be wondering where you are."

"Same time tomorrow?" Rayna smiled knowingly. Bit by tiny bit she'd begun peeling away the layers of his disbelief. Soon he'd be ready to hear and accept the entire truth.

"Of course. I'll meet you at the wolfens' pen."

"Maybe we can go for a long walk—" Rayna stiffened and glanced around, her sentence left hanging in midair.

"What's the matter?" Lett asked, alarmed by her expression.

Rayna peered into the shadowy trees, nostrils flaring as she caught the first trace of a familiar, masculine scent. A knot wedged in her throat. "He's here," she whispered hoarsely.

"Who's here?" Lett stared wildly at the dense-packed trees. He couldn't see anything.

"Count Vahnti." Instinctively, she drew a hand to her

chest, protecting the small black pouch hidden beneath her silky robe. "He's been watching us."

Lett's heart missed a beat. The thought that the count might have witnessed him handing Rayna the amulet gave him a terrible start. But that wasn't possible. Rayna's senses were far keener than an ordinary human's, and she would have ferreted out his presence long before now. Still, the idea that they were being watched made him distinctly uncomfortable.

Rayna climbed to her feet and stared at a particular tree, her back as stiff and rigid as her expressionless face.

Dax stepped from the shadows around the base of the tree and walked into the clearing, leading a sweaty and lathered Blackfire behind him. He strode toward the center of the oval clearing, cold, angry eyes trained on the girl standing so defiantly at its heart.

"Count Vahnti," Lett said, but could think of nothing further to say. The dark scowl on the warlord's face boded ill for them both. Lett shifted nervously, pushing and smoothing at his wayward hair.

Rayna held her ground, her chin lifting a notch higher as he neared. She had managed to avoid a face-to-face meeting with him for so long that she'd lulled herself into believing that he was avoiding her, too.

He came abreast of Lett Bahleigh and paused, his eyes still fixed on Rayna with unswerving intensity. A muscle twitched angrily along Dax's jaw, moving back and forth in tandem with the beat of his pulse. He'd watched from the shadows as she'd smiled and lifted a hand to Lett's cheek, fingers moving gently over the doctor's youthful flesh. "Have you finished your session, Doctor?" he said tightly, still caught in the blaze of white-hot fury he'd felt when that slender hand had lifted to another man's face.

Lett cleared his throat. The count had never even glanced his way. "Yes, my lord," he answered, shifting his feet again. "We're finished for today."

"Good." He looked Bahleigh full in the face and handed him Blackfire's reins. "Walk him back to the stables, will you, Doctor? I'd like a word alone with my young houseguest."

Lett swallowed hard, and his hand closed around the length

of leather. "Of course, Count. I'd be glad to." He threw a final, worried look in Rayna's direction and moved away, the horse walking tiredly behind him. In truth, he was glad for an excuse to escape the warlord's scrutiny. Daxton Vahnti's pale eyes had been dark with some heated emotion. Lett paused a moment and glanced over his shoulder at the silent couple standing in the middle of the clearing. His brow furrowed. It was anger that he'd seen in the count's glacial eyes, anger and a hot surge of something vaguely akin to outright jealousy.

Chapter Eleven

Lett Bahleigh vanished into an inky pool of shadow, as if man and horse had suddenly been swallowed whole by the dense stand of trees. Then the steady rustling of hooves through fallen leaves faded into nothingness, too.

Rayna stood very still, fighting an almost irresistible urge to flee. The Vahnti count was standing before her, cold and openly hostile, the gold braid on his shoulders glittering fiercely in the morning light. "What do you want with me?" she demanded in a voice as curt and cool as his eyes.

His lips thinned, and his gaze narrowed even more. Her tawny hair was disheveled, leaves and snowy seed fluff caught in the curly strands. "I want to know exactly what you and Dr. Bahleigh were doing."

"Doing?" she said incredulously. "We were doing exactly what the mighty Vahnti count instructed us to do! The very same thing we've done each morning for the past three weeks."

"I saw you touch him, Rayna. I saw the way you were looking at him." He'd moved heaven and hell to find time to be with her, ridden away from the castle with the intention of beginning a swift and gentle courtship that would culminate with her coming willingly to his bed. Instead, he'd found her fawning over the idealistic Bahleigh, a sight that had sent him into a rage. "Have you allowed Bahleigh to have his way with you?"

She took an angry step forward and glared up at him. *How dare he?* Lett was a decent, honorable man, nothing like the foul-tempered oaf standing before her. "What is it that you're insinuating?"

"I asked you a simple question," he said in a lethal voice. "Answer me."

She flashed him a look of utter disdain. *The gall of him!* "Such a question deserves no answer."

Raw fury scalded his cheeks with red. Had Lett Bahleigh tasted the sweetness he'd been hoarding for his own private use? If so, the good doctor didn't have much longer to live. "No one touches what is mine, Rayna," he said between clenched teeth. "You belong to me, and no woman of mine shall ever be touched by another man."

Furious, Rayna lashed out with a hand, but the blow never reached its mark. Instead, he grabbed her arm in a viselike grip and twisted her elbow behind her back.

"I warned you not to try to strike me again." A sudden rush of excitement shone in his eyes, and his lips curled in a dangerous smile. "Now you'll have to pay the price."

He pulled her roughly against his chest, his thoughts walking a razor-edge between violence and unbridled lust.

Rayna gasped and tried to break free, worried that he might discover the amulet. "May the spirits damn you for the demon that you are, Daxton Vahnti!"

He gave her a wicked grin. "I'm sure they will." He loosened his hold on her elbow and pulled her closer, drawing a quick, sharp breath when her breasts pushed against the hardness of his chest. On impulse, he bent low and kissed her, his lips grinding against the fullness of hers in a ruthless display of proprietorship. A shock of desire ran through him, and his kiss suddenly deepened, an insistent exploration that made him want even more.

Rayna longed to pull free and wipe the taste of him from her lips but she was powerless even to try. When his mouth claimed hers she'd felt an inexplicable thrill, the birth of something hot and primitive low in her stomach.

A breath of wind curled around her ankles, and she realized that he'd somehow managed to lift the hem of her robe, tugging the silky blue material up to the tops of her thighs. Rayna tried to slip away from him, but his hold on her grew as insistent as his lips.

Dax was beyond caring what she thought or felt. His universe had narrowed to one of sensation and animal need. He shoved the silky folds of fabric aside and explored the soft mound of flesh hidden beneath.

At his touch, the ache in Rayna's stomach turned to scalding heat. She arched against his hand instinctively, wanting to draw him nearer, yet hating herself even as she did. Why did he have such an effect on her? Why couldn't she find the strength to resist?

She moved against him, and Dax almost lost complete control. He longed to free them both from the confines of their clothing, throw her to the ground, and take her again and again in the field of sweet-smelling flowers. He made a tortured, animal-like sound low in his throat. As much as he wanted to, he knew that he couldn't. Not here. The castle grounds were under constant surveillance by the security force, every square foot diligently surveyed by scores of robotic eyes. He stepped away from her and smoothed the flowing skirt of her robe back into place. He'd made enough of a fool of himself for one day, humiliated them both by his inability to control his temper and runaway lust. Deep within the bowels of the castle, an amused Haywood was probably sitting in front of a monitor screen, having a good laugh at his warlord's expense.

Struggling to catch her breath, Rayna stared at him in mute confusion. She touched a finger to her swollen lips, wondering why he had stopped. If truth were known, she wasn't sure whether it was relief or anger that she felt when he'd ended his attentions so abruptly. In the end she decided that she was greatly relieved.

Dax straightened his uniform jacket, angry at himself for letting her get to him once again. Haywood had said that he was obsessed with her, had insinuated that his interest might have even deeper roots. Was that why he had flown into such a dark rage when he'd seen her touch Bahleigh's face?

A brooding frown settled over his sharp-planed features. The girl had indeed muddled his senses, beguiled him with her maidenly body and mysterious ways. She was like a dangerous toxin, quick-acting and lethal whenever she touched his skin. He fought down his uncertainty and desire, pushed them deep within the folds of his mind where they hovered, dark and determined, waiting like patient predators for the opportunity to strike once again.

He gritted his teeth in frustration and turned his thoughts to other, safer matters, but the memory of how she had looked at Bahleigh refused to recede. Half expecting the madness to overtake him once again, he grabbed her by the forearm and held her tightly, an owner claiming title to what was his. "For the next few days," he told her in a cold tone, "a security guard will accompany you and Dr. Bahleigh on your excursions." He tugged on her arm, forcing her to start the long walk back to the castle.

"Why?" She stumbled a step and threw him a daggerlike look, sharp enough to gouge a hole in solid stone.

"Because I wish it." Dragging her along, he stalked to the edge of the clearing and into the woods, the cool air tinged with the sour, bitter scent of the oozing tree sap. Around them, the white-trunked trees towered toward the sky like columns of dark-veined marble. "But it's also for your protection."

She was nearly running to keep pace with him. "The only one I need protection from is you!"

He tightened his hold on her arm. "Wrong, pet." The woods began to thin, and the long stretch of open grass surrounding the castle was visible between gaps in the trees. "Guests will be arriving at Drakken tomorrow, quite a few of them. And I don't want you wandering about without an escort while they're here."

Rayna snorted. "What's the matter? Does the Vahnti count fear that I might plunge a knife into one of his noble guests?"

He stopped suddenly and turned to face her, a bemused smile playing across his lips. She actually thought he was concerned about the safety of his guests, when in fact the reverse was true. "How shall I put this . . . ? Let's just say that some of my compatriots are somewhat jaded in their attitudes, and I'm more worried about their actions than yours."

Rayna stared at him blankly.

"Given the opportunity, one of them might get the notion to plunge something into you instead." His smile widened. "And the weapon they'd use wouldn't be a knife, though it might resemble one in some ways."

A rush of crimson rode up her cheekbones.

"Understand now?"

She nodded woodenly.

His smile faded, and his expression turned somber and darkly intent. "As I said, no one is allowed to touch my possessions. If they did, I'd be forced to kill them, and it wouldn't be very polite of me to eviscerate one of my guests. To do so might even raise an unpleasant political stink. But mark my words, if forced to I would, without the slightest shred of guilt or remorse."

His eyes held hers. "The same holds true for any member of my clan foolish enough to attempt such a thing . . . the good doctor included."

Rayna stared back at him, fantasizing about the longed-for moment when she would carve out his black heart. No one was immune to his wrath, not even Carlo or Dr. Bahleigh. This was the black, evil side to the Vahnti warlord that had been whispered of over campfires, the hateful, vengeful man who killed animals for sport and humans for petty revenge, the demon who would uproot an entire culture and plunder a continent for the sake of a few precious stones. At that moment, Rayna would have gladly sold her soul in return for a sharpened blade.

A sudden, unnatural quiet descended over the copse of trees. Rayna pulled free of his grasp and wheeled around. The birds and foragers had ceased their incessant chatter, and the acrid scent of ozone hung thick and still in the morning air. Fear prickled the skin along the nape of her neck. When animals fell silent, danger was near.

Dax watched her curiously. One moment she'd been giving him a daggerlike look; the next she'd stiffened and begun casting wild, almost frantic looks about the quiet landscape, as though she were bracing for an unseen attack.

The ground shuddered beneath them, and a low-voiced rumble trembled across the quiet landscape. Rayna froze, paralyzed by fear.

Dax cocked his head toward the north, listening carefully for the screech of the earthquake alarm, but the strident sound never came. Another shock shuddered beneath them, more a quiver than one of the major temblors that rocked the region every few months or so. Then the ground stilled abruptly, and the birds found their voices once again, filling the air with the sound of their frightened calls.

"It's over now." Dax gave her a probing look. Had she somehow known that the quake was about to strike? "We would have heard the alarm if it was going to be worse."

Blood pounded a timpani in Rayna's ears. *Run, run,* the thrumming seemed to urge. "Were those earthquakes?" she managed to croak. She placed a hand against the pouch secreted inside her robe, drawing comfort from its presence. Reality shifted, and she was a child again, the years slipping away from her as if they had never been.

"Minor ones." Dax shoved his hands in his pockets and shrugged. "This region has dozens of them a day. But those were larger than most. Usually you can't feel them at all."

Only once had Rayna experienced a quake, a memory that had haunted her since the age of four. There'd been many a night when she'd woken damp and screaming, images from that day as fresh and horrifyingly clear as when they occurred. She could still remember how they'd run for the open grass, her mother urging her to greater speed . . . a jagged wound suddenly opening in the ground beneath them.

Rayna squeezed her lids shut to block the terrifying images, force them back into the bowels of her memory. But she could still see the stunned look of surprise on her mother's face as she tumbled into the yawning chasm. Still hear herself screaming and screaming . . .

"Rayna?" Dax frowned and grabbed her arm to steady her. She was swaying slightly, as if she were about to faint, and her face had turned a chalky ghost-white. "What's the matter?"

She swayed into him and buried her face against his chest, the memories coming fast and hard. She didn't care that it was his arms that closed about her. His touch was warm and human, a connecting thread with the here and now.

He could feel her trembling against him, violent shudders that racked her body from head to toe. "What is it, Rayna?" Lines of concern gathered across his brow. "What's wrong?"

For a moment she didn't speak; then she lifted fear-glazed eyes to his face. "My mother . . . she died in an earthquake when I was a child," she said in a voice roughened by emotion. "I haven't felt one since that day."

"I'm sorry." His embrace tightened. On this matter, at least, they shared common ground. He tilted her chin and met her gaze. She was so young, hardly more than a child now. "How old where you when it happened?"

"I was only four." She took a shaky breath. The ghosts were finally beginning to recede.

The wind lifted a strand of her hair, curling it about her face. Without conscious thought, Dax smoothed the strand back into place. "I know what it's like to lose a parent unexpectedly," he said in a quiet tone. "I lost both of mine in a ship accident fourteen years ago. Caccia and Carlo's parents died at the same time." He was silent for a moment. Then a shiver seemed to move through his body and he spoke again. "My younger sister and I were supposed to be on that ship, Caccia and Carlo as well. But Carlo became ill, and our parents decided to leave us behind. The four of us were standing atop a roof turret, watching as the flight took off. A few moments later the ship exploded." He turned toward the south, a faraway look in his pale eyes. "A breach in the reactor core, the experts said. They never stood a chance."

He rubbed at his temples wearily, his gaze still fastened on the distant horizon. "I was about your age then, more child than man, but I was forced to grow up overnight, take charge of the clan, my sister, and my cousins . . . whether I wanted to or not."

Rayna saw the grief reflected in his eyes and knew without

a doubt that the story was true. "I didn't know about your parents," she murmured. Actually, she knew very little of his background, only the horrifying tales of Vahnti arrogance and knavery recited over Lakota campfires, snippets of information that had fed her hatred through the years. The thought that he might have assumed the mantle of warlord reluctantly was unsettling, much less that he was capable of feeling grief. It was a side of him she'd never seen, utterly at odds with the coldhearted nobleman of legend and lore. "I didn't know that you had a sister, either. Is she here at the castle?"

"No," he said in a strained voice. "Alexandra's ship was lost in an ion storm some years ago."

"Do you still miss them?" It was a foolish question, Rayna knew, but oddly, she felt the most perverse urge to comfort him somehow.

"Yes, sorely at times. It's hard dealing with the memories . . . and the guilt. I should have died along with my parents." He pulled away from her and stared at the sunlit trees, surprised at himself that he had opened up to her this way. What kind of hold did she have on him? It wasn't like him to share his thoughts and feelings with anyone. "But I'm alive and they're dead."

He'd given voice to the same thoughts that had plagued Rayna long ago. Even though she'd known better, she'd tortured herself with the hideous notion that if she'd done something different, reacted differently, her mother might be alive today. Javan had set her straight, guided her through the morass of grief by instructing her in the ways of the Inner World. It was the truths he'd taught her that she attempted to share with Daxton Vahnti. "The physical bodies of your parents and sister were fated to die, as was my mother's. But their souls, their essence, have passed into the spirit world now, where they've joined the peace and harmony of the Universal All. Their spirits are part of the web of life now, individual threads woven into the tapestry of all life."

Dax laughed abruptly. The sound of his startled laughter drove a covey of birds from the trees and shattered the moment of calm between them. "I don't believe in your so-called spirits, my dear, nor in that tired old concept of universal harmony. We live; then we die—it's as simple as that. After a few years our worm-eaten flesh crumbles into bone dust, but that's the only metamorphosis we undergo. We're all doomed from the moment we're born, dying by slow degrees from the very instant we come squalling into life.''

Her mouth flattened, and her gaze turned stone-hard. He was mocking her, and her beliefs, and that was the one thing she could not abide. Why had she been so foolish as to try to comfort him? Her anger grew, feeding on his arrogant smirk. ''Mock me if you wish, Vahnti demon, but do not mock that which you know nothing about. The tapestry of the spirit world is all around us, from the trees to the smallest blade of grass, in the helpless creatures you so callously hunt. It even dwells within you, I'm sorry to say.''

An amused smile ruffled the edges of Dax's lips, but inwardly he cursed himself for spoiling the brief moment of understanding between them. Still, how could anyone hold to such nonsensical beliefs in this day and age? Three thousand years of scientific and technological advancements had freed humankind from the yoke of superstition, peeled away the mysteries of the universe one by one until all that was left was a single, inescapable truth: life was no more than a cosmic accident. There was nothing spiritual or harmonious about it, no matter what the foolish Nirvannans believed.

''If I had my way, pet, whoever filled your pretty head with such silly drivel would be thrown out an air lock into the vacuum of space.''

Her face hardened, and her eyes thinned to glowing slits. Enough was enough. It was time Daxton Vahnti began to learn the power of the Inner World. She touched the amulet hidden beneath her robe, then lifted a hand to her temple, her eyes never leaving his arrogant face.

A rustling of leaves and a chorus of angry cries rose from the nearby trees, the squawks of a hundred creatures shrieking in unison. Wings fluttered, beating furiously against the crisp fall air as the birds took flight and gathered in a frenzied swarm that darkened the morning sky.

Dax stared upward, startled and amazed by the peculiar sight. ''What in space . . .''

A fat tree hen broke free of the swarm and daggered downward, followed quickly by several more. Dax ducked reflexively and tried to cover his head, but the tree hen still struck, pecking and stabbing at the top of his head with its arrow-thin beak. The others landed on his back and shoulders, cawing and tearing at strands of his flowing hair.

The attack ended as suddenly as it had begun, the tree hens spiraling back into the sky with their stolen booty of hair. The swarm thinned, then vanished altogether, the birds settling back onto nests and branches.

Speechless, Dax glanced around in wide-eyed amazement. Save for an occasional bird chirping and darting from limb to limb, the sky was peaceful and silent once more. As if the attack had never occurred. He winced as he touched his fingers to a sore spot on his head, then glanced at Rayna from the corner of his eye. She had escaped the attack completely unscathed, as if the birds had purposely focused their ferocity solely on him. His brows drew downward in a suspicious frown. Why hadn't they attacked her as well?

A slow, secretive smile tugged at the corners of Rayna's mouth. Now that she had the amulet back there was nothing to stop her. She'd teach him how wrong he was, make the Vahnti warlord wish he'd never heard of a planet named Nirvanna.

Chapter Twelve

The atrium was ablaze with light, pinpoints of vibrant color that seemed to dart and weave through the tangle of trees and vines like thousands of incandescent flameflies. Rayna lifted a hand in wonder and allowed a single ruby light to drift through her fingers. It hovered for a moment, nestled like a feathery insect in the palm of her hand, then floated upward, slowly rising through the dense jumble of limbs toward the crystal ceiling a thousand feet above.

Hoverlights, Lett had called them, mindless robotic ornaments that were sometimes loosed in the atrium to adorn the demon lord's parties. Rayna stared at the fairy lights, mesmerized by the shimmers of color.

Beside her, the gi chirped in protest and batted at a drifting circle of blue with a tiny paw. The light descended, brushing against the mossy ground, then rebounded past the startled gi. The creature squawked and leaped into her lap.

"It's all right, little one." She stroked the gi's dark fur soothingly. "It won't hurt you." Rayna sighed and leaned her back against a hollow tree. Poor little gi. He hadn't adjusted well at all to being the demon lord's captive. But at least he was still alive, and free to roam the confines of the castle's atrium. He'd even begun to build a burrow inside the hollow tree trunk.

A strange, plaintive sound suddenly filled the air, an endless string of mournful notes that rose and fell on a distant echo. Rayna cocked her head and listened. Music. A reed instrument of some kind, lower-pitched and far more poignant than the joyful sounds made by a Lakota flute. She could hear other sounds now, too, the steady rush of the waterfall as well as the distant murmurs of voices raised in conversation.

The shadow of a frown moved across her brow. The warlord's party had begun, the first of many scheduled to celebrate the Vahntis' annual hunt. Her lips curled in disgust. A steady stream of ships had been landing at Drakken Castle for the past two days, disgorging scores of richly clothed and jewel-bedecked nobles who'd come to spill the blood of innocent creatures for the sake of a Vahnti tradition.

She clutched the helpless gi tight against her abdomen. Cold-blooded killers, who, according to Lett, would butcher as many as a hundred animals before the hunt day was over. There was no justification for what they planned. If just one human were felled by a predatory animal, there would be a great hue and cry for revenge. Were a hundred little deaths of any less value than the death of a solitary human?

Furious at the prospect of what the new day would bring,

she reached inside the hollow of the tree to place the gi inside the entrance of his new home, but drew her hand back in surprise when her fingers brushed across something soft and leathery. Frowning, she leaned around and peered inside the oblong hole, fingers groping for the object half-buried in the rich black soil.

Rayna tugged the article from its hiding place and lifted her discovery into the glow cast by the hoverlights. Her frown turned to an expression of bewilderment as she brushed a fine layer of dirt from the leather of a pouchlike case. The front was richly tooled, the soft black leather embossed with the familiar Vahnti crest. She glanced around to make sure no one was watching and lifted the flap, her curiosity winning out over suspicion.

A gasp escaped her lips as the contents spilled on the mossy ground. "Oh, my," Rayna said softly.

The gi chirped excitedly and scampered around beside her, running toward, then dancing away from the silver knife lying in the thick yellow moss.

Rayna's heartbeat accelerated, and her hand shook as it closed around the hilt of the filigreed knife. Tears stung the corners of her eyes. Her knife. A gift forged from Nirvannan silver long ago by Javan's loving hands. She closed her lids a moment, fingers wrapped tight around the familiar blade, and whispered a silent prayer of thanks to whatever spirit had prompted its return.

The gi chirped again, drawing her attention to a small black device no larger than her hand, as well as a thin scrap of parchment that had fallen from the case along with the knife. Rayna unfolded the parchment with trembling hands.

The device is a key to open a doorway through the shield wall. There are a goodly number of money chits secreted inside the case as well. Make your way southeast over the nearest chain of mountains to a small settlement named Argossa. A ship will be awaiting your arrival, but you must act soon. When you reach Argossa, use the chits to bribe the ship's captain. Buy transport as far from Hellfire as possible.
    A Friend

Rayna read the note over and over until the contents had been etched into her memory. Finally, the parchment still clutched in her fingers, she leaned her head against the tree trunk and allowed the tears to fall unhindered.

"Lett . . ." she whispered to the gi. It had to be. Lett had found and returned the amulet. Now the knife. He'd placed himself in terrible jeopardy to arrange her escape from Drakken Castle. And if the Vahnti count ever discovered what he'd done, the courageous doctor would surely die. "Spirits protect him. . . ."

Hope burned bright in her tear-glazed eyes. With the knife, key, and chits Lett had hidden inside the tree, she and the animals could escape from Hellfire. "We'll be able to leave soon," she told the gi. She blinked away the haze of tears and tried to focus her thoughts. Now was not the time to give in to her emotions. There was too much at stake. Too much to plan. "Tomorrow, maybe, or the day after."

A furtive rustling of leaves warned her that someone was on the pathway that angled to the left of her hiding place. Rayna's heart thumped against her rib cage. Quietly, she slid the knife, key, and parchment back into the case, then stuffed the leather bag inside the hollow and buried it beneath a thick layer of dirt.

A limb snapped, the brittle sound even closer than the rustle of leaves. She clutched the gi tighter and crouched low, hiding within the tree's muddy shadow as she peered through gaps in the dense wall of greenery.

A young security officer crept into view, her dark armor gleaming dully in the artificial light. She paused for a moment, hardened, warrior eyes searching back and forth across the dense tangle of foliage for a telltale movement. Rayna crouched even lower, allowing the tree's shadow to envelop her completely. It was Sub-Leftenant Anwell, the officer in charge of the security detail that had dogged her footsteps night and day since the castle's guests began to arrive. After hours of plotting and planning, Rayna had finally managed to slip away from Anwell's cohorts and make her way to the atrium, but judging by the officer's determined expression, her next escape would prove a more difficult feat to achieve.

Armor creaked as Anwell dropped to her knees and began peering into the jumble of greenery, no more than a dozen feet from where Rayna was hiding.

"Anwell?" On the pathway, Dax ground to a sudden stop and lifted an ebony brow. The young officer was on her hands and knees, crawling through a bed of creep-vines rimming the walkway. "What's going on here, Sub-Leftenant?"

Anwell bolted to her feet, her face reddening with embarrassment that she'd been caught in such an undignified position by the count himself. "Count Vahnti, sir . . ." Her jaw stiffened, and she reddened even more as she gave him a swift salute. "I regret to report that Miss Syn slipped away from the detail that I assigned to watch over her. We believe she's in here, sir, somewhere in the atrium. We're attempting to locate her now."

Dax's brows drew downward in an incredulous scowl. The central portion of the atrium was brimming with scores of royal guests who'd gathered for the prehunt dinner, and now Rayna was loose in the very same room, roaming around at will. "The guards *lost* her?" he nearly shouted. "Inside the atrium?"

The sub-leftenant stiffened and steeled herself for a dressing-down. "They lost track of her in the main corridor, my lord. A security eye positioned at the western doors recorded her passage into the atrium itself."

Dax's face went very still. Over two hundred of the Dominion's "finest" were wandering about the atrium, most blind-drunk on Logo wine and other mind-altering chemicals. There was no telling what would happen if one of them happened to stumble upon Rayna. "I'll find the girl myself, Sub-Leftenant," Dax ordered tersely. "In the meantime, I want the security detail stationed at the atrium's western doors. Once I find Miss Syn, you are to escort her back to my suite and lock her inside. Absolutely no one is allowed in or out except me. Is that understood?"

"Yes, sir." Anwell struck her fist to her chest in a hasty salute and quick-stepped down the pathway.

Dax huffed out an angry breath. Rayna was somewhere inside the junglelike atrium, alone, the very thing he'd hoped to avoid by assigning the guards to watch over her. Muttering beneath his breath, he slipped the small tracker from a pocket and cupped it in his palm. A tiny light turned from red to green as he pressed a pad at the bottom of the disc-shaped device. He studied the disc's flat surface, watching as the tracker began homing in on Rayna's sensor cuffs. A split second later a series of coordinates flashed across the small readout screen.

His anger suddenly faded, and he suppressed an amused smile. Close. No more than twenty paces to the right from where he stood. He glanced at the thicket of vines out of the corner of his eye. "I know you're in there, Rayna. Come out now and it will go better for you."

The only sounds he could hear were the steady drone of his guests' conversation and the distant, plaintive notes of an old Earth ballad the flutist was playing.

"Why do you insist on defying me, Rayna?" he told his unseen captive. "I told you why I was ordering the guards to watch over you. It's for your own protection."

She still didn't answer.

Dax sighed and rechecked the tracker's readout screen. She'd moved deeper into the foliage, backing away from him another ten steps or so. "All right, then. I'm coming in after you." He dropped to all fours and crawled into the creep-vines snaking around the pathway, the very same position he'd found Anwell in just a few minutes before.

There was a faint scratching sound to his right, much like a creature of some kind sharpening its claws. Beside him, a patch of vine leaves trembled as something small and dark scurried through the undergrowth. Dax frowned and peered at the vines.

A hissing noise was his only warning as the creature launched itself from under the leaves. Razor-thin teeth dug into his hand, a sensation he'd become all too familiar with just weeks before. Dax jerked upward in surprise and let out an oath as his skull collided with a thick limb hanging above him.

"Damn it all," he muttered darkly, and pried the animal's jaws loose from his thumb. Recognition flared in his eyes as his hand closed around the hissing puff of fur and teeth. "You!" Man and gi glared at each other. "What fool let you loose in my atrium?"

Still hissing, the gi squirmed from his grasp and scampered away. Dax winced and wiped away the droplet of blood that had seeped from his thumb. His scalp hurt worse than the tiny puncture wound, though. He'd managed to scrape his head in the exact same spot where the tree hens had attempted to snatch him bald. He stared into the thicket suspiciously. For just a moment there, while he was busy dealing with the gi and vine, he had thought he'd heard a faint peal of feminine laughter.

He rummaged through the leaves until he found the tracker. A new string of coordinates appeared on the screen. Rayna was moving again, slipping soundlessly through the verdant jungle toward the western doors, exactly where he wanted her to go.

"Dax, darling," a voice said from behind him. "Whatever are you doing?"

Dax stopped cold and shook his head. *Wonderful.* He extricated himself from the web of vines and climbed slowly to his feet. Rayna would have to wait.

Flavian Modalbeau, warlordess of the Modalbeau clan, arched a blondish brow and wagged an admonishing finger, her lips curling downward in a pouty smile. "You should have called me, Dax." Her smile turned sultry. "I would have been more than glad to crawl around the bushes with you . . . for as long as you wanted."

"I was looking for something, Flavian." He straightened his formal uniform jacket and squared his shoulders. He'd managed to avoid running into Flavian ever since she'd arrived the day before, but there was no escaping her now.

"Really?" Flavian stepped into the greenery beside the pathway, nimbly placing herself between the Vahnti count and his only avenue of escape. She ran a long, golden nail down the length of his arm and brushed away a hoverlight clinging to the front of his uniform. "We can look for it together." The fingernail moved to his neck, tracing a thin trail up his throat to his chin. Desire flamed to life inside her gray eyes.

"I don't mind if we miss that boring dinner, Dax. I'd much rather spend the time with you." She wound her arms around his neck, her slender fingers moving through the thick queue of ebony hair tied at the base of his neck. "It's been so long since we were together." She pressed herself against him, eyes turning dark and boldly sensual at the prospect of feeling his hard flesh once again. "Remember how it was between us, Dax? The games we used to play?"

He pushed away from her gently. "I remember it well, Flavian." A muscle knotted along his jaw. They'd been together for only a few short weeks, but in the two years since, Flavian had exaggerated their brief relationship into some sort of grand, long-term love affair. Granted, Flavian Modalbeau was a desirable woman, with an expertly sculpted body that would heat the blood of any man. Her exotically chiseled face was quite pleasing, too, the best that money chits could buy. But there was something rather cold about her, an emptiness deep inside her, as if the bioengineers who'd done such a remarkable job on the outside had made a muddle of her interior.

She smiled and pointed toward the greenery with an elegant finger. "We could just disappear for a while. No one will even notice that we're gone."

"You know me, Flavian." Dax had no intention of making the same mistake twice. He no longer desired her, and the warlordess of the Modalbeaus was far too valuable as an ally to risk their clans' relationship with another meaningless dalliance. "Once I've seen the contents of a box, I have no desire to look inside again." Her features tensed, and he smiled to soften his comment. "I'm sorry, Flavian, but the answer has to be no. Although I must admit your offer is quite tempting."

"Oh, well." Flavian sighed and shrugged. "Nothing gambled, nothing gained . . . isn't that how the saying goes?"

"I think so." Dax grinned and studied her attire with an appreciative eye. She was dressed in a billowing overrobe shot with woven gold, an effect carried through by the fine sprinkling of gold dust that glittered on her face and elaborately coiffed hair. A thick gold chain hung from her neck, trailing downward to a flat crystal pendant suspended between her ample breasts. "I like the robe, Flavian. It suits you."

A flicker of emotion passed through her eyes. She'd worn it for him, wasted half the afternoon preparing to see him again, then spent additional hours wandering about the mausoleum of a castle in hopes of catching him alone. "Why, thank you, Dax," she said in a disinterested voice, though inwardly she rejoiced that he'd noticed at all.

"Was there something you wanted, Flavian?" Dax glanced at the dense foliage, then at the tracker cupped in his palm. Rayna was still moving. "I have a few matters to tend to before dinner."

Her eyes narrowed slightly. That wasn't the first time she'd caught him glancing at the snarl of vegetation, as though whatever object he'd been searching for was far more important than a conversation with her. She forced her mouth to bend into a tight-lipped smile. "Can you spare a moment for a little business talk? I've been trying to set an appointment with you ever since I arrived, but your aides haven't been very forthcoming about your schedule or whereabouts. I was beginning to think that you were purposely avoiding me."

"Never, Flavian." He touched her elbow and guided her back to the pathway, hoping whatever she had on her mind wouldn't take very long. "I haven't been keeping much of a schedule the past few days. Even a warlord or warlordess deserves time off every now and again. Don't you agree?" he said absently.

"Of course." She eyed him long and hard, all trace of softness fading from her elegant features. Something had changed about him since the last season at court. He looked relaxed, as close as she'd ever seen him to happy. The Daxton Vahnti she knew was prone to black moods and periods when he became an unsociable recluse. But his clan and clan business always came first. He often drove himself and others to the point of physical collapse, a man who didn't suffer fools, or any form of sloth. He would never just take a few days off, not without a damn good cause.

Flavian was quiet for another moment, studying him curiously, but when she saw an impatient frown sweep across his brow, she got on with the business at hand. "I need a favor, Dax," she said gravely.

137

His gaze moved from the greenery to Flavian's face. The word *favor* wasn't taken lightly in Dominion society. "I'm listening."

"I've heard that the Lyseene trade ambassador has been on Hellfire for nearly a week to negotiate a compact on mineral rights from the Nirvannan system. I've also heard that you've delayed finalizing the agreement until after the hunt."

Dax gave her a veiled look of surprise. "You're very well informed."

"You know how it is, darling." She smiled engagingly. "There are no true secrets within the Dominion. Rumors travel from clan to clan at the speed of light. In fact, I knew about the proposed compact before the ambassador ever arrived."

"So? What does the Lyseene proposal have to do with a favor to the Modalbeaus?"

Flavian turned to face him and touched his arm, gold-tipped fingers sliding over the braid on his sleeve. "Don't sign with the Lyseenes, Dax. My clan needs that duranium, as well as a hundred metric tons each of platinum and tritinium. I'm prepared to pay three million chits for the rights, but I can go no higher."

"Flavian, that's not even market value. The Lyseenes have offered top chits—ten percent above fair market. They might even increase their bid if I press."

Flavian glanced around to make sure no one was listening, then lowered her voice to a near whisper. "I'm in trouble, Dax. My clan is teetering on the verge of financial collapse. We've had crop failures on three colony worlds, and our reserves of chits and natural resources are close to depletion. If I don't get those ores to keep my factories running, we'll be ruined."

His brows angled downward in a troubled frown. "I knew there were problems, but I had no idea they had reached this magnitude."

Flavian drew in a shaky breath. "You know what will happen, Dax. Once word gets out, those Dunstan carrion will pick the bones of my clan clean."

"Why didn't you come to me sooner, Flavian?" he asked

curiously. "I would have been glad to loan you enough chits to see you through the worst of it."

She shrugged and glanced away. "Pride, I suppose." She should have gone to him at the first inkling of trouble, but it was too late now. Had been for a number of months. "Things just progressed so fast." Flavian fell silent for a second, her eyes shifting this way and that, fastening on a tree, a tangle of vines, anything but his face. "It's far too late for just a bridge loan now. I need access to those ores, Dax." Her troubled gaze finally focused on him. "I need it now."

Dax sighed and rubbed at the ache building behind his temples. How could he refuse such a request? The Modalbeaus had been allied with the Vahntis for close to a thousand years, true friends who'd stood by his family's side more than once during the Dominion's tumultuous history. He couldn't stand by and let their clan fall to ruin. But the economic well-being of clan Vahnti was his top priority. He would help the Modalbeaus obtain the resources they needed, render whatever aid they required, but it was his duty to further his clan's interests in the bargain.

He smiled inwardly. Besides, once his own clan's shortfall of strategic ores had been righted, there would be more than enough to share with Flavian. And the true value of the Nirvannan system had never rested solely on its stockpiles of valuable minerals. The real value of the star system lay on the planet itself. Everything else was secondary.

He pursed his lips and considered. "I'll need a concession from your clan," he said finally. Flavian was well aware that he would ask for a favor in return, and probably already knew which one it would be. A favor for a favor. Tit for tat. The philosophy was the engine that drove the Dominion economy. And there was only one thing he truly wanted from the Modalbeaus, an agreement his family had been trying to negotiate for over two hundred years. "I can't justify throwing away the proposed compact with the Lyseenes without some sort of compensation, Flavian. There are too many chits at stake, as well as my relationship with the Lyseenes. Even though we don't have a signed agreement yet, Edgar won't be very happy if I back out of the deal."

"Fair enough." Flavian arched a brow expectantly. "What sort of concession did you have in mind?"

"Something I've wanted for a long, long time," Dax said quietly. The Gamma system was located on the fringe of Modalbeau territory, a crucial nexus that abutted Dunstan space. If his clan had a forward base on Gamma Three, Alfred and his brood couldn't make a single move without him knowing in advance. And with several brigades of troops prepositioned there, the Dunstans would be rendered impotent. He would be able to counter any movement of troops and supplies that Alfred contemplated, prevent the Dunstans from spreading their growing web of influence any farther.

He stared into the distance, thinking. His troops were already stretched thin along Vahnti borders, and if he sent additional brigades to Gamma Three, they would be stretched so thin that large sections of his territory would be open to attack. But if Flavian was willing to agree to the concession, he would be a fool not to seize the opportunity.

"I want a Vahnti base on Gamma Three," he demanded. "As well as Modalbeau permission to station up to three brigades there for the next ten years."

Flavian nodded slowly. "Done." He'd asked for no more than she had expected. "The Modalbeaus agree to your terms."

A glint of triumph filtered through his eyes. "Tell your negotiators to meet with mine tomorrow. They can work out the details during the hunt."

"Thank you, Dax." She pressed cool lips against his cheek, then quickly drew away from him, her taut face smoothing into soft lines once again. "You don't know how much this means to me."

"My pleasure." He inclined his head in a short bow. "Now, if you'll excuse me for a moment, I must have a word with the security detail before the dinner begins."

"By all means."

Dax hurried away, taking the nearest cross path to hasten the long walk to the atrium's western doors.

Flavian watched his progress until she was sure that he'd really gone, then touched the tip of a nail to a tiny depression hidden on the band of an emerald ring. A privacy field shimmered to life around her, a thin bubble of energy that would repulse the signals of any listening device.

She picked up the crystal pendant nestled between her breasts and glared into its opaque depths. "Well? Is that what you wanted?"

"An inspired performance, my dear, truly inspired." Alfred Dunstan puckered his mouth in distaste and leaned away from the viewscreen, mildly repulsed by the distorted image of Flavian Modalbeau. "But I do wish you wouldn't stare down into the lens like that, Flavian. I just had dinner, and I don't wish to spoil my digestion with a close-up view of the inside of your nostrils."

She scowled and pulled the lens up higher. "Better?"

"Much." Now he could see her entire face. "I especially enjoyed the part when you all but threw yourself upon the count." Alfred made a sad, sighing sound. "Too bad he didn't take you up on your generous offer." Witnessing their coupling would have been the high point of his day. But then, being an unseen guest inside Drakken Castle for the past two days had been remarkable fun in itself. It even made up a bit for the fact that he'd never been invited inside Drakken's towering black walls, an insult he would soon set right. "I would have really enjoyed watching the two of you."

Flavian shuddered, and the edges of her lips curled in an artificial smile. For a single foolish moment, when she'd first spotted Dax crawling around the bushes, she had forgotten about Alfred Dunstan, and his watching eye. "Yes, too bad." If Dax had just been a little more receptive, if he had offered the slightest encouragement of any kind, maybe she could have found the courage to extricate herself from this predicament. "I had so hoped . . ."

"Still carrying a candle for him after all this time?"

"No," Flavian lied. "That was over long ago."

He lifted a corpulent hand to the flat wall screen and traced a finger down the image of her jaw. "I'm glad to hear it, my dear. Very glad."

The taste of bile rose in her throat. She could almost feel the clammy touch of his finger through the tiny screen. "I did what you wanted, Alfred. A favor for a favor." She had struck a bargain with the Dunstan devil in order to save her clan, agreed to Alfred's demands in return for economic salvation. "Now tear up my clan's loan notes as you promised."

"All in good time, Flavian. You're not quite finished yet."

Flavian closed her eyes. She'd become Alfred's puppet, a marionette dancing to his perverted little tunes.

"Why such a sad face?" Alfred said cheerily. "You'll get your notes back, and you'll soon have a massive infusion of Vahnti capital at little or no interest, as well as a shiny new military base on one of your worlds. Think about it, Flavian. All those riches in return for just a few minutes' work."

She wrapped her arms about herself as if to ward off a sudden chill. "What else do you want me to do?"

"You still have to find that girl I spoke to you about—and be sure you're wearing the pendant when you do. I want to have a good, close-up look at the mysterious Rayna Syn."

She frowned into the pendant. Why was Alfred so interested in this girl? "I haven't seen a single new face since I arrived, Alfred. How am I supposed to find her if I don't even know who she is?"

"Forgive me, Flavian; I thought you already knew." Alfred grinned maliciously. He so loved being the harbinger of bad news. "Rayna Syn just happens to be your ex-paramour's latest love interest. A beautiful creature, from what I've been told. People are even saying that the elusive count is so smitten by her that he's moved her into his personal suite." His grin stretched even wider. "Who knows? She might even become a permanent fixture around Drakken Castle."

Flavian visibly paled.

"I think it's past time that Daxton settled down." Alfred chuckled gleefully. "Don't you agree?" He touched a pad on the console and ended the transmission abruptly.

Flavian dropped the pendant as if it held some gruesome insect. She clenched her hands into tight fists, the gold-tipped nails digging into the flesh on her palms. The chain swung back and forth across her chest as she began walking toward the distant sounds of music and laughter.

Chapter Thirteen

The bugler sounded the call, a low-pitched clarion note that hung in the morning air. At the base of the stone staircase leading to the castle's entrance, a chorus of hounds howled in anticipation, straining against leashes held by a dozen young kennelboys. Farther away, a small herd of dark-hued horses were being led toward the steps, their sleek, curried hides shining with meticulous care.

From his position atop the terrace, Dax leaned against a buttress and surveyed the scene contentedly. Nothing could darken his mood this day, not even Rayna, who was watching the proceedings with a tight-lipped expression, obviously revolted by the whole idea.

The day itself had dawned bright and clear, the crisp fall air almost free of volcanic dust. Guests clad in the traditional colors of black and red were pouring from the massive main doors, an excited, chattering mass of humankind who began milling in animated groups along the length of Drakken's esplanade. Only a handful would actually ride the hunt, a carefully chosen few experienced in the ways of horses, as well as the ways of their prey. The others would simply await their return, eager for the opportunity to be a part of Dominion tradition, and to join in the after-celebration.

Dax's hold on Rayna's elbow firmed, as much to keep her by him as to prevent her from running away. He wanted her to see and experience the sights and sounds, wanted her to try to understand the meaning of the tradition.

It was hunt day—a long-running custom that harkened back to the very first Vahntis and the Dominion's grimmest time, when a colonist's life was cheap and death a constant companion. The key to survival had been cooperation, an unswerving bond between the small bands of colonists who'd struck

143

out from Earth to forge new lives on strange, alien worlds closer to the Milky Way's starry core, thousands of light-years from humanity's spawning ground along the galaxy's outer rim.

His pale eyes were drawn upward, to the stone gargoyles perched atop the buttresses on either side of Drakken's doors. The gargoyles had been placed there centuries before as permanent testament to those first colonists' tenacity, and to the human will to survive and endure.

Rayna followed the direction of his gaze and grimaced. She hadn't noticed the hideous stone creatures before. The catlike animals were grotesque, with large, misshapen bodies and blunt-faced heads. Twin fangs curved downward from their open mouths, and thin, sheathlike wings fanned outward from vestigial hands that were more talon than paw.

Curiosity won out over her desire to ignore Daxton Vahnti. ''What are they?'' she asked him in a quiet voice.

''They're vampire-cats, pet. That's what we'll be hunting today.'' His face settled into somber lines. ''Through the centuries, those creatures killed more of my ancestors than disease and war combined. They're the reason why the annual hunt was begun, why the Dominion itself was formed. Hellfire was teeming with those ugly beasts when the first Vahnti ship arrived. They attacked without provocation, and soon developed a taste for human blood. The fangs secrete a neural toxin that paralyzes its prey; then it simply sucks the victim bone-dry. A vampire-cat can drain a human of blood in less than five minutes.''

The blue of his eyes deepened as he recounted this small portion of Vahnti history. ''The early colonists fought them constantly, but it was a losing battle until other clans pitched in and devised the annual hunt. Without the shield wall, and the hunt to thin the numbers of vampire-cats, every human on Hellfire would have been dead long ago. There are fewer of them now, but still enough to pose a danger to anyone who wanders around outside the wall.''

She thought of the distant predator scent she'd picked up when she and Lett were in the clearing. Was it a vampire-cat she'd smelled? Rayna shivered slightly, her thoughts veering to the next day, when she and the animals would use the hidden key to make their escape through the shield wall. Would the vampire-cats attack them, or let them pass unmolested? It was hard to say. Her ability to communicate with animals was not completely reliable, depending on the creature's mood and temperament, as well as its intelligence. The strange scent had been dark and malignant, a terrifying smell filled with loathing and lust.

Dax felt her tremble and pulled her closer, tucking her hand securely within his. "I didn't mean to frighten you, but I wanted you to understand the reason for the hunt. You seem to think we do this just for sport."

She gave him a sharp look, trying desperately to ignore the heat generated by the mere touch of his hand. "What of the other animals you kill? Surely all the creatures on this planet don't bear you ill will."

He sighed and glanced away, nodding a greeting to the Lyseene warlord as he walked by. Edgar Lyseene threw him a scorching glare in return. Dax straightened from his slouch against the buttress. The Lyseenes had obviously gotten wind of his impending deal with the Modalbeaus, and weren't very pleased with the news.

Nearby, Caccia and Flavian Modalbeau strolled onto the esplanade side by side, their heads bent close as they carried on a low conversation. Dax lifted a brow. What conspiracy were the two of them brewing?

Rayna's body went rigid when she spied Caccia Vahnti and a fair-haired woman she'd seen from a distance in the atrium. The pair had turned in her direction and were staring at her openly with hard, appraising eyes. For over a week now she had managed to avoid an encounter with the demon lord's spiteful cousin, who seemed to take special glee in tormenting her again and again.

"I'd like to leave now," Rayna told the Vahnti count. "I've seen what you wanted me to see. There's no reason to keep me here any longer."

His expression turned angry. Did she think she could pick and choose which orders to obey? "You have no say in the matter, Rayna. I may pretend to the others that you're my guest for the sake of convention, but remember, in reality you're not a guest at all.''

"Dax, dear!'' Flavian Modalbeau bullied her way through the throng, a sour-faced Caccia following close behind. "There you are.'' She ground to a sudden stop, her red hunt capelet billowing around her tall frame in the stiff morning wind. "I've been looking for you since breakfast.''

From the corner of his eye, Dax glanced at Caccia, who had puffed up like a petulant toad and was staring daggers at Rayna.

"You're still here?'' Caccia snapped, glaring malevolently at the Nirvannan girl.

"Unfortunately,'' Rayna retorted. "Your cousin seems to think my presence is necessary for some reason.''

"I can't imagine why.''

"Neither can I.''

Dax ignored them. "What can I do for you, Flavian?''

"I just wanted to tell you that my trade negotiators will be meeting with yours within the hour,'' Flavian said, intrigued by the current of tension flowing through their little group. She cast a covert look toward the copper-haired woman standing next to him. This was the girl Alfred was so interested in seeing? The same one Dax was lavishing his attention on? Granted, she was pretty in a natural sort of way, a look that might appeal briefly to a man such as Dax, who relished the new and different above all else. Still, save for those glittering green eyes, there was nothing truly remarkable about her that Flavian could discern. The girl's features had never even been enhanced. "The contracts should be ready for your signature by the end of the hunt.''

"Fine.'' Dax knew the conversation was just a pretext. Flavian's sharp eyes had lingered on Rayna far too long, and he guessed he had sweet Cousin Caccia to thank for that. "We'll sign before the banquet tonight.''

"What contract?'' Caccia's face had turned a ghostly shade of white when she heard the word.

He gave her a knowing grin. For the most part, Caccia had been on her best behavior since he had threatened her with Petwitt's offer. "Not to worry, cousin. It's not at all what you're thinking.'' His smile turned gleeful. ''But I do sign contracts every day and there's no telling what the next one might contain.''

A flush of red rode up her snowy cheeks. ''You're talking nonsense, Dax.'' Her chin lifted to a haughty angle. ''I haven't the slightest idea what you're referring to.''

''Really? Come to my office tomorrow, and I'll be more than glad to refresh your memory.''

Flavian waited for the conversation to continue or for Dax to offer a formal introduction to his latest conquest. But he and Caccia seemed to be having a private battle of wills and words that no one else was privy to. When Dax stubbornly refused to follow protocol, she took matters into her own hands. ''I'm Flavian Modalbeau, dear.'' She angled her body toward the girl, positioning herself so that the pendant was directly facing her. ''And you are . . . ?''

A cold, deathly chill crawled down Rayna's spine as her gaze traveled over the heavy pendant hanging on the woman's chest. ''Rayna Syn,'' she answered in a wary voice. Sunlight brushed the crystal's facets, turning the surface into a rainbow of color. But the beautiful exterior masked something darker inside, a strange, chilling emptiness that she couldn't ignore. She had the oddest sensation that the pendant was watching her, like some loathsome, mutant eye. Rayna tried to pull her arm free, wanting to flee as far as possible from the woman and her necklace, but the warlord's grip held her firmly in place.

''So you're the little Nirvannan girl I've heard so much about,'' Flavian said coldly. She shifted her body a fraction more, her movement mirroring the girl's, then gave Dax a knowing smile. ''Where have you been hiding this adorable child, Dax? I can see now why everyone says you've been so preoccupied of late.''

''I'm not hiding anything, Flavian.'' Dax cleared his throat but said nothing more. Flavian had placed too much emphasis on the word *child,* as if there were something indecent about it.

Rayna's senses sharpened, warning her that something was amiss. The crystal-thing was shimmering brightly, the facets turning a deep, hideous pink. She averted her face abruptly to break her gaze on the pendant, unconsciously moving closer to Dax Vahnti as she did. She clutched at his shoulder fearfully. There was something malevolent about the crystal, something that made her want to snatch it from the woman's chest and crush it beneath her heel.

Dax blinked in amazement. What had caused the sudden change? After weeks of cringing away from him, Rayna was clinging to his arm and shoulder as if her life depended on it. He smiled slowly. Whatever the reason, she'd reached out to him of her own volition. Just in time, too. He'd promised Haywood that he'd settle things by the end of the hunt, and the guests would be leaving in only two short days. He wound his fingers through a thick strand of russet hair. Tonight then, at the latest tomorrow.

Flavian's mouth tightened at the sight of him pawing at the girl's hair. So did Caccia's.

The bugler sounded the call to mount up, eliciting another round of deep-throated howls from the pack of hounds. The riders began making their way down the long flight of steps, triangular crossbows clutched in eager hands. Caccia and Flavian stalked off to join the throng of hunters moving toward their mounts.

Dax pulled away from Rayna gently and smoothed her unbound hair. "Be strong, pet." He trailed a fingertip along the curve of her jaw. "I know you'll miss me, but I'll be back soon."

Rayna gathered her scattered wits and gave him a hostile glare. What was wrong with her? She'd been so frightened by a bit of glass that she'd thrown herself into the demon lord's arms. "If I'm lucky you won't come back at all."

Dax laughed and hurried down the staircase, taking the steps two at time. He turned back for a moment before mounting his horse, and gave her a mocking salute.

The crowd cheered as the hounds were loosed, the animals baying excitedly as they raced down the winding pathway toward the distant shield wall. The riders thundered after them, each eager to bag the prize for the first kill of the day.

Rayna glanced to her right, where the security guards assigned to her were busy watching the beginning of the hunt. Haywood March was there, too, as well as Carlo, but their eyes were fixed on the herd of riders racing down the gravel road. She moved in the opposite direction, slowly at first, slipping from shadow to shadow along the side of the castle. She weaved through a cluster of onlookers, then quickened her pace, confident that she'd moved past the guards' line of sight.

If she hurried, she could cut through the woods and beat the riders to their destination, watch from the tiny clearing as they opened the shield wall. Learning how to operate the key beforehand would aid in her escape. She picked up the hem of her cumbersome robe and lengthened her stride.

Leaves crunched underfoot as she raced through the woods, darting unerringly between the white-barked monoliths. Beyond the curtain of trees, she could hear the steady tattoo of hoofbeats pounding through gravel as the riders neared the wall.

She could see the shield now, a thin patina of gold undulating against the southern sky. Farther away, the dark chain of volcanoes she would have to cross baked like hot coals beneath Hellfire's sun.

Huffing for breath, she threw herself behind the cover of a tree just seconds before the riders came to an abrupt halt at the wall. The sound of laughter drifted toward her. She watched as Dax Vahnti grinned in response to an unheard jest, his perfect smile a flash of white against his dark face. It was Flavian Modalbeau who'd captured his attention. The women was regal, beautiful, and obviously anxious to please. She sidled her horse closer and rested a hand on his upper thigh.

Rayna's eyes thinned. "Arrogant worm," she whispered. "Get on with it."

He pulled a small device from his tunic, a twin to the one hidden in the hollow of the tree, and pointed it toward the section of wall at the end of the pathway. Rayna scrutinized his movements carefully as he touched the base of the device. There was a short, high-pitched hum like the buzz of an angry insect; then a small, clear circle suddenly appeared in the golden wall, its diameter blooming outward until it became a tunnel-like hole.

A chaotic mass of baying hounds and excited riders swarmed through the newly formed hole, emerging on the opposite side of the shield wall. The demon lord was the last to go through. From her hiding place, Rayna watched as he pointed the device at the wall again, and the hole collapsed on itself, vanishing as swiftly as it had appeared.

After watching their progress for several minutes, she sank against the trunk of the tree, satisfied that she could master the use of the shield key. Only one obstacle remained now—the hunters' prey. Rayna settled herself more comfortably to await their return. No matter how much the idea revolted her, it was vital that she see a dead vampire-cat firsthand so she would know what sort of foe she and the animals would be up against.

A small, fuzzy creature poked its head up from a nearby burrow, round eyes blinking in the glare of the sun. Rayna smiled and stretched out a welcoming hand. The animal stared for a moment, then padded to her side and crawled into her lap, turning in quick circles until it found a comfortable spot. She stroked its soft fur absentmindedly, consoling herself with the knowledge that the hunters were wreaking their bloody havoc outside the shield, not inside where the constant presence of man had tamed the animals to the point that they had lost all fear.

There was a whisper of sound and movement, like the faint flutter of a bird's wing brushing against rock. Dax cocked his head and listened, crossbow ready in his hand. Blackfire jerked his head, flanks twitching nervously. "Steady," he whispered, and kneed the horse forward, urging him to move another few steps toward the outcropping of dark volcanic rock. Another sound, fainter, but much closer this time. Adrenaline surged through his bloodstream as he lifted the crossbow, his finger slowly closing around the trigger. Vampire-cats usually hunted in packs. He could expect two or three to stage a concerted attack. Any more than that and he would be in serious trouble.

The onslaught came sooner than he expected. The first cat sprang from behind the rocks, a fanged, screaming arrow daggering through the air. Two more rose from the heart of a chasm on his left, thin gray wings beating furiously as they targeted him for attack. Dax aimed and fired, three quick blasts of laser energy that felled them in midair. The sizzling carcasses tumbled to the ground, charred to blackened gristle.

A muffled shout warned him that he was about to be attacked again. Dax heard the beat of wings, smelled the stink of carrion flesh, so close he felt his own flesh crawl. Jaw clenched, he wheeled the horse around and fired the crossbow at point-blank range, the flash of laser energy so near and bright that it left an afterimage behind his eyes.

Blackfire reared and danced away from the charred thing that fell directly in front of him. Dax stared down at the steaming carcass and drew a ragged breath. That one had almost gotten him.

Flavian reined her horse to a stop, her face pale and worried. "Are you all right, Dax? The thing couldn't have been more than two feet from your face when you fired."

He managed a feeble smile. "I'm okay, but I'll probably be seeing that flash behind my eyes for quite a while."

"I don't doubt it." Flavian shook her head, the pendant catching the sunlight as she moved. She'd never seen anyone make a shot like that. The cat would have had him in another second.

"Thanks for the warning," Dax said in a somber voice. "You saved my skin."

She lifted a brow suggestively. "Remember that the next time I want to crawl around in the bushes with you."

Hoofbeats clattered over the rocky ground as a group of riders approached. Dax turned in the saddle, his mouth flattening when he saw Caccia give her reins a vicious yank.

Caccia ignored the cat bodies strewn on the ground and gave her cousin a sullen glare. "I want to go back to the castle, Daxton. The sun is just far too bright today." She pressed a hand to her cheek. "It makes my skin feel hot."

"Be my guest," he told her sharply. Even sunlight annoyed her now. "But you can't head back alone. There're still a number of cats in this area." Dax wondered why she insisted on coming in the first place. Year after year it was some variation of the same whiny story. Too hot. Too cold. Too everything.

"I'll be glad to escort her back," Edgar Lyseene offered. A dark scowl stole across his fleshy face as he glanced at Flavian, then Dax. "I've had more than enough myself."

Several others agreed to return, too, all members of the Lyseene clan. Dax gave them an appraising look. Two of them he recognized as having been Caccia's lovers at one time or another. The other was Lyseene's eldest son, a sour-faced boy whose expression reminded him of Caccia's.

Dax sighed. The Lyseenes were angrier than he'd thought. "Very well." He pulled a spare key from his pocket and tossed it to Caccia. "The rest of us won't be far behind."

The clatter of hoofbeats startled Rayna from an untroubled sleep. She blinked herself awake, taken aback that she'd managed to doze so deeply beneath the towering white tree. The tiny animal that had been curled in her lap squeaked and darted away.

Shifting quietly, Rayna peered around the tree trunk just as a small group of hunters trotted through a hole in the shield wall. Her mouth flattened. *Caccia.* There were four other riders with her, but no dead vampire-cats were slung across their saddles. A puzzled frown flitted across her brow. Had the hunt been unsuccessful, or had they left the bloody corpses where they'd fallen?

A fat tree hen squawked and flapped its wings in a nearby tree.

Edgar Lyseene tugged on his reins and lifted his crossbow. "Look at that, would you?" Eyes on the tree, he drew a bead on the plump bird. "It's just sitting there, right in my crosshairs."

A minor noble in his clan gave him a warning glance. "Don't do it, Edgar. Dax has some sort of prohibition against shooting inside the shield wall."

Caccia huffed out a furious breath. "Drakken is mine, too, I'll have you know." She waved a hand imperially. "If Edgar wants to shoot the bird, he has my permission. Dax isn't the only Vahnti on Hellfire."

Edgar inclined his head, gladdened by the opportunity to tweak the Vahnti warlord's nose. "Thank you, Lady Caccia."

Violating Dax's prohibition might even help assuage his anger at losing the Nirvannan deal. A vindictive smile tipped his lips as he touched the crossbow's trigger and fired.

A pulse of green energy lanced upward, and a charred lump plummeted from a limb, landing with a sickening thud near the base of the tree. Scorched feathers drifted in its wake.

"Good shot, Edgar!" Caccia gushed. "There's nothing left but a few stray feathers!"

Rayna's shock quickly yielded to white-hot fury. Never in her life had she witnessed such a cruel and callous act. Her lips already moving in a soundless chant, she closed her eyes and touched the amulet secreted beneath her robe, gathering the threads of nature's energy to inflict a vengeful blow.

Birds squawked angrily in the trees, a thousand high-pitched voices crying out their fury at once. Animals swarmed from lairs and nearby burrows, a seething, snarling mass of fur and reptilian skin that began crawling toward the gravel pathway from every direction.

Edgar Lyseene froze, his senses shouting a dozen conflicting warnings. He turned his horse in a slow circle and glanced around wildly. There was movement and sound all around them.

"What's that noise?" Caccia shouted in alarm, struggling to make her voice heard over the crescendo of sound. Birds were gathering above them, so many they threatened to blot out the sky.

Her horse bucked furiously, then angled his head around, huge white teeth snapping at the folds of her robe. A bird landed on her head, then several more, claws and beaks ripping at her coiled hair. Caccia squealed in terror.

Fighting to keep his horse under control, Edgar Lyseene swatted at several furry things nibbling on his legs. The crossbow slipped from his grasp and fell, vanishing beneath a roiling mass of animals swarming across the pathway. Something leaped onto his back, sharp claws tearing at his capelet. A bird screamed in his ear. He dug his heels into his horse's flanks and shouted for the others to make a run for the castle, but his voice was lost in the cacophony of animal noise. The horse reared and Edgar tumbled backward, landing in an ungainly heap atop a squirming layer of furious beasts.

"Get them off me!" Caccia screamed as an army of black rock-lizards crawled up her robe.

The noise suddenly ended, the absence of sound so swift and complete that it took a few moments for Caccia and Edgar to realize that it was over. The birds took wing, fluttering toward the treetops, and the animals beat a hasty retreat, moving quickly for the cover of the woods.

Caccia started sobbing incoherently.

Behind her, a new hole formed in the shield wall, and the rest of the hunters poured through, the hounds darting ahead to see what the commotion was about.

Dax reined Blackfire to an abrupt stop and stared around in disbelief. There were animals everywhere, running for the woods or scurrying up the trunks of nearby trees. Hundreds of them, of all shapes and colors. A swarm of birds was circling overhead as well, but their numbers were dwindling by the second.

He urged the horse forward. "Caccia?" Her face was buried in her mount's thick mane, and she was weeping uncontrollably. Lyseene's sour-faced son was lying facedown in the gravel nearby, bawling like an infant.

"Gods," a stunned Flavian said behind him. "What went on here?" Other hunters began whispering back and forth, talking in low, puzzled voices.

His clothes in tatters, Edgar Lyseene scraped himself from the ground and lurched toward the Vahnti warlord. His face darkened with rage. "You bastard!" he shouted at Dax. "You treacherous, backstabbing bastard! I don't know how you did it, Vahnti, but I know it was you! No one insults my clan like this. No one!"

Dax's jaw tightened, and his eyes turned a chilly shade of blue. "What are you talking about, Edgar?"

"You trained those filthy animals to do what they did! Admit it! I violated your prohibition against hunting inside the wall, so you sicced them on me in retaliation."

"Edgar, I assure you, I had nothing to do with this." But

he was beginning to suspect who had. Dax rubbed at the knot of tension building behind his forehead. *Rayna.* Deep inside he knew it was her, knew it with a certainty that hovered between awe and dread.

Chapter Fourteen

A violinist strolled down the length of the banquet table, the sweet, perfect notes of a centuries-old ballad harmonizing with the fluid sounds of the waterfall rushing down the atrium wall. Above, hoverlights of alternating hues drifted through the treetops, the vivid points of color a stark contrast against the artificial night sky. A silent army of servers clad in black and gold hovered behind the banquet guests, replenishing a goblet here, offering a canapé there, their movements perfectly timed and orchestrated.

Scowling, Dax slouched back in his chair at the head of the table and tossed down the remainder of his wine, then held out his goblet for a server to pour him more. Too bad the servers' efforts had been in vain. What should have been a joyous culmination to his guests' time on Hellfire had disintegrated into a dismal, nerve-racking affair punctuated by awkward silences and cold, accusing stares.

His pale gaze moved down the length of the table, lingering on the abundance of unfilled chairs. The entire Lyseene clan was gone, as well as the majority of their allies, their ships lifting off from Hellfire within an hour of Edgar's accusations about the animal attack. The outraged Lyseene warlord had adamantly refused to believe the attack wasn't a staged event, no matter what assurances Dax tried to give, and had ended the confrontation by storming from the castle and leaving Hellfire in an aristocratic snit. Now there would be bad blood between the Vahntis and the Lyseenes for generations to come because of the imagined offense. Even Caccia, who'd taken to her bed upon returning to the castle, refused to believe that he hadn't trained and provoked the animals to attack. She'd gone so far as to accuse him of doing it out of spite.

He gulped down another glass of the potent Logo wine, his mood darkening with every sip. His peaceful, well-ordered life had been turned upside down since his first encounter with Rayna Syn. How could he have been so blind, or so foolish? Nirvannan mysticism was no myth . . . Rayna was living proof of that. Somehow, *she* was responsible for everything that had happened. She'd whipped the animals into a feral frenzy that night on Nirvanna, caused the birds to try and snatch him bald, and had instigated the attack on Caccia and the Lyseenes as well. But other than himself and Lett Bahleigh, no one in their right mind would give credence to such an outlandish tale.

I didn't do it, Edgar . . . the girl did. She has some sort of mystical power over beasts and told them to peck at your pompous head.

Dax snorted to himself. Giving voice to his suspicions would have elicited an even worse reaction, and made him the laughingstock of the entire Dominion Court.

"More wine, Count Vahnti?" a server asked quietly, and proceeded to refill the goblet Dax lifted in response.

Dax stared at the contents of his goblet absently. Now that he knew what Rayna was capable of, what in space was he going to do with her? At the moment she was locked inside his suite, an entire squad of guards stationed outside the doors, but for all he knew she was up there waiting for him, like a spider in some lavish web patiently awaiting the chance to strike again.

In the chair to his right, Flavian Modalbeau cleared her throat and leaned in Dax's direction, the crimson peak of her elaborate headdress almost brushing the side of his face. "Dax, darling," she whispered, "you really must put on a show of joviality for your guests' sake if nothing else." She cast a covert glance at the long row of solemn faces lined down her side of the table. A few of the guests were talking quietly among themselves, but for the most part the richly adorned lords and ladies were eating their meal as swiftly and silently as possible, eager to end the ordeal and be on their way. "Your black mood has cast a pall over everyone here."

"Everyone left, you mean." Dax gave her a tight-lipped, cynical smile. "The Lyseenes obviously have a lot of friends."

Flavian lifted one shoulder in an offhand shrug, the pendant glittering as she moved. "What happened this afternoon was just a freak of nature. Anyone with a whit of common sense knows that."

"A freak of nature," a minor member of Flavian's clan echoed.

"Of course." Dax tossed down another glass of the sweet blue wine. "Just a natural phenomenon." His lean frame sank a little deeper into the high-backed chair. "Easily explained."

"No doubt," another lord murmured. "Must admit, though, that I've never seen the like. Some of those creatures almost looked as if they were marching in formation."

"Odd," Flavian's half brother added. "I noticed that, too."

"For heaven's sake!" Flavian interjected. "The two of you are as bad as that dimwit Lyseene. You sound as if you're insinuating that those filthy beasts staged some sort of planned revolt."

"I was merely making an observation, Flavian," Tay Modalbeau retorted.

Dax swallowed down the rest of his wine in one gulp. He'd hoped that he had been the only one to notice that the animals had seemed to align themselves in columns according to size.

"Well, keep such drivel to yourself," Flavian snapped back. "Personally, I believe that Lyseene staged all this himself in retaliation for losing the Nirvannan deal. He's pulled off a few underhanded stunts before. I wouldn't put it past him."

Dax gave his Modalbeau ally a bleary smile. Her defense of him was impassioned, but misplaced. Blame for the fiasco lay at Rayna's feet, not the Lyseenes'.

A grim-faced Haywood appeared at Dax's elbow and waited patiently for the Vahnti warlord to acknowledge his presence.

Dax cocked his head slightly and grinned, the contents of his goblet sloshing over the rim as he moved. "Haywood . . . where've you been all night?"

Haywood's gaze flitted over the stream of blue liquid before shifting back to Dax's bleary-eyed face. The soldier suppressed a sigh and leaned close to his ear. "I need to speak with you, Dax."

"Can't it wait?"

"We received a communiqué a few minutes ago that you need to review right away. I had it decoded and transcribed for you."

"So give it to me." Dax swayed sideways in the chair.

Haywood's mouth tightened. He would have preferred that Dax read the contents of the message alone, out of earshot of the banquet guests. "Very well, if you insist." He handed over the folded slip of paper.

Curious, Dax unfolded the note and blinked to focus his eyes.

My Dear Count Vahnti,

I regret to inform you that after careful deliberation, the Dominion High Council has decided to proceed with a formal investigation of your recent activities. Based upon information contained in grievances filed against you by Clan Dunstan, you now stand accused of moral and ethical turpitude pertaining to your treatment of a colonist named Rayna Syn, a female of less than eighteen years, the legal age of consent within the boundaries of Dominion space.

Be advised that my ship shall arrive at Drakken Castle two days hence, whereupon I shall endeavor to conduct my own investigation of these charges by interviewing the minor in question, then render a swift and summary legal judgment in regards to this distasteful matter.

Yours very truly,
Archduke Luc Davies,
Overlord and Chieftain of the Dominion clans.

Dax cursed and bolted from his chair, the crumpled missive wadded in his fist. The upended chair clattered to the stone floor behind him, but Dax was too caught up in his rage for the sound to penetrate. "Damn you, Alfred Dunstan!" he raged at his startled guests, and hurled the wad of paper to the floor. The marriage contract had been an elaborate ruse. Petwitt had come to Drakken in hopes of finding something to use against him, and he'd found it in the form of Rayna Syn. "Damn you and your accursed son to hell!"

A tense, awkward silence descended over the banquet table. Several clan lords shifted uncomfortably, embarrassed that they'd witnessed the unseemly display of anger.

Flavian pressed her hand against the pendant instinctively, blocking the lens with the flat of her palm. Alfred would be infuriated that she'd impeded his view of Dax's outburst, but that was just too bad. He'd have to get his jollies some other way. "Whatever's wrong, Dax?" she asked quietly.

"Nothing." Dax snatched his goblet from the table and staggered around the overturned chair. Had anything in his life gone right since he found Rayna? "Nothing I can't fix." His features dark and rigid, he stalked away from the banquet table.

Sighing, Haywood scooped up the wad of paper Dax had thrown and shoved it inside a pocket, then dipped his head in silent apology to the startled guests and hurried after Dax, who had stormed down a pathway that led to the atrium doors. "Dax!" he called when he finally spotted him. "Wait up!" The soldier swore under his breath. He didn't like the look he'd seen in Dax's eyes. "Where are you going?"

"Leave me be, Haywood."

Footmen rushed to open the doors as the scowling count approached.

Dax strode through the doorway and into the corridor beyond, his footsteps ringing against the cold black stones.

Haywood grasped his shoulder as Dax ground to a halt at a lift-tube. "I want to know what you plan to do."

"If you really must know"—Dax slammed his fist against the "up" pad—"I'm going to do what I should have done weeks ago . . . what you've been advising me to do all along." His pale eyes turned a flat, chilly blue. "Why not? I've already been charged with it anyway."

Rayna twisted the ornate door handle for what seemed like the hundredth time. Still locked. She pressed an ear against the heavy wood and listened. At least seven, maybe eight guards were posted outside the doors, several moving about and talking quietly among themselves.

"Now what?" Rayna murmured to herself. She had been waiting for an opportunity to make her escape ever since the demon lord had returned from the hunt and ordered her locked inside his suite again. But the opportunity had never come. She'd screamed and pounded on the door repeatedly, even tried to feign illness to trick the guards into unlocking the latch, but they'd been unmoved by her ploys.

She walked to the tall bank of windows overlooking the courtyard hundreds of feet beneath her. Even if she could manage to break a window there was nowhere to go. There were no buttresses, turrets, or porticos on this side of the castle, nothing she could try to jump to. Nothing but a sheer drop to the flagstones in the courtyard far below.

A salty haze of tears burned in the corners of her eyes. She had to get out before the demon lord returned. The knowing look he'd given her when he came back from the hunt still clung to her memory, the dark expression on his face replaying over and over like an afterimage dredged from some terrifying dream. Cold and brittle and stone-hard. Those pale, flinty eyes had been filled with distrust, as well as utter conviction.

She clutched her little bundle of clothing and pilfered food tight against her chest. He knew. The demon lord knew. She started pacing the confines of the sitting room, prowling about the interior without thought to her direction. She had to escape before he returned.

The latch clicked, and Rayna's gaze snapped to the doors, the sound of her heartbeat like the rumble of thunder in her ears. Light from the corridor spilled across the carpet as the door swung inward and a muddy shadow flowed through the crack. Seizing the chance, Rayna rushed toward the opening, but came to a terrified halt when Daxton Vahnti stepped into the room.

Dax stared at her for a long moment, his chilly gaze flickering over the small bundle clutched so tightly in her arms. He smiled grimly. Clothes and food, probably. According to Sub-Leftenant Anwell, Rayna had been trying to lure the guards into opening the doors for hours, using every ploy imaginable. He glanced over his shoulder at Anwell. "Dismiss your squad, Sub-Leftenant. The regular night watch will be sufficient on my floor for the remainder of the evening."

Anwell signaled the guards with a wave of her hand. "Yes, my lord." All but two of the soldiers headed down the corridor.

Dax slammed the door shut and started toward the girl standing so rigidly in the center of the room, weaving a bit as he made his way around a brocaded settee. "What's in the bundle, Rayna?" He finished the wine in his goblet and flung the chalice to the floor. "The potion you used to drug those beasts?"

Her chin lifted a notch, and she cradled her provisions protectively. "There's nothing in here that concerns you."

"Everything within Drakken's walls concerns me." Dax came to a stop directly in front of her and snatched the bundle from her hands. "Especially when it might affect one of my guests." He flung the fabric parcel to the carpet, spilling a loaf of dark bread and several rounds of elk-cheese.

"I'm not your 'guest,' " Rayna snapped, "and never have been." A chill rode up her spine as she eyed the goblet and provisions he'd tossed to the floor. There was something different about his eyes and wine-dulled voice, a sharp edge of anger and resolve that hadn't been there before.

"When I spoke of guests, I wasn't referring to you, Rayna." For a split second of time Dax lost himself inside those luminous green eyes; then his features darkened with anger once again. He stripped off his uniform jacket and flung it carelessly to the floor. "Do you have the slightest idea what sort of trouble you've caused me? Do you even realize that your foolish stunt today might effect my clan for generations to come?"

"I don't know what you mean." Her eyes cut right, then left, searching for an avenue of escape. She gathered herself to make a lunge toward the door, but he belayed her by grabbing her shoulder.

"Don't lie to me, Rayna." Dax lifted a length of her hair and twisted it around his fingers. "It was you all along . . . on Nirvanna, then that day with the birds, and now this afternoon.'' His throat tightened. The scent of her hair was drifting around him, an intoxicating fragrance that reminded him of Arkanon wildflowers blooming on a warm spring day. He lifted the curls to his face and breathed deeply. Even now, knowing what he knew, he still wanted her in the worst sort of way. ''I was just too blind and stupid to see what you really are.''

She took a half step backward, but his hold on her hair kept her from retreating any farther. ''And what is that?''

His fingers moved from her hair to her throat, sliding down the slender column of flesh to the collar of her jewel green robe. ''You're a temptress,'' he said in a ragged voice, ''a siren sent to lure me into a hell of my own devising.'' He wound his arms around her and drew her closer. Expectation glittered in the depths of his azure eyes. ''But the game is over, pet. . . . It's high time I claimed my prize.''

He pulled her to the floor so swiftly Rayna didn't have time to resist. The air rushed out of her lungs as he pinned her body beneath him and buried his face in her hair. Gasping for breath, she pushed against his chest, trying desperately to free herself from the bone-crushing embrace. ''Get off me, you drunken oaf!'' Rayna managed to croak. She flailed at his back and shoulders with her nails and fists.

Oblivious to her struggles, Dax ran a hand down the length of her leg and nuzzled the base of her throat. He was drowning in the tangle of silky hair, her heady fragrance, the feel of her loins crushed against his own. ''I'm drunk with need,'' he whispered gruffly, and pushed the flowing skirt of her robe up to her thighs. ''You're so very beautiful. . . .'' His fingers clawed at the intricate fastenings adorning the front of the brocade robe. ''Make love to me, Rayna. . . . I'm tired of waiting.''

A wave of revulsion twisted across her features, and her eyes turned a smoky, rage-filled green. ''Make love to you?'' she said incredulously. The stench of wine hovered about his clothes and body like a cloying cloud. ''Is this how the noble Daxton Vahnti shows his love?'' She jerked her head sideways, away from the sickening feel of his lips against her throat, and shoved at the deadweight of his body with all her might. But he was too heavy, too sotted for her to budge. "You sicken me." She glared into his lust-glazed eyes. "You don't have the slightest idea what the word 'love' means."

A fastener at her waist gave way, another at her breasts. Salt stung the corners of her eyes as he forced a hand through the opening, his fingers gliding down her abdomen. Her rage and revulsion were replaced by a stony acquiescence. No matter what she did he intended finally to have his way with her, and there was nothing she could physically do to stop him. "Do what you want," she said in a dull, emotionless voice. "I won't fight you anymore." She bit back the tears and willed her body to remain completely still. "But don't dare couch this moment in terms like 'love.' I feel nothing for you but contempt."

His hands stilled, her cold words cutting so harshly and deeply that they were like daggers slicing into his bones. He blinked to clear the fog of wine and anger from his mind and stared into the innocent face just inches beneath his own. His desire flagged abruptly. Her slender form was pinioned beneath his bulk, the skirt of her flowing green robe bunched around the tops of her thighs. No trace of movement was visible in her exotic features, no sign of emotion save for a deathly stoicism that made him cringe with self-disgust. Her eyes were vacant, staring. Though he could still feel the steady rise and fall of her chest, nothing remained of Rayna Syn, as if her spirit had fled to some far-off place where emotion no longer existed, and he was trying to force himself upon a hollow shell.

Cursing himself for ten kinds of depraved fool, Dax rolled to one side of her and sat, his movement as swift and sudden as it had been when he had pinned her to the floor. Anger and self-loathing furrowed his brow. Had he sunk so low that he had to try to take from her what other women freely gave?

He sucked in a shuddering breath and drew his knees up to his chest. "Don't worry," he whispered hoarsely. "I don't need any woman enough to take her by force." There was a flicker of movement in her almond-shaped eyes, the only sign that she was listening, the only sign of animation in that lifeless face. For a moment he was still and utterly silent. He had never intended for things to come to this. "I wanted . . . I had hoped . . ." His sentence trailed off in a frustrated sigh.

Rayna's eyes sought and captured his, drawn by the raw edge of emotion she'd heard in his voice. She stared up at his mercurial features, a bewildered frown inching across the width of her brow. From the moment she had awakened aboard his ship to find him watching her, she'd been trying to fathom the reason behind his interest in her. Did he keep her near just to torment her or was it something else? If it was solely a matter of lust, she would not have survived this night or any other with her maidenhood intact. "What is it that you want from me?" she asked quietly. It was a question she had no answer to. But she needed to know, had to know.

He lifted one shoulder in a half shrug, his brooding gaze drifting to an elaborate fresco adorning the high ceiling. A thoughtful expression stole across his shadowed features. What did he want from her? "An amusing distraction . . . my own particular form of revenge . . ." *Liar,* his mind whispered. *Tell her the rest of it. Tell her how she skews your senses when she enters a room, how your body aches with desire whenever she's near. Tell her how much you want to hold her, touch her, feel those lush lips upon your skin.* "Perhaps it's simply the thrill of knowing that at any given moment you might try to plunge a knife into me again." He said the last to shock her, to stave off further probing, but in the end he shocked himself because there was far more truth in the comment than he cared to admit.

His callous words caused a knot of fury to coil in Rayna's gut, but then the anger suddenly faded, and she gazed back at him in mute wonder. What sort of twisted mind could find pleasure in that? "You've actually *enjoyed* thinking that I might make another attempt on your life?"

He blew out a short breath, a small sound laced with self-derision. "You find that so hard to believe?"

"Yes," she said sharply.

"Then you don't understand the sort of life I lead. I'm surrounded by people seeking to curry favor with me, or to bring me to ruin, as well as an army of aides and servants eager to fulfill my slightest whim." He shrugged fatalistically.

"I relieve the stress and monotony by taking risks, whether from flying too fast—or in keeping an assassin close by my side. It doesn't matter. I take my pleasure when and where I find it."

No matter how twisted his reasoning, deep down Rayna knew it was true. The more she had fought him, the more heated his interest in her had become, as if her very resistance had stoked the flames of his desire. Comprehension inched through her veins. He wanted her because of that resistance, and because she had neither sought his favor, nor catered to his every whim as others did. If she didn't resist, would his interest begin to wane? "And you've found such pleasure in me?" she asked quietly.

He shrugged again, but didn't answer for a moment; then he turned toward her slowly, a distracted smile playing across his lips. "More than you can possibly imagine." He'd felt more alive these past weeks than he had in many a year, as if her very presence had somehow filled the dark, lonely hollow that lay hidden in his soul. "With you, I know exactly where I stand, Rayna. There's no equivocation in our relationship, no need to question your motivations, or to wonder if your every word veils some hidden machination. You're different from the others. You hate me and want your freedom, nothing more. Is it so very hard to understand why I would find pleasure in your company?"

A shadow of uncertainty moved through her eyes. His reasoning was dark and distorted, yet strangely, it made sense in a tangled sort of way. He'd found comfort and pleasure in the surety of her hatred, a momentary escape from the threat of treachery that was part and parcel of Dominion life. At that moment she pitied Daxton Vahnti, pitied his clan and people for what they had become. They were prisoners, too, in an odd sort of way, shackled by tradition and expectation to live out their lives in a universe corrupted by wealth and power.

And with that realization came the first glimmering of understanding. Beneath that cool veneer of detachment, Daxton Vahnti was a rebel, a man trying desperately to free himself from the shackles of his life by courting disaster at every opportunity. A man who'd learned from experience to trust the hatred of his enemies far more than the endearments of a friend or lover. "I feel sorry for you," Rayna said suddenly. "You have everything, yet nothing in life that truly matters."

A quick flash of anger sharpened his eyes and voice. He didn't want or need her pity. "So tell me, what is it that truly matters in life, Rayna?" The corners of his mouth lifted in a derisive smile. "Contemplating the beauty of a tree? Belief in some preternatural afterlife? Tell me what the secret is."

Rayna sat up abruptly, the contempt and challenge in his tone giving rise to a surge of anger that more than equaled his own. She grabbed his hand from atop his knee and lifted it into the air, pressing it palm-to-palm to hers. "This is what matters!" She pushed against the flat of his hand with all her might. "Do you feel the warmth of my flesh against yours?"

He stared at her curiously, both startled and fascinated by her vehement gesture. The fire in her eyes came from within. Pure, hot, and fever-bright.

"It's human flesh," Rayna said in an impassioned tone. "Not wealth or power—or anything that can be bought. It's simply the touch of another human. Without it, we cannot exist as a race. It's not in our nature." Her forearm trembled from the strain of pushing against his hand. "It's the only thing that gives meaning to our lives!"

For a moment there was silence. Only the shallow sounds of their breathing intruded as Dax held that jewellike gaze. *Such passion. Such utter conviction.* Her palm was still crushed flat to his, fingers splayed and quivering from the effort of trying to move his hand. The air itself seemed to crackle with the force of her energy. And in the depths of her well-deep eyes the Vahnti count caught a terrifying glimpse of himself—a lonely, troubled man who had lost the ability to touch another human long ago.

He pulled his hand away, unwilling to look upon the truth, to see himself as she saw him. She was right to pity him. His lids drifted closed. He couldn't look into those preternatural eyes again, didn't want to face her pity or the truth. "You leave tomorrow," he said in a whisper. What he truly wanted from her, she would never willingly give. "Go . . . I don't want you here anymore." He sighed deeply, a poignant sound weighted with sorrow. She'd been punished enough, and so had he. "I'll tell Haywood to arrange transport for you."

Rayna held her breath, daring to hope, yet frightened to believe that he'd just announced that she was free. "I'm free to go?" she finally managed to ask. "To return to Nirvanna?"

"Wherever you want." Dax opened his eyes, but he refused to meet her startled gaze. He couldn't bear to see the wild surge of elation in her eyes, didn't want to know how joyful she was to finally be rid of him. "Take your things . . . your clothing, and just go," he said in a dead voice. "I want to be alone."

Rayna stiffened suddenly, and her joyous smile vanished as quickly as it had come. He'd said nothing about the animals. She drew a breath to steel herself and rose to her knees, shifting her body so that she faced him head-on. "I cannot leave here without the wolfens and the gi."

When he didn't answer, Rayna edged closer. He was staring out the bank of windows, his brooding gaze dark and preoccupied, seemingly absorbed with the plethora of stars spattered across the night sky. A thick strand of ebony hair had slipped from his queue and was hanging loosely in front of his eyes. The beginnings of a frown crept across her shadowed face. There was something mournful about his look that troubled her deeply, an air of sadness and sorrow that tugged at her emotions. She lifted a hand to brush the errant lock from his face, but was loath to do anything that might cause him to take back his promise of freedom. Still, she had to. She was responsible for the animals' lives. She touched his forearm lightly. "Count Vahnti . . . I am responsible for the animals' being here. You must give them their freedom as well." Her voice was calm and controlled, but it was edged with determination. "I won't leave Hellfire without them."

His gaze moved from the stars to her defiant face. Even now, with her freedom close at hand, her thoughts were more focused on the well-being of the creatures she so dearly loved than the possibility that he would change his mind. He stared at her for long seconds, forcing himself to look into those hypnotic green eyes one last time. He drank in her youthful beauty, her quiet courage, the serenity of spirit that seemed to flow around her like an aura of light. And he knew, suddenly and totally, that he cared for this woman-child, that foolish as it was, he did have feelings for her and would miss her presence in his life. She was everything that he was not, his complete opposite, yet strangely, he knew that deep inside she was more like him than anyone he had ever known.

He sighed, a sad, heavy exhalation of air laced with regret. "Take them," he told her quietly. "Haywood will make the arrangements."

A grateful smile lifted the edges of her lips, but inwardly she felt as if she had been cast adrift. "Thank you." She wanted to say something more, a word, a gesture of some kind to show him that she was indeed grateful, but in the end she did nothing, said nothing.

The flowing gown rustled and moved around her as she gathered the heavy folds in preparation to rise. Dax watched, acutely aware that this would be his last sight of her. Her silky hair was loose and tangled, falling about her slender form like a copper veil. The brocaded gown was crumpled and askew, the front gaping at her chest and abdomen where he'd torn the ornate fasteners loose. As she struggled to rise, her foot snagged in the flowing hem and she stumbled slightly. The fastener at her neck gave way, then the one beneath it, giving Dax a last, tantalizing glimpse of her sun-burnished flesh. His brows lowered, and for the space of a single heartbeat, his mind refused to comprehend the meaning of what he saw.

His face went rigid and still. Deathly still. His eyes narrowed slowly, dark and icy blue as he stared at the familiar bit of black leather suspended between her breasts. A chill crept through his body, and he choked down a cry of rage. The amulet she was wearing had been locked inside his desk, inside an office suite protected by layers of security fields and a contingent of guards day and night. There was no way Rayna could have stolen through the maze of sensors and alarms, retrieved the amulet, then escaped undetected. That entire floor of the castle was sacrosanct, access restricted to all but a select few among his clan. He'd been betrayed by someone close to him, someone he trusted—a member of his own clan.

"Where did you get the amulet, Rayna?" he asked in a cold, lethal voice.

She blinked and stopped moving abruptly, her face turning a ghostly shade of white. "I . . ." Her heart missed a beat as her gaze flicked downward, just long enough for her to know that he had indeed seen the amulet.

A muscle trembled along the line of his jaw. He'd revealed himself to her, given voice to some of his most intimate thoughts and feelings. "I thought you were different." Dax shook his head, the rage and shock of betrayal visible in his eyes and pain-roughened voice. "What a fool I was to think such a thing. You're no different from the others."

He lashed out with a hand, his strong fingers closing around the amulet with so much force that Rayna was jerked to her knees. "Where did you get it, Rayna?" he demanded. "I know you didn't steal it yourself. Who helped you? Who are you working with?"

She stared at him in mute horror, the air rushing in and out of her lungs in panicky little gasps. If she told him the truth Lett would surely die. "No one," she said in a fearful voice.

"You're lying!" Slowly, deliberately, his fingers edged up the length of the leather cord until he'd pulled it taut around her throat. "By the gods, you'll tell me or I'll wring your lovely neck. Do you understand me? I'll not have a traitor walking free within my clan!"

She cried out in alarm as the cord tightened around her throat.

"Who are you protecting?" Dax bellowed. "Your friend Dr. Bahleigh?" An even darker thought suddenly jelled in his mind. Perhaps her innocence was a ruse in itself, an insidious ploy used to lull him into complacency. "You're one of Alfred's puppets, aren't you?" He twisted the cord even more. "Damn you, Rayna, tell me!"

"No!" she yelled back at him, then clamped her mouth shut. She'd rather die than tell him.

He flung her to the floor, fingers still latched around the cord at her neck. A cold, deathly smile stole across his lips. "Then I guess I'll have to leave it to Haywood to loosen your tongue. There are ways, pet, many ways to deal with spies.

All of them unpleasant. You'll talk, more quickly than you think. There's even a device that can rip the truth from your brain if the chemicals fail."

A shadow of fear passed across her eyes. They were going to force her to talk, sift through her mind with chemicals and technology until she told the truth—and condemned Lett to a quick and certain death.

"You should be scared," he told her, gratified by the glint of fear he'd seen in her eyes. "The security force has been eager to get their hands on you for a long, long time." The lines of his face hardened, becoming a death mask carved from stone. "And if they discover that you're one of Alfred's operatives, you'd better call on your spirits to protect you, because I swear before the gods that I'll kill you with my own hands!"

Rayna glanced wildly about the room, but there was nowhere to go, nowhere to run. She had to get away, break free of his deathly embrace before he turned her over to the security guards. Her eyes suddenly sharpened. There was a way. A desperate, dangerous ploy, but she had to try. She willed her lids to close, her mind to concentrate. It was her only hope. Lett's only hope. Her fingers closed around the amulet, and she began the thready whisper of a chant, calling on the strength of the Inner World in her time of need, drawing the faint wisps of nature's energy that flowed through the castle into her body and mind.

Thin strands of energy gathered around her until they formed a writhing tidal wave of power that rushed into her body like a river of light, a force more powerful and unpredictable than any she had ever managed to conjure. Her eyes reopened slowly, limbs trembling as her mind gave direction to the energy, calming, shaping, and guiding it to do her bidding.

Dax released the cord as if it were a serpent that had bitten him. He stared down in disbelief as her delicate features transformed beneath him. Her eyes turned an eerie greenish gold, and her sun-touched skin vanished completely, replaced by a thick sheen of golden fur. His heart rate accelerated as he felt her body lengthen beneath him, grow larger and heavier. A muzzle suddenly sprouted where none had been. Knife-sharp fangs glistened wetly, iridescent in the peculiar haze of light that seemed to hover around her like a filmy cloud.

"Oh, my god," he whispered hoarsely.

Chapter Fifteen

Too stunned to react, Dax simply stared, his shocked gaze riveted on the wolfen sprawled beneath him. Until this moment he had thought that shape-shifters existed only in legend, mythical creatures conjured by dreams and human imagination. Not so. The transformation he had witnessed was all too real.

Impossible, he told himself. He closed his eyes for a split second, convinced that his wine-dulled brain had produced some sort of hallucination. But when he opened his lids again the creature was still there, watching him with the savage fixity of a predator about to devour its prey. Yet at the same time he saw a trace of something else in that green-gold gaze, a familiar glint of fierce intelligence and untamed innocence.

His doubts and uncertainty gave way to utter conviction. Rayna was a shape-shifter, able to transform her lithe body into the flesh of an animal in no more time than it took him to draw a single breath. And with that startling realization his overwhelming belief in a well-ordered, rational universe was shattered forever. Every belief, every single tenet of science and nature that he'd once thought immutable had been ground into cosmic dust. If Rayna was capable of achieving the impossible, what other marvels did the universe hold?

"Rayna?" he said quietly. The wolfen was indeed blood and bone, but what of Rayna? Was the essence of her still there, encased within that facade of animal flesh and fur? Or had she indeed become a wolfen, in thought as well as appearance? If so, he was in mortal danger of losing his life. "Is that truly you?"

A throaty growl rumbled from the creature's mouth.

Dax froze, the flesh along the nape of his neck prickling in response to the feral sound. The fangs were only inches from his throat, those luminous eyes so close to his own that he saw the vertical pupils contract in the room's half light. So close those wet, white fangs could rip his throat out before his brain even registered the fact that he'd been attacked.

There was another growl, and a rush of apprehension slithered down the length of his spine. Mesmerized, Dax stared into her wolfen face, unable to tear his gaze from those eerie eyes, and certain that if he did glance away, even for a fraction of a second, he would surely die. He'd never felt as close to death before, nor as filled with such a sense of awe and amazement. But if he did die, here and now, he would embrace death with the sure knowledge that the universe was even stranger and more magical than he had ever envisioned.

His apprehension faded away, replaced by a fatalistic sense that he was meant to be here, meant to see and experience this moment in time. And in his heart of hearts, he was gladdened by the knowledge that he had finally learned the wondrous truth about Rayna Syn. Slowly, warily, he lifted a hand and touched the silken fur along her muzzle, reassuring himself that his eyes had not betrayed him. Thick golden hair drifted through his fingers. It was soft and velvety. Real.

At his touch, Rayna's nostrils flared. His throat was so close, tantalizing her with the sweet scent of salt and warm human blood. The hunger was like a living thing crawling through her veins, urging her to tear the flesh, taste the blood. *No,* she screamed at herself, instinct and intelligence warring for control. She was human, not wolfen. The bloodlust ebbed, and reality returned by slow degrees.

"I'm not afraid, Rayna," Dax told her in a soothing voice, and oddly, he wasn't, though he knew that he should be. "If you want to hurt me, I know I can't stop you . . . not as you are." Her eyes had softened, turning more green than gold. Human green. He moved his head slightly, exposing the skin on his throat even more. "But I don't think you will. I don't think you want to."

She regarded him carefully. Curiously. The demon lord was offering himself to her, giving her the choice whether he lived or died. It was the moment she had hoped for, the goal she'd strived so single-mindedly to achieve. Her decision. Her choice. With his death the prophecy would be fulfilled, and Nirvanna freed from his control.

A flash of uncertainty glimmered in her predatory eyes. She didn't know how or why or when, but sometime in the past few weeks her desire to kill him had quietly withered. He was still the Vahnti demon lord, her sworn enemy, but not the evil creature she had thought him to be. He was simply a man, no worse than many others of his kind. Did he deserve to die simply because he'd sprung from noble loins? No, she admitted to herself. He had been born to be exactly what he was, as had she.

Along with that revelation came another, swifter and more terrifying. Against all logic and reason, she had grown to care for Daxton Vahnti. In another time and place she could have loved this man. But they were from different worlds, different cultures.

Her eyes turned a green-flecked, brittle gold. Though she couldn't kill him, he was still her enemy, and always would be. She buried her newborn feelings deep inside her wolfen heart. Nothing had changed between them. She was still his captive, the same woman he had vowed to turn over to his security guards only minutes ago. Escape was even more important now. He had seen her transform, knew the secret she'd shared with no human save Javan.

She snarled suddenly and lunged from beneath him, her powerful forelegs flinging him aside with no more effort than needed to swat a flamefly.

Dax crashed into a settee and fell to the floor, stunned by the force and abruptness of the impact. "Rayna!"

She rose to stand on all fours, huge and fierce, the hackles along her back lifting into angry tufts of golden fur.

Their eyes met for a long moment, animal gold and startled,

human blue; then she charged to the door, turning the handle with one swipe of her powerful jaws.

"Rayna, don't!" Dax heaved himself upright and staggered toward the rectangle of light spilling through the open doors. There were armed guards in the corridor. "Wait!" he yelled, but it was too late.

Dax rushed through the doorway and froze. The guards stationed at the lift-tube were staring at the growling wolfen in shock, their faces gray and clammy with fear.

Rayna paced back and forth across the corridor as she waited for the lift-tube, but her golden eyes never wavered from the terrified guards. She gave them a low, challenging growl, daring them to interfere in any way.

The doors finally opened, and she leaped inside.

Their shock subsiding, the guards jerked their weapons free and fired blindly at the lift-tube. Streams of blue-green light sizzled across the inside.

"No!" Dax shouted. "Cease fire!" He knocked the pulse gun free of Anwell's hand as the lift-tube began descending. "I order you not to fire!"

Claws clicking and sliding on the polished stone, Rayna rushed down the central corridor, a panting blur of gold racing headlong toward the castle's atrium. There was a shout as she swept past a startled guard, a screech of alarm from a wide-eyed nobleman who flattened himself against a corridor wall.

Her lungs strained for air. She was tired, so tired, but she forced the powerful body to run faster, willed herself to hold the wolfen form just a little while longer. But with each passing second, she could feel the thin currents of energy that sustained her form dwindling into nothingness. Soon she would lose the ability to hold the wolfen form at all. But she had to hold on long enough to retrieve the shield key and escape the castle.

Two footmen stared at her in stunned surprise as she barreled through the atrium doors. She angled down an overgrown pathway, dodged a group of noblemen clustered near the waterfall, and swept past the banquet table. Guests still lingering over their after-dinner wine scurried for safety, overturning chairs and bumping into each other in their haste to flee.

A young lord screamed, long and hideously loud, then leaped atop the banquet table, scattering plates and serving dishes as he scuttled down its length on his hands and knees.

The hysterical shouts and screams finally began to fade with distance. Rayna plunged into a thicket of creep vines, emerging from the tangle of vegetation in the shadowy clearing surrounding the hollow tree. The gi was waiting, its tiny legs and claws encrusted with dirt from digging up the leather pouch.

At a glance from Rayna, the furry creature dove into the pouch, curling and shifting around until it found a secure position inside. She lifted the pouch with her fangs, cast a final wary glance down the nearest pathway, then raced toward the western doors and freedom.

"I want this castle searched from top to bottom!" Haywood yelled into his wristcom. "Every floor, every room without exception!" His mouth compressed into a hard white line as he marched toward a lift-tube, a squad of battle-armored security guards trailing on his heels. "I don't care how long the security sweep takes! Just get it done! And tell Anwell not to leave Count Vahnti's side, no matter what he says!"

"Right away, Commander," a tinny voice said through the wristcom.

Static crackled as the frequency shifted, and a different voice filled Haywood's ears. "Footmen stationed at the atrium doors report the creature ran past them a short while ago, Commander. They say the beast was clutching something in its jaws."

"Find it then!" Haywood barked. The entire castle was in an uproar, with hysterical guests running this way and that while frustrated guards tried in vain to herd the panicked aristocrats into a secure location. He just hoped it wasn't some hapless nobleman's head or severed arm clutched in the animal's jaws.

"Damn it all to hell," Haywood muttered under his breath. He ground to a halt in front of the lift-tube that would take him to Dax's floor and pounded the controls with his knuckles.

In a security crisis, his first duty was to see to the safety of the Vahnti warlord. As the translucent door slid open, he motioned toward the waiting security guards. "Fan out and take up positions at every lift-tube leading to the count's floor. The top level of the castle is now sealed. No one is allowed access until further notice."

As the lift-tube began rising, Haywood closed his eyes and took a calming breath. First the fiasco with the Lyseenes, now this. How could so many things go so terribly wrong in the space of a single day? He tapped the side of the wristcom. "Leftenant Robichau, report. I need to know what you found at the kennels."

A mile away, Robichau clicked the safety off on his rifle, his nervous gaze shifting back and forth across the shadowy darkness. The beam from his hand torch cut a white swath across the pile of stone and bent steel that had once been the gate to the wolfen pen. "They're definitely loose, Commander. The gate is nothing but a pile of rubble. Looks like the creatures threw their weight against it until the bars collapsed outward."

"Any sign of them?" Haywood asked. The hounds were baying in the background, a nerve-racking chorus of excited yips and howls.

"No, sir." Robichau swung the light downward. "Just pawprints leading away from the pen."

"Which direction do the prints lead?" Haywood demanded.

Robichau frowned and stared at the huge pawprints again. "That's what's strange, sir. There are three sets of pawprints leading toward the shield wall, *not* the castle."

"Three? That's impossible." Haywood's brows bunched together in a puzzled frown. There were only two wolfens. What was going on here?

"There's something else, Commander," he announced in an ominous tone. "Sensors picked up a six-second fluctuation in the shield wall's energy level a few minutes ago. Residual scans indicate an unauthorized exit. Someone used a key to open a doorway in the wall—a key that was reported missing by Captain Remi a few days ago. He reported the loss as soon as he realized it was missing from his rooms, but thought he might have misplaced it. Now we're not so sure."

Haywood's expression turned rigid. Remi would never misplace a shield key. It had been stolen, most likely. And since the wolfens couldn't use a key themselves, the third set of tracks was probably a ploy to veil the thief's movements. Haywood's eyes hardened. If he was right, they had a traitor in their midst. A very foolish *human* traitor. There was only darkness beyond the safety of the wall, and a horde of hungry vampire-cats waiting in the shadows. "Are you sure the missing key was used, Leftenant?"

"Very sure."

As the lift glided to a stop, the Vahnti military commander switched off the transmission and stepped into the corridor outside Dax's private suite. He glanced around. Two nervous-faced guards from the night watch had taken positions on either side of the double doors, their weapons trained on the tube and the corridor beyond.

Haywood hurried through the open doors and blew out a relieved breath when he spotted a scowling Dax prowling about the sitting room in a flurry of activity, obviously annoyed that Anwell was watching his every move. But at least he was alive, and unharmed.

"I suppose you've heard about what happened in the atrium," Haywood said. He surveyed the room but there was no sign of the girl.

"I heard," Dax answered absently. He dumped a saddle-pack atop a tall wing chair, along with a change of clothes, and rushed to an ornate wall cabinet beside the windows on the opposite side of the sitting room.

Haywood's gaze thinned with suspicion when he noticed Dax's attire. The Vahnti count had shed his formal uniform in favor of a pair of well-worn breeches, a dark, loose-fitting tunic, and a quilted flak vest. Traveling clothes. The soldier tensed as Dax pulled a laser crossbow from the cabinet, his fingers moving over the curved metal with cool precision as he checked and rechecked the weapon for any sign of malfunction.

A lump of fear crawled up Haywood's throat. There was only one thing the bows were used for—vampire-cats. His back stiffened with anger. The wolfens were on the loose, the girl had yet to make an appearance, and Dax was packing for a journey outside the shield wall. A simpleton could put the pieces together. Rayna Syn had made a run for it and Dax planned to go after her.

The crossbow emitted a metallic clack as Dax released the safety. He looked up at Haywood, his face taut and grim, his pale gaze fiercely determined. The obstinate set to Haywood's shoulders told him that his friend had figured things out. Some of it, at least.

Dax turned to Anwell and jerked his head toward the door. "You may leave, Sub-Leftenant." If he and Haywood were to have a confrontation they would do so in private. "Commander March will see to my safety now."

Anwell nodded and moved into the corridor, closing the doors behind her.

The soldier stared at him woodenly, an angry flush riding up his cheekbones. Dax had pulled some foolish stunts through the years, but why would he even contemplate risking himself in such a manner?

"Don't try to stop me, Haywood," Dax said calmly. "I've thought it over carefully." He tossed the bow onto the wing chair, as well as a shield key and a traveling cloak. His face settled into tight, unyielding lines. "I'm going after her—alone." He frowned and glanced out the windows for a moment, staring at the dark, the dense wash of golden light visible in the galactic core. "I have to," he said quietly.

A muscle bunched along Haywood's jaw. "By the gods, why?" he nearly shouted. "You have more than two million soldiers at your disposal, ready and willing to die at your slightest whim! Send them to hunt her down if you want! Send them *all* if you want! Why risk yourself this way?"

Dax turned suddenly, fury etched in stark lines across his face. "Because it's my fault she's out there alone!" He slammed his fist against the window frame, so hard the sound reverberated through the armored glass. "She doesn't realize the danger she's in. She doesn't understand about the cats!"

Confusion flickered in Haywood's eyes. "All the more reason to send out the guard force. She couldn't have gotten far.

We'll track her and those creatures down and have them back before dawn."

"No," Dax said harshly. He pushed away from the window and stalked back to the wing chair, hurriedly shoving his equipment inside the saddlepack. For a single second he considered telling Haywood, confiding what he had discovered about Rayna, and why he felt such an overwhelming compulsion to go after her. But how could he explain what he didn't truly understand himself? "I have to do this myself."

"Why?" Haywood demanded. "To prove that you've taken leave of your senses?"

Dax shook his head slowly and slung the pack and bow across his shoulder. The stablehands would have Blackfire saddled and waiting by now. "You're just going to have to trust me, Haywood." His expression hardened. "I know what I'm doing."

"Dax, please, I'm begging you." The soldier lifted his hands imploringly. "Think of the clan! If the cats don't get you, the girl or those damnable wolfens will. What then? Do you think Carlo or Caccia is actually capable of taking your place?"

Any reservations Dax might have felt about what he planned vanished entirely. "Don't you see, Haywood? That's the problem." A blend of determination and serenity showed in his eyes. "For close to twenty years now all I've thought about is the clan. It's long past time that I thought about myself . . . what *I* want—as a man, not as the Vahnti warlord." Oddly, by admitting those few simple words, he felt more at peace with himself than he could ever remember. "And what I want is her," he announced quietly. "I want her back, Haywood. I can't let her go. . . . I don't think I'll ever be able to let her go."

Haywood clenched his hands in frustration. He'd waited years for this moment, to hear Daxton Vahnti admit that he cared a whit about any woman, to know that finally Dax might be ready and willing to plant his seed and produce an heir for the clan. And now that he had heard those long-awaited words, the only thing he felt was a cold, bone-chilling dread. Rayna Syn, the Vahnti warlord's would-be assassin, might soon become a permanent resident of Drakken Castle. "You can't be serious," he whispered in disbelief.

"I've never been more serious, or more certain about anything in my life."

Haywood shook his head and clenched his fists tighter. "That she-devil has you under some kind of spell, Dax. She's got some sort of strange hold over you."

The Vahnti count walked to the doorway and stopped. For a moment he just stood there; then he turned back to Haywood, a slow, cynical smile playing across his mouth. "You know, I think you're right."

Chapter Sixteen

Steam plumed from a distant volcano, gouting from the cone in a thick column of milky gray that climbed for thousands of feet, then suddenly mushroomed outward, forming a huge cloud that nearly blanketed Hellfire's southern sky. Rayna paused a moment to catch her breath and surveyed the dusty, blackened terrain, squinting to see in the fierce morning sunlight.

The ridge of mountains that stretched before her was dark and forbidding, but if Lett's directions were accurate, Argossa lay just beyond them, along with the ship waiting to transport her to freedom.

A wolfen whined beside her, a tired, plaintive sound that caused her to throw a worried glance at the exhausted creature. Both wolfens were sprawled on the uneven ground, panting heavily, hunched together in a narrow spot of shade cast by an outcropping of volcanic rock.

"Rest a moment," she told the wolfens, and sank to the ground beside them. The gi scampered from the pouch, seemed to think better of the idea, and darted back inside for protection from the heat and glare.

Sweat trickled down her forehead in small, salty rivers. It had been cool before dawn, but as the sun broached the horizon they had encountered a thick wall of steamy heat that was slowly sucking them dry of moisture and strength. And the farther south they traveled, the more unbearable the heat became, as if the area surrounding Drakken Castle was a tiny oasis in the midst of a nightmarish hell.

Rayna leaned her head against the outcropping and looked around tiredly, willing her body not to succumb to sleep. She was drained, as close to collapsing from heat and exhaustion as she'd ever been. The strain of performing the long-term shift the night before had taken a heavy toll. In truth, she didn't know how she had managed to hold the wolfen form as long as she had. Her parched lips thinned. Terror, most probably, fear of what the demon lord would do if he caught her in human form.

But even that hadn't sustained her for long. Though not unexpected, the reverse shift had come upon her so abruptly that the transformation left her confused and disoriented, stumbling around in the pitch-dark like a blind woman who'd imbibed too much wine. It had happened as they'd neared the shield wall. One moment she had had four legs, the next only two. She was human again, weak and vulnerable, unable to see in the dark with her animal eyes, her senses reeling from the mind-numbing shock of shifting unexpectedly. If it hadn't been for the wolfens guiding her, she would have never made it through the shield. Not alive, at least. But combined with the tremendous distance they'd traveled during the night, the strain of shifting back and forth had left her in such a weakened state that she wondered if she still had the strength to make it across the mountains to Argossa.

She sucked in a deep breath. She'd made it this far. The only obstacle that now stood between her and the waiting ship was a single ridge of mountains.

As the minutes passed her breathing slowed to a nearly normal rhythm. Beside her, the panting wolfens began to doze, their sides still heaving in and out at a furious pace. "Let's rest a little while longer," she whispered to the weary animals, allowing them time to recoup their strength. The nearest wolfen had a pink-stained paw, the pad scraped and bloody from climbing over the endless rocks that littered the moonlike terrain. The charred stones were strewn everywhere, grotesque-shaped things spewed from Hellfire's bowels in some ancient cataclysm.

Rayna glanced down at herself. She was no better off than the wolfens. Her hands were scraped and cut from climbing the rocks, the heavy brocade robe stained and torn in a dozen places. Worse, the dainty green slippers had proved no match for Hellfire's treacherous terrain. As a result, her feet were raw and blistered, making every agonizing step she took an ordeal in itself.

A self-mocking smile lifted the corners of her mouth. She had planned every detail of her escape, right down to the last second, but in the end nothing had gone according to plan. The change of clothing and provisions she'd packed were strewn across the carpet in the Vahnti count's sitting room. But then, she should probably be grateful that she still had clothing at all. When Javan had first taught her how to shift, she had returned from her early attempts as naked as the day she'd been born. It had taken years of concentration and practice to bring back her clothing, too.

She glanced down at the thin gold bands encircling her wrists. Unfortunately for her, she'd mastered the technique all too well. The hated sensor cuffs were back as well.

The sight of the cuffs brought on thoughts of Daxton Vahnti, troubling memories from the night before that etched a frown across her sweaty brow. She remembered the hurt she'd seen in his chiseled face when he'd found the amulet, how those cool, pale eyes had burned with the thrill of discovery when she shifted beneath him. Most troubling of all was her last sight of him, the fear she'd seen in his eyes when the guards fired at her, how he had knocked the weapon from Anwell's hands to keep her from shooting again. As though he cared, as if he had made a conscious decision to save her life. She shook her head in confusion. Daxton Vahnti was a study in contrasts, a living, breathing contradiction that she would not understand.

A brief flash of pain shadowed her eyes. Her escape had

changed nothing. In some ways she was still his prisoner, bound to him by the tangle of emotions that raged inside her even now. Those feelings refused to die, no matter how deep she tried to bury them inside her heart. Could things have been different between them? On some level, had she wanted it to be different?

Maybe, she admitted to herself, but there was no use fretting over what would never be. Besides, she was too tired to think about it now. Her lids drifted closed, and her head dipped toward her chest. The siren call of sleep was luring her into darkness, a cool, quiet place where thoughts of Dax Vahnti wouldn't intrude. She shifted her arms and legs around and pillowed her head on the wolfen's furry back, the metal bracelets jangling against each other as she moved.

The discordant sound jarred her into wakefulness. The sensor cuffs . . . Her eyes snapped open, and the dull fog of exhaustion lifted from her brain. He could use the cuffs to follow her if he wanted, home in on their signal and track her every move.

She grabbed the pouch and bolted to her feet, her heart rate accelerating. "Come on, boys. Up," she urged the wolfens. "We have to keep moving." The huge creatures climbed upright and flexed the stiffness from their muscles. Tongues hanging, the wolfens stared at her with golden eyes and waited obediently. "If we don't he might find us."

The wolfens turned instinctively toward the southeast and padded off in the same direction they'd been moving since exiting the shield wall. Rayna trotted after them, climbing or leaping over the odd-shaped rocks strewn in her path, the possibility that he was tracking them urging her to greater speed.

As the landscape sped by, Hellfire's swollen white sun began edging toward midsky. And as the hours and miles slipped by, the terrain became more rugged, the small rocks turning into dark cliffs, the outcroppings into glassy monoliths whose magma-stained peaks narrowed into volcanic cones.

Every now and again the wolfens would sniff the dust-fouled air, the fur on their backs stiffening in response to some invisible threat. Rayna would stiffen, too, wondering if they'd caught the scent of a vampire-cat. But after tense seconds the wolfens would relax their hackles, as if the threat had moved away.

She kept going, one bone-numbing step at a time. Footing that had once been treacherous became nearly impossible as they made their way up the side of a towering cliff. A maze of thin ledges veined the cliff face, one leading upward another few feet, the next turning into a blind alley, forcing them to backtrack and lose precious time.

But after long hours the ledge beneath them suddenly widened, and Rayna almost cried in relief. She half walked, half crawled the short distance to the top of the ridge, grabbing handholds in the cliff face to keep her balance.

A freshening wind curled about her as she climbed the last few feet to the top of the cliff, expecting to see Argossa shimmering like a dusty jewel in the valley below. She stopped and stared around, blinking in the glare of Hellfire's boiling sun.

"No . . ." Rayna whispered in disbelief. She felt dead inside, as dark and dead as the sight that greeted her eyes. "It can't be." There was no valley, no settlement. Beyond the narrow plateau she was standing on lay an endless chain of glistening mountains, the dark, jagged peaks cresting above a sea of volcanic steam. She staggered toward the edge of the plateau, hoping against hope that what she sought would be there when she glanced down. But the shelflike plateau simply fell away into a yawning chasm, a stream of red-hot magma snaking down the length of the fissure's wide belly.

She did weep then, the bitter tears hot and scalding against her sun-flushed cheeks.

Dax reined the lathered horse to a stop in the shadow of a cliff and pulled the tracker from a pocket in his vest, studying the small readout screen for perhaps the hundredth time since he'd ridden through the shield wall. He shook his head and frowned, puzzled by the course Rayna had taken after making her escape. She was still heading southeast, the worst direction she could possibly choose. The charred terrain was harsh and mountainous, riddled with volcanic fissures and sheer black cliffs. And she was heading right into the heart of a five-hundred-mile dead zone that had been declared too dangerous for human habitation over a thousand years before.

His frown grew more pronounced. Why had she come this way? It didn't make the least bit of sense, especially not for someone on foot—and she was on foot, not paws. He'd spotted her small footprints before he'd even passed through the shield. Human prints interspersed with the huge paw marks left by the two wolfens.

Dax sighed and patted Blackfire's sweaty neck. He was astounded by how fast and incredibly far Rayna had traveled since her escape. More than thirty miles now, an amazing feat for someone on foot and unequipped to deal with Hellfire's inhospitable landscape. "She's led us on a hell of a chase, hasn't she, boy?"

The horse nickered softly in response.

He glanced at the tracker again. The electronic blip indicated that she'd stopped moving, the second time she'd done so since daybreak. He'd almost caught up with her then, but she'd taken off again, braving the worst terrain Hellfire had to offer, while he in turn had zigzagged west, taking an easier, more cautious course up to Dead Man's Plateau. He'd realized she was heading there early that morning and had changed course to intercept her.

It wasn't a brilliant deduction on his part. The narrow plateau stretched for more than a hundred miles in either direction, as well as the wide volcanic fissure that lay just beyond it. Once she reached the plateau she'd be cut off, unable to go forward, too tired to go back. And that was where he'd catch her.

He studied the string of coordinates displayed on the readout screen. She'd reached the plateau, which explained why she had stopped so abruptly. After slipping the tracker back into his vest, he unslung the crossbow and made sure the controls were set on rapid fire. He'd already killed five cats since daybreak.

"Just a few more miles," Dax said, and nudged the horse into a walk by flexing his knees. He headed toward an ancient lava tube, a wide, smooth channel that curved around the brow of a mountain and offered an easy ascent to the top of the plateau.

The sun was sliding toward the mountains huddled along the horizon as Rayna climbed tiredly to her feet, her face streaked with dust and the remnants of her tears. She stared at the landscape with dull, vacant eyes. How could Lett have done this to her? There was no settlement, no waiting ship, and never had been. She knew that now.

The note had been a lie, a deadly ruse used to fool her into risking life and limb for the promise of freedom. And she'd believed, grasped desperately at the thread of hope the note represented, and made herself a willing victim of the malicious ploy. Her belief in Lett, in the possibility of freedom, had condemned both her and the animals to certain death. She peered down at the stream of lava inching through the chasm. Because of her they were stranded at the edge of hell. No food, no water, their bodies too exhausted to survive the dangerous trek back to Drakken Castle. They had a day left, maybe two. The heat, thirst, or vampire-cats would get them eventually.

"I'm sorry," she told the wolfens, who were sitting nearby, watching and waiting. "It's my fault." How could she have been so foolish as to place her faith and hope in Lett's note?

She frowned suddenly. Actually, there'd been no signature at the bottom of the note. She'd only assumed that Lett had written it, an assumption made because the only friends she had at the castle were him and Carlo, and Lett had been the one who'd found and retrieved her amulet. Her eyes narrowed. The person who'd written that note was no friend.

Behind her, the wolfens sprang to their feet and cocked their ears, listening for a sound, testing the wind for a threatening scent. A few feet away, the gi leaped out of the pouch and chittered nervously.

Rayna turned from the chasm and scanned the landscape, but there was no sound, no trace of movement of any kind. Her heartbeat quickened. It was too quiet, far too still.

The plateau shifted beneath her, a violent, rolling motion that heaved the ground sideways, then back. A deep, vibrating rumble filled the air, a noise so loud and furious that Rayna clapped her hands to her ears.

Quake, her mind shouted, the single word paralyzing her with fear. She sucked in a terrified breath, unable to move or think, her legs refusing to heed the hysterical voice in her head that kept screaming for her to run.

A jagged fissure opened in the rock near her feet, wisps of dust and steam gushing upward as the rift crackled along the edge of the plateau. A massive boulder toppled from the top of the mountain, careened across the shelf of rock, and rolled off the edge, spinning out of sight into the chasm below.

The groanlike rumble increased to a deafening roar as the earthquake intensified. The plateau heaved and pitched, entire sections lifting at sharp angles then slamming downward again, collapsing into smoky heaps of jagged rubble.

The small fissure widened, and the ground beneath her suddenly tilted. Unable to keep her footing, Rayna slid backward and fell. She clawed at the slippery rock for a handhold, fingernails digging into small depressions in search of something to stop her downward slide. The surefooted wolfens clambered past her and scrambled for the safety of level ground. They leaped across the widening fissure and stopped, refusing to retreat any farther until she joined them.

Rayna lost her handhold and started sliding, flailing vainly to stop her fall. Terrified, she craned her neck sideways and glanced behind her out of the corner of her eye. The edge of the plateau was just a few feet away now. She slid another few inches as a shower of gravel rained down on her from above; then she slipped even more, the edge so close her legs dropped over the side.

She gazed up at the wolfens. There was no reason for the animals to die with her. "Run!" she yelled at them. "Get out of here!"

Rayna closed her lids as the ground tilted even more. Strangely, she felt no fear. An odd sense of peace had washed through her when she realized that death was only seconds away. Somehow it seemed right that she would die the same way as her mother.

The slab of rock she was clutching crumbled beneath her

fingers and she began to fall, her body tumbling through empty air. For a moment she felt like a bird.

Dax lurched to his feet and swayed against the frightened horse. A sticky trail of blood was running down his cheek from a cut on his forehead. He squeezed his eyes closed to clear his vision and rubbed at the cut with the back of a hand. A rock had hit him and knocked him from the horse. Or something. He couldn't really remember.

Blackfire danced sideways and snorted, ears flattened to his head. Dax stroked the horse's quivering neck. "It's over now," he reassured him, "at least for a while." Judging by the size of the quake, there would be plenty of aftershocks for days to come.

He surveyed the plateau. Mammoth boulders had been tossed around like childrens' toys, and steam hissed from a weblike maze of small fissures that crisscrossed the blackened rock. Farther away, a thick pall of dust hung across the shattered landscape like a smoky blanket.

Dax reached for his wristcom to call the castle and swore beneath his breath. The rectangular face of the device had been shattered in his fall from the horse, the wafer-thin biochips crushed to an unrecognizable pulp. He tapped at the ON switch just to be sure, but the wristcom was completely dead.

"Wonderful," he muttered to himself. It had been his own idea to go after Rayna alone, without interference from Haywood or the guard force. Now he had to pay the price for that decision. He couldn't contact the castle to check on the quake damage, and they couldn't contact him. In a few hours, after things had settled down at the castle, Haywood would become frantic and send out a search party. But until then, he was completely on his own, and he'd yet to find Rayna. She could be badly injured for all he knew. Or worse.

He took out the tracker to check her coordinates, his brow knitting in a troubled line as he studied the small screen. She was less than a mile away, but he was receiving a signal from only one of the bracelets. The other was as dead as his wristcom.

The first aftershock jolted the plateau—a mild one, for

which Dax was thankful. His frown deepening, Dax grabbed Blackfire's reins and led the horse toward the east—and Rayna.

An hour later Dax heard the wolfens. The sound of their howls drifted toward him on the dusty wind, mournful cries that sent a shiver down his spine. He clucked to Blackfire and quickened their pace. The golden-haired beasts were pacing back and forth along a flat section of rock near the lip of the plateau, stopping every so often to stare into the depths of the chasm itself.

The sound of his heartbeat drummed in his ears as he dropped the reins and started running. "Not that," Dax whispered to himself. "Please not that."

He jumped a small fissure, slowing only when he reached the flat shelf the wolfens were standing on. Dax glanced around wildly, but there was no sign of Rayna save for a leather pouch lying near a slab of rock that had cracked and tilted toward the edge of the ravine. "Where is she?" he demanded, as if the animals could actually answer him.

The tiny gi darted around his legs, chirping frantically. It scrambled down the slanted stone to the rim of the chasm and peered over the side.

His jaw tightened. The animals were behaving as if Rayna had indeed gone over the edge.

Giving the giant wolfens a wide berth, Dax slid and picked his way down to the rim of the abyss, half expecting the wolfens to attack the moment his back was turned. But oddly he sensed no danger from the monstrous beasts. As if they knew what he was doing and approved.

When he reached the rim he paused for a moment and shut his eyes, not wanting to look, but knowing that he had to. He drew in a deep breath to steel himself and opened his eyes again. The bottom of the chasm was choked with dust and debris, a dark, smoky haze tinged orange-red by the slow-moving lava stream. His gaze shifted, moving up and along the sheer wall of the ravine.

And then he saw her, about thirty feet below and to his right. He expelled a ragged sigh, his relief so fierce that for a few seconds he couldn't draw another breath. She was huddled on a narrow shelf of rock protruding from the chasm wall, her small form scrunched tight against the side of the ledge. Her gaze was fixed entirely on something at the opposite end of the shelf, as if whatever it was needed her full attention.

"Rayna!" Dax shouted, his deep voice echoing down the wide ravine. From what he could see, she didn't look badly injured, but from this distance he couldn't really be sure. "Are you hurt?"

Rayna flinched in surprise and risked a quick glance upward, just long enough to prove to herself that she hadn't imagined the familiar voice. Daxton Vahnti was on his hands and knees, peering down at her over the edge.

Her wary gaze flicked back to the other end of the ledge, to the small black crevice gouged in the chasm wall. She concentrated on the hole intently, a small, sad smile lifting the corners of her mouth. A week ago that deep, rich voice would have made her cringe in terror, but now, just knowing that he was here filled her with a different kind of fear.

"I'm all right," she shouted back, her voice trembling with emotion. "But there's nothing you can do for me! Just leave—while you still have the chance! And take the animals with you if you can!"

Dax laughed and leaned a little farther over the edge to get a better view. "Sorry, pet," he yelled. "I have no intention of going anywhere." Ever defiant, his little captive was determined to drive her would-be savior away. "Since I don't intend to leave, why don't you just turn yourself into a bird and fly up here? I promise I won't bite."

"I can't!" Rayna cried weakly. Her hands knotted in frustration. It would be days before she was strong enough to try to shift again, into any form. "I don't have the strength."

"Well, I don't have any climbing gear to hoist you up, so you're going to have to sit tight and enjoy the view. Help should be here around morning."

She bit back a haze of tears. He didn't understand. He hadn't felt the presence of the terrible things lurking in the bowels of the crevice. She tried to block the malignant sensations that kept slithering through her thoughts, the dank emanations pouring from the hideous creatures inside the hole.

They were watching her with sly, dead eyes, savoring her fear, letting the scent of it grow and build around her until she could almost smell it herself—like malevolent children toying with an insect before they squashed it again and again beneath their heels.

She lifted her gaze upward and met the Vahnti count's eyes. "I won't be here in the morning." Her voice echoed back to her from across the chasm.

Her words and hopeless tone sent a ripple of fear up the base of Dax's neck. "What do you mean?" he called, growing more alarmed by the second. Her upturned face was drawn and ghostly white—the color of bleached bones.

"I'm not alone down here. . . ."

Dax went cold inside.

"There's a hole at the other end of the ledge," she called more softly. "I think it's a nest."

His heart missed a beat. *Vampire-cats.* "Dear gods," he whispered to himself. What was he going to do? He had left the castle in such a rush that he'd foolishly left behind his climbing gear. He couldn't hoist her up, and there was a thick overhang sheltering all but a tiny portion of the ledge, which would prevent him from shooting into the nest.

"Don't move, Rayna," he told her as quietly as possible. "Don't do anything to attract their attention."

Rayna tilted her head even more, her gaze stilling on his chiseled features. "It's too late." And it was, for many things. "They already know I'm here." She stared at him for a long moment. "They'll be coming for me soon," she announced calmly. "I can feel it. . . . I can feel their hunger and loathing." A bewildered look touched her face. She'd never sensed such depravity in a creature before. "It's as if they're feeding off my fear . . . amusing themselves by making me wait for the moment of my death."

Dax's expression darkened, and he slammed his fist against a stone in frustration. Her voice was filled with an eerie calmness, as though she had made peace with herself and was embracing the notion of death. "Listen to me, Rayna. You're *not* going to die! Do you hear me? I'm not going to let you die down there, so don't you dare give up!"

"There's nothing you can do." She choked back a fresh rush of tears as she sensed a glimmer of movement inside the crevice. Malformed bodies and wings were twisting, shifting, moving slowly toward the entrance of the hole. They were tired of playing their vicious little game and had decided to come for her. "Just go. . . . Get away from here as fast as you can!"

Dax bolted to his feet and stumbled up the tilted slab, his eyes dark with fear and grim determination. He had to do something, anything, and do it now. His hands shook as he ripped the tracker from his vest and stabbed at the controls, locking Rayna's coordinates into the device's memory. The string of numbers began glowing red on the tiny readout screen. He snatched his saddlepack and crossbow from Blackfire's back and slung them over his shoulder, then jammed the tracker and his broken wristcom inside a carry-pouch near the pommel of the saddle.

Time was the enemy now. Rayna wouldn't survive the next five minutes, much less stay alive until morning. Dax slipped the bit from Blackfire's mouth and gave the horse his head. "Go home, boy! Home!" He slapped the horse across the rump. "Yah!"

The animal bucked and cantered off, picking his way westward across the rugged terrain. To the west lay the lava tube and a safe descent from atop the plateau. Odds were that the horse would be felled by vampire-cats or catch a hoof in a hidden fissure long before he made it out of the mountains. But if by some miracle he did make it to open ground, Haywood and the security force would stand a better chance of spotting the horse or picking up the tracker's signal and homing in on their location.

The wolfens were standing at the edge of the chasm as he hurried back down, the golden fur along their backs stiff and rigid. The one nearest to him snarled, its long, thin fangs bright white in the waning sunlight. Dax approached the wolfens warily, but their fury was focused on the creatures threatening Rayna.

A cool twilight breeze curled around his body as he stood on the edge of the abyss and looked over the rim, carefully gauging the distance down to Rayna and the ledge. Her life depended on what he did in the next few minutes, and he was damn well determined that he was going to do it right. He switched the crossbow's sight to infrared and made sure the weapon was ready to fire.

There were sounds below, faint and tenuous, like the quick rustlings of a bird's wings. Dax lifted the sight to his eye and waited.

Rayna screamed, an endless, terror-filled cry that reverberated over the canyon walls. A vampire-cat swept from beneath the overhang, then another, batlike wings flapping furiously in the fading sun as they hovered just beyond the ledge.

The crossbow made a humming sound as Dax squeezed off two quick shots, sizzling the bulbous bodies in midair. Two charred gray lumps plunged end over end toward the chasm floor.

Rayna cried out again, more a sob than a scream. He angled the bow downward and sighted along its length but couldn't get a clear shot at the others because of the overhang. "Cover your head, Rayna!" he shouted down to her. "Keep them away from your throat!"

Cursing silently, he hitched the bow and saddlepack over his shoulder. The breeze buffeted him gently as he inched closer to the rim, the toes of his boots loosening a dusty shower of gravel and small stones. What he planned was risky and very stupid, but his options had long since run out.

Dax sucked in a deep breath to brace himself—and jumped.

The wind roared in his ears, and the sour taste of bile rose in his throat as the chasm wall rushed past at a heart-stopping speed. For a split second he felt a surge of panic, thinking he had misjudged the distance, but the thought died abruptly when his body collided with the rocky ledge.

The air rushed from his lungs, and his knees and ankles buckled, unable to absorb the force of the violent impact. Tumbling sideways, he crashed against the side of the ledge and came to a stop, his right foot bent beneath the other at an unnatural angle. The saddlepack careened over the edge and fell out of sight.

Rayna ducked as a vampire-cat dove past her head, then

lifted her eyes and gaped at the man beside her in stunned surprise. Like some great black bird, the Vahnti count had just fallen from the sky, landing in a crumpled heap on the narrow ledge.

The startled vampire-cats took to the air in a flurry of squeals and wings. They hovered uncertainly, fangs extended, gathering together to stage a concerted attack.

His face taut and white with pain, Dax rose on his elbows and lifted the bow. A cylindrical bolt of blue-green light daggered outward. The first cat dropped like a stone, flopping and twitching near the edge of the shelf. He kicked it over the side with his good foot and fired again. The shot went wide, and the intended target arrowed toward him, screeching furiously as it closed on its prey.

Dax fired three times in rapid succession, killing one but only searing a wing off another. The half-dead creature squealed in pain and careened toward him, spinning in circles as it fought to stay airborne. He didn't have time to fire again. The single wing beating furiously, the vampire-cat hit him square in the chest and tried to dig its talons into his flesh, fangs and putrid mouth snapping at his throat. He flailed at the thing feverishly, wincing as a needlelike fang grazed the side of his neck.

There was a sharp cry beside him, a savage yell laced with fury and fierce determination. From the corner of his eye he saw Rayna rise from the shadows like an avenging angel, arms trembling as she lifted a huge rock over her head and heaved it sideways. The stone hit its mark with a dull, bone-crunching thud.

Rayna shoved the stone and the remnants of the cat over the edge and scanned the shadows beneath the overhang with wary eyes. "That's the last of them, I think," she whispered shakily.

For a moment Dax just lay there, too exhausted to move. His fingers found the spot of blood on his neck and explored a small, perfect circle of swollen flesh. His hand stilled, and he blew out a shuddering breath. "Gods," he whispered to himself. The fang had broken the skin. "Rayna . . ." he called softly, his voice dark with despair. "You have to make sure we got them all." He slid the bow toward her. "Fire into the nest. Keep shooting until you're sure there's nothing left alive."

She nodded woodenly and picked up the bow. "How do I fire it?"

"There's a pad midway up the stock." He blinked to focus his eyes. "Just press it when you're ready."

"All right." She crept toward the crevice, found the pad he'd indicated, and started firing, searing the interior of the hole with a constant pulse of greenish heat. There was no trace of movement inside, no angry squeals of pain. She quit firing and moved back to Dax's side, placing the bow within easy reach between them.

"It's done," she announced quietly, and fell into a numb silence, knowing she should say something, but too tired and confused to think of the proper words. The Vahnti warlord had taken a terrible risk on her behalf. She didn't understand why, yet deep down, the knowledge that he had risked himself to save her caused a tiny thrill to sweep through her blood. "You saved my life." She gave him a shy, probing glance. "Why?"

"It seemed the thing to do at the time." His mouth curled slightly, more a grimace than a smile. "A little gratitude would be nice."

"Thank you."

"That's better." His chest rattled as he drew in a raspy breath.

Rayna's glance sharpened when she heard the sound of his shallow breathing. She studied him more closely. His olive skin was pale and clammy, the flesh stretched taut across the planes of his face. Her heart beat faster, and her anxious gaze moved downward to survey the rest of his body. His dark quilted vest was shredded and torn, small splotches of blood seeping through the fabric where the creature's talons had clawed at his chest. A worried frown settled over her brow. "You're hurt." It was a statement of fact, not a question. His right foot was caught under the other, twisted outward at a painful angle.

He tried to smile, but the muscles around his mouth had

gone numb. "I guess you could say that." His entire body was a mass of aches and pains, but that was changing swiftly, one nerve ending at a time. Soon he wouldn't feel anything at all.

She pulled his boot off gently and ran a hand down his shin and ankle, strong, deft fingers probing along the length of bone. "I don't think anything's broken."

"Feels like it is," he said hoarsely. His right foot had taken the brunt of the impact when he'd jumped onto the ledge. "I'll be sure to bring a rope next time." He gritted his teeth as she examined the swollen flesh along his injured ankle.

"Don't move." She knelt on the ground beside him and placed her hands beneath his calf and heel. "I'm going to try to straighten your foot."

His eyes widened. "Do you know what you're doing?"

She snorted quietly. "Enough to ease your pain a bit. My grandfather is a medicine man—a healer. He taught me a lot of things." She jerked twice, hard. His ankle snapped back to a more natural position.

The bolt of pain he'd anticipated never came. Oddly, his ankle did feel better. He stared at Rayna in fascination, wondering what other secrets were hidden behind those vivid green eyes. Secrets he'd never bothered to try to discern. He scowled, furious with himself and the perversity of fate. So many things he would never know.

She continued to study his injuries, frowning at the bloody gouges in his chest. "How soon can we expect help to arrive?" she said in a voice edged with concern. The puncture wounds weren't too severe, but she didn't like the shallow, huffy sound of his breathing, or his ghostly pallor.

"Morning, I think." Too long, Dax thought darkly. He couldn't feel his arms anymore, and the ice-cold numbness had begun to inch into his hands. "Maybe later in the day." Tremors ran through his fingers when he tried to flex them.

Dax swallowed. Even that had become difficult. "Rayna . . ." His voice was raspy, thick. "We need to talk." It was time to tell her, prepare her while he still had the chance. "There's something you need to know."

She glanced up from his chest. "What is it?" she said uneasily. His husky words had been spoken in a calm, carefully measured voice. Ominously calm.

"There's a good chance I'll be dead by morning."

Her face went very still. "What do you mean?"

He tried to shift his head to show her, but he couldn't move the muscles in his neck. "The cat . . . it scraped my neck with a fang. I took some venom." He paused a moment, tried to swallow. "My body's going numb. Pretty soon I won't be able to move at all. I might stay conscious, but my muscles will be completely paralyzed for around six hours."

She leaned forward, her fingers groping and pulling at his collar and tousled hair until she exposed the skin underneath. There was a small, blackened circle of flesh near the base of his throat. The skin around the puncture was swollen and mottled with angry splotches of purple, red, and black.

"There's nothing you can do, Rayna." He sucked in a rattling breath. "If I got enough venom to shut down my heart and lungs, I'll die."

She stared at him mutely.

"You're going to have to stand watch tonight." Hellfire's fiery sun had slipped beneath a distant mountain ridge. A still, dusty twilight was gathering around them. "Chances are we got all the cats, but we can't be sure, not with a nest nearby."

Her lids drifted closed for a short length of time, but when they reopened, her expression was as carefully composed as his voice. "I'll be ready." She gripped the stock of the crossbow tightly.

"If I die, tell Haywood I said to set you free. . . ."

"I'm not going to let you die!" she told him fiercely, echoing the impassioned words he'd shouted from atop the cliff.

He tried to frown, couldn't, and settled for staring at her for long seconds. It took several tries to make his tongue and mouth work in unison. "I thought that's what you wanted."

Rayna glanced away, breaking contact with that cool, hypnotic gaze. "Not anymore," she said in a whisper.

"Good . . ." The raspy word came out thick and slurred, and Dax knew it was the last one he would utter for a good while. He continued to watch her, fascinated by the tangle of emotions playing across her dust-stained face. A tear slid down her cheek, and he watched the bead of moisture fall and spread atop his outstretched hand. Had she shed that tear for him? he wondered silently. No. It couldn't be. But the possibility was intriguing, and shook him to the core of his soul.

The muscles in his lids suddenly froze, and he was glad that his eyes were open when it happened. If he died in the coming hours, his last glimpse of the living world would be of her.

Rayna sighed, long and deep, and glanced back at his face. A chill of fear rippled down her spine. His features were slack, devoid of all expression, his glassy eyes open and staring.

She leaned over him and pressed an ear to his chest, blowing out a shuddery breath when she heard the shallow rattle in his lungs. He was alive, and she planned to keep him that way.

"I forbid you to die!" she yelled suddenly. She clutched at the fabric of his collar and shook him violently. "Do you hear me, Daxton Vahnti? You die on me and I'll carve out your black heart and feed it to the wolfens!"

For one quick second, a glint of amusement seemed to flare in his pale, glassy eyes. If not amusement, at least a glimmer of intelligence. And if he was still conscious, there was hope.

A dense, heavy darkness settled over the mountains, the only light the reddish glow of the magma coursing through the chasm below. Shadows stretched and lengthened, and somewhere above the narrow ledge, the wolfens began to howl at the approaching night.

"Listen to their howls," Rayna told him. "They're hungry, eager to taste a plump Vahnti heart, so you'd best try to stay alive." She peered into his face, but this time there was no answering glint in his eyes.

As her fear and the darkness deepened, she jerked the leather cord from around her neck and opened the tiny black pouch, spilling the contents of the amulet into the palm of her hand. She laid a small purple rock atop the swelling on his neck, as well as a precious mito feather, then carefully covered the wound with a fine layer of gritty powder made from the seed pods of Nirvannan grass. When ground into a powder, the mysterious pods had curative powers, promoted healing by making a wound impervious to infection, and acted as a powerful stimulant to the brain.

Rayna closed her eyes and whispered a healing chant, drawing and focusing the full force of nature's energy toward the man beside her. A wisp of smoke rose from his neck, and the mito feather burst into a single tongue of blue flame, darkening and curling until all that was left was a smoldering cinder.

When she was finished, she reopened her eyes and clutched the cold steel stock of the crossbow tightly. Five hours, maybe six, and then she'd know whether he'd live or die. She scrunched closer to his cold, still body and began her vigil, watching the shadows, watching him.

She had to keep him awake, conscious, his mind and body focused on staying alive. And so she began to talk, the quiet flow of words slow and awkward at first, then gaining momentum as the minutes passed.

Chapter Seventeen

She talked for hours, until her throat was raw, her voice hoarse and strained. She spoke of her childhood, her mother's death, the father she never knew, the ancient grandfather who'd taught her Lakotan mysticism, trained her young mind to project an illusion made of flesh and bone. She described what it felt like to run barefoot across the plains, about the times she'd gone into the hills alone to commune with her chosen spirit guides, the fearless wolfens.

The words poured from her parched lips in a soft, steady stream, tales of brave warriors and fair maidens who set forth from the scarred, war-torn world of their birth in search of a new world where it was prophesied that they would live much as their ancestors had, free of the taint of civilization. She told him the rest of the prophecy as well, how they'd always known that someday a fierce serpent would descend on them from the night sky, a dark and powerful demon with eyes of ice who could wither Nirvanna's life-giving grass with a single frozen glance.

And through those long, lonely hours, she knew he listened. Staring at nothing, at everything, as much a captive to her words as she was to him. Four hours? Five? She'd lost all track of time. The star-filled core had long since risen, washing the night-shadowed mountains in a haze of gold. In the distance, thin fingers of glowing magma striped the darkness with bands of red.

The ground had rumbled many times with the thunder of aftershocks. Boulders crashed in the darkness, tumbling and grumbling as they were swallowed by the chasm. Scary sounds. Sounds that made her heart leap with fear, and clutch the man lying beside her tighter still.

She had lost her fear of the vampire-cats long before. If they came, she wouldn't be able to stop them. Not in the dark. Not alone.

Her moments of fear and hopelessness were reserved for Daxton Vahnti, and so she waited for the hours to pass, the coming of the distant dawn. She prayed for a sign that he would live, a change of some kind that would give her reason to hope.

Twice now he'd stopped breathing completely, and she'd pressed her lips to his and filled his chest with air from her own lungs until the crisis passed. At other times, when she sensed him beginning to slip away, she would slap his face and scream in his ear to force him back from the brink of death.

When she ran out of words she'd done other things. Strange, desperate things like trying with her body to entice him to live. He might not be able to feel, she'd reasoned, but he still had his sense of sight, and she would give him something to see. So she'd stripped down to her thin white underrobe and leaned close to his face, slowly pulling the filmy fabric lower to expose the curve of her breasts. She caressed him, trailing her fingers down his still flesh, her lips across his face. Once she'd even picked up his cold, limp hand and crushed his palm against her breast, moving it around and around the peak of her nipple.

The very memories made her cheeks flush with shame. But worst of all, the touch of his hard male flesh against her own had left her breathless and hungry for more.

Tired and frightened, Rayna lay in the darkness, huddled against him, and ran her fingers through his silky hair, toying with the ebony strands. He had such beautiful hair, thick and silky, like a woman's in some ways. The color suited him. So did his eyes.

"You're a very handsome man," she told him dreamily. "Too much so, I think. Sometimes I catch myself watching you. Just staring like some idiotic fool." She blinked and frowned in the darkness, horrified that she had blurted aloud something so intimate, yet strangely, she couldn't seem to stop herself from drifting down that embarrassing chain of thought. "And when you touch me . . ." Her eyes shut tight, and a pained expression stole across her shadowed features. "Oh, gods, I just want to push myself against you to stop the ache inside me. I want to touch your body in ways I've never dreamed of before. . . ."

She realized then that her body had reacted instinctively to her hushed words. She was moving against him, her breasts brushing his forearm and chest, her loins pressed tight to the curve of his hip. She knew it was insane, but she didn't care. If Daxton Vahnti died here, in this terrible place, he would do so in her arms.

He made a small sound beside her, a gaspy, sighing expulsion of air.

Rayna flinched and sat upright, her heart pounding in fear. It was the first sound he'd made in hours. "Dax?" she said in a small voice. She ran her fingers inside his shirt, placed her palm flat against his chest, and expelled a sigh of relief. Death hadn't come to claim him yet. "I wish I knew what to do for you." She checked his vacant eyes and lifted his hand, idly stroking his chilly skin. "I can't even tell if you're still conscious."

Dax wished he was unconscious. He was beyond mere pain. His body was in agony, a hideously exquisite misery the likes of which he'd never suffered before, and prayed he never would again. Her hands had been all over him for hours. At first it didn't matter because he couldn't feel a thing. But as time passed, the venom had begun to loosen its paralyzing hold. Though his muscles were still useless, every nerve ending in his body had come alive with a terrible, screaming vengeance long ago. Was it because of the venom, the powder from the amulet that she'd poured on his neck? Or was it the feather that had mysteriously burst into flame on his throat, nearly scaring him out of what was left of his wits?

Whatever the reason, his senses were heightened, sharper than they had ever been in his life. Especially his sense of touch. And oh, gods, how she'd been touching him, with her hands, her mouth, those lush, ripe breasts, and other secret parts of herself that he didn't care to contemplate. He had never been so aroused before, hadn't thought such a driving, furious need was humanly possible. But the worst of it was that there was absolutely nothing he could do about it.

When she was certain his breathing had resumed its shallow rhythm, Rayna settled back into the crook of his arm and trailed her fingertips down the length of his torso. She sighed and stared at the star-drenched sky, the lava streams staining the night with red. "Hellfire's actually beautiful in a strange kind of way," she said quietly. "I'm beginning to see why you like it so much." She picked up a long lock of his hair and played with it absently, draping the ebony strands over her face and lifting it into the air.

Dax broke out in a sweat, the cold, clammy moisture beading on his brow and cheeks. Death almost seemed preferable to the torture she was putting him through. His skin was on fire, his blood near to boiling. He tried frantically to lift his hand, but all he could manage was a single twitch of a thumb. Please, he prayed, just make it stop.

Suddenly, maddeningly, a large section of his torso began to awaken from its venom-induced sleep. The muscles tensed and spasmed from his collarbone down to his thighs, the ligaments kinking, then loosening as the toxin's grip slowly faded. But just when he thought the worst was about to pass, Rayna touched him again, and a searing bolt of awareness began to knot inside his loins. He felt himself harden, go rigid with terrible, aching need, and at that moment, Dax was sure he was going to die.

Her nail singed a pathway down the side of his face, and a soft, young breast brushed against his arm. He worked at moving his jaw, managed to slip his tongue between his teeth, and bit down until he tasted a warm gush of blood. His body began to tremble, the muscles strung as taut and rigid as his loins.

Rayna felt him shudder and lifted her head, an anxious frown building along her brow. His entire body was trembling, quivering feverishly from head to foot. She peered into his face worriedly. His eyes were still the same glassy blue, but his forehead, cheeks, and neck were slick with sweat. Unsure if the changes boded ill or not, she shoved her hand inside his shirt to check his breathing again.

He gasped suddenly, his lips moving to form the sound. Muscles in his neck and throat tightened, flexed, and blessedly relaxed. "Stop. . . ." he finally managed to croak.

At the sound of his raspy voice, Rayna burst into a storm of tears. She slumped atop him in relief and clutched at his shoulders, weeping grateful tears against his chest. "I thought you were going to die!" she said in a sob, her voice muffled by his sweat-drenched shirt. "I was so scared."

Dax made a tortured sound low in his throat. If there truly was a hell, he'd found it. "Rayna," he whispered. He didn't know how much more he could stand. "Get off me. . . . Now."

She pulled up to her elbows and turned to face him, tears glistening on her cheeks. "I'm sorry." The weight of her body must have been pressing into the wounds on his chest. "I didn't mean to hurt you." Concerned that he might be bleeding again, she worked the fasteners loose on his vest and shirt and pushed the material aside to examine the torn flesh.

"Don't touch me," Dax ordered, grimacing as her fingers grazed bare flesh. He flexed his arms, stretching out the kinks, and opened and closed his fingers, testing his strength, his ability to reach out and drag her into his arms. "If you do, I don't think I'll be able to stop myself."

She blinked in the darkness, completely baffled now. There

203

was a dangerous edge of urgency in his voice that she didn't understand. "Stop what?" Was he delirious? Suffering from the aftereffects of the venom? "Are you in pain?"

It was too much. She was hovering over him, her face close to his, those innocent green eyes wide and beckoning. He could hear himself breathing faster. She shifted slightly, and the front of the thin underrobe gaped open, granting him a perfect, maddening view of her softly mounded flesh.

"Yes, I'm in pain!" he snapped harshly, the words exploding from between clenched teeth. "You've been touching me for hours, brushing yourself against me, and I felt every single hellish moment of it! Just get away from me and stay away!"

She jerked away from him, hurt and humiliation deepening the color of her eyes. A hot rush of embarrassment rode up her neck and cheekbones. She glanced downward, a tangled curtain of hair falling forward to veil her reddened face. "I'm sorry," she managed to whisper. "I had no idea just touching you would cause such pain."

Dax laughed, a hoarse, raw sound that caught in his throat and turned into a choked gasp. She had absolutely no idea what he was talking about. "You're so damnably innocent, Rayna. . . . I wasn't speaking about that kind of pain."

She looked up then, eyes hidden behind the tumble of hair, understanding what he'd meant with a sudden, horrifying clarity that stained her cheeks a deeper shade of red. In her desperation to keep him alive, she had purposely tantalized him with her body, enticed him with the knowledge that she was doing so of her own accord. A pulse beat at the base of her throat. She had known he could see her but had never dreamed that he could feel her touch as well.

Dax watched her closely. The tense set to her shoulders told him that she finally understood. *Good*. She'd stay away from him now, scurry to the opposite end of the ledge to keep her maidenly body far away from him. It was just as well. He was in no mood or condition to deal with a quivering, frightened virgin. The numbness had mostly faded, but he felt drained, unable to move his arms or head more than an inch or so. But he was still in agony. Just the sight of her crouched beside him, copper hair streaming about her shoulders, the swelling of her breasts visible beneath the thin robe, was enough to make him die a little more.

Rayna pushed a lock of hair from her face and gazed at him steadily. He'd warned her, told her to move away from him—given her the final choice. Just as he had when her wolfen fangs were grazing the side of his throat, and she was considering whether he should live or die. But this was a far different choice from that. Daxton Vahnti wanted her. She could hear it in his husky voice, see the naked need glittering like quicksilver in his pale, anguished eyes. And if he weren't so weakened by the venom coursing through his veins, she knew the Vahnti count would have taken her this very moment. Without reservation. Without the slightest trace of regret.

And she didn't care. All the awareness and desire she had forbidden herself to feel because of who he was, what he was, came to an abrupt, tumultuous boil. A small, hot shiver stirred deep within her veins. She wanted him, too, without a shred of reservation or regret.

She stood up slowly, her gaze still locked with his, and slid her arms from the underrobe, pulling the wispy material over her head. She tossed it aside and stared into the depths of his heated eyes.

"I've made my choice." She had the oddest feeling that something monumental had just occurred, as if the thin web of energy flowing around her had suddenly shifted, the tangled currents of life and nature rearranging themselves into a strange, unfamiliar pattern. "I think I knew what my decision would be from the moment I first saw you."

Dax stared at her raptly. She was standing before him, grave, fierce, and proud, yet still the utter innocent in an age when the idea of innocence held no meaning at all. Behind her the sky and mountains were a dense, empty black crisscrossed with veins of glowing magma, still bolts of crimson lightning that seemed to lead nowhere, come from nowhere. A cloud parted in that vast stretch of nothingness, and a rush of starlight brushed her bare skin with pale hints of gold. Dax drew in a breath and held it there. She was wonderfully, gloriously naked, everything he had ever wanted in a woman and more. And she was offering herself to him at last.

Rayna knelt down beside him, a silken tendril of hair falling atop his chest. She lifted a hand to touch him but stopped herself, feeling unaccountably shy.

A pained grimace twisted his features. "This is not the time nor the place for maidenly games, Rayna," he said in a low, urgent voice. He hardly had the strength to lift his head, much less the energy required to cajole and seduce her virginal flesh. "Don't even touch me if you can't see it through to the finish. We play for keeps tonight."

Her emerald gaze held him captive for a long moment; then she moved to straddle his body, her knees biting into the stone beneath them. She slowly lowered herself onto his abdomen.

Dax made a small, animal-like sound as her warm flesh settled around him. He'd waited so long for this moment, so terribly long. She'd finally come to him of her own volition, but his first taste of victory was bittersweet. Now that he had her, he knew he could never let her leave.

Rayna held her body stock-still. She could feel the proof of his desire beneath her, a hard ridge of flesh generating a fierce heat that rivaled Hellfire's midday sun. The heat spread to her own loins with the quickness of a grass fire, tendrils of flame that singed fiery little trails up the center of her body. She drew in a sharp breath and dropped her hands to his chest, fingertips exploring the hard-planed, muscular flesh.

At her touch, Dax rose against her desperately. His fingers clenched and unclenched, nails digging into his palms as he tried to lift himself onto his elbows. He cursed in frustration and allowed his arms to fall back to the ledge. "Rayna . . . I can't lift my arms. . . . My breeches."

Careful not to disturb his ankle, she edged backward until she reached his knees, and began fumbling with the fasteners. Her hands shook violently as she tugged off his remaining boot, then carefully pulled the breeches down and off his legs. "What now?" she whispered hesitantly, her gaze trained on his face.

"My tunic." His misery was acute now, reaching such a feverish state that he would soon lose control. "Help me get it off." In all his years he had never been so aroused, never wanted or needed a woman as much as he wanted her. He moaned softly as she pushed the tattered material aside and freed his arms, her fingertips currents of electricity against his bare skin.

Rayna moved back over him and laid her head atop his chest. A pulse at her throat quickened. Her breasts were crushed against him, his lungs rising and falling beneath her in a ragged rhythm that matched her own panicked breathing.

"Oh, sweet heavens," Dax whispered. Her soft, slender body was stretched full-length against him, and he was hungry to touch and taste every enticing inch of her beckoning flesh. "Kiss me, Rayna."

She lowered her mouth to his, tentative, uncertain. He caressed her gently with his lips and tongue, a relentless exploration that quickly moved to the sides of her neck, the thready pulse beating in the hollow of her throat. Her lips suddenly captured his, probing deeply, and Dax knew that her uncertainty had faded, replaced by a rush of desire that nearly equaled his own.

"I never knew that a kiss could be so pleasurable," she said softly against his cheek. A sense of urgency was building inside her. She ran her fingers through his hair, her lips along the line of his jaw.

His heartbeat accelerated to a maddened pace. Trembling from the strain, grimacing from the sheer effort it took to move his weakened limbs, Dax lifted his arms and locked his hands around her shoulders, pulling her forward. Closer. He made a hoarse, tortured sound as his mouth closed around a satiny breast, tugging and suckling fiercely at the crest of her nipple.

Rayna gasped in surprise but didn't flinch away. His tongue was moving in steady, fevered circles, the embrace of his lips growing deeper and more urgent as the interminable seconds passed. The sensation spread downward, a warm, aching heat that left her breathless with desire. She arched her neck and pushed herself against him, closer to his hungry lips, her fingers threading through his night-black hair, tightening her hold on the silken strands as the warmth built to a crescendo inside her.

Dax released her abruptly, gasping for air, and shifted his attentions from one lush mound to the other, moaning against her skin with every breath he drew. His hand slipped between them, sliding downward along the curve of her breast, heating a slow, trembling trail past her waist and abdomen to the silky warmth between her legs. He explored her gently, carefully, kneading the sensitive flesh in tiny circles until she quivered beneath his touch and cried out for more.

Her sharp cry of pleasure shattered his tenuous control. He forced her hips lower and thrust deep inside her, unable to stop himself, unmindful of anything except his own primitive need. Dax felt the fragile barrier give way, heard her pain-filled cry, and only then did he find the strength and will to slacken his frenzied pace.

Blood pounded in his ears as he stared up at her shocked face. It cost him every last pitiable scrap of his strength to regain some semblance of control. He pushed into her gently, his movements carefully measured, heaving a gratified sigh as the taut flesh enfolding him began to loosen and relax.

Rayna moaned softly as the pain began to drift away, and a tight, searing heat flared to life inside her. The narrow ledge of rock and Hellfire's star-strewn sky faded into a formless haze of shadows. His pale, piercing eyes and sharp-angled features became her only reality, the sole inhabitants of her newfound world. She lifted herself instinctively, straddling his hips, and arched her neck and back, plunging her body down the hard length of him until the blaze filled her completely.

Dax drove into her, his hands sliding up her velvety skin to cup her swollen breasts as the rhythm of her movements quickened to match his own. "Rayna . . . oh, gods." He was falling into an abyss, a dark, primal place where nothing existed beyond her willing flesh and his savage need for release. "I never thought . . . never dreamed it would be anything like this."

Rayna stiffened suddenly, her features knotting with pain and exquisite pleasure. She stared at him for a timeless moment, gold-flecked eyes wide and preternaturally bright, glazed with silent wonder.

The first of her tremors tightened around him, and Dax cried out fiercely, joyfully, thrusting himself deeper to claim his own fevered release. His body shuddered, and the abyss closed around him, a dark, rapturous void he knew he would seek again and again.

After long minutes, Rayna slumped against him and curled herself beside his warm, lean body, still quivering with the aftershocks of their coupling. She lay in the predawn darkness and listened to the slow, even sound of his breathing, uncertain whether he had slipped into the black folds of unconsciousness or the quiet arms of sleep. Whichever it was, his body needed the brief respite. And she needed time to be alone with her thoughts, time to come to terms with the tumultuous feelings he had aroused. Even so, his very presence was somehow comforting, the coiled strength of his body a safe haven from the emotional storm brewing inside her.

Turning slightly, she pillowed her head in the hollow of his arm and studied the clear-cut lines of his profile. How and why she'd fallen prey to Daxton Vahnti's dubious charms was a complete mystery. Outwardly, he was arrogant, vain, and coldly manipulative, but there was another, carefully hidden side of him as well. Perhaps it was that secret side that attracted her so, the brooding, joyless man struggling beneath the burdens placed on him by birth. Or perhaps it was simply a matter of her weak flesh and his darkly handsome looks. She stared curiously at his elegantly sculpted face. He had such a striking, noble face. Strong. Aristocratic.

Her thoughts stilled and her blood went cold as the reality of her situation returned in a mind-numbing rush. She had given herself to the Vahnti warlord, wantonly and foolishly gifted her flesh to her captor, her enemy, the most feared and hated man on Nirvanna. The darkling count who had claimed her as his property and somehow stolen her heart, the man whose briefest touch made her pulse quicken with need and lust. She was his property in more than name now, bound to him forever by the flood of emotions coursing inside her. She hated him and loved him. She wanted to flee, and she wanted him near, inside her once again, as firmly bound to her as she was to him. Her heart beat faster. Just the memory of his hot embrace was enough to make her long for more.

She squeezed her lids shut, trying to force back the tears,

trying not to give in to the grief and pain. Nirvanna was lost to her now. She was an outcast, a traitor branded for life by the Vahnti count's sensuous lips. By allowing him to lay waste to her body and heart, she had committed the ultimate betrayal. The young Lakotan adept who had rushed headlong into the night to save her people had instead condemned an entire culture to destruction at her lover's powerful hands.

She turned away from him, crying softly.

The dark fog of unconsciousness gradually lifted from Dax's mind. He opened his eyes and frowned, confused for a moment by the crust of rock above him, the sight of Hellfire's starlit sky. He remembered then. *The vampire-cats . . . Rayna.* A wave of erotic images flashed through his thoughts, heated memories of the past few hours that made him all too aware of the young woman lying quietly beside him. He winced in dismay, both astounded and chagrined by the effect she'd had on him. In all his years no woman had ever driven him to such a frenzy that he actually blacked out from sheer rapture. The very idea was embarrassing.

It was the cat venom, he tried to convince himself. The venom, exhaustion, and twisted ankle would be enough to make any man pass out. But then he had never made love to a shape-shifter before. For a fraction of a second, just as she'd reached to claim her release, he'd seen her eyes change from green to luminous gold. His imagination? Perhaps, but the sight had created a niggle of uncertainty in the back of his mind, a tiny thrill of fear that had added an element of danger to their joining and heightened his rapture all the more. The corners of his mouth curled in a cynical smile. If Rayna was indeed to blame for his moment of weakness, there was only one way to prove it for sure. A tremor ran through his body. It was a mystery he planned to solve many times over in the coming days.

Dax turned toward her slowly and drew her into his arms, burying his face in the sweet bliss of her luxuriant hair. He sighed deeply. Her back was snug and warm against him, tucked securely along his chest. A perfect fit.

It was then that he realized she was weeping, her slender shoulders rising and falling in time with her silent tears. His elation withered abruptly, and a stab of guilt knotted in his throat. She was crying because of him. But what else should he have expected? That she would throw herself into his eager arms and declare her undying passion? A scowl passed over his face, and he cursed himself soundly. He had taken away her world, her life, stripped her of everything she held dear, and tonight he'd robbed her of her innocence as well.

His arms tightened around her, and he pulled her closer, cradling her against his chest. A bleak expression settled over his sharp features. What a clever trap he'd set for himself. He had brought his would-be assassin back to Hellfire simply as a brief diversion, a pretty little plaything to cure his boredom. It had amused him to have an innocent around, to see how long it would take before she succumbed to the infamous Vahnti count.

He sighed raggedly and tried to block the wrenching sounds of her quiet weeping. She had finally succumbed, given him exactly what he wanted, but perversely, he found that was no longer enough. The rules had changed in midgame. He had staked his claim to her virginal body, branded her as his, but he still didn't own her heart and soul. And he wouldn't rest until he possessed those as well.

The sky above him turned a quiet, milky gray, seeming to pause for an uncertain moment between night and day. Dax stared into the distance as Hellfire's sun broached the peaks of glassy mountains, searing the landscape with a violent shade of purple-red. If fortune favored them, help would be arriving soon.

He shifted her body until she was facing him and locked his arms about her slender form. She was still crying, very softly now, the flow of tears finally beginning to ebb. He stroked her hair gently. "It's all right, Rayna," Dax whispered. "We'll be going back to Drakken soon."

He felt her shoulders tense at the news, and his mouth settled in a resolute line. A decent, honorable man would have kept his promise to free her. "You'll be staying with me permanently," Dax told her, determined to make it so. He had never claimed to be a decent or honorable man.

To his surprise, Rayna's only response was a silent, wooden nod against his chest.

A triumphant smile tugged at his lips. She was his now, and he wasn't going to let her go. Ever. The archduke and the entire High Council could go straight to hell, and take the Dunstans with them. He'd kill anyone fool enough to try to take her away.

Chapter Eighteen

"If those ugly beasts so much as twitch an ear, scatter their atoms from here to kingdom come," Haywood ordered quietly.

The nervous guard sighted down the length of her pulse rifle. "Gladly, Commander."

Haywood eyed the wolfens suspiciously. The yellow-haired creatures were standing near the edge of the chasm, growling and tracking the movements of the rescue team with equally suspicious eyes. The officer's mouth thinned. If it had been up to him, the wolfens would be dead already, but orders were orders.

His hard gaze shifted back to the rim, where a huddle of guards were busy winching up the metal basket containing the injured count. Haywood spat into a narrow fissure. They were hoisting up the she-cat, too. "Hurry it up there!" he yelled. "The count needs med attention straightaway!"

As the first basket swung into view, Haywood heaved a sigh of relief and turned to the man standing quietly beside him. "Check him over, Doctor, but leave it at that for the time being if possible. The sooner we get him back to the castle, the better off he'll be."

Lett Bahleigh nodded and slung the med-kit over his shoulder. "Fine by me." Lowering his head into the dusty wind,

Lett picked his way through the rocks to a level area, where he planned to examine his patient.

Haywood shook his head in disgust. Chaos, he thought darkly. First the set-to with the Lyseenes and the scene in the atrium, then Dax foolishly charging off to recapture the girl—alone—like some demented knight chasing after his ladylove. And then the earthquake, the biggest one to strike the northern polar region in over two hundred years. Haywood narrowed his eyes and frowned. An awful, nagging feeling in the pit of his gut kept whispering that the worst was yet to come.

He gave the wolfens another suspicious look. The brutes were still standing sentinel along the chasm rim, showing their teeth and glaring at the guards, but they'd yet to make an aggressive move. As if they were waiting for something, or heeding a strict command not to attack. "Ridiculous," he muttered to himself as the winch arm finally swung toward the plateau and the basket bumped to a jarring stop.

Still muttering, Haywood walked to the edge and surveyed the scene while the guards shifted the battered count from the basket to a med-litter. Dax was bloody, bruised, and gouged, but at least he was alive. He hated to think what might have happened if a patrol ship hadn't spotted the horse running loose on the open plain and homed in on the tracking signal. Sighing, Haywood folded his arms and shook his head in reproach. "Glad we can still count you among the living, Dax."

The Vahnti warlord managed a feeble grin. The scowl on Haywood's face spoke volumes. He would be forced to suffer through endless lectures on proper security protocol in the coming days. "We can argue over my shortcomings later. Give me a status report on the quake damage."

"A few broken bones, some bloodied heads, and minor damage to the castle itself. Two spires and a turret tumbled, but that's about all structurally."

"Good." Dax blew out a grateful breath. Due to his ancestors' foresight, the entire foundation of the structure floated inside a thick bed of silicon gel that allowed the castle to shift and sway with the movement of the gel, not the quake itself. "What about the interior?"

"Some broken vases, that sort of thing. The worst problem

was the herd of rattled aristocrats stampeding about. They caused more damage than the quake. A few clans stayed to help out, but most of your noble guests grabbed their luggage and hightailed it off-planet before the first aftershock hit.''

Dax snorted. He had expected as much. Fortitude wasn't a common trait among the Dominion aristocracy. ''What about the outlying settlements? Any damage estimates yet?''

The soldier didn't answer. Haywood's full attention had shifted to the chasm as the second basket swung over the ledge. A guard rushed to open the metal gate and offered a steadying hand to help the basket's cargo climb out.

Anger flared in Haywood's eyes. The girl had obviously weathered the ordeal far better than Dax. He squared his shoulders and placed his body between her and the litter. ''That's twice now that you've failed,'' Haywood whispered furiously. ''You won't get another chance.'' His hands bunched into fists. ''I'll see to it personally.''

Rayna held her ground against the towering soldier. ''What makes you think I tried again?'' She lifted her chin and returned his accusing glare measure for measure.

''Because I know you're out for blood.'' His face reddened with fury. ''I can see it in your eyes.''

''Let her be, Haywood!'' Dax said sharply.

''Dax—''

''There is absolutely nothing to discuss.'' The Vahnti count's eyes turned deathly cold. ''Rayna is my concern, not yours. Is that clear?''

The feeling of foreboding gnawed at Haywood's gut again. He glanced at his injured friend, then at the disheveled girl, eyes narrowing in comprehension when he realized her dusty garment was nothing but a scanty underrobe. His foreboding turned into sickening certainty. Dax had finally had his way with her, and judging by the fierce, possessive look on his face, it had only served to make his obsession with the girl that much stronger.

''I hope it was worth it, Dax,'' Haywood said quietly. ''You almost got yourself killed.''

The edges of Dax's mouth curled in an enigmatic smile. ''There's more than one way to die, Haywood.''

Haywood arched a questioning brow but said nothing. It was probably better if he didn't know. He shook his head and motioned to a cluster of guards. "Take Count Vahnti up to the doctor and be quick about it. The rest of you, gather the equipment and reload the ship." His eyes swung back to Rayna. "Dr. Bahleigh will see to your needs—after he's finished with Count Vahnti."

Rayna's gaze snapped around at the mention of Lett's name, finally coming to rest on the familiar man standing atop a patch of level ground. Her mouth compressed, and a wave of uncertainty flickered through her eyes. Was it Lett who'd left her that fateful note, pretended friendship, then tried to send her to her death? Or someone else entirely? Haywood March, perhaps? His hostility was a tangible thing, a dark cloud of rage that seemed to seep from his pores every time he happened to glance her way.

She shook her head and clambered up the tilted rock as Lett bent to examine his patient. It could have been anyone within Drakkcn's walls. She stopped a few feet shy of the litter and stared into the Vahnti count's dirt-grimed face. If not for him, if he hadn't risked his life to save her, she would be dead already, the vampire-cats feasting on her dessicated corpse.

As Bahleigh poked and prodded at the wounds in his chest, Dax turned his head to the side and glanced at Rayna. She was standing nearby, watching him shyly, a lost, little-girl look of uncertainty clouding her exotic features. "Rayna, come here," he called softly. She moved closer, and he reached up and clasped her hand, a calculated gesture on his part, one designed to lay her fears to rest, and to show anyone watching that her position in his household had been permanently altered. His pale gaze flicked from Haywood to Bahleigh, conveying a silent challenge.

Lett stiffened and cleared his throat, startled by the sudden flare of warmth and protectiveness he'd seen in Vahnti's chilly eyes. Was it possible that the coldhearted count actually had feelings for Rayna? He discarded the possibility and went back to his examination, his fingers moving along a section of the count's leg. "Your ankle looks bad, Count, but nothing that a stasis cast and regenerative therapy won't cure. Your leg will need to be immobilized for about five days, though. It would be best if you cut your work schedule to a minimum and stayed off it completely while the cast is on.'' He studied the fang mark in the count's neck again, puzzled by his rapid recovery. The puncture wound was still mottled and puffed from the dose of cat venom, but the very fact that Dax Vahnti was alive and breathing proved that his body had already shrugged off the worst of the effects. He shouldn't have survived at all. ''The bed rest will do you good, Count. It will be at least a week until the venom is out of your system completely.''

Dax threw Rayna a heated look and brushed his lips across the back of her hand. The idea of lying abed with her for five days was appealing in the extreme. ''I'll be sure to take your advice to heart, Doctor.''

He smiled inwardly and glanced at Haywood, the beginnings of a plan suddenly taking shape in his mind—an eminently satisfying solution that would solve all his problems in a solitary stroke. ''You never finished your report. What sort of news have you received from the northern settlements?''

Haywood's bushy brows pulled downward in a worried frown. ''It's not good, Dax. Argossa's gone. Flattened.''

A chill prickled down Rayna's arms when she heard the name of the settlement and that it lay to the north. The note had contained instructions to head southeast, in the opposite direction. She studied Lett out of the corner of her eye, watching for any visible reaction to the exchange. His long face remained cool and placid, unchanged in any way.

''The epicenter was only a few miles south of the settlement,'' Haywood continued. ''Most of the people managed to make it into the quake shelters, but there're at least five hundred confirmed dead and well over seven thousand injured.''

''Damn.'' A bleak, tight-lipped expression settled over Dax's features. ''What have you done so far?''

''I ordered a battalion of engineers and emergency response techs in yesterday. I also dispatched assessment teams to the smaller settlements east of Argossa, but the damage isn't nearly as heavy in that area.''

Dax sighed in frustration. He should have been at the castle where he belonged. His grip on Rayna's hand tightened. "Send in another battalion of engineers. Tell them I want that town completely rebuilt within sixty days. Winter's coming, and I'll not have those people shivering around campfires in the cold like refugees on some forgotten Dunstan world." He winced and drew in a sharp breath as Bahleigh shifted his ankle. "I want them to have a clean start, Haywood, with enough chits in their pockets to see them through the worst of it. The same goes for the other settlements."

A small smile tugged at Haywood's mouth. He had expected no less. "I'll see to it."

"And arrange an inspection tour for me," Dax ordered, "but wait until the rescue operations have been completed. I don't want my presence to hinder the aid efforts in any way."

Rayna stared at him curiously. She'd seen many layers and levels of his personality in the past weeks, from arrogant nobleman to passionate lover. But she had never suspected that the Vahnti warlord possessed a smidgen of compassion for the people he ruled.

"I'll arrange it." Haywood paused a moment and cleared his throat, looking distinctly uncomfortable. "There's one other thing you should know."

"Yes?" Dax didn't like his tone of voice or the way he kept shifting from foot to foot, as though this bit of news would be even worse. "Out with it."

The soldier's mouth curled downward in a disgusted grimace. "Archduke Davies and his entourage arrived a little after dawn this morning. Petwitt Dunstan's with them. They're at the castle now—waiting for your return."

Dax let loose with a string of invectives and tightened his hold on Rayna's hand. He didn't give the slightest damn what the council said or ruled. Rayna was his, and would remain so with or without their approval. "I will not allow that bunch of simpering fools to interfere with my personal life!" He tried to sit up, struggling to free himself from the litter and Bahleigh's restraining hands. "I will not give in to them, no matter the cost!"

"Count Vahnti!" Lett grabbed at his shoulders. "Please! If

you keep flailing around like that you'll worsen your condition.''

As his anger flagged, Dax fell back against the litter and clenched his jaw in determination. ''Damn you, Alfred Dunstan,'' he muttered to himself. ''I'll get you yet.''

Lett threw him a probing look but wasn't fool enough to comment. He glanced up at Haywood. ''We need to get him on board the ship, Commander.''

Haywood jerked his head, and the guards lifted the litter. ''Gently now. Take him aboard but don't jostle him any more than you have to.'' He turned to Rayna. ''You, too.''

Rayna slipped free of Dax's grasp and shook her head. ''I'm not leaving.'' The gi scurried from beneath a boulder and threw itself into her arms, winding its long body around her neck. She stroked the creature's glossy brown fur. ''Not without the animals. They'll die if they're left here.''

Haywood's jaw dropped open. She was talking about the wolfens. ''Have you lost your wits, girl?'' He jerked his thumb toward the waiting ship, a curved-wing scad-about equipped to carry a complement of only thirty troops, no more. ''There aren't any cages aboard that ship, and I'm not about to let those brutes dine on our gizzards.''

The guards carrying the litter stumbled over a rock, banging Dax's foot against the side. He swore under his breath and lifted a hand to belay them from carrying him off.

''They won't harm anyone, Commander,'' Rayna told him in a confident voice. Her chin lifted a little higher. ''I swear it.''

''Not a chance!''

''Let the wolfens aboard, Haywood,'' Dax said abruptly. ''Rayna says the beasts won't attack, and I have no reason to doubt her word.'' His gaze caught and held hers for a long second. Her eyes posed a silent question, a glint of surprise that he had interceded on her behalf. He gave her a lazy smile in return.

She grinned back, then ran to get the wolfens.

Haywood stared in disbelief as the guards carried the litter up the ramp and disappeared inside the scad-about. Dax had lost his wits, too. He rubbed at his forehead, feeling a headache building behind his eyes, and kicked at a pile of stones in disgust. The rocks scattered, revealing an object that had been half-buried beneath the stones and a thick layer of ashy dust.

Frowning, Haywood stooped low and picked it up, studying the black leather pouch with wary eyes. It looked fairly new, as if it had been lying in the dust for only a day or so. Dax's? The girl's? There was only one way to find out.

His face went still as he opened the flap and examined the contents, fingers moving slowly over the hilt of the silver knife tucked inside. There was no doubt about the owner's identity now.

"Count Vahnti, I beg you, please reconsider!" Lett Bahleigh's plea reverberated down the castle's central corridor, a sound that seemed to treble in volume as it ricocheted off the stone arches and walls. "Just wear them, sir." Lett clutched at the sleeve of Dax's uniform jacket and held out the metallic boots. "All this trudging about to inspect the quake damage isn't doing your leg a bit of good. Your cast hasn't even had time to tighten properly."

The stern-visaged count ground to an abrupt stop and leaned heavily on the head of his cane, eyeing the half-gravity boots in distaste. "The matter is settled, Doctor. Don't try to press the issue with me again." The temperature in hell would fall to absolute zero before he ever put those things on his feet. "I'd sooner have my foot rot off than glide around looking like that snake Alfred Dunstan!"

Lett stiffened and moved back. "It was not my intention to offend you, Count. I was only concerned about your welfare."

Dax lifted the cane and took several halting steps toward the atrium doors, wincing as his entire weight fell on the heel of the tight stasis cast encasing his leg from toe to knee. Several security guards moved forward to lend a hand, but Dax waved them away. "Don't concern yourself with me, Doctor. As you can see, I'm getting around just fine with a cane." He tapped the end of the cane against a block of stone for emphasis. "Sometimes the old ways are best."

"Very well." Lett tucked the boots beneath his arm as Haywood and another squad of guards strode into view. "But I still wish that you had put off this meeting until you'd had a chance to rest."

"The archduke isn't known for his patience." Dax straightened the braid on his jacket and smoothed back a thick strand of hair that had slipped from his queue. "But if it will set your mind at ease, I do plan to take your recommendation for a lengthy bed rest as soon as the archduke has left Hellfire." His lips curved in an unconscious smile. "Five days . . . that's what you advised, isn't it?"

A flush of heat crawled up Lett's face. The count's expression was darkly sensual. "Yes, sir," he said tightly.

Dax glanced up expectantly as Haywood approached. "Well?" He lifted an inquiring brow.

"You're not going to like it." Haywood pursed his lips and gave him a level stare. "According to our spies, Petwitt and the archduke were together for more than an hour this morning, arguing inside a high-level privacy field our listening devices could penetrate for only a few seconds at a time." He hesitated for a short moment. "We picked up enough to know that Petwitt has already filed a motion on his father's behalf to have her removed from Hellfire immediately if the archduke's decision goes against you."

A surge of rage flared to life inside Dax's eyes. "They *what?*" His bellow echoed down the cavernous corridor.

Haywood winced and straightened his shoulders. "The Dunstans claim that by holding her as a captive you've demonstrated a flagrant disregard for current law and a lapse in ethics that merits severe penalties from the council." He paused a beat, swallowing nervously. There was no telling what Dax would do when he heard the rest. "The motion contends that if the girl is simply set free and returned to Nirvanna, you might be tempted to do her or her people harm in retaliation. So to protect her, Lord Alfred has *generously* offered to become her guardian until such time as she can safely be returned to her homeworld."

"Her guardian!" Dax slammed the cane against a wall. Whispers about Alfred's treatment of women in his household had been drifting around for years, nightmarish stories of depravity and murder that couldn't be substantiated but continued nonetheless. There had even been whispers about the disappearance of one of Dunstan's own sons. The line of his mouth flattened even more. "I'll see Alfred in hell before I allow him to touch Rayna!"

"Dax," Haywood said grimly, "a majority of the High Council is already leaning toward granting the motion. Alfred has garnered support from the Lyseenes and several other clans with an ax to grind against you. The only thing standing in Alfred's way is the archduke himself. He was overheard telling an aide that he knows this whole business is just some sort of ploy by the Dunstans, but if you don't present an adequate defense, he's legally bound to side with the majority."

"Damnation." Dax blew out a furious breath. Alfred was using Rayna as a pawn in their ongoing chess game, a hapless piece being moved about in some grander scheme. But what did he hope to gain?

His eyes darkened dangerously. Alfred's true intentions would become clear to him in the future, but the threat to Rayna had to be dealt with here and now. "Place the troops on full alert. I'm going to offer a legal solution to the archduke that should be more than acceptable, but I want the troops ready in case he rules against me."

Haywood's features visibly tightened. "You're courting disaster, Dax! If the High Council discovers that we've placed our armies on a war footing while the archduke is inside our borders, they'll consider it a treasonable offense."

A blaze of anger shadowed Dax's eyes and voice. "Then so be it. This is one battle I will not allow Alfred to win—no matter the consequences!"

Haywood stared at him in disbelief. Was the Vahnti warlord willing to risk a full-scale war for the sake of a single girl? "Just answer one question," he said in a hushed tone that only Dax could hear. "Is this a matter of principle . . . or is it personal?"

For an instant, Dax's features knotted with uncertainty. Why was he so determined not to relinquish Rayna? Was it his hatred of the Dunstans, or something else entirely? She'd tried to kill him once, could actually transform herself into a fanged beast and do so again. He fought the need to reach inside himself and discover the reason for his obsession, but the question kept echoing through his mind, demanding a truthful answer. The battle raged for long seconds, but in the end he finally lost.

Because you love her, you stupid fool, he admitted to himself. She was exciting, intriguing, magical, and so damned desirable that he might not even survive another night of passion with her. But he wanted to try. He'd been dead inside for more years than he cared to remember, cold, hard, and wary of anyone who dared to try to wheedle their way into his life. But with Rayna he felt reborn, a man who'd suddenly realized that the universe was truly a magical place where anything was possible—even love. And he wanted her to have the same feelings for him. He wanted to look into her preternatural eyes, see those same feelings reflected in their jewel-green depths, share himself and his life as he never had before.

He glanced up at Haywood then, cool and detached as always, but the tautness in his face had given way to a look of quiet confidence, the expression of a grimly determined man who knew where he was going in life and why. "It's personal, Haywood." He would go to war if he had to because he couldn't abide the thought of Rayna being touched by another man. "Very personal." Her magic was for him and him alone.

The soldier expelled a ragged breath and nodded woodenly. He wished he hadn't asked. "I'll place the troops on alert immediately."

Dax heard the sound of light footsteps nearby, the silky rasp of fabric swishing against stone—sounds he'd been waiting for. He shifted the cane and turned, a slow smile of approval curving the corners of his mouth when he spotted Rayna coming toward him on Carlo's arm. He had placed an eager Carlo in charge of preparing her for the meeting with the archduke, a task the boy had obviously taken to heart. The heavy black robe he'd chosen for Rayna was simple yet breathtaking, with tapered sleeves and a high, fluted collar that folded outward to encompass her neck completely. The severity of the color and design was relieved by a floor-length overvest shot with gold thread embroidered in an elaborate pattern of flowers and vines. But the crowning glory was her russet hair. Clean and unbound, it was streaming down her shoulders and back in a shining veil of thick curls.

Dax stared at her raptly, transfixed by the transformation from the dirty, dust-grimed woman he'd last seen to the elegant creature who now stood before him. She looked exotic and regal and utterly sensuous, a devastating fusion of beauty and simmering passion that any man would be loath to resist, even Luc Davies.

A hint of color rose in Rayna's cheeks in response to his lengthy scrutiny. His eyes burned with a silent message, a promise of what the night would bring.

"You look beautiful, Rayna," he told her quietly, and caressed a silky curl.

She fiddled with the overvest self-consciously, her heartbeat quickening. "Thank you." She'd forgotten how tall and striking he looked in the formal black uniform, how intimidating.

Carlo cleared his throat. The heat they were generating was almost tangible. "I take it you approve of the robe I chose, Dax? This is something like what you had in mind, isn't it?"

Dax forced his eyes to Carlo's face. "Exactly." Luc Davies was expecting to see a frightened, bedraggled child, not the elegant young woman he was about to meet.

"It's the robe she's been posing in for my painting," Carlo explained. He touched Rayna's hand reassuringly. "I thought it might suffice for the . . . occasion."

"Most definitely." Dax's eyes narrowed in appreciation. "I can't wait to see the painting itself."

"A few more sittings and it will be done." Carlo's gaze wandered to the ceiling, to a small, perfect triangle at the nexus of an arch. He frowned, studying the shape intently. There was music in geometry. "I believe I'll give it to you when I'm finished. A fitting gift to mark the day."

"I'd like that," Dax said quietly. His cousin's eyes had taken on that distant, glazed look that he'd come to recognize in the past few years.

Rayna tilted her head and looked at Carlo curiously. Though his eyes were vacant and listless, his face was wreathed in a beatific smile, as if he were the sole witness to some profound event beyond mere words. It was odd that she hadn't noticed it before, but there was something strangely familiar about his look. She just couldn't pinpoint what it was.

"Rayna?" Dax held out his arm.

She blinked the thought away and turned her attention back to the Vahnti count. He was staring at her expectantly, his features shadowed by some undefinable emotion. "Yes?" He seemed almost hesitant, unsure of himself.

"Last night, when I said that you'd be remaining here with me, you didn't protest. I need to know if you still feel the same way. . . . I need to know now."

She gazed at him curiously, losing herself in the depths of those cool blue eyes. The events of the previous night were imbued with a dreamlike quality that was almost surreal. Yet she could still feel the touch of his lips, his strong hands, remember every blissful moment in exquisite detail. She remembered her grief as well, the aching sense of loss she'd felt when she realized that Nirvanna was gone from her life forever. "I have nowhere else to go," she said softly, but deep inside her a tiny voice kept whispering that there was nowhere else she wanted to be.

It wasn't the answer Dax had hoped for, but it would do for now. In time she would grow to care for him. He would see to it. "Let's go, then." He took her arm from Carlo, tucked it securely within his own, and hobbled toward the atrium doors.

Footmen pulled the doors outward, and his little party filed inside, a dozen soldiers forming up to follow.

Lett Bahleigh glanced up a pathway, saw a cluster of waiting noblemen, and hesitated near the doors.

Haywood stopped and frowned. "Coming, Doctor?"

His fingers clenched nervously. "Of course."

"I fear Daxton has completely lost his mind, Flavian." Caccia puckered her mouth in distaste. "It's that hideous girl. There's no other explanation for his behavior."

Flavian Modalbeau flashed her teeth in an artificial smile. "Perhaps you're right. It must be that wretched girl's influence."

"Of course it is," Caccia said knowingly. "Why else would Dax abandon his guests in their hour of need and run off into the mountains to track her down?" She made a sad little sigh. "I thought he'd be glad to be rid of her—good riddance to bad rubbish. I never dreamed he would do something so foolish!"

Flavian stared absently at the atrium waterfall over the peak of Caccia's headdress, only half listening to the litany of complaints about Dax's behavior. Caccia, the poor dear, didn't have the slightest clue as to what had motivated her cousin. Flavian's perfect mouth hardened. But she knew. Rayna Syn had somehow managed to burrow her way through that veneer of detachment Dax clung to like a suit of armor.

The rouged line of her mouth thinned even more. The snickering and snide laughter had already started among the Court. Flavian Modalbeau, warlordess of the Modalbeau clan, had been bested by a nobody, an untitled, chitless colonist from some obscure border world. She stared down at the pendant cradled between her breasts. Alfred was indeed her only hope now, her only chance to salvage her clan and regain some semblance of dignity.

On impulse, Flavian jerked the chain over her head and stuffed the crystal inside a pocket. Alfred might have turned her into a spy, but she was sick and tired of him spying on her as well. She'd kept her part of the bargain. If he wanted more from her, he'd have to pay.

"Look, Flavian," Caccia prattled on, "I believe the archduke is watching me. I've caught his eye on me more than once this morning." She smiled prettily and shifted her shoulders, presenting a better view of her plunging neckline.

"I've noticed that, too," Flavian lied. She glanced at the archduke and Petwitt, who were standing near the waterfall, and snorted inwardly. The archduke was staring at the trees with a rapt expression, oblivious to Caccia's presence. Petwitt on the other hand, could hardly tear his eyes from her. He'd been drooling after her for hours now, watching her slender body like a viper preparing to strike. Petwitt glanced their way, and Flavian gave him a brittle smile. He and Caccia deserved each other.

Petwitt lifted a brow and gazed at Flavian steadily, curious as to what had prompted that secretive little smile from his erstwhile ally. He shrugged off the thought and turned his full attention back to the mercurial archduke, vacillating over whether he should interrupt his reverie or not. Vahnti would be arriving before long, and he needed to throw a few more darts in case the archduke was wavering.

Nearby, Luc Davies folded his hands primly and watched a scarlet-plumed bird flit from limb to limb in the bower of a tree. The archduke ignored the pompous nobleman who'd been hovering around him all morning and concentrated on his surroundings. He could hear rustlings in the thick vines, the sort of sounds tiny creatures might make as they moved about, the quiet music of water cascading down the atrium wall into a grottolike pool. Restful, comforting sounds.

"Revolting, isn't it, Your Grace?" Petwitt Dunstan said, misjudging the archduke's expression. He flicked a hand in a dismissive arc that encompassed the entire atrium. "Personally, I believe the existence of this monstrosity alone is proof of Vahnti's unbalanced state."

The archduke turned slightly, annoyed at the interruption, yet not so much that he would give Dunstan a dressing-down. "Do you mean that Daxton himself is responsible for creating this atrium?"

Petwitt smiled thinly. Another point scored. "So I've heard."

Luc stared at the waterfall wistfully. "We weren't aware of that." He wasn't really surprised. The Vahntis had always been innovators and experimenters, strong-willed people who were willing to spend centuries to bring their ideas to fruition. "Must have taken him years to build it."

"Undoubtedly." Petwitt cleared his throat and decided to force the topic of conversation in the desired direction. "Might I impose upon you for a small favor, Your Grace?"

The archduke sighed. "Our answer would depend in part on the favor asked, Petwitt."

"Just a brief word alone with Count Vahnti before your interview. Lord Alfred still hopes for an amicable solution to this sordid affair, and has empowered me to speak on his behalf to our dear friend Daxton."

"Very well." Luc Davies lifted a graceful hand in a grand gesture of dismissal. "The favor is hereby granted."

"Thank you, Your Grace. Clan Dunstan is in your debt." Petwitt gave him a piercing look. "If by chance a measure to increase your stipend soon appears before the council, Lord Alfred plans to look quite favorably on the appeal."

"Yes, yes." The archduke smoothed the silky folds of his flowing robe and adjusted the monogrammed train to the left so that he'd have a better view of the shimmering fabric. He loved the way he looked in gold. "We shall endeavor to remember your father's offer."

The rhythmic sound of soldiers marching down a nearby pathway caught the archduke's attention. He cocked his head and listened. "Perhaps you're about to get the opportunity for that private chat, Petwitt."

"Oh?" Petwitt glanced up as a squad of Vahnti soldiers appeared on a walkway, clearing an open path through a gaggle of noblemen so their limping warlord could walk through unimpeded.

Petwitt's jaw sagged, and his breath caught in his throat when he caught sight of the magnificent creature on Vahnti's arm. Was this the same enchanting waif he'd seen in this very room little more than a month ago? There was nothing childlike or savage about her now. This was a woman in full, passionate bloom, an auburn-haired temptress whose mere presence would be the stuff of many a late-night fantasy when darkness fell this day.

Incredulous, the archduke swung his gaze to Petwitt, his face clouding ominously. "Tell us, Petwitt, is that the *child* whose welfare Lord Alfred is so concerned about?"

Petwitt stared back helplessly. "It's the dress, Your Grace," he finally said, floundering for a plausible explanation. "Vahnti simply gussied her up in order to deceive you that she was older."

"Oh, we see." Luc Davies sighed heavily. What sort of contretemps had the Dunstans embroiled him in now? "Seek your private audience with Count Vahnti and attempt to settle this matter without involving us further.''

"Right away, Your Grace.'' Petwitt bowed and hurried toward the hobbling count, his gaze sweeping over the Vahnti entourage curiously. Bodyguards, mostly, and Haywood March, the Vahnti count's diligent shadow. That half-wit Carlo, an aide or two, and ... Petwitt's nostrils suddenly flared, his only outward display of surprise. He stared in disbelief, trying his utmost to pretend that he wasn't, then finally allowed himself the tiniest of smiles. He would have to congratulate his father upon his return to Malcon, and remember never to underestimate him in the future. Alfred had outdone himself this time. He'd even managed to surprise his own son.

Petwitt's step was lighter, his chin set at a more arrogant angle as he strolled toward Vahnti, finally waylaying his quarry near the edge of the clearing.

"Count Vahnti,'' Petwitt said, and inclined his head. "I'm gratified to see that you survived your latest ordeal. And you, Miss Syn, you look as if the count has been taking remarkably good care of you. Perhaps too much care?''

Dax's eyes turned glacial blue. "What do you want, Petwitt?''

"Just a moment of your time, with the archduke's permission, of course.'' His gaze roved over the girl's face, lingering on her full lips. "Privately.''

Rayna resisted the impulse to back away from Petwitt Dunstan's loathsome perusal. Even now, she could still remember the awful, icy feel of his mouth slithering across the back of her hand.

A muscle tightened along Dax's jaw, and his hand closed around Rayna's arm possessively. "If you want to speak with me, do so here and now, Petwitt. The archduke has been waiting long enough.''

"Very well. My father sends his greetings—and a message.'' His gaze lingered on the girl again. "Lord Alfred fears that you are dragging your feet over my proposal to marry Lady Caccia, so he has very generously offered to withdraw the motion for guardianship over the lovely Miss Syn in exchange for your swift approval of my upcoming nuptials.''

Rayna gave Dax a startled look. "What does he mean?"

His hold on her arm tightened a fraction more. "He means, pet, that if I don't sign the marriage contract between him and Caccia, his father intends to punish me by taking you for himself. Lord Alfred wants to become your guardian for a multitude of reasons." Dax's gaze rested on Petwitt. "But most of all, he wants to take care of you in his own very special way."

Anger crackled in the depths of Rayna's eyes. There was no mistaking his meaning. "Who is this Lord Alfred? I've never even met him before!"

Dax stroked her arm. "And I plan on keeping it that way. He's not a very nice man, Rayna." He jerked a thumb toward Petwitt. "His son here isn't much better, I'm afraid. Come to think of it, I don't believe he would be a suitable choice for a husband—even for Caccia."

Petwitt's composure slipped, and a crimson flush crept up his cheekbones from beneath his manicured beard. "If you refuse to sign the contract, we shall press the issue before the entire High Council immediately." His mouth curved in a tight-lipped smile. "We already have the votes, Count Vahnti. The matter is completely out of your hands."

The grin Dax gave him in return was amiable enough, but his eyes conveyed an entirely different message. "Sorry to disappoint you, Petwitt. But I've never taken kindly to blackmail." A dark, deadly expression swept over his face. "You've said your piece; now get out of our way."

Dax brushed past him, elbowing him aside with enough force to push Petwitt back a foot or so. He half dragged Rayna toward the waterfall.

"I don't understand." Rayna tried to pull her arm away and stop, but he refused to relinquish his hold. "What does all this have to do with me?"

"Nothing, really. They're simply using you for leverage, Rayna, a political weapon against me." He stopped and placed his hands on her shoulders. "By taking you from your home-world and placing a forfeiture claim against you, I opened myself up to charges of misusing my authority." He sighed deeply. "The Dunstans' charges are simply a means to an end, blackmail designed to force me into signing that contract. Pet-witt wants to marry Caccia, more than likely as a preliminary move to killing me and taking over Clan Vahnti.''

Rayna's eyes widened in horror. "Killing you? You make such goings-on sound like everyday occurrences." But then such a goal shouldn't come as a terrible surprise. She had tried to do the very same thing herself.

Dax smiled ruefully. "The Dunstans are my enemies, Rayna, and since I'm warlord of the Vahnti clan, that makes them your enemies, too. Never forget that. They'll stop at nothing to get what they want, and at the moment, Lord Alfred has decided that he wants you."

Rayna shook her head in confusion. She would never understand these people or their convoluted way of life. "But why?"

"I thought that would be obvious." Dax touched her cheek lightly. "He wants you because you're mine." A blend of concern and conviction darkened the hue of his eyes. "Just know that I have absolutely no intention of letting him have his way. I have a counterplan that should settle the situation quite nicely. Alfred will never get his filthy hands on you." He smiled slowly and tugged on her hand. "So let's take care of this business once and for all, shall we?"

Rayna allowed him to pull her along, casting wary glances at him as they walked toward the waterfall. The secretive smile he'd given her had been almost gleeful.

Dax drew to a stop a few feet shy of the gold-clad archduke and bowed formally, then straightened and shifted a goodly portion of his weight to the head of the cane. His leg was starting to ache abominably. "I apologize for the delay, Your Grace." His fingers tightened around Rayna's arm. "I was unavoidably detained."

A crowd gathered nearby, anxious to hear the exchange. Petwitt pushed his way to the forefront.

Luc Davies studied Dax through slitted eyes. "We're gratified that your injuries don't appear too serious, Count Vahnti. Your death would have been a regrettable event."

"I'm not an easy man to kill." He cut a glance at the woman beside him and slid his hand down her arm, wrapping his fingers about her own. "As any number of people will undoubtedly attest."

Rayna arched a brow at his comment, but remained silent, focusing the full force of her gaze on the strange man standing before them like some glittering bird with golden plumage. This was the legendary Luc Davies? The fearsome ruler of all the Dominion clans? She swallowed a startled laugh. The archduke was small, pale, and extraordinarily thin, with a round, cherubic face topped by a thick crown of snow white curls.

Luc Davies straightened his back, a bit disconcerted by the girl's unwavering scrutiny, as though she had passed judgment and found him wanting in some way. "You think we are strange to look upon, child?"

Rayna continued to stare. "You're not at all what I expected."

He rearranged his face into a pinched smile. "Neither are you, my dear." She had such remarkable eyes—an eerie, fathomless green so bright it seemed to capture and reflect all trace of light. "We were expecting someone far less . . . womanly." He lifted a brow. "How old *are* you, child?"

"I'm a woman, not a child," Rayna said indignantly. "I have already seen eighteen summers."

Dax winced. That meant she might be only seventeen.

The archduke sighed melodramatically and threw Dax a sharp look. Undoubtedly Count Vahnti had personally seen to her transformation from child to woman. He decided to dispense with the pleasantries and get to the matter at hand. "Womanly or not, the fact still remains that Count Vahnti has acted most abominably by making a forfeiture claim against a minor's life, regardless of any illegal act you might have committed to spur his claim. The laws of forfeiture were enacted during a barbaric period of Dominion history, a less genteel time when assassination was an everyday occurence." A brittle edge of irony crept into his voice. "Ours may not be a perfect society, but such unsavory behavior has been relegated to the past." That was news his food and wine tasters would be surprised to hear, as well as his bodyguards. "We humans are far more civilized now."

Dax snorted beneath his breath.

The archduke fixed Dax with an artificial glare, amused that the scoundrel had actually had the temerity to steal the young beauty from her homeworld and claim her as his own. His gaze swept over the girl again. If he'd been a bit younger, he might have been tempted to steal her himself.

Luc flicked at an imaginary speck of lint on his train, annoyed that he'd been forced into the awkward position of passing moral judgment on one of his favorites for something he might have done himself. But the Dunstans had left him little choice. He tilted his head and forced himself to glower. "Count Vahnti, you had no right to twist an outmoded law to suit your own purposes, and we're here to see that your wrong is set right. To that end a motion has been filed to forcibly remove this *child* from your keeping and declare Lord Alfred Dunstan as her guardian until she has reached the age of legal consent. Do you have any final comment before we render our judgment?"

"Your Grace," Dax said in a carefully measured voice, "I respectfully demand that you declare all motions null and void immediately."

The archduke flushed angrily, a tidal wave of pink against his alabaster skin. "You demand?"

"Yes." Dax stared at him intently. "And rightly so."

Luc's flush receded. There had been a subtle flaring of mischief and triumph in Daxton's cool eyes, a silent warning that the Dunstans were treading on perilous ground. "Oh?" The archduke decided to play along. It would please him greatly to see that offal Petwitt get his comeuppance. "Be so kind as to explain yourself, Count Vahnti."

Dax smiled and wrapped an arm about Rayna's slender waist, pulling her tight against him. "Because I cannot and will not allow Lord Alfred to assume guardianship over my future wife."

Rayna gasped and stared at him in disbelief.

There was a screech nearby and a dull, fleshy thud, followed by a ripple of movement as a bevy of noblemen rushed to Caccia Vahnti's aid.

Haywood winced and shook his head. Only Carlo seemed unsurprised. He was standing on the fringes of the crowd, grinning, as if he'd known all along what Dax intended.

The archduke gave Daxton Vahnti a covert smile. An elegantly simple solution, to be sure, but one the council and the Dunstans would be forced to accept, especially if he gave the union his blessing. "We must admit, Count Vahnti, that your little announcement has taken us completely by surprise." He inclined his head toward the group of noblemen fawning over Caccia Vahnti. "As well as certain members of your own family."

"So it would seem."

Luc Davies's gaze swept over the cause of all the commotion. The Nirvannan girl was white-faced with shock, staring at the man who'd just announced that he planned to marry her as though she'd suddenly been rendered deaf and mute. "And the young lady in question? How does she feel about your intentions?"

Dax studied her face carefully, searching for any outward clues as to how she felt. Her heart-shaped face was devoid of any expression, but her eyes held a glint of shock as well as something akin to silent wonder. He raised a brow. At least she hadn't run screaming from the atrium, which was what he'd feared most, and why he hadn't warned her beforehand. He bent toward her, so close his lips brushed across the lobe of her ear. "You said you would stay," he whispered to her. "I'm simply holding you to your word."

She caught and held his pale gaze, her brow clouding with an uncertain frown. "By wedding me?" she managed to whisper.

"It's a workable solution, Rayna," he said in a hushed tone. "If I wed you, the charges will have to be dropped, and Alfred will have no claim over you."

A shadow of pain moved across her eyes. For a fleeting moment, she'd foolishly thought that he might actually care for her. But emotions had played no part in his decision. He wanted to marry her only in order to extricate himself from a political dilemma, a convenient ruse designed to prevent the Dunstans from achieving their goal.

Her mouth compressed in a grim white line. If he could be that cold and calculating, so could she. "And what of me?

233

What benefit would I receive for agreeing to this scheme?''

At her words and tone, there was a subtle tightening along his mouth that mirrored her own. *How ironic.* After years of running from just such a moment, the woman he'd finally chosen to be his wife had responded by making demands on him. "What do you want?" he whispered hoarsely.

"I'll stay here with you—I'll even wed you—but only if you promise to stop forcing my people to leave the plains." Her chin inched higher. "You also have to promise that you'll put a stop to your clan's mining operations on Nirvanna immediately."

Relief washed over him. She wanted nothing for herself. "You have my word," Dax said swiftly. The concession to halt the relocations was a small price to pay in order to win her trust. And the mining activities on Nirvanna had already shifted from the planet's surface to its ore-laden moons. Such an agreement might even work to his advantage. If putting a stop to the relocations stopped the fighting, perhaps he could negotiate an agreement with Rayna's people, elicit their co-operation instead of their animosity. His clan was set to begin harvesting Nirvanna's reedlike grass in a matter of weeks, a monumental task that would span an entire continent. Perhaps the Nirvannans could be induced to temper their objections and aid in the harvest itself. "On my honor as the Vahnti warlord."

"Agreed," she said in a tiny voice. By wedding him, she could save her people, her entire way of life, as well as safe-guard the plains for future generations. In years to come perhaps those partial achievements would balance out against her betrayal. And as the Vahnti countess, she might be able to influence his future actions in some small way, even if their marriage was in name alone.

He expelled the tense breath he'd been holding. Now he had to prove to her that he could make a halfway decent hus-band—a formidable challenge. "I promise you won't regret it, Rayna."

"Count Vahnti," Luc Davies said impatiently, "we asked a simple question and are waiting for your reply. We did not expect you to engage in protracted negotiations."

"The young lady in question will answer for herself, Your Grace."

Rayna lifted her gaze and met the archduke's head-on. "I have chosen to remain on Hellfire . . . and to marry Count Vahnti."

A murmur ran through the crowd. Flavian turned a deathly shade of white.

The archduke pursed his lips in a small smile. The day's events would be grist for talk among the court for months to come. He had overheard enough of their whispered conversation to know that Daxton had been reduced to bargaining over his proposal. "Have you made this decision of your own free will?"

"I have," Rayna answered gravely.

"Then the union has my blessing. All motions and charges brought by Clan Dunstan are hereby declared null and void." He straightened his train. Thank goodness this business has been settled. Maybe now he could have a bite to eat. "We would be honored to host an engagement celebration for you and your future countess, Daxton. In one month's time, perhaps?"

Dax would have preferred to marry her here and now, but the archduke had other ideas, and he was in no position to object. "Thank you, Your Grace. That's very kind of you."

Petwitt pushed past a stone-faced Flavian and shouldered his way toward the archduke, his face turning a florid shade of red. "This is an outrage! Clan Dunstan objects, and will not allow this matter to be swept under a mat on a sham legal technicality!"

The archduke's round face went completely still. "It was at your behest that we came here, Petwitt. By what right do you now object to the decision that you forced us to render?"

Petwitt bit down on his lower lip to silence himself. Plots within plots, he reminded himself. All wasn't lost. The entire affair had simply been a distraction, and on that level it had worked admirably well. "I apologize for my outburst, Your Grace." The timetable would have to be stepped up, but Caccia Vahnti would still be his before the year was out. They had to move fast, though, before Vahnti wed his beautiful little captive and produced an heir.

Dax gave Petwitt a victorious smile, then turned back to the archduke. "Would you care to join us for a light repast before you leave, Your Grace?" He tucked Rayna's hand within his own and shifted his weight to the cane.

"By all means." The archduke adjusted his train and started walking toward the pathway Daxton had indicated, a bevy of courtiers following at a discreet distance.

Petwitt glared after them, lingering near the waterfall long after all but a few stragglers had made their way to the doors. He strolled toward the miserable-looking young man loitering near the pathway, doing his best to act nonchalant for the security eyes.

He surveyed the area surreptitiously as he neared the young man, just to be sure no one was watching, then touched a pad on his wristcom. A privacy field shimmered to life, enveloping them both. For years he'd wondered about the identity of the high-level spy Alfred had managed to slip into Clan Vahnti. Now he knew. "Hello, brother."

Lett wheeled around, his eyes widening in horror. "Are you mad?" he hissed quietly. "You're going to get us both killed!"

Petwitt smiled. "Don't worry. I turned on a privacy field."

Lett's face was gray with fear. "Do you think that matters? The Vahnti security force can cut through most any field in existence."

"Oh, don't be too concerned. This will only take a moment. Besides, I'm sure the count's little announcement has created such a stir that we're the last thing on anyone's mind." Petwitt arched a brow. "I must admit I was surprised to see you here. Everyone thought you were long dead."

Lett's expression darkened. "I'm sure you did." It had been Petwitt who'd encouraged him to bed their stepmother, and was probably the one who'd seen to it that they were caught in the act.

"After all," Petwitt went on, "Father is not known for his compassion—especially where his wives are concerned."

"Compassion had nothing to do with it. This is my penance. Either I agreed to Father's demands, or he was going to have me killed. I wasn't ready to die."

"Wise decision." Petwitt's mind raced. There had to be a way that he could use Marcus's position to his own advantage. "Your partner in crime recently suffered a very unfortunate fate. Sadly, Father is now a widower again, but I'm sure we'll have a new mother again soon . . . very soon, if he has his way." He had seen the hunger in Alfred's eyes when he saw the first holos of Rayna Syn. She had swiftly become the star of his father's virtual fantasies. The fact that she belonged to Vahnti had only served to make her all the more desirable.

Sweat beaded on Lett's forehead. He didn't know which fate was worse—worrying about the possibility of his own father having him killed, or being unveiled as a Dunstan spy. Either way he would end up very dead. But right now, discovery was the most immediate threat. He closed his eyes and turned away from Petwitt, pretending to stare at a tree. The conversation had gone on too long. Someone was bound to notice. "What do you want, Petwitt?" he whispered. "Make it fast."

"Since the archduke saw fit to rule in Vahnti's favor, Father has issued a new set of instructions." It was an outright lie, but Marcus wouldn't know that. By the time he did, it would be too late. Plots within plots. He had no intention of allowing Alfred the chance to act out his virtual lust and make Rayna Syn his new stepmother. She was too much of a variable, a very real threat to his long-term plans. "As soon as the opportunity presents itself, you're to kill the count's intended wife."

Lett spun back around, his face twisting with shock and horror. "No!" he said furiously. "I won't do it!" Anguish welled in his voice and eyes. "I can't!"

Petwitt understood instantly. Poor foolish Marcus had done it again. He gave his brother a vicious smile. "I see your propensity for lusting after unattainable women hasn't changed. A dangerous habit, Marcus. I thought you would have learned your lesson the last time."

237

A look of abject misery passed over Lett's face. "I can't kill her."

"Then kill the count instead," Petwitt said casually. "Just do it fast." That would work, too.

Chapter Nineteen

"He *what?*" Alfred Dunstan reddened and exploded from his chair. "Marry her!" His fist collided with the top of his private dining table, causing several passionberries stuffed with Andwillian chocolate to leap from his plate. "I won't allow it!"

White-faced servants scurried quietly toward the doors, their bodies hunched low to make themselves as small a target as possible. In a fit of pique, Alfred snatched a goblet from the table and flung it at a servant's retreating back. The old man yelped and scuttled faster. "I will not allow that Vahnti bastard to steal what's rightfully mine!"

Petwitt blinked at that. His father's reasoning was hopelessly obscure at times.

His eyes flattening dangerously, Alfred lumbered around the circular table to confront his son, wincing from the strain when he realized that he'd neglected to switch his half-gravity boots on. "It's been days since you left Hellfire! Why didn't you warn me of this before, Petwitt? The least you could have done was to send a comm message from your ship!"

Petwitt suppressed a smile. Comm his father the news and miss seeing his reaction firsthand? "Forgive me, Father. I simply assumed that Flavian or one of your other spies had already informed you of Vahnti's plans."

Alfred glowered at his son. "How many times do I have to tell you, Petwitt? Only fools and half-wits make assumptions! No one told me a cursed thing, including that bitch Flavian!" He lifted his gaze toward the gold-plated ceiling, as if to plead with a higher being to end his suffering. "I'm surrounded by incompetents!"

"Again, Father, I apologize for my oversight." Petwitt's dispassionate gaze drifted over his father's corpulent body and rage-ruddied face, which had turned an unhealthy shade of red. Terminally red? As he watched, Alfred's complexion faded to a more normal hue. Petwitt sighed inwardly. *Too bad.* He'd been hoping for years that Alfred's violent temper tantrums and obsession with food would lead to a convenient demise, but so far his father's constitution had proved immune to both.

"Perhaps another bite of sweets would make you feel better," Petwitt suggested. "I'll have the servants send in a new tray if you wish." Surely his body couldn't stand much more. "All your favorites."

"Don't tell me what to do, you ungrateful oaf!" Alfred's face settled into petulant lines. "Damn that Vahnti! This changes everything. If he dies with an heir, your marriage to Caccia will be meaningless! The title and clan holdings will pass to a blasted infant!" He lifted a hand and shook his fist at empty air. "And rest assured, with Vahnti dead, Haywood March will make certain that no assassin ever gets close enough to the mother or infant to rid the universe of them!"

Petwitt's mouth tightened. His marriage to Caccia was the culmination of all his aspirations. With Vahnti out of the way, the pliable dimwit would assume the title, and he would become the de facto ruler of her clan. Then, when Alfred died, either on his own or with a bit of assistance, he would claim his rightful position as Dunstan warlord as well—making him the richest and most powerful man in all the Dominion. No mewling infant was going to stand in his way. "Then I suggest that we step up the timetable and dispose of Vahnti as soon as possible." He didn't add that he'd already instructed Marcus to do just that, though chances were that his miserable excuse for a brother wouldn't go through with it. Marcus had never had the stomach for murder. "The count doesn't have the slightest intention of signing the marriage contract, no matter what inducements we offer, so I think we should just kill him and be done with it—before he has a chance to plant his seed in the girl's belly."

Alfred rolled his eyes. "Think, Petwitt! Caccia would never marry you if she suspected that our clan was involved in her cousin's death. Haywood March would make sure of that, too."

"I've already considered that, and come up with a viable solution." He would just have to coax Caccia into marrying him by other means. Blackmail possibly. A simple enough task considering how endearingly stupid she was. "Blame for his death could be placed elsewhere, Father, perhaps squarely at the feet of those pesky savages on Nirvanna. They already despise Vahnti anyway. How hard would it be to stage a little insurrection to cover up his death?" He shook his head in mock sadness. "War is such hell. Poor Haywood March might even be killed in a vain attempt to save his warlord's life."

Alfred pursed his lips and thought. For once Petwitt had come up with a workable idea. In one bold stroke he could have everything he'd ever wanted—and more. Nirvanna, Vahnti's death, and the lovely Rayna Syn as well. "Hmmm. It might work at that." If Vahnti was enamored of the girl enough to marry her . . . "Even the vilest of creatures is attracted to the scent of musk," he mused aloud.

"The girl?"

"Of course. She'll be the bait we use to lure Vahnti into a trap." Alfred stroked the virtual headset hanging from a cord on his neck, absently caressing the slick black metal. Ever since his first glimpse of Rayna Syn through Flavian's pendant, she had held the lead role in his virtual illusions, a luscious blend of innocence and sultry vixen he found completely irresistible. And once Vahnti had been permanently dispatched, she would be his to do with as he pleased. In the flesh. Alfred smiled suddenly. If she pleased him greatly, he might even make her the new Lady Dunstan for a while.

Still mulling over the possibilities, Alfred moved back to the table and eased his bulk into the chair. His original intent was to marry Petwitt off to Caccia, quietly dispose of Vahnti, then take Nirvanna for himself, each event carefully timed to take place over a period of months to avoid suspicion. But if he used the girl as a lure, he could reverse the order of events and accomplish it all in a solitary day. And then there was

Flavian, of course. The contracts between the Vahnti and Modalbeau clans were signed, and several brigades of Vahnti troops would soon be on their way to the new treaty base on Gamma Three, effectively dividing Vahnti's forces. Alfred snorted to himself. He'd known Daxton Vahnti wouldn't be able to resist the temptation of acquiring a base on Gamma Three in return for aiding Flavian, even if such a move would leave his clan's territory vulnerable to attack.

Alfred made a contented sound. All he needed now was a tantalizing morsel of bait to set the trap. He popped a passionberry into his mouth and gave his son a predatory grin. "We'll have to steal the girl, of course."

Petwitt gave his father a benign smile in return. "That shouldn't present too much of a problem. Vahnti can't keep her locked inside the shield wall forever—and I hear she's on very friendly terms with a certain doctor named Bahleigh." He inclined his head slightly, a wordless acknowledgment of Alfred's tactical brilliance in sending Marcus to Hellfire. "Perhaps the good doctor could be induced to lend his assistance."

Alfred glanced at him sharply. So Petwitt had discovered that Marcus was still alive, and on Hellfire. He lifted one shoulder in a diffident shrug. "Perhaps."

"And if something goes awry," Petwitt added, "the unfortunate doctor can be held responsible."

Alfred suppressed a snort of amusement. His eldest son never tired of plotting ways to dispose of his siblings. "The success or failure of a covert operation can never be trusted to a single intelligence asset." He fell silent for a moment as he thought. Flavian would prove useful in the endeavor, especially if she thought she'd be reunited with Daxton Vahnti as a reward for services rendered. Poor, love-starved Flavian wouldn't be told that the object of her desire would be dead within weeks anyway. "This will be a concerted effort, with you acting as my personal liaison to our operatives on Hellfire. That will increase the chances of success, and if anything does go wrong, the blame will be cast in more than one direction."

Petwitt's eyes narrowed slightly, but he kept his face expressionless. Just as long as his father didn't throw blame in *his* direction. If Alfred made him a scapegoat, Vahnti would hound him to the edge of the galaxy in order to extract his revenge. A chill slithered up Petwitt's backbone. That would never do at all. "There is another possibility, Father. The girl has already made at least one attempt to escape Hellfire and return to Nirvanna. What if we plant evidence that her next disappearance is simply a repeat performance? That way Vahnti will suspect no one—until it's far too late."

After pouring himself another goblet of wine, Alfred arched a brow and lifted the golden chalice toward his son in salute. "I must admit, Petwitt, you do have occasional moments of absolute genius."

Petwitt's left eyebrow lifted in an exact replica of his father's expression. He smiled slowly. "Why, thank you, Father. It's an inherited talent."

"Naturally."

Caccia hesitated outside the library doors and sighed melodramatically. Rayna was in there, as well as her blithering idiot of a brother. Sitting for that damnable painting again. Caccia gave the woman standing next to her a baleful glare. "Do we really have to go in there, Flavian? I'm not particularly thrilled at the prospect of seeing either one of them right now."

"Protocol, dear." Flavian smiled slightly. "I must take my leave of Rayna before Commander March and I depart for the new base on Gamma Three. She is the Vahnti warlord's future wife, after all."

"Pah!" Caccia puckered her mouth in distaste. "Not if I have anything to say about it!"

"You don't," Flavian said in a matter-of-fact tone. "Dax is your liege lord. If he wants to marry some lowly little nobody, there's absolutely nothing you can do to stop him." Her features hardening, she glanced down the corridor covertly, then leaned toward Caccia until her mouth was almost even with her ear. The pale gold sheen of a privacy field shimmered into existence. "Without help, that is," Flavian whispered softly.

Caccia's eyes widened, and a swift, probing smile feathered

her generous lips. "What sort of help?" she whispered back, careful to keep her voice as low as Flavian's.

"I have friends, Caccia . . . powerful friends who are no more pleased about Dax's plans than you. They stand ready and willing to offer their assistance. All you have to do is give the word."

"And you, Flavian?" Caccia watched her expression carefully. "What do you hope to gain?" The Modalbeau warlordess never embroiled herself in any scheme unless she had a personal stake in the outcome.

A flicker of emotion darkened Flavian's eyes. "That's none of your concern."

Caccia smiled knowingly. It was common knowledge that Flavian had been enamored of Dax for years—a dogged, valiant pursuit that had proved fruitless so far. "I see. . . ." Rayna Syn was now a major obstacle to Flavian's long-term goal of becoming the next Vahnti countess, a union that would improve her own position as well as her clan's. But with Dax's intended wife permanently removed from the scene, Flavian's path would be clear again. "Just how do your 'friends' hope to accomplish this remarkable feat?"

Flavian eyed her guardedly. The less Caccia knew, the better for all concerned. "Certainly not by placing a foolish note inside a hollow tree." She flashed her teeth in a sly smile. "That was very indiscreet of you, dear. You should have never done the deed yourself. I'm surprised you weren't caught."

Caccia's face turned a deathly shade of white. "How did you know?" she said without thinking, then cursed herself soundly for blurting out her guilt.

"If you really must know, a member of my clan saw you sneaking around the atrium and decided to investigate. But don't worry. I'll keep your dirty little secret—if you'll promise to keep mine." The Modalbeau warlordess smiled again, a hard, thin smile that never reached her deep-set eyes. "Our goals intersect, Caccia. You want the girl gone, and I want Dax. An alliance would be beneficial as well as practical."

A shiver crawled along Caccia's arms. If Dax ever discovered her part in this . . . "Dax can never find out," she said in a breathless whisper.

"I assure you he won't. The girl will simply disappear. Dax will think she's just run off again, but this time he won't be able to find her."

A pulse beat at Caccia's temple as she weighed her decision. "All right," she said finally. "What do you want me to do?"

"Befriend her. Stay as close to her as possible. If she leaves the protection of the shield wall for any reason, be sure you're with her; then wait."

A look of excitement flitted across Caccia's face. "What am I to wait for?"

Flavian pulled the pendant from a pocket and pushed it into her hand. "Just wear the pendant at all times. When the opportunity presents itself, my friends will know . . . and act."

Caccia's excitement rose to a fever pitch. She slipped the chain over her neck and stared at the crystal in awe. "It's a spy device, isn't it?" She laughed and cupped the pendant in her palm possessively. Who would have ever imagined that she would end up being a Modalbeau spy? "Oh, what great fun this is going to be!" She was going to make such a wonderful spy. Clever, astute, and beautiful as well. Men would be powerless to withhold their secrets from her.

Flavian's eyes narrowed. The girl was a complete idiot. Didn't she understand the risks inherent in such a venture? She sighed inwardly. She should have never let Alfred talk her into this insanity. But if she truly wanted Dax, it was the only way.

"Compose yourself, Caccia," Flavian ordered. The fool was dancing about and admiring her reflection in the crystal's surface. If she only knew who might be gazing back at her in return. "You must conduct yourself as if nothing out of the ordinary has occurred."

Caccia's amusement faded. "Of course. How silly of me." She was a spy now. She had to act the part.

Flavian switched off the privacy field and inclined her head toward the library doors. "Shall we?"

"By all means."

Hands folded behind his back, Haywood stood at parade rest and waited for Dax to respond in some way, just as he had for the past five minutes or so. The absence of noise in Dax's cavernous office suite was almost like a sound in itself, and with each passing second, the Vahnti count's silence became colder and more lethal.

Dax glanced up finally and stared. A credit chit clutched in his hand fell to the top of his desk, clinking against the polished obsidian.

Haywood steeled himself. "I thought you should see the evidence before I left with the troops for Gamma Three," he said in his own defense. "I know I should have given the pouch to you before now, but I wanted to see if I could come up with a reasonable explanation first."

"And did you?" Dax said tightly. Haywood had waited two weeks before presenting him with the pouch. Time that he'd used to try to prove Rayna was a spy.

"No . . . There's only one explanation for everything."

Dax fingered the delicate filigree etched into the hilt of Rayna's knife, as well as the large stack of credit chits that had tumbled from the pouch Haywood had placed on his desk. There was indeed a spy within Drakken's walls, either that or someone so cruel and malicious that their perfidy had very nearly cost both him and Rayna their lives. The proof was sitting atop his desk in the form of the stolen shield key, the generous supply of chits, and the false instructions scribed on the thin sheet of parchment secreted in the pouch along with the knife.

All trace of animation withered from his face. Someone he trusted was involved in this, had been since the amulet first disappeared, someone capable of slipping into his office at will. And whoever it was, Rayna was possibly covering for them, either out of a misplaced sense of loyalty or deathly fear. She had never said a single word about the pouch or the false directions, and still refused to tell him how she had gotten the amulet, adamantly insisting that if blame was to be cast, then it should be thrown at her.

Dax gazed up at his military commander for a full ten seconds, his hard, probing stare more ominous than his silence had been. "Why did you take so long to give these to me, Haywood?" Was there another, darker reason other than trying to prove Rayna's guilt? "I should have been informed immediately."

Haywood cleared his throat and shifted uncomfortably. "Because I was positive that Rayna was involved in some way, Dax. You have to admit that a lot of strange things have happened since she came to Hellfire."

"And now?"

"I think she's the focal point of these events for some reason, but not the root cause." His shoulders rose in a slight shrug. "The contents of the pouch speak for themselves. Whoever did this went to a lot of trouble to set her up. They managed to steal a shield key from the captain of security, generate an untraceable computer note, as well as break into your office to get the knife. And judging by the number of chits hidden in the pouch, it was someone with access to unlimited funds." Haywood pursed his lips. "Rayna was definitely manipulated," he said finally, "either by a professional or someone with enough intelligence not to leave tracks. I don't know which, but whoever it was wanted her dead."

Dax's eyes turned a flinty, glacial blue. Haywood, perhaps? His hatred of Rayna bordered on obsession. But then again, the guilty party didn't necessarily have to be someone inside Clan Vahnti. Scores of hunt guests had been roaming Drakken's halls at the time. "I want to know who did this," he said in a voice as cold and sharp as his eyes. "And I want to know why."

"I have a few suspicions, but no proof at all." Haywood sighed in frustration. "As for why, who knows? Perhaps someone thought you were growing too close to her, or a member of the security force decided to take his own revenge for what she did on Nirvanna. Rayna may even have enemies we're not aware of—or it could be a feint for an attack against you."

Dax's forehead clouded with a sudden frown. He hadn't considered the possibility that Rayna might have enemies herself. Beyond her connection with him, what could anyone hold against her? Once they were married, she would indeed wield significant political power, but until then she was a relative unknown, a simple colonist from a Vahnti border world. His thoughts stilled. Rayna was no simple colonist. She was a shape-shifter, a strange and perilous ability that might be perceived as a threat by some, a valuable commodity by others. For the past two weeks he had simply assumed that he was the only one who knew, and had planned to keep it that way. Always. But what if someone else had discovered her secret and passed the word along? Who had gotten close enough to Rayna to discover such a thing? Haywood, with his constant spying? Or Carlo with his soothing words and gentle ways? Certainly not Caccia, who had bared her hatred for all to see.

"Lett Bahleigh," Dax said quietly.

"Impossible." Haywood shook his head vigorously. "I did the background check on him myself when he applied for clan membership. His scientific and medical credentials are impeccable."

"What of his family?"

"The Bahleighs are a nonaligned tribe from Janus Four who declared their neutrality over eleven generations ago. They specialize in the sciences and offer their loyalty and service to other clans in return for a generous stipend."

"What else?"

"Nothing unusual. He checked out clean."

"Dig deeper," Dax ordered, uncertain whether his motivation came from jealousy or suspicion. "I want to know more."

"All right, but I don't think you'll find anything there. The Bahleighs have never been involved in any sort of clan chicanery."

"There's always a first time." Until he got the report, Dax would keep a much closer eye on young Lett. "In the meantime, I want the guard force assigned to Rayna doubled."

Haywood nodded. "I'll see to it before I leave. Watch yourself while I'm gone, Dax." Gamma Three was light-years from Vahnti space. Too far to make a hasty return should the need arise. "Stay close to the castle."

"I go to Argossa in five days, then on to the northeastern settlements to inspect the quake damage."

"Cancel the trip and stay inside the shield wall."

"I've waited long enough as it is. I need to make an appearance to show those people they haven't been forgotten.''

"Then promise me that you'll take along a sufficient guard force to counter an attack.''

"I plan to.'' Dax decided to take Rayna along, too. He'd rather have her with him and know that she was protected than leave it to chance.

"I have an itchy feeling about all this, Dax. I fear there's more trouble on the way.''

"So do I.'' Dax pressed his lips flat and frowned, brooding over the possibilities. No one had ever been foolish enough to stage a direct assault against him on Hellfire. But there was a first time for everything.

Chapter Twenty

A freshening wind curled through treetops dappled with the rubicund hues of Hellfire's approaching winter. Flameflies weaved and arced through the swaying grass, gracefully darting through the thick sea of yellow stalks at the edge of the clearing. Dax lengthened his stride, glad finally to be free of the castle and the hated stasis cast, eager to see and be with Rayna again.

His pulse quickened when he caught a glimpse of her. She was sitting at the center of the clearing, eyes closed, arms outstretched to catch the wind, at one with herself and her surroundings. Nearby, the wolfens lay in a patch of sunlight, vigilant ears cocked in his direction, guarding their youthful mistress while she lost herself in some unseen rapture. The look on her face was blissful, enchanting, so utterly compelling that he was powerless to resist.

On impulse he tapped a switch on his wristcom. It was early yet. He still had an hour before the servers arrived with his surprise—the table, chairs, and special luncheon he'd ordered brought to the clearing for their midday meal. Time enough for what he had in mind.

"Yes, Count Vahnti?" a voice answered.

"Turn off the eyes around the southwestern clearing."

"Sir, Commander March said—"

"Turn them off, Robichau, and order the security detail to withdraw to the far side of the woods." To hell with Haywood's admonitions. The wolfens would be security enough for a while.

A muffled sigh whispered through the tiny speaker. "As you wish, my lord."

"Thank you." Grinning, Dax stepped from the shadow of a tree and strode purposefully toward the center of the clearing.

Rayna lowered her arms and turned, a shiver of awareness spiraling through her blood. She had sensed his presence long before she'd withdrawn from the Inner World and opened her eyes.

He waved a hand toward the silent wolfens, who had tensed and risen to their feet. "I hope they aren't planning to make a meal of me," Dax said lightly.

"Only if I tell them to." She watched him approach curiously. His ebullient expression was vaguely disquieting. It reminded her of the fresco in his bedroom, the eager-faced hunters immortalized above his bed. "Is there something wrong?" No one came to the clearing when she was here anymore—not even Lett, since the announcement of her impending marriage. It was the one place she was always assured of solitude within the confines of the castle's shield wall.

"Nothing's wrong." Dax shrugged and sat down beside her. "I just wanted to see you."

"For what reason?" Her suspicion increased. In the weeks since that night on the ledge she had shared his meals and bed, made love to him more times than she could remember, but he had never really spent idle time with her. The Vahnti count was always working, thinking, brooding, constantly busy both mentally and physically.

"Must I have an ulterior motive to see my future wife?"

"Any other man, no." Rayna gave him a mocking smile.

It still felt odd to have him describe her as his future wife. "But you . . . ?" She left the question hanging in midair.

Dax winced inwardly and sighed. So far he had obviously done a poor job of proving his worth as a husband. "If you really must know, I planned to wine and dine you here in the clearing, then seduce you and present you with a gift."

Her brows lifted. He had given her many a command or ultimatum, but never a gift.

He brushed his fingers through a lock of her wind-tousled hair. "But I suppose I could always give you the gift first." He fished inside a pocket of his tunic, withdrew the black-and-gold ring, and slipped it onto her finger. "It's a tradition that dates back to old Earth."

For a moment, Rayna just stared at him, glancing down at her hand every so often with an expression that vacillated between bewilderment and dismay. The ring curving around her finger was made of heavy gold and obsidian, a raised Vahnti serpent with ruby eyes fixed atop the flat, shiny surface. "What sort of tradition?" Did he truly expect her to wear a Vahnti crest—his personal brand?

"Once the man makes his intentions known to his future wife, he gives her a ring that's symbolic of the vows they've made to each other." A note of pride crept into his voice. "The ring was my mother's, and her mother's before that. It's been worn by every Vahnti countess for almost fifty generations now."

"Oh." A family brand then, not specifically his.

"Will you wear it?"

She twisted the band back and forth across the width of her finger. There had been no vows between them, no whispered words of love. The bargain struck inside the atrium had been forged in the needs of the moment and mutual lust. But at least he had asked, and that was a beginning. "If you wish me to."

"Always," he said softly against her ear.

The single word caused a tiny thrill of hope to bloom deep inside her. There was a hint of forever in the simple word, a promise of far more than a judicious bargain. She lifted her gaze to his, searching for the truth within the shadowy coolness of his eyes. But she found no answers hidden there, only the same unquenchable hunger she felt herself whenever he was near.

"Make love to me, Dax," she whispered, praying that the tenuous roots of their relationship would deepen someday. If not, the future would be a very lonely place indeed. She wound her hands around his shoulders, drawing him closer, her fingers loosening the strip of braid tied at the base of his neck. His hair slipped free, the coal black strands twining around her fingers. "Here, in the clearing."

A rush of desire flared to life in his eyes. Her shyness and uncertainty had faded with the passage of time, the look of infant passion she used to wear permanently replaced by an ardor that more than equaled his own. He nuzzled her cheek and throat, relishing the clean scent of flowers and earth that seemed to drift around her like a fragrant cloud. "I plan to . . . again and again."

The clearing was in full shadow when Rayna opened her eyes. It was late—almost night, judging by the dusky gloom settling over the copse of trees. A wolfen rose to his haunches, eyed her for a moment, then lay back down and continued his perusal of the darkening woods. Beside her, Dax slept peacefully, sated by the elaborate meal and their endless lovemaking.

She smiled to herself and curled closer to the warmth generated by his body. It had been a glorious day. Daxton Vahnti had been attentive, tender, and so very passionate, as if his hidden self had been granted freedom to leave the prison of his title and live the life of an ordinary man.

For whatever reason, he had tried to prove that he cared for her, to demonstrate by word and deed how blissful a life with him could be if she gave it half a chance. The Vahnti count appeared ready and willing to accept her as she was, despite their differences. He even seemed to relish the preternatural elements of her nature, as though her mystical side served to heighten his interest all the more. And if he was willing to forget the past, could she not find the strength to do the same?

She stared at the darkening sky, considering. Javan had once told her that love and hatred were inexplicably intertwined, two halves of a deeper, nameless emotion that, when joined, became something new and unexpected. She could and would find the strength to meet him halfway, to build a new, unexpected future atop the wreckage of her past.

She closed her eyes and placed a protective hand over her abdomen, dreaming of that future, of the seed she had long sensed growing in her womb. She had to try, for all their sakes. Her hand stilled on the ripening curve of her belly. Soon she'd have to tell him. In a week or so, perhaps, but not today. But when she did, she'd know for certain whether his commitment to her went beyond mere words and deeds.

Dax stretched and yawned, instinctively reaching to pull her tight against his hip. He glanced around the clearing in surprise. Full night was only an hour or so away. "We've been here all afternoon," he said ruefully. The security force was probably in a dither by now, feuding over whether they should disobey his order to stay away from the clearing or not.

"You sound as if you regret it."

He blew out an amused breath. "Not quite." Only a madman would regret spending such an afternoon with Rayna at his side. He traced the outline of her breast with the back of his thumb, wishing he had the time to remove her cumbersome robe all over again. "In fact, I think we'll have to make this a regular event." The notion of making love out-of-doors had never particularly appealed to him, but with Rayna it was different. She seemed happier, more at peace outside the confines of the castle walls, a part of nature. "One afternoon a week, perhaps."

"I'd like that," she murmured, gratified that he planned to spend more time with her. A covey of tree hens took flight, skimming the tops of white-skinned trees to arc across the dusky sky. "I love this clearing."

He pulled up on an elbow and propped his chin in his hand. She had always been attracted to the clearing, ever since her first days on Hellfire. "I've never understood that." The small oasis was pretty, but nothing out of the ordinary. "Why is it so special to you?"

A chill gust of night wind sighed across the billowing grass, rustling and whispering through the tall yellow stalks. "It's the grass. . . ." She took a deep, shuddering breath. "It reminds me of Nirvanna. You've been to the plains before; you saw how peaceful and beautiful it is. In some areas the grass is like a living, breathing ocean stretching from horizon to horizon. It's all you can see, all you can hear," she said wistfully. "The grass is sacred to us, as much a part of our heritage as Earth ever was."

His brow knotted in surprise. "Sacred?" No one had ever told him this before. "In what way?"

"Like the buffalo of old Earth." She cast him a probing glance, wondering why his face and voice had suddenly tensed. "Without the grass, the colony would have failed long ago. It almost did at first. Many of the early settlers died before they discovered what could be done with the grass. We use it for everything now—to build our homes, weave our clothing, to make medicines that heal almost any ill. The taste is foul and bitter, but in times of famine we even harvest it for food. Nothing is ever wasted. There are countless uses for every part of the plant."

Her glance sharpened. He was just staring at her, blank and unmoving, as if he didn't quite comprehend the meaning of her words. "Nirvanna saved my ancestors from certain death, blessed us with the bounty of the life-giving grass."

Why was he looking at her as though she had suddenly lost her mind? Impatience flickered like green fire in the depths of her eyes. "Don't you understand? It's why we fought you . . . why we refused to leave the plains. The grass has enabled us to survive for over a thousand years. It's the soul of the planet, the voice of our spirits. We couldn't stand by and do nothing when your soldiers and digging machines began plundering the plains and threatened the grass itself. We had to try to protect the soul of our world."

For long seconds, Dax continued to stare, too astonished to speak; then he stretched full length in the wind-ruffled grass and dissolved into a fit of laughter.

Rayna's face darkened with rage. She'd been wrong to think that he had changed. "I see nothing amusing in what I said." Her voice was flat and angry, ominously so.

Tears streamed from the corners of his eyes. "Gods," he finally managed to say in a gasp. "The irony . . . it's too good to be true." He clutched at a stitch in his side, unable to stop another paroxysm of laughter. Her people had fought and died to protect "nature's bounty"—Nirvanna's plentiful grass.

"What do you mean?" Birds were gathering in a nearby tree, and a wolfen bolted to his feet. Rayna took a calming breath to cool her thoughts, afraid that she would soon lose control.

"You really don't know, do you? I thought your people would have at least suspected."

"Know what?" she demanded.

"Rayna, your sacred grass . . . nature had nothing to do with its creation. It's man-made . . . *Vahnti*-made."

It was her turn to stare blankly. "What are you saying?"

"Nirvanna was nothing more than a barren rock when humans first arrived in this region. My family claimed it and terraformed the entire surface of the planet over the next thousand years: insects, soil, flora, fauna—the entire ecosystem. They even had to create an oxygen atmosphere to make Nirvanna fit for habitation."

Her stricken expression sobered him abruptly. He grasped her hand gently, trying to soften the blow, to make her understand. "It's not all that unusual, Rayna. We've terraformed dozens of worlds. Most of the clans have. If we hadn't terraformed in the early days, humankind would have never survived out here. Earth-type worlds are far more rare than most people realize. We're by-products of our homeworld, unsuited biologically to adapt to such alien environments."

Rayna jerked her hand away and blinked back a gush of tears. The very idea ran counter to everything she had ever believed. The wonders and beauty of nature they had always held sacred weren't natural at all. Nirvanna was artificial, a glorious, living lie.

No, she told herself. *It can't be.* But if it was true, then everything she had ever believed about the Vahntis was wrong as well. She had told him that he could use his technology to reshape, remold, and imitate to his heart's content, but only nature could *create.*

She sat up slowly and stared into the gathering night, her features shadowed with confusion and despair. Wasn't that what Javan had taught her? That nothing of true value and beauty could be created by technology? "The grass is everything to us. . . . How can it be artificial?"

Dax pursed his lips and sighed. He hadn't realized that his revelation would bring her so much pain. "Rayna, the grass has so many uses because it was designed to be that way."

"I don't believe you," she whispered miserably, but deep inside she knew it was true. "The grass was a gift from the spirits, a sign that Nirvanna wanted us to survive."

"It was an experiment, Rayna, genetically engineered insurance against a time in the future when a new resource might be needed." Dax gentled his tone and chose his words with care. He was treading on treacherous philosophical ground, in danger of destroying everything she held dear. "Humans came to this part of the galaxy because Earth's star system was almost dead, sucked dry of resources by an ever-increasing population. In time the same thing will happen here. It's already beginning. My family wanted to delay that time as long as possible, so they began experimenting with organic materials that might be transformed into renewable resources. The Nirvannan grass was one of the first of those experiments, and so far the most successful. The stalks were impregnated with living polymers—organic plastic—that can be used for almost anything," he attempted to explain. "To make shelters, weave fabric, build tools, even eat, if the need arises. There are probably a million other uses that we haven't even considered yet." Its use in healing was one, he thought to himself. Though unexpected, it did explain the rumors and legends of spontaneous cures on Nirvanna. "But the real beauty of it is that the grass is a renewable resource that can be harvested and replanted again and again."

He fell silent for a moment, allowing her time to absorb the impact of his words. "Rayna, your grass might have been created artificially, but does that make it any less real, any less a part of nature? The true beauty and power of nature lies in its existence, not in the method of its creation."

She squeezed her eyes shut and considered his words. From

her earliest days she had been taught that the Vahntis and their use of technology would bring about the same destruction that had doomed distant Earth. Perhaps it was so. But did that mean that *all* technology should be rejected in order to coexist with nature? The same technology that could wreak such terrible destruction could also create, give life to entire worlds where none had been before.

Shaken, she turned and studied the lines of his face. Because of their beliefs, her people had despised and rejected everything the Vahntis stood for—the very same family whose tools, wealth, and ingenuity had enabled her people to survive on Nirvanna for a thousand years.

"It was not my intention to hurt you, Rayna."

"I know that." Their eyes met and locked. "But the truth hurts at times." A wormlike lie ate at the heart of her entire way of life. "You were right . . . it is ironic. Nirvannans fought and died, spilled Vahnti blood in order to protect a technological creation." She shook her head sadly. "Why didn't you tell us? The truth might have put an end to the bloodshed."

Dax's brows pulled downward in a worried frown. "I cannot even begin to tell you how valuable the grass is, as well as the process that created it. It could be the salvation of us all. But if the wrong people discover the truth before enough of my troops are repositioned to defend the planet, no one on Nirvanna will be safe. We had hoped that your people would be moved out of harm's way long before the first harvest began and any of the other clans found out." He gave her a small, rueful smile. "Our agreement changed that. But the remainder of your people still on the continent should be safe enough. A large force of Vahnti ships and troops are preparing to leave for the Nirvannan system in a few weeks. They'll be there well before the start of the harvest to defend against any invasion attempt."

Rayna suppressed an irrational urge to laugh, or to weep hysterically—she wasn't sure which. Her people had sacrificed themselves in order to defend Nirvanna and its grass from the evil Vahntis, while they in turn had come to do the same, but from a far greater evil. The perversity of it all was beyond belief.

"Do you really think another clan might try to invade?" she said anxiously. She would never understand clan squabbles or politics, but a threat to Nirvanna and her tribe, from any quarter, was cause for concern.

"The Dunstans, most likely. When Alfred learns about the grass he'll make a move of some kind against me. He covets what others possess." He gazed at her steadily, conveying without words that she was included in that description. "It's not in his nature to stand by and let us begin the first planetary harvest without reacting. But I hope to belay him with a show of force he can't ignore."

Dax climbed to his feet and brushed flecks of grass and withered wildflowers from the legs of his breeches. He glanced up at the night-black sky, at the golden bands of starlight wheeling around the distant core. Talk of Nirvanna and Alfred had made him uneasy, as if he could sense a current of danger riding on Hellfire's wind. "It's late, Rayna." He needed to get back to the castle, check with the security force to make sure that all was well. "We need to get back." Maybe then he could lay his fears to rest.

"Andwillian eggs, my lady?" Vannata asked smoothly. "They're especially fresh this morning." She held the serving tray out for inspection. "Only a month old, judging by the smell."

Rayna flinched and fought down the urge to gag. The bright blue eggs had been steamed and fluffed into a smelly mush. "No," she said more forcefully than she had intended. Bile rose in her throat. "Take it away. Please."

"As you wish." Vannata placed the offending tray on a sideboard. "Count Vahnti has ordered me to see that your every whim is fulfilled. If the breakfast isn't to your liking, I'll instruct the kitchens to prepare an alternative for you."

"That won't be necessary." Rayna pulled in a steadying breath. The hideous smell was beginning to fade. "I have no whims in need of fulfillment." A tremor ran through her hand as she lifted the porcelain cup and took a sip of the soothing mint tea. She closed her eyes for a moment, savoring the warmth, but wishing she had taken the tea in the solitude of their rooms. Having Vannata, Caccia, and a multitude of servants watch her every move was not an auspicious way to begin a day. Worse still, Caccia had taken to wearing the Modalbeau woman's gruesome pendant everywhere she went, as if she couldn't abide the thought of taking it off. Rayna grimaced. She couldn't shake the feeling that it was watching her, too.

Vannata cleared her throat. "Are you ill, my lady?" Her gaze bored across the width of the table. "You look a bit pale."

Rayna's eyes flew open, and a flush crawled up her neck. "I'm just not hungry today." She wasn't about to admit that she had morning sickness with Caccia seated across the table from her. "Nothing's wrong."

Caccia peered at her intently. "You do look rather pale this morning, Rayna." She pursed her lips and studied Rayna's wan face in the light cast by the dining room chandelier. "Pasty, in fact." Actually she looked almost fashionable for a change. Close, but not quite. Rayna still had that outdoorsy, peasant look of a woman who enjoyed grubbing for roots. "Are you sure you're all right?" Caccia pitched her voice a notch higher, conveying just the right mix of anxiety and concern. "You seem so preoccupied this morning."

"I'm fine," Rayna said irritably. She took another sip of tea, eyeing the other woman suspiciously. She was preoccupied, but that was none of Caccia's concern. Her entire universe had been turned inside out by Dax's revelations. "Don't concern yourself on my account." Even her memories of Nirvanna were different now, tempered with the knowledge that many of her beliefs had been based on a technological lie.

"I was just trying to be your friend," Caccia said defensively. Rayna was ruining everything. How was she to befriend her if she was rebuffed at every turn? "Can't you at least meet me halfway?" She forced her mouth to tilt in a smile. "I'm just trying to make amends for my past behavior."

Rayna's gaze thinned. The old, spiteful Caccia was far more

trustworthy than this one. At least she knew where she stood with that Caccia. The new one was friendly and concerned, always seeking to curry favor, always lurking about with that loathsome crystal and an artificial smile. "You've made it very clear that you don't like me. Why would you suddenly want to be my friend?"

Caccia's practiced smile remained firmly entrenched, but inwardly she was seething. Even a spy could take only so much. How dare Rayna question her motives? "Well, if you really must know the truth, I don't think I have a choice in the matter. You and Dax will be married soon, so we'd best try to get along." She dabbed at her mouth with a square of linen. "For Dax's sake, if nothing else. He wants so much for us to be friends."

A dubious frown angled over Rayna's features. Since she'd come to Drakken, Dax had rarely spoken Caccia's name and seemed inclined to avoid her company whenever possible. Still, what harm would there be in trying to lessen the tension between them? "If that's what you want, I'm willing to try."

Caccia gave her a cheerful smile. "How wonderful. Why don't we start this afternoon? I hear Dax is going somewhere for a few days. It will be the perfect opportunity for us to spend time together."

Rayna shook her head, relieved that she had an excuse to put her off for a while. "I'm going with him."

"Away from the castle?" Caccia's dark eyes smoldered with sudden glee, and her hand moved unconsciously to cup the pendant glittering between her breasts.

"Dax said it would be a short trip. We leave this morning for Argossa and some other settlements. I don't know their names." She rose from the straight-backed chair. "He told me to be at the shuttle pad at half past nine."

"His inspection tour . . . how silly of me to have forgotten." Caccia's mind raced. It was almost nine already. "Vannata," she said casually, "would you have my personal server pack a travel bag for me?" She had to be on that shuttle.

"Yes, my lady, right away."

Caccia smiled at Rayna benignly. "Dax is always telling me that I should take a more active role in clan affairs. The least I can do is to show those poor, suffering people that Caccia Vahnti cares about the tragedy that's befallen them.'' Her smile widened. ''And just think, while Dax is busy doing whatever it is he does, you and I will have plenty of time to spend together.''

Rayna felt ill again. ''Of course.'' Until now she had been excited by the prospect of venturing outside Drakken's walls, of spending time alone with Dax.

''See you on the shuttle.'' Caccia bolted from her chair and careened through the doors.

As the servers began clearing the table, Rayna walked toward the doors and into the corridor beyond, pausing for a moment to get her bearings. The cavernous hallway stretched as far as she could see in both directions, the triangular ceiling adding to the impression that she was staring down a tunnel into the depths of infinity.

Lost in thought, she turned left and headed toward a distant lift-tube that would take her to the castle battlements and Dax's private shuttle pad.

Boot heels scraped on the stone behind her. ''Rayna!'' a voice whispered urgently, so close the hairs along her neck rose in response.

Startled, Rayna pivoted, her heart drumming erratically. ''Lett.'' The thunder in her chest slowed. ''You scared me.''

''I'm sorry.'' His hand shook as he grabbed her elbow and forced her into the shadow of a stone pillar. ''I've been waiting for you.'' His gaze darted left then right down the empty corridor, searching for guards and the ever-present robotic eyes. ''We need to talk . . . now.''

Rayna frowned and edged a step backward. Lett had avoided her company since she'd made her escape attempt, and she had tried to avoid him as well, fearing a confrontation over the contents of the note. Her expression turned wary. ''About the note?''

''What note?'' he said, flinching at the sound of a door slamming in the distance.

''The one in the pouch.'' She watched his expression carefully, but she saw no guilt buried there, only the vague, distracted look of a man fearful of his surroundings. "The one you left in the tree."

Lett's brows knitted in bafflement. "I didn't leave you any note, Rayna."

She continued to watch him for a few seconds, then exhaled in relief. It wasn't Lett. She could sense the truth, see and hear it in his face and muffled voice. "Then why did you want to talk with me?" A guarded frown swept across her features. And why did he seem so frightened?

Sweat beaded on his high forehead. "We need to talk about us, Rayna," he said breathlessly. "I've made all the arrangements. A ship is waiting for us, but we have to hurry." He pulled her deeper into the shadow and lifted a clammy hand to stroke her cheek. "The captain will wait only one hour, no more."

She stared at him in confusion. "What are you talking about?"

His nervous gaze darted up and down the corridor again, then settled on her face. "Don't you understand? I've made all the necessary arrangements," he said in a hushed tone. "We can disappear together, go where no one will ever find us . . . not Count Vahnti, not even my family. We'll be together, just the two of us." He pulled her tight against his chest, arms quivering with fear and longing as he wrapped them around her slender body. "I love you, Rayna." He buried his face in her hair. "I think I have since the first moment I saw you aboard the count's ship."

Shock drained all trace of color from her face. She wiggled free of his embrace and backed away. Never in her wildest imaginings had she thought he harbored feelings for her beyond friendship. "Lett," she said gently, "I'm to marry Count Vahnti in a matter of weeks. We made a bargain. I gave him my word."

He shook his head violently. "Don't you see? You don't have to keep that bargain now!" He trapped her hands inside his own, squeezing fiercely. "I'm offering you the means to escape him, to escape everything. But we *must* go now while you still have time."

She untangled her hands from his and pulled away, retreating from the intensity of his eyes, the naked longing visible in his face. "I'm sorry, Lett, but I can't go with you . . . especially now."

"Why?" Lett demanded, clutching desperately at her sleeve.

She averted her gaze, unwilling to witness the pain her admission would bring. "I've grown to care for him, Lett, more than I ever thought possible." She took a deep breath and held it. "And I carry his seed as well," Rayna announced quietly.

Lett staggered sideways and grabbed at the column for support. "Oh, gods, no." He pressed his forehead against the cool black stone, eyes shut tight to block the sight of her face. She was carrying the count's child, the heir to Clan Vahnti. A knot of foreboding wedged in his throat. "You've just given him another weapon," he muttered darkly. "He'll use it, too . . . against all of you."

Rayna swallowed and reached out to touch him, console him in some way, but withdrew her hand abruptly. "I'm sorry, Lett." She hadn't meant to hurt him, didn't want to be the cause of such pain, but it was not her place to console him. "We won't speak of this again." She turned and ran down the corridor.

"Rayna, wait!" Lett cried.

She kept running.

Chapter Twenty-one

A cloud of dust and smoky ash still clung to the ruins of the once-thriving settlement, wrapping Argossa inside a murky skin of grit and powdery sand. Wide fissures snaked down the dusty remnants of a grassy promenade and gouged a zigzag course through block after block of buildings destroyed by the quake.

As the scad-about arced around for another fly-by of the

settlement, Dax drew in a shaky breath and stared out the viewport morosely. "It's worse than I imagined. This will take at least a year to rebuild, maybe more." The expenditure of time and manpower alone would be enormous. "If it can be rebuilt at all."

In front of him, Caccia squinted out the viewport next to her seat. A gray pall of dirt and dust hung over the settlement's skeletal remains. "Why bother trying to revive the corpse?" she said over her shoulder. "Seems like a waste of chits and time to me. You ought to just force all those people to move to another part of the planet and forget about this place."

Dax glared at the back of her dark head. Why had Caccia insisted on coming along? Diplomacy and compassion were alien concepts to her. "Argossa is their home, Caccia. And in case you've forgotten, Hellfire doesn't exactly have an abundance of arable land."

"Well, I still think trying to rebuild would be a terrible waste."

Rayna turned sideways and studied the clear-cut line of Dax's profile. This was a man who could accomplish anything he chose to. "You'll do it," she told him quietly. "You have the means, as well as the will to see that it's done."

He glanced her way and arched an ebony brow. Rayna never ceased to surprise him. "Do I take it that you might actually have a little faith in the evil demon lord?"

"More than a little." She met his cool blue gaze, her own eyes shining with absolute certainty. The shadow cast by the troubling scene with Lett had finally lifted from her thoughts. Everything seemed so clear to her now. Her future was here, with Daxton Vahnti. "But he's not evil. A lord, maybe, even an arrogant demon on occasion, but not evil."

Dax sighed contentedly and lifted her hand from the seat, cradling it inside his palm. This was the life he'd envisioned for himself, a blissful future with a lover and helpmate firmly at his side. A woman who believed in him. He pressed a gentle kiss against the back of her wrist, his lips moving over the sliver of flesh where the sensor cuff had been. "You know, the night you tried to kill me might have been the luckiest night of my life."

"For me as well," she admitted, to herself and to him.

Caccia rolled her eyes and glared at the scad-about's low ceiling, wishing she had a set of ear mufflers to block their nauseating conversation. She lifted the crystal and squeezed it with all her might. Flavian's mysterious friends were her only hope now, the only chance to rid her clan of Rayna Syn before it was too late.

The outskirts of Argossa came into view as the scad-about slowed and dipped lower, circling hundreds of feet above a refugee camp that had risen from the ashes along the settlement's southern rim. Dax peered out the window at the confusion below. Thousands of people were running through a hodgepodge of flimsy tents and geodesic survival domes littering the flat terrain, all rushing toward the clearing where his ship would land.

"It appears they have faith in you, too," Rayna said in awe. Tens of thousands were cheering, frantically waving squares of black-and-gold fabric at the ship flying overhead.

Dax pursed his lips, chagrined by the enthusiastic greeting. "So it seems."

At the front of the cabin, the small contingent of security guards shifted uneasily, watching the chaos below with anxious eyes. An even larger number of refugees had gathered around the clearing, a writhing, churning sea of humanity desperate to catch a glimpse of the reclusive Vahnti warlord, the man who'd promised to rebuild their lives.

The scad-about hovered for a moment, its landing thrusters blowing a thick cloud of chalky dust over the crowd, then settled onto the ground with an audible thud.

Leftenant Robichau swallowed nervously and leaped from his seat, fingering the pulse gun slung over his shoulder. "Look alive," he ordered the guards, dreading the moment when the air lock opened. Insuring the count's safety was difficult enough without allowing him to walk into the arms of a mob. "I want a security cordon of twenty feet around the count at all times. Settlement officials are the only exceptions."

"Just look at them all," Caccia said, grimacing at the viewport. "Do I have to go out there?" A shiver ran down her arms. "They're so dirty . . . and close."

Dax glowered. "You're the one who insisted on coming, Caccia. The least you can do is put in a brief appearance."

"Oh, all right." She unstrapped herself and climbed from the upholstered seat. Actually, she wouldn't miss it for the world. "If you insist."

"I do." He stood and clasped Rayna's hands. "Stay with Caccia and don't venture far from the ship. I'll have to go off for a while to attend meetings with settlement officials. But I want the two of you close enough to run back on board at a moment's notice if the crowd gets out of hand."

She smiled reassuringly. "I'll be fine."

Dax gave her a quick kiss, straightened his uniform jacket, and strode to the air lock, giving Rayna one last glance over his shoulder as the roar of the crowd reverberated through the cabin. He disappeared down the gangway, along with the majority of the guards.

"I just hope none of them touch me this time." Caccia walked toward the open hatch. "I hate it when they do that."

Rayna followed along behind her, feeling slightly foolish at being in such a situation. She was neither noble-born nor noble-raised and had no experience with Dominion pomp and ceremony. For once she would have to follow Caccia's lead, stay close to her, as Dax suggested.

She hesitated at the top of the gangway, disoriented by the rush of sound, the press of moving bodies, the sudden glare of Hellfire's sun. She caught a glimpse of Dax's dark head in the distance. He was smiling as he exchanged formal greetings with a small knot of officials, his party completely encircled by a line of Vahnti guards.

Caccia motioned to her impatiently, and Rayna walked down the gangway to the outskirts of the waiting throng, intimidated by the kaleidoscope of movement and deafening sound. Eager hands slipped out to touch her robe, her hair, any part of her they could reach. She stared around in amazement. No one even knew who she was, yet they were according her the same reverence given the Vahntis simply because she'd been aboard the warlord's ship.

There was a flash of light in the crowd nearby, then another, like a huge diamond glinting in the glare of Hellfire's sun. Rayna stared at the light in confusion, wondering what it meant. Around her, people began wriggling through the cordon of guards, pushing their way closer. The hands became more insistent.

Caccia grabbed her by the elbow and shouted something next to her ear. Rayna shook her head in frustration. Caccia's mouth had moved, but she couldn't hear a single word. Dax's cousin grinned and tugged on her arm, leading her toward the flashes of light. A guard tried to push his way toward her, his head wobbling back and forth as if to tell her no, but the crush of bodies soon swallowed him whole.

The crowd surged around them, folding them inside a screaming blanket of flesh. Rayna's heartbeat accelerated, and a sudden rush of fear swept through her blood. She couldn't see beyond the bodies pressed against her, the ocean of faces swimming in front of her eyes. But through it all, she felt the steady pressure of Caccia's fingers on her arm, guiding her, leading her to safety.

Someone grabbed the back of her hair, and a hand moved along her neck. Rayna felt a sting on the side of her throat, much like the bite of an insect, and tried to flinch away from the anonymous hands. Her vision suddenly dimmed, and she had the sensation of falling. The darkening sea of bodies seemed to jostle closer, spinning above her.

Caccia's face appeared in the dimness, smiling. Happy. The crystal pendant was hanging down, glinting malevolently as it twisted around and around. Rayna stared up at the glittering pendant. She couldn't move, couldn't speak, could hardly see anymore. Was this how Dax had felt when the cat-venom had taken hold?

Still smiling, Caccia leaned close and waggled her fingers in a delicate little wave. " 'Bye, dear.''

Dax continued to pace, his relentless stride carrying him back and forth along the length of the ship's exterior. The glow of a thousand hand torches bobbed and weaved in the surrounding darkness, moving methodically through the refugee camp and the ruins of Argossa.

At the slightest sound or movement, Dax would stop and glance up expectantly, hoping against hope that Rayna had been found. But the search had proved fruitless so far.

He shoved a dusty lock of hair from his face and rubbed at his eyes tiredly, then resumed his restless pacing. How much longer should they search? His eyes turned a searing, pain-filled blue. How much longer before he could accept the truth?

"Dax, please stop doing this to yourself," Caccia pleaded. He had actually gouged a trail in the dirt with his pacing. "She's gone, and there's nothing you can do about it." She pulled her knees up to her chin. "I'm tired. I want to go home."

He turned and scowled at his cousin, who was sitting at the base of the metal gangway, her body slumped against the guardrail. She had been there for hours, either weeping or whining since early afternoon. His hands bunched into fists at his sides, tensing then relaxing in an obsessive rhythm. "Tell me again."

Caccia threw up her hands. "Why? I've already told you a hundred times!"

"Do it, Caccia!" Dax shouted. "I want to hear it again!"

"All right," she said in a clipped voice. "If that's what you want." Glaring, she placed her elbows on her knees and propped her chin in her palms. "Like I said, there were people everywhere, pawing at us, touching us all over, but Rayna kept moving deeper into the press. I couldn't stop her, so I just clung to her arm for dear life and followed." She paused a moment to collect her thoughts, to remember the exact words she'd used before. "A man dressed in a dark robe appeared beside us. He was big and muscular with long brown hair, the type of ruffian you might find in the crew aboard a merchant freighter. He smiled at Rayna and she smiled back; then she reached inside her robe and handed him a small black pouch. He nodded once, and she turned to me and yelled, 'He won't find me this time.' Then she took the man's hand and ran into the crowd." Caccia lifted her shoulders in a small, helpless shrug. "I never saw her again."

Dax stared into the darkness. He didn't want to believe, couldn't abide the possibility that Rayna had run from him again. Not now. His shoulders sagged under the weight of his grief. Caccia's version of events had been verified by several witnesses, and a woman fitting Rayna's description had been seen getting into a waiting vessel, hand in hand with a man clad in a dark robe. Dax started pacing again. The ship had left Hellfire within minutes of Rayna's disappearance, a mystery ship with fake registry, a fake flight plan, and an unidentified crew—vanished into a million light-years of empty space.

Robichau trotted out of the torchlit darkness, huffing his way toward the Vahnti count.

Grim-faced, Dax stopped pacing to await the news. "Well?" he demanded impatiently.

"Nothing, my lord." Robichau shook his head and blew out a weary breath. "Nothing beyond what we already knew."

A line of muscles spasmed along Dax's jaw. "I won't accept that! No one can just disappear!"

Robichau swallowed and met the count's angry gaze. "Maybe in the morning . . ." His voice trailed off miserably.

Dax choked down a cry of rage. Did Rayna hate him so much that she would trick him into thinking that she cared? Lull him into relaxing his vigilance, then bribe her way to freedom? *Yes,* his mind whispered. She hated him enough to try to kill him, enough to wheedle her way into his life, then betray him. Perhaps he'd been wrong about her all along. Perhaps there had never been a spy in Drakken Castle save for Rayna herself.

"Call off the search," Dax whispered hoarsely. He felt hollow inside, cold and empty. "It's time to go home."

Rayna moaned softly and rolled onto her back. She could feel the wind brushing across her cheeks, hear it ruffling the tops of nearby trees, cool and sharp, yet strangely sterile, devoid of any natural smells. There was another sound as well, an unfamiliar rumbling that seemed to advance then recede from her in a deep, basso rhythm. Like waves pounding against a quiet beach. Not the clearing then, or Argossa. She worked her mouth, trying to make her throat and tongue form intelligible sounds. "Dax?" she finally croaked. "Where are you?"

"I'm here, my darling."

Her lids snapped open. The voice did not belong to Dax. His pitch was lower, smoother. This voice was mocking and contemptuous, the directionless sound drifting toward her from nowhere and everywhere. She pushed up on her elbows and glanced around, blinking to acclimate herself to the darkness, the strangeness of her surroundings. Three moons hovered in a star-filled sky, forming an uncertain triangle above a sickly orange sea. Her confusion increased. The nearby trees were puny and ragged, the wind-torn foliage and slender trunks an unnatural shade of purple-blue.

A flash of terror glittered in her eyes. This wasn't right at all. The last thing she remembered was dry, dusty Argossa, how Caccia had dragged her into the crowd, the sting on her neck, the vertigo and darkness dragging her downward, Caccia's malevolent smile floating above her. . . . "Caccia?" Her voice swelled on a wave of fear, strident and demanding.

"I'm afraid I'm the only one here."

Rayna jerked in surprise and scrabbled around on all fours, her hands and knees sinking in thick, muddy sand. She stared up in horror. The creature standing before her was pale and hideously bloated, his monstrous body swathed in a voluminous red robe. "Who are you?"

The flesh on his face rearranged itself, and his mouth parted in an indulgent smile. "How droll of me. I've known you so long that I forgot we had never truly met. I'm Alfred Dunstan, of course."

"Dunstan?" A dark chill crawled up Rayna's arms. Dax's enemy, and Petwitt's father.

"I see you've heard the name."

"I know who you are." Her mouth curled in revulsion. "That dung worm Petwitt is your son."

"Oh, my." Alfred shook his head in mock sadness, enjoying himself tremendously. The girl had beauty, spirit, and taste as well. Far more than he'd bargained for. But with proper discipline the spirit-thing could be brought to heel. "Daxton has obviously been spreading lies about us again."

"Somehow I doubt they are lies." She risked a quick glance at the purplish trees and the odd-hued sea, searching for an avenue of escape. The water lay to her right, Alfred Dunstan directly ahead. She could either retreat down the beach or make a dash for the scraggly trees.

Alfred chuckled in delight. His little passion play was progressing just as he'd envisioned. "Don't bother trying to escape, my dear." He stretched his arms out wide, the sleeves of his robe billowing in the artificial wind. "This is my world. You've nowhere to run."

Her eyes thinned speculatively. He was so immense there was no way he could catch her if she did run. "Watch me." Rayna bolted to her feet, took three quick steps toward the trees, and fell, her legs mired in the muddy sand. Slithery, snakelike things latched onto her ankles, dragging her backward. She clawed frantically at the sand, at the roots ensnaring her ankles, but each desperate movement only entangled her more. She stopped struggling and cried out in frustration.

"You see?" Alfred said huskily. "I told you that you couldn't escape me." He stared down at her prostrate body, drawing a ragged breath to control his growing lust. His little wood nymph was facedown in the sand, the back of her robe rucked up to reveal satiny thighs. "Now that you've learned your lesson, let's get down to business, shall we?"

Alfred touched a finger to his forehead, and the roots released her, slithering back into the ether from which they'd crawled. "Take off your robe," he ordered. "Then kiss my feet."

Aghast, Rayna scrambled around to face him. "Are you mad? I'd sooner die than take off my robe for you!" She glanced down at the mounds of sweaty flesh that passed for his feet. The other demand didn't even bear consideration.

A frown flitted over his face. She wasn't supposed to say that, wasn't supposed to argue at all. "I'll overlook what you said because I'm in a generous mood tonight." His expression turned devious. "In fact, if you please me greatly, I might even let you keep breeding, even though the seed planted in your belly belongs to that devil's spawn, Daxton Vahnti."

Her heartbeat accelerated to a fever pitch, so loud she could hear it drumming in her ears. He knew. She swallowed hard, trying to dislodge the lump of terror caught in her throat. "I don't have the slightest idea what you mean."

"Don't lie, my dear. It's so unbecoming. A med scanned you days ago, so I know the truth." He smiled slyly. "Of course, if you refuse to cooperate I can always change my mind. . . ."

The silent threat hung between them, dank and malignant. Her hands moved lower, shielding her abdomen protectively. There was no doubt in her mind that he would gleefully kill her child. "All right," she whispered. Her voice was low and carefully measured, laced with just the right amount of despair. "I'll cooperate. Just don't hurt my child." Her gaze thinned as she tugged at the buttons at her throat to open the front of her velvet robe.

"That's much better." Alfred's eyes glazed as the dark blue robe slipped to her waist. He'd known she would give in. Real or not, they all did eventually. "Now do as you were ordered and kiss my feet."

"Yes, my lord." She lowered her head to his feet, her eyes turning a bright, gold-flecked green as she sank her teeth into the top of his foot. Bile rose in her throat as she felt the flesh give way, but oddly, she couldn't taste his blood.

Alfred squealed in pain and tried to kick her away, but her teeth just clamped down harder. "You're not supposed to do that!" He stumbled back a step, his heel catching in the hem of his robe, then tumbled sideways, landing on the beach in an ungainly heap.

Rayna released his foot and sprang atop him, fingers digging into the soft folds of flesh engulfing his throat. "Filthy offal! Touch me again and I'll kill you!" Her death-grip tightened. "I swear it on my mother's bones!"

Terrified, Alfred stared into her rage-filled face, watching in horror as her eyes seemed to change from bright green to a glowing, beastly yellow. He screamed again and grabbed at his forehead, fingers fumbling for the off switch.

The virtual beach vanished abruptly, and the real world re-formed around him at the speed of light. Dazed, Alfred blinked in the sudden glare and sighed in relief. He was on board his ship again, crumpled on the floor of his private cabin. But at least he was safe. He dabbed at his sweaty face with the sleeve of his robe, then grabbed the side of the chaise he'd fallen from, grunting as he strained to lift his ponderous form.

"Trouble in paradise, Father?" Petwitt watched his contortions in amusement, deciding the Dunstan warlord looked much like a beached sea-slug trying to flop back into water.

Alfred's head jerked around. Petwitt was lounging against the cabin doors, obviously enjoying his predicament. Cursing himself for forgetting to change the privacy codes again, Alfred glowered at his firstborn son. "How long have you been here?"

"Long enough to see you fall out of the chaise and thrash around on the floor." His brow climbed. "What went wrong, Father? Didn't she like playing your virtual game?"

Alfred turned and stared at the unconscious woman lying atop his bed, the neural stimulators still strapped to her forehead. "She attacked me!" he said incredulously. "Bit my foot and tried to strangle me!" Though his injuries were only virtual, his pain and fear had been all too real.

Petwitt snorted. "I told you it wouldn't work. Her body might be virtual while she's in there, but not her mind. In the future, you'd be wise to stick with your programmed playthings. Miss Syn doesn't have the slightest idea that she's trapped inside the setting of your fantasy. If you go back for another visit, she'll probably attack you again."

Alfred's lips compressed, a determined slash of pink set against his orb-shaped face. He'd find a way. Force the meds to increase the amount of drugs flowing through her blood. Dull her brain into acquiescence. If Vahnti could take her willingly, then by the gods, so would he. "I don't remember inviting you into my cabin to give unwanted advice, Petwitt," he snapped harshly. "What are you doing here?"

Petwitt dipped his head in apology, though it irked him to do so. "Forgive the intrusion, Father. I meant no offense." He cocked his head toward the motionless woman atop Alfred's bed, his bearded chin lifting to a disdainful angle. "While you were otherwise engaged, we received a comm signal that the last of our fleet has managed to slip past the Vahnti border patrols undetected.''

"Excellent!" Alfred's jubilation gave him the strength to finally heave his body atop the silk-covered chaise. "How soon until they reach the prearranged coordinates?"

"The entire fleet is converging on the dark side of Nirvanna's moons as we speak. Our troops await only your signal to strike."

Alfred's teeth gleamed in a dazzling smile. Vahnti would be caught unawares, as well as Haywood March, who was twiddling his thumbs on Gamma Three along with the bulk of Vahnti's forces, light-years away from their count. No one could save Clan Vahnti now. Once his own forces had taken Nirvanna, he'd send the message that would seal Daxton Vahnti's fate once and for all: *I have your world, your woman—and your heir. Come to Nirvanna, alone and unarmed, or watch them die.*

Alfred chuckled. He'd keep Nirvanna, of course, no matter what Vahnti did, and the girl as well. She would be his keepsake to mark the occasion, a living reminder of a job well done. A spasm of laughter rumbled up from his chest. This was the most satisfying web he had ever spun. Within days, Daxton Vahnti would be dead, his noble body putrefying in a shallow grave beside his unborn spawn.

Dax slouched against the high leather chair, propped his boots atop the desk, and continued to stare at the oil painting on the far wall of his shadowy office. A single light shone down on the portrait, illuminating Rayna's face from above and setting the cascade of auburn hair aflame with golden highlights. Carlo had captured her in profile, standing in front of the library windows, her features half in shadow, half in a sheen of radiant light cast by Hellfire's setting sun. She was gazing out at the hellish landscape, erect and defiant, yet strangely morose at the same time, a golden knife dangling from her slender hand.

His hawkish face darkened as he finished off a bottle of Logo wine. Was that the knife she'd used to carve out his heart? Sunder him so completely that he'd been reduced to sitting here in the shadows, unable to do much of anything except drink and stare?

He resumed his perusal of the painting, his pale, bloodshot eyes glazed by wine and endless hours of trying to understand, to come to grips with the knowledge that the future he had envisioned would never be. Rayna was gone. Forever. And nothing could change that one simple fact.

"Damn you, Rayna," Dax whispered, staring at the lines of her face, an image frozen on Carlo's canvas for all eternity. "Why did you leave me?"

He sagged deeper into the chair, absently trailing his thumb around and around the lip of the empty bottle. Had he done or said something to cause this himself? Been too self-absorbed to realize that their growing intimacy was only a sham? He shook his head in frustration. The questions only led him to more questions, all unanswered.

In a fit of rage, he slung the bottle at her portrait, where it shattered in an explosion of sound and slivered glass. "I loved you, dammit!" Dax railed at the painting. "I loved you!"

He wanted to shout his outrage at the universe for torturing him so, rip her painting from the wall and burn her memory from his mind. But in the end he just sat there, staring at the portrait, unable to rouse himself to do anything at all.

The chime on his office doors sounded, perhaps the hundredth time it had rung in the past two days. A frown rippled over his face. Or was it three days? Four? He couldn't remember anymore. Didn't really care.

"Go away!" he bellowed in a voice sure to send his aides scurrying for safety. "I don't want to be disturbed!"

"Dax, it's me, Carlo." In the corridor beyond the doors, Carlo motioned for the guards to move away and rang the chime again. "Release the lock and let me in," he yelled through the armored doors.

"I said go away!"

Carlo flinched but held his ground. "Not until I see you face-to-face." Worried lines built across his forehead. Dax had been locked inside his office suite for the better part of a week. He punched the chime three times in rapid succession, wishing

Haywood wasn't light-years away. The soldier would know how to handle Dax far better than he.

Dax sighed and brushed a lank strand of hair from his eyes. Carlo could be just as pesky and determined as Caccia at times. He pounded a pad on his desk with the heel of a fist to release the privacy lock.

Carlo steeled himself and walked into the shadowy room, leery of what sort of reception he would receive. Since Rayna's disappearance, Dax had been alone inside the suite, unsealing the doors only to receive an occasional delivery of wine. "Dax?" he said cautiously, peering into the gloom. The only source of light was a small sconce above Rayna's portrait. "What do you want?"

He wheeled in the direction of the slurred voice, squinting to see into the shadows. Dax was half sitting, half lying in a chair, his long legs draped across the top of the polished stone desk. "Would you mind turning on some lights? I can hardly see in here."

Dax punched another pad, and the room filled with artificial light.

"That's better." Carlo moved in front of the huge desk, his gaze widening in alarm when he caught sight of his cousin's haggard face. His ice blue eyes, usually so cool and self-assured, were now blank and empty, rimmed with exhaustion and a look of defeat. "I think it's past time that you rejoined the living world, Dax." Wine bottles were strewn everywhere, littering the floor around the desk. "Wallowing in wine and self-pity won't do you or the clan a bit of good."

Dax snorted and rubbed his eyes. "Maybe not, but it helps pass the time."

Carlo studied him for long seconds, still stunned by his unkempt appearance and ghastly pallor. His fastidious cousin looked as if he hadn't slept or eaten in a week. "Get on with your life, Dax. Don't let this turn you into even more of a recluse than you already were."

"Strange advice coming from you," Dax said crossly.

Carlo shrugged. "Maybe it is. But then I'm not the Vahnti warlord. You are, and the sooner you remember that the better off we'll all be."

He glanced over Carlo's head and stared at the painting morosely. "I just don't care anymore."

"If you don't, who will?" Carlo snapped.

Dax's empty gaze met Carlo's for a timeless moment, the only indication that he'd even heard. He sighed, long and painfully deep, but there was a hint of resignation in the sound, as well as acceptance.

Carlo smiled in relief. It was a start. "I'm going to tell Vannata to send a tray of food up to you right away." His first priority was to get Dax fed and rested. Once he exited his self-imposed prison, they would speak of Rayna Syn. "Eat, then get some sleep, Dax. I'll be back to check on you in a while."

The Vahnti count nodded shortly.

Elated, Carlo hurried through the doors and rushed down the long corridor. Perhaps everything would be all right after all. He lengthened his stride and turned into a secondary passageway, eager to reach a lift-tube that would take him to the lower floors and the castle's kitchens.

The cold black stone beneath his feet gave way to plush blue carpet as he made another turn, muffling the clatter of his rapid footsteps. Graceful columns jutted from the floor at regular intervals, climbing up the walls to merge with the arches soaring overhead. Shadows cast by the columns pooled in thin rectangles along his path, each the same precise length, the same width apart. Carlo slowed his pace to admire the view, losing himself in the symmetry of the shadows, the perfect harmony of it all.

Sounds echoed off the columns and sweeping arches, stealthy whispers coming from a small alcove a short distance ahead. Carlo forced himself to concentrate and focus on the whispering.

"You're the one who's insane now," a man's voice hissed, his low words accompanied by a sharp crackle of static. "Don't speak of such things inside the castle! You're putting us both at risk!"

"I don't care!" a voice whispered back. "Just tell me what I want to know!"

Frowning, Carlo paused at the base of a column, uncertain

whether he should make his presence known or hide until they had continued on their way. Had he stumbled into a family dispute? Some sort of quarrel between two guards?

"Need I remind you that you're in no position to make demands of any kind? A single word from me and he'll order your death."

"Sooner or later he'll do it anyway, and you know it," the man said quietly. "I've outlived my usefulness here."

"What's the matter?" There was a trace of glee in the droll voice. "You scared he's actually going to do it this time?"

"Listen, you arrogant bastard, you promised that if I helped with the arrangements that you'd tell me where she was. You swore that Rayna would be mine when the two of you were finished playing your sick little games. I held up my end of the bargain; now it's your turn."

"And you actually believed me?"

Carlo choked back a startled gasp and edged deeper into a puddle of shadow, flattening himself against the dark stone wall. He took a deep breath to steady himself. One of the voices belonged to Lett Bahleigh, and he had spoken of Rayna as if he knew what had happened to her. But who was the other person? The man's hushed words were low and tinny, as if they were being filtered through a transceiver from a distance away. But something about the distorted voice struck a chord in Carlo's memory. He'd heard it before. Somewhere.

Lett Bahleigh forced himself to calm down, to try to sound resolute even though he didn't feel that way at all. "I swear, if you break your promise to me, if either of you harms her in any way, I'll tell Count Vahnti everything I know. It's not too late to put a stop to this."

"You pathetic fool," the man said icily. "It's too late for Vahnti already. Too late for you as well. If he doesn't send an assassin after you this time, I will. No one threatens me." A dull hiss of white noise signaled that the channel had been cut abruptly.

Carlo's heart drummed against his rib cage, and his chest heaved in and out at a frantic pace. What did he mean that it was too late for Dax already? He clutched at the column for support and struggled to control his raspy breathing, terrified that Lett might hear.

For a few seconds, Lett just stared at the tiny transceiver clutched in his hand, wondering how long it would take Petwitt or his father to send an assassin for him. He switched off his privacy field and chewed on his lower lip thoughtfully. No more than a day or so, he decided.

Lett shoved a lock of hair from his eyes and gazed at the stone ceiling absently. He'd told Rayna how he felt about her, tried his best to make her understand that running away with him would be for her own good. But she'd spurned him, made it abundantly clear that she cared for Count Vahnti, not him, and was actually carrying the Vahnti heir. That should have settled things then and there, but he couldn't seem to stop worrying about her. He shook his head slowly. It didn't really matter anymore. Rayna was gone, and he was a marked man.

He stared at the stone arches a few seconds longer. It was time to make a run for it, to slip away to a quiet little border world before his "loved ones" sent an assassin to do him in. He would simply vanish as he'd originally planned, only he'd have to do it by himself now. Rayna was on her own. He had done all that he could for her, foolishly involved himself in matters that were none of his concern. Maybe Petwitt was right. Maybe he did have a weakness for unobtainable women. He slipped out of the alcove and into the corridor, swearing to himself that if he survived the next few days, he would avoid such dangerous entanglements in the future.

The soft rasp of a boot brushing across the deep carpet was Carlo's only warning that Lett had turned in his direction. He flattened his body against the wall even more, praying that Lett kept his eyes straight ahead and passed the column without noticing him.

Cold sweat beaded on Carlo's forehead as the muted footsteps grew louder, almost even with his hiding place. He had to get to Dax, warn him about Lett, let him know that Rayna hadn't run away. Trembling with fear, Carlo drew in a frightened breath and waited.

Lett's gaze swept past a column and paused. His eyes narrowed, darkening with surprise and a touch of sadness. Another hour or two and he would have been gone from Hellfire forever. He sighed. Too bad it was Carlo who'd discovered him. He'd always sort of liked the boy. "How long have you been hiding there, Carlo?"

Carlo froze, his mouth silently working up and down, his feet rooted to the floor.

"I see." Lett touched a strap on his wrist and freed the stiletto from the scabbard hidden up his sleeve. "I really hate to do this, Carlo. I might be a doctor, but I've never been very comfortable with the sight of blood." He sighed again. "Unfortunately, you haven't left me much choice, not if I want to get off Hellfire alive."

Carlo stared at the cold length of steel, paralyzed by fear. "Then don't do it," he whispered hoarsely. "I swear I won't tell anyone until you're safely away."

The dull black metal blended with the shadows as Lett hefted the finely hewn blade. "Come on, Carlo. You and I both know that you'll run straight to the count as soon as my back is turned. And I don't have any intention of being handed over to the Vahnti security force." A cynical smile lifted the corners of his mouth. "I'm not ready to die yet."

He drew back his arm to throw the knife, and Carlo bolted, turning and ducking left just as Lett's hand swept toward him in a tight arc. A bolt of pain daggered through Carlo's shoulder as he started running.

Lett cursed under his breath. Carlo had twisted around just as he released the knife, throwing his aim off.

Carlo stumbled once and dragged himself upright, staying on his feet by sheer force of will. He grabbed at the columns and walls for support as he careened down the corridor. "Dax!" he screamed, the sound echoing back to him over and over again. The pain was sharper now, a burning throb that seemed to reach into his bones.

Lett started after him, but stopped short when he heard a familiar whisper of sound above him. He glanced up and muttered another curse. A tiny sphere was hovering above him, the concave lens of the security eye homing in on his face. An alarm sounded as another eye sailed past, the robotic device hurtling down the corridor to track Carlo's movements.

Lett went cold inside. Too late. He lunged toward a lift-tube, but knew he'd never make it out of the castle alive.

Breathing heavily, Carlo turned into the main corridor. A knot of guards was visible in the distance, grouping into defensive positions around Dax's office doors.

"Dax!" he called again, but his voice was smaller, weaker. Carlo sank to his knees. He could hear the clatter of boot heels pounding against stone, an officer shouting orders.

"Carlo. . . . ?" Dax caught him just before he crumpled to the floor. A thick stream of sticky, warm blood ran down his hands and arms. "Oh, gods." He stared in horror at the stiletto buried in Carlo's shoulder. "Get the meds up here!" Dax bellowed, and rushed back to his office, Carlo cradled tight against his chest.

He gently placed the boy atop his desk and jerked the blade from his shoulder. Blood gushed from beneath his tunic, collecting in a small puddle on the gleaming obsidian.

Carlo moaned softly.

"Who did this to you, Carlo?" Dax prodded as he pressed the heel of his hand against the puncture to stanch the flow.

Dazed, Carlo blinked several times.

"Who stabbed you?"

"Dr. Bahleigh . . ." he finally whispered.

"Lett?" Dax's hands knotted into fists. His instincts had been right all along.

"I think he's a spy," Carlo went on, his voice growing stronger as he talked. "He caught me listening to a transmission between him and someone outside the castle. It was a man, but I didn't recognize the voice." He coughed weakly and grabbed Dax's sleeve. "Something's going on, Dax. You're in danger . . . maybe the entire clan, but I don't know from who—or why."

Dax had a pretty good idea. Lett had known the truth about Nirvanna, and if Alfred Dunstan was his spymaster . . . "An attack, you think?"

"I don't know." He shifted his body and winced. "There's something else. . . . They both mentioned Rayna. Lett talked as if he knew what had happened to her."

Dax's face went cold and deathly still. If it was true . . . He closed his mind to the possibility, to the sudden surge of hope flaring to life inside him—and the sickening realization of what that possibility signified.

"She didn't run away from you, Dax. I'm sure of it. And from the way they talked, I think she's still alive." Carlo was quiet for a moment, mustering the courage to say what had to be said. He finally met Dax's grief-shadowed gaze head-on, but the pain in his own dark eyes equaled his cousin's. "You know what it means, don't you?"

Dax sighed raggedly and nodded. "Caccia lied."

A bevy of meds rushed into the office to tend their patient. Dax stepped away from the desk to give them more room and surveyed the flurry of activity, his face and demeanor deceptively calm. Only his eyes betrayed him. They were hard and icy-cold, brimming with a rage so fierce that when someone happened to glance his way they quickly averted their gaze.

Robichau hurried into the room. "A security eye recorded part of it, my lord. Dr. Bahleigh stabbed Lord Carlo in the west corridor, then fled to the upper floors in a service lift-tube." He shook his head, still incredulous. "If I hadn't seen a replay of the vid with my own eyes, I would have never believed it."

"Search his rooms," Dax ordered, although he didn't think the search would turn up any evidence. "Hunt for anything that might point to his master's identity." A spy who could successfully ply his trade for years inside the enemy camp would never risk detection by leaving evidence lying around. "Have you caught him yet?"

Robichau nodded. "We took him into custody up on the battlements. He was trying to break into the air lock on your ship."

"Place Hellfire under a planetwide security alert," Dax said quietly. "Then bring Bahleigh to me." The rage in his eyes was like a cold blue fire, so hot and bright it seemed to suck the air from the room. "Bring Lady Caccia to me as well. I don't care if you have to drag her here by the hair; just do it. And I want her suite searched along with Bahleigh's."

Robichau saluted stiffly. "Right away, my lord."

A young med cleared his throat to catch Dax's attention.

"Lord Carlo is going to be just fine, Count Vahnti. The blade missed puncturing a lung by a hair."

Dax let out the tense breath he'd been holding. "Can he travel if necessary?" It was possible that Bahleigh wasn't the only spy roaming Drakken's halls. If there was an attack, Carlo would be a primary target. And with the castle's security in disarray, the boy would be safer with him.

"Yes," the doctor said dubiously. "If it's absolutely necessary."

"It might be a matter of life and death," Dax replied darkly. He turned slowly, his attention shifting to a commotion near the doors. Lett Bahleigh was being led into the crowded room by a detail of heavily armed guards. Dax took a step forward, then stopped himself, afraid that if he moved any closer his rage would get out of hand. He gritted his teeth and stared coldly. Bahleigh was slumped forward, his gaze riveted on the floor, his hands firmly bound with repulsor cuffs that restricted movement of his arms to a few degrees up or down.

The guards moved away from him, leaving Lett standing alone in the center of the room. Lett lifted his head slowly and flinched. Daxton Vahnti was only a few steps away, the fury simmering in his icy eyes as powerful as a physical blow. The prospect of death at an assassin's hands seemed distant now. Judging by Vahnti's expression, the count planned to kill him himself.

"Who are you?" Dax hissed quietly.

Lett lifted his head a notch higher. He would never leave this room alive, so what harm was there in telling the truth? "Marcus Dunstan."

A ripple of shock swept through the room. Guards reached for their weapons uneasily, but no one made a sound. The muscles in Dax's shoulders shifted and tensed. Marcus . . . the son rumored to have been killed by his father some years ago. "You're Alfred's son." His voice was low and calm, eerily so, but inwardly he was battling the urge to kill the spy where he stood. "The one who offended Alfred in some way?" For Rayna's sake he had to take things slowly. Marcus Dunstan was his only clue to her whereabouts.

Marcus dropped his gaze to the stone floor. "Yes," he admitted in a near whisper.

Dax started pacing, his footsteps carrying him from one side of the room back to the other. Alfred had made a perfect fool of him and his clan's security force by placing his own son inside the castle itself. He had to hand it to him. The sheer audacity of it all was mind-boggling. "Surely you knew what would happen if you were ever discovered. What sort of inducement did Alfred offer to make you take such a risk?"

"He offered me my life." Marcus shrugged. "I could either die at his hands, or risk discovery by you. I chose to take my chances with you."

There was a squeal in the corridor, followed by a scuffling sound. "Remove your hands from my body!" Caccia screeched. "I want to see the count immediately! When I tell him how I've been treated, he'll flail every one of you within an inch of your lives!"

Sub-Leftenant Anwell shoved her inside the doors. Caccia took a stumbling step, then recovered her balance and her dignity. "Dax! Thank goodness you're here." She smoothed her rumpled brocade robe. "Those filthy beasts actually dragged me from my suite!"

His fists knotted so tightly that tremors ran up the tendons in his arms. The rest of Marcus Dunstan's interrogation would have to wait. "They were simply following orders ... cousin."

Caccia's head snapped up, and her eyes narrowed with suspicion. Dax's ominous tone warned her that something was amiss. She swallowed and glanced around. At least thirty people had gathered in the room, all dour-faced and watching her every move. "Whatever do you mean?"

"You lied to me, Caccia."

She flicked at a crease in the skirt, nervous eyes darting this way and that. Why were Lett Bahleigh's hands bound with security cuffs? And why was Carlo sitting atop Dax's desk, staring at her with those huge, mournful eyes? "Dax, you're not making any sense. I haven't the slightest idea what you're talking about."

"Why did you lie about Rayna?"

"What about her?" Caccia's features froze in a bland expression. The eerie calmness of Dax's voice was belied by the anger smoldering in his eyes.

Anwell cleared her throat and stepped forward. "We searched Lady Caccia's room and found this, my lord." She opened her hand to reveal several bits of shimmering crystal cupped in the center of her palm. "An active spy lens and transceiver were imbedded inside the whole crystal. I had to destroy it to disable the transceiver."

Dax's control finally snapped, and he crossed the distance to Caccia in two angry strides. "What have you done?" He grabbed her by the shoulders and shook her hard. "Tell me now or I swear I'll turn you over to security for interrogation!" He shook her again, more roughly this time.

Caccia started bawling, great hiccuping sobs that shuddered up from her chest and exploded from her throat in childish wails. "Flavian promised you'd never find out!" she cried. "She promised!"

Dax jerked his arms from her shoulders as if he'd been burned. "Flavian!" he yelled in disbelief. She'd worn a crystal pendant that night in the atrium. How far had Alfred's tentacles slithered into his life? "What does she have to do with this?"

"She said her friends were willing to help me! All I had to do was wear the pendant and accompany Rayna when she went outside the shield wall." She tried to clutch at his sleeve but he flinched away from her touch. "What was I supposed to do, Dax? I managed to get rid of her once before; then you had to go running off the day of the quake and bring her back again. Don't you see?" she said desperately. "You're so much better off without Rayna. She's a nobody, completely unsuitable for you. And Flavian still loves you. She'd make such a wonderful countess. Both of us just wanted what was best for you."

"You little fool," Dax said in a choked voice. He'd walked right into a trap baited with the only lure he could never resist—a base on Gamma Three. His deal with Flavian had been an elaborate ruse, one designed by Alfred to tempt him into dividing his forces, making the rest of his territory vulnerable to an all-out Dunstan attack. "Do you know what you've done? Do you have the slightest idea who Flavian's *friends* are?"

Caccia looked at him blankly.

He motioned to the guards. "Get her out of my sight," he ordered in a dead voice. Forgiveness would be a long time coming, if at all. His own cousin had sent Rayna off to certain death on Dead Man's Plateau, then when that failed, allowed herself to be used as a Dunstan dupe to get rid of her again. "Lock her up somewhere until I have time to decide what to do with her."

Caccia's jaw dropped in horror. "Lock me up!" Her gaze cut left, to where Carlo was sitting atop the desk, his head bowed low to avoid her eyes. "Carlo, stop him." She struggled to free herself from the hands restraining her arms. "He can't do this to me! I won't allow it!"

"Get her out of here." Dax started pacing again as a squad of guards dragged her from the room, the sound of her wails echoing in their wake.

Dax sighed, a hollow, empty sound that dug down to his soul, but when he opened his lids again, his eyes were clear and focused, glittering with defiance. There was still time, still hope. The game wasn't over yet.

His gaze swept over Marcus Dunstan. For a spy he had been remarkably candid so far. But could he trust information revealed by a Dunstan? "I'll offer you a trade," Dax said, deciding he didn't have much of a choice, though the thought of such a trade galled him in the extreme. "Information in exchange for your life."

Marcus glanced up incredulously. Was it possible the Vahnti count might let him live? He nodded quickly. The thought of betraying his father and brother didn't grieve him at all.

"Where is Rayna?"

"On my father's ship."

"Where are they bound?"

He shook his head slowly. "Petwitt refused to tell me. All he ever said was that they planned to use Rayna as bait to lure you into a trap. He said she would be in the one place you would be sure to look.''

Comprehension flared in Dax's eyes. *Nirvanna*. It had to be. He could feel it in his bones, in the way the pieces of Alfred's puzzle had begun to slip into place. Alfred planned to attack Nirvanna first, cut Vahnti territory in half before Haywood had a chance to intervene, and use Rayna to lure him from Hellfire into the arms of waiting troops.

''Send an emergency comm to Gamma Three,'' Dax ordered tersely. ''Tell Commander March to abandon the base immediately and move his brigades to the Nirvannan system. Tell him to burn out his ships' jump engines if he has to, just to get there within the next forty-eight hours—but not to breathe a word of his plans to the Modalbeau clan. And signal our troops on Nirvanna; inform them that a Dunstan attack is imminent.''

Several officers ran from the room.

Marcus took a deep breath to brace himself and turned to the Vahnti count. ''There's something else you should know.'' The count had given him back his life, a chance to start anew, far more than his own family would have done. He owed him something in return.

''Yes?'' Dax eyed him steadily.

''I spoke with Rayna the morning you left for Argossa.'' He swallowed hard. ''She told me that she's with child. By now Alfred and Petwitt know it, too.''

Blood pounded in Dax's ears. ''Oh, gods . . .'' He lifted his gaze to the portrait, the thrum of his heart the only sound to penetrate the stunned hush that had fallen over the room. ''Have my ship readied for immediate liftoff,'' he said hoarsely. His features darkened with grim determination. ''We leave for Nirvanna within the hour.''

''No, Count Vahnti!'' Robichau objected. ''You heard the spy. It's a trap!''

A bleak expression passed over his features. ''I know.'' Alfred had designed the perfect trap. The Dunstan warlord had the woman he loved—and his heir.

Chapter Twenty-two

Stars streamed past the viewport, thin ribbons of light that bowed and stretched as the ship hurtled through light-days of hyperspace. Dax prowled from one side of the control deck to the other, willing the ship to move faster, even though he could already feel the stressed rumble of the engines vibrating beneath his boots. He smacked a fist against his armored thigh in frustration. The jump engines had been pushed far beyond their design limits the moment the ship broke free of Hellfire's atmosphere. If he pushed any harder, they would implode.

"Try again," he said impatiently, eager for news. Any news. They had lost contact with Nirvanna nearly a day ago, an ominous event that probably coincided with the first wave of Alfred's attack.

The communications officer glanced up from her console. "Nothing, my lord. Nirvanna is still being jammed. I can't break through the interference to any of our brigades."

Dax swept a lock of hair from his face and started pacing again. They were so close, so damnably close. Only minutes away from Nirvannan space. He just hoped they weren't too late.

An air lock opened and Carlo stepped onto the deck, the sling on his arm the only outward sign of his injury. He stared at his grim-faced cousin.

Dax stopped beside him, his fist still slapping against his thigh.

"You'll find her, Dax," Carlo said reassuringly. "I can feel it. You and Rayna were meant to be."

He gave Carlo a sidewise, cynical glance. "Fate?"

"Something like that."

Dax snorted. "This isn't about Rayna, or the child."

Carlo smiled knowingly. "Isn't it?"

Dax didn't answer. Carlo was right, of course.

"Thirty seconds to drop coordinates," the navigator declared.

Dax tensed and gazed out the viewport, waiting for the moment when the ship would drop out of hyperspace and they'd have their first look at Nirvanna.

Beyond the viewport, the thin bands of stars collapsed and widened, expanding into elongated splotches of brilliant light. As the stars finally stilled, Nirvanna's twin moons swelled into existence, peaceful crescents shining white above a madman's version of hell.

Carlo gasped. The helmsman cried out in horror.

Nirvanna's night sky was pockmarked with pulses of moving light, the quick green flashes of a thousand laser cannons being fired at once. Dozens of Dunstan warships were streaking in and out of the planet's atmosphere, strafing the surface with pulse fire, then darting back to the safety of space.

"Helmsman," Dax ordered, "get us down to the surface now! Head for the northern polar region and set us down behind our lines." Nirvanna's northern reaches were alight with the steady pulses of Dunstan cannon fire. "That seems to be where the majority of their fire is directed." He grabbed a console as the ship angled downward, diving into Nirvanna's atmosphere. "Send a message to the rest of our ships. Order them to take out as many Dunstan warships as possible; then go down and provide air cover for our brigades."

Carlo clutched at the back of the navigator's seat. Although he had never been in the thick of battle before, he knew they were outnumbered a dozen to one, outgunned so much that the numbers didn't even bear consideration. "Dax, what can you hope to accomplish against that?" he murmured, gesturing to the chaos on the viewscreen.

The angle of descent flattened out. "Maybe nothing," Dax said grimly. Nirvanna's rolling landscape was visible now. "Maybe everything. We're arriving days earlier than Alfred expects." Dax just hoped that Haywood and the bulk of his forces would arrive in time as well. The small number of troops and ships accompanying him now could do little to halt the Dunstan juggernaut. "If nothing else, we'll shoot his time-table to hell and back."

A laser flash lit up the viewport, the fiery blast searing a trail across the ship's thick metal underbelly. Bulkheads trembled and groaned.

"And what of Rayna?" Carlo asked in a low voice, clinging to the chair back to keep his feet.

Anxious lines furrowed Dax's brow as the landing thrusters fired and the ship settled onto the hilly terrain. "She's here somewhere," he said, hoping it was true. "Alfred won't be able to resist. If his past behavior is any indication, he'll have hidden his ship near the main battle so he can witness the carnage firsthand, but far enough behind his lines to avoid endangering himself."

Dax snatched his helmet and battle gloves from atop a console and stalked into a curving corridor.

"I'm going with you," Carlo yelled after him, and hurried to catch up, pushing through a knot of battle-armored soldiers waiting for the air lock to open.

Dax stopped and eyed the boy. "Suit up then." He pointed toward a supply locker. "You're not going out there without body armor."

Carlo nodded and ran into the locker.

The air lock hissed and dilated open. Soldiers pounded down the gangway and spread out around the ship. Carlo reappeared at Dax's side, his dark eyes wide and frightened behind the helmet's visor. The Vahnti count gave the boy's metal-clad shoulder a reassuring slap, then descended the gangway into the dark bowels of Alfred's hell.

The night sky and tall Nirvannan grass were alive with sound and frenetic pulses of brilliant light. A thick pall of dust and acrid smoke hung above the darkened landscape, debris churned into the atmosphere by the searing heat of Dunstan's laser cannons. There were shouts in the distance, the clatter of armor, screams of fear and pain lost within the smoke and all-encompassing grass.

Grim-faced, Dax stared into the smoke. A bedraggled line of soldiers from a Vahnti brigade were staggering out of the tall grass, their armor charred and battle-torn, faces glazed

Jan Zimlich

with shock and defeat. Other soldiers stumbled out of the darkness.

Dax cursed beneath his breath. Troops and supplies were pouring from his ships, but he knew it was too little, too late. The northern brigades were in full retreat. Even worse, his communications net was still jammed, and there was no way to get word to the front lines that he had arrived with reinforcements.

"Get those soldiers some med attention; then send couriers out to find the brigade commanders!" he shouted to his officers. "Tell them fresh troops and supplies are being brought up to the front and to hold out as long as they can."

Soldiers raced off into the smoke and grass to stop the pell-mell retreat as Dax slung a rifle over his shoulder and strode toward the towering grass.

"Dax, where are you going?" Carlo called, afraid that he already knew.

He paused a moment to slip on his gloves, his stark features backlit by a flash of greenish light. "To the front lines. The retreat has to be stopped or we don't stand a chance." He turned back to the thick grass and flinched in surprise, squinting through the smoky haze to make out a shadowy figure looming in his path.

For a fraction of time, Dax thought he saw luminous yellow eyes; then the smoke thinned, curling and drifting around the figure's lean body in feathery wisps. A gust of wind touched long strands of snow white hair, curling it about the apparition's stooped frame. Laser light pulsed in the distance, illuminating the Nirvannan's black-painted face and simple clothing. Dax stared at him curiously. The grizzled old man was just standing there, silently watching him, his gnarled fingers clutching a long wooden staff. He seemed oblivious to the fact that he was standing in the middle of a war zone.

Behind him, Dax heard a Vahnti soldier cry out a warning when he noticed the old Nirvannan, and the telltale clicks of weapons being primed and aimed. He lifted a hand to belay his troops. "Hold your fire," he ordered. "This man has done nothing." So far he'd done nothing at all but stare at him with those knowing green eyes.

The Nirvannan's ancient gaze narrowed and stilled, searching the Vahnti count's sharp features. "I have been waiting here in this place for you to return," the old man said calmly. "So long that I had begun to fear that the spirits might be wrong." He flattened his lips and clutched the carved staff tighter. "Doubt is for the aged and nonbelievers. Perhaps my mind is feeling the passage of years."

Dax frowned uncertainly. There was an air of power and serenity about the old man that he found hard to dismiss. "Who are you?"

He lifted his head even higher, his chin jutting up to a defiant angle. "I am Javan, shaman of the Lakotas, spirit-speaker for the seven human tribes of Nirvanna."

The frown cutting across Dax's forehead deepened. Rayna's Javan, the old shaman his troops had been unable to capture? His gaze swept over the tall grass uneasily. "What do you want with me, Javan?"

Laser light flashed across the night sky, bathing the old man's leathery face in a ghostly haze of green. "The evil times foretold in Nirvannan prophecy have come to pass," Javan said in a strong, clear voice. He took a step closer, peering into the Vahnti warlord's face intently. "The heart of the serpent has finally been sundered by the daughter of a shaman. His blood now mingles with ours. . . . The fruit of his seed is now that which binds Nirvannan and Vahnti as one."

Dax stared for long seconds, puzzling over the old man's strange words; then the first faint glimmer of comprehension showed in his eyes. If he was the serpent, then . . . "Rayna?" he said softly.

Javan dipped his head in a slow nod and touched a fist to his frail chest. "The heart of my heart, daughter of my daughter, has fulfilled the ancient prophecy."

"She's your granddaughter?" No wonder Rayna had tried so hard to protect him.

Javan nodded again.

Carlo and a knot of soldiers clustered around them, listening curiously.

Dax stared at Javan with a dubious expression. How could the old man possibly know that Rayna was carrying the "fruit of his seed"? Even he wasn't sure about that. Of course, he'd learned from painful experience not to blithely dismiss the notion of preternatural abilities out-of-hand, especially when it came to Nirvannans. Still, the whole thing didn't make sense. Why had the old man risked arrest by coming to find him? "Other than the obvious, what does this all have to do with me?" He waved a hand toward the laser-lit sky, the steady stream of injured soldiers stumbling out of the surrounding grass. "And why have you come to tell me this tonight, of all nights?"

"Because you are the sword forged by the spirits to save us all. You are the tiller of the sacred garden." Javan closed his eyes a moment, remembering the final passage of the prophecy unknown to any save the spirit-speaker of the Nirvannan tribes, a safeguard practiced for centuries lest the knowledge change the future in some way. "The seeds of our future, our peoples' great destiny, shall ripen and bloom within the shaman's daughter. And once sundered, the serpent with eyes of ice shall become more powerful than before, and return to protect the garden he has sown from the demons who walk the night."

A chill rippled down Dax's spine. Could the old shaman actually know what he was talking about?

Carlo grabbed his cousin's elbow and squeezed. "He's talking about fate, Dax." His dark eyes glittered with excitement. "You and Rayna were destined to be together. I've always felt it."

Javan glanced at the boy curiously, wondering if he was the one the spirits had promised would soon arrive. Possibly, he decided, then lifted his gaze to Nirvanna's blazing sky. "There are many demons here this night, Vahnti count. So many I fear a single sword cannot fell them all." His hypnotic green eyes shifted back to the Vahnti nobleman. "I have come here tonight because of those demons. You and I are brothers in blood now, each of us caretakers of the sacred garden. To save our future, Nirvannans must join their hands to yours and help guide your sword. Only then will your aim be sharp and true."

Dax tried to keep his voice steady. "Are you saying that your people are willing to join us as allies?" Though the Nirvannans were armed only with spears and arrows, Haywood had said they were the best guerrilla fighters he'd ever seen.

"Joined in blood and spirit." His aged eyes drifted over the dark-haired boy again, appraising, studying. The spirit world was strong within him. "In this and many things to come."

Dax heaved a sigh of relief. He reached out and clasped Javan's hand tentatively, the old man's flesh thin and papery beneath his fingers. He had reason to hope now. Javan wouldn't stand by and allow his granddaughter to die. "How many of your tribe will be willing to fight with us?"

Javan lifted the staff over his head and shook it high in the air. Thousands of voices screamed in response, an eerie flood of human sound that thundered across the Nirvannan night. Deep within the shadowy grass, countless torches flamed to life, their numbers swelling with each second that passed. Cinders from the torches danced and spiraled on the chill northern wind. "All of them," Javan said as the war cry faded into an expectant silence.

Dumbfounded, Dax turned in a slow circle, trying to discern how many Nirvannans had been hiding in the towering grass. There were thousands of torches flickering in the darkness, far too many to count. The rustling grass was also thick with the luminous glow of nocturnal eyes, the quick dartings of thousands of animals amid the reedlike stalks. He gaped in disbelief. Had the beasts come to fight as well?

Startled Vahnti soldiers began dropping into defensive positions around the ships, lifting pulse rifles to their shoulders. "Lower your weapons!" the Vahnti warlord shouted. "Our clan will shed no more Nirvannan blood! These people have come to us as allies, and I have accepted them as such . . . animal and human alike!"

Vahnti troopers glanced at the Nirvannans uncertainly, perplexed by the turn of events. A throng of Lakotan warriors edged from the torchlit grass, eyeing their former enemies with an equal amount of trepidation.

"Cast your differences aside and work together!" Dax told the listening crowd. "The past is over and done with." He lifted a hand and pointed to the battlefront, the flashes of green splotched across the horizon. "Somewhere out there, hidden in the darkness, Alfred Dunstan is sitting aboard his warship awaiting news that we have been defeated, word from his army that this world has fallen at his feet.'' His hand fell back to his side, and a sudden glint of pain shadowed his face. "He also holds a prisoner there, a Nirvannan captive who is very precious to me . . . to Javan. We must find that ship . . . for all our sakes.''

Dax was quiet for a moment; then he pulled in a breath and raised his voice, his deep, dulcet tones echoing across the cannon-lit night. "Tonight we must fight for the future of this world, the destinies of both our peoples.'' Dax moved through the press of bodies, extolling, persuading, trying to rally them for the coming battle. Golden-furred wolfens and a host of smaller creatures were slinking through the shadows, gathering in the darkness, silently watching him with glowing animal eyes. "Tonight we fight for Rayna, the woman who will be my countess . . . the mother of the Vahnti heir!''

Lakotans shouted eagerly, and the glazed looks of defeat faded from Vahnti faces, replaced by a steely, battle-hardened air of resolve.

"If we fight together, no Dunstan army can stand in our way!'' Dax shouted. "Break through their lines and find Alfred's ship! If we cut off the snake's head, the body will wither and die!''

Soldiers and Nirvannan warriors roared in approval and charged into the smoke and grass, a yipping, snarling swarm of night creatures leading the way.

The Dunstan field marshal came to stiff attention, his dour features knotting with worried lines. The dull thuds of distant cannon fire sounded closer than before. "My lord,'' he began nervously, "I regret to inform you that sensors have detected a large fleet of Vahnti ships entering the Nirvannan star system.''

Annoyed, Petwitt Dunstan pursed his lips and scowled at the medal-bedecked officer. "So? What are you bothering me about it for? I only stepped outside the ship for a bit of air.'' He flicked at the soot and dust clinging to the hem of his robe. "Save such unpleasantness for my father. It's his war, you know.'' He yawned in the man's face, bored beyond endurance, and walked several paces toward the gangway leading back into his father's warship. ''Besides, we've won the battle already. The arrival of additional Vahnti troops will simply afford us the opportunity to do away with them as well.''

''But my lord, you don't understand. The battle—''

Petwitt wagged a finger to cut him off. ''There are no buts about it, Field Marshal. I've grown quite weary of you soldiers thinking every mindless word that falls from your tongues is worthy of my attention.''

The officer's face reddened, but he said no more. His uneasy gaze shifted back to the darkness, calculating the trajectories of the cannon fire glowing along the horizon. His anxiety turned to outright fear. The front lines were moving, falling back toward the center on both the right and left flanks.

''I shall be in my father's cabin in case of a true emergency,'' Petwitt said in a droll voice. Careful not to drag his hem, he started for the gangway, grimacing in disgust when a small puff of fur darted across his path. ''Filthy beast,'' he muttered, and lifted his robe higher, wishing he were anywhere in the universe other than this dirty little world.

Another furry creature skittered past, squeaking and glaring at him with sullen yellow eyes. A third charged up and snapped at his slipper. Petwitt froze. Dozens of the filthy things were scuttling around him, so many the ground seemed to be moving.

An animal growled in the darkness, the low rumble of something large and feral. Panicked, Petwitt swung his head in the direction of the sound. Other creatures were pouring out of the dense grass, slinking toward him and the ship. Ahead of him, a sentry cried out sharply, staggered for a moment, then collapsed facedown, a thin shaft of wood protruding from his neck.

Petwitt gaped in horror as a screaming horde of black-painted savages suddenly leaped from the grass, all charging directly toward him. A spear buried itself in the dirt near his feet, and a laser bolt streaked past his ear. Lifting the robe to his knees, Petwitt hurtled the dead sentry, shoved the field marshal and several Dunstan soldiers from his path, and careened up the gangway for the safety of the ship.

White-faced with terror, he hammered a switch and sealed the heavy air lock behind him, ignoring the frightened cries of the Dunstan troops left stranded outside. Petwitt took a deep breath to compose himself and dabbed at the sweat on his face with an elegant hand. Fists pounded on the closed air lock as he scurried toward his father's cabin, but he ignored that, too.

A klaxon sounded and alarm lights tinted the passageway bright red as he frantically punched the access code into his father's door lock, praying that Alfred wasn't off on one of his fantasies again.

The doors slid open and Petwitt barreled inside. To his relief, Alfred was standing at an intercom console, minus his headset, shouting and cursing for someone to answer him. Beyond him, the girl lay motionless in the center of the massive bed, neural sensors still attached to her temples.

Alfred glanced up at his son, his features mottled with rage. "Why in the hell are the alarms going off, Petwitt?" The stupid klaxon had gone off just as he was about to pay another visit to his pretty little guest, drink a bottle of wine in celebration of his conquest, and transmit the text of his message to the Vahnti count. "I can't get any of those damn fools on the bridge to answer the intercom!"

"Order the captain to lift off immediately, Father," Petwitt said in a quavering voice. "The ship is being attacked by painted savages and a host of nasty beasts. They were shooting pointed sticks at me, and one of those creatures actually nipped at my slipper."

Alfred laughed incredulously. Leave because of a few beasts and savages? "Are you mad or just a coward, Petwitt? We have the battle well in hand. The Vahntis are on the run, fleeing through the grass like a herd of terrified ground-toads."

"Not anymore, I'm afraid." Petwitt swallowed. "A fleet of Vahnti warships has already entered the star system. They'll be here anytime now."

Alfred's eyes bulged, and his face turned a lethal shade of red. "Why wasn't I told of this?"

Petwitt gazed at him steadily. "I haven't the slightest idea."

Infuriated, Alfred snatched a marble bust of himself from a

table and smashed it against a bulkhead. He pounded the intercom with his fist, but this time there was an answering chirp. "Report!" Alfred shouted.

"We're under attack, my lord!" an officer shouted back. "The ship is surrounded by natives and enemy troops! And there are creatures swarming over the top of the hull!"

Alfred glowered. Where had the Vahnti troops come from? "Well, what are you waiting for, man? Just blow them into cinders and take off! Tell the captain to set us down farther from the battlefront next time."

"But the engines and weapons systems are off-line! We think they've been sabotaged from outside the ship!" An edge of hysteria filled the man's voice. "What do we do, my lord? The field marshal commed the ship a moment ago and claimed he'd been taken prisoner! He said Vahnti troops demand that we surrender ourselves immediately!"

A crackle of static shot through the intercom and the device fell silent. Alfred pounded the switch again to no avail.

A low, vibrating shudder trembled through the deck plating, the sound growing in intensity. Bulkheads shivered violently, and a thunderous explosion rocked the ship. The lights dimmed, then returned to their normal level.

Petwitt's jaw went slack. "What was that?" he whispered, glancing around nervously.

The Dunstan warlord clamped his mouth shut, his eyes darkening ominously. "They've breached the hull." No savages or beasts had done that. The explosion had been caused by a sonic charge—a device favored by Vahnti himself as a prelude to boarding a ship. And only he could have stopped his troops from retreating and rallied them for a counterattack. "Vahnti's here," Alfred said in a hiss, cold fury turning his face bloodred. "That bastard is here . . . I can feel him."

Petwitt's stomach clenched, and his bowels turned watery. "On Nirvanna?" The words came out in a high-pitched squeak. "But you haven't sent him the message yet. How could he be here already?"

"Does it matter?" Alfred roared. Vahnti could have discovered his plans in any number of ways, most likely by interrogating a captured spy. He slammed his fist against the dead console. He'd been so very careful, planned it all so well, considered every variable except finally ordering the termination of his treacherous son.

The Dunstan warlord's mouth flattened, almost disappearing inside the folds of his cheeks. He hadn't counted on Marcus's betraying him again. "I've lost," he whispered bitterly. "Lost everything." Vahnti wouldn't rest until the Dunstan armies and war fleets were completely destroyed, his clan in economic shambles. Then the outraged count would haul him before the High Council, force him to resign as warlord, and impose ruinous sanctions in retaliation for the sneak attack. And not a soul would try to stop him. His weak-willed allies would melt into the shadows when they heard the news.

The glum expression brewing on his father's face made Petwitt's chest constrict with fear. For a moment he thought he might faint. If Vahnti was really here . . . His frightened gaze darted back and forth, finally settling on the motionless figure in the bed. "We still have the girl," he said desperately. "Maybe we can negotiate . . . trade her for generous terms of surrender."

Alfred's gaze swung around, and his eyes narrowed on the girl. "Yes," he said slowly. Vahnti would pay anything, do anything to protect his precious heir. Perhaps the girl as well. His actions tonight had proved that beyond a doubt. "Maybe we can negotiate." A tiny smile crept over Alfred's face. He still had one final hand to play. "Go out there and surrender yourself, Petwitt. Open up a dialogue with the bastard. Tell him I'm ready to barter for favorable terms." *Keep him occupied*, he added silently.

Petwitt's mouth sagged open. Surrender himself? Like the proverbial lamb? "You can't be serious!"

"It's your duty, you sniveling coward!" Alfred reached inside a storage drawer and extracted a dagger, the same blade he'd used to rid the universe of his bitchy first wife. There was a certain symmetry in using it on her son. He glided toward his firstborn, his movements quick and menacing. "Do it or there'll be nothing left for you to inherit." His features stilled, and his voice turned malevolent. "Do it or there won't be enough left of you to bother burying." The curved blade gleamed in the artificial light.

Petwitt's heart gave an erratic little jump. What an insidious choice. Face Vahnti's wrath, or his father's. He opted for neither. "Very well. If you insist, Father." He released the nervous breath he'd been holding. There was an escape hatch two levels down, hidden beneath the deck plating in the oxygen plant. If he could make it there quickly enough, slip through the hatch, and steal a Vahnti uniform, he might have a chance. "I'll try to speak with Vahnti." Petwitt eased toward the doors, careful to keep the knife and his father in view at all times. "I'll do it for us . . . for the clan."

Alfred's fingers tightened around the hilt. "Don't disappoint me."

The doors sealed behind Petwitt with a pneumatic snick. Alfred stared at the knife, the locked doors, then smiled and glided to the bed. "Your lover's outside," he whispered to Rayna, easing his bulk onto the bed beside her. "Did you know that, Rayna?" Alfred stroked her silky hair, running it through his stubby fingers. "Of course you didn't. I've talked to you so much in the past week that sometimes I forget your mind is someplace else." He gazed at her heart-shaped face, the slightly parted lips, the way her long lashes feathered against her cheeks. Such an enticing little thing. No wonder Vahnti seemed so enamored of her.

"Sorry things have to end this way, my dear." Alfred picked up his headset. "But you see, your lover has left me little choice. You're my designated pawn, Rayna. And I can't stand by and let him win the endgame without a final move, not when I still have a piece in play." He sighed contentedly and put the headset on. "It's poetic justice in a way. Vahnti managed to wriggle out of my trap, so I'm going to retaliate by killing the bait. Tit for tat. We'll both be losers."

He adjusted his grip on the dagger. "But first we're going to have a bit of fun." He took a long, shuddering breath. "I'm going to take you virtually—and in reality—all at the same time, and then I'm going to kill you the same way." Anticipation flashed in the depths of his eyes. "Doesn't that sound exciting? It does to me. In fact, I don't know why I haven't thought of it before.''

He positioned the knife over her chest, the hooked tip of the blade barely grazing the bodice of her robe. ''Ready or not, here I come.'' Chuckling, Alfred switched on the headset, and the world reformed around him. He was back on his private beach, the wind curling around him, the stars and moons wheeling overhead.

Enjoying the view, Alfred set off down the beach, following her footprints in the artificial sand. It took him only a minute or so to find her. She was sitting among the trees, her back resting against a spindly trunk as she stared absently at the umber sea. The hand holding his virtual knife stole behind his back. ''Miss me, Rayna?''

Rayna jerked her gaze toward the familiar voice and bolted to her feet. ''You again!'' He had returned several times to torment her, saying vile, hateful things about Dax and their unborn child. But so far he hadn't tried to touch her again. She edged around the tree, painfully aware that escape was out of the question. No matter how many times or how far she'd run down the strange beach, she always seemed to end up in the exact same spot. ''What do you want this time, you stinking dung worm?''

''How touching.'' Alfred smiled and took a step closer. ''You did miss me.''

''I want out of this hideous place,'' Rayna demanded, edging back a bit farther. She didn't like the sly look on his face or his contemptuous smile. It reminded her of Caccia.

''Sorry,'' Alfred said smoothly, ''but I think I like you better in here.''

Rayna glanced at the odd-colored sea, the garish, sickly trees. What was this place, and why did she feel that nothing around her was actually real? Even time seemed suspended, compressed into a single moment and place for all eternity. She wasn't even sure how long she'd been here. ''Where is *here?*'' she shouted at him.

''Inside my world, my thoughts.'' Alfred gripped the knife tighter. ''You're just an actor trapped inside the theater of my mind, doomed to repeat the same scene over and over again until you get it right.'' He smiled again and touched his forehead.

Limbs slithered down the scraggly trunk, winding around her arms and shoulders. Rayna cried out in surprise and tried to jerk away, but the snakelike appendages had a death grip on her arms. Another crawled around her neck, binding her head against the tree trunk. She pushed and twisted with all her might, but the more she flailed, the tighter they wrapped around her.

Alfred laughed and pulled the blade from behind his back. He waved it back and forth in front of her face, testing the weight, the feel of the hilt in his hand. "My world, my thoughts," he said in a silky voice. "I control everything here."

Rayna gasped for breath as the limb dug into her neck, squeezing her airway shut. A wave of fear swept through her eyes. One way or another he planned to kill her, either with the knife or by strangling her to death.

"I'm afraid this is your final scene, my dear, so try a bit harder to get it right this time." He moved closer and caressed the limb knotted around her neck, his fingers inching down the moist length of wood to the pulse pounding frantically at the base of her throat. "I want it to be enjoyable—for both of us." A rush of desire roughened his voice. "And when I've had my fill, I'm going to kill you, very slowly, then Vahnti's spawn. A parting gift for your loving count."

Rayna stiffened and pushed her head against the tree trunk, freeing her neck a tiny fraction. Enough to draw a feeble breath, enough that she could speak. "Don't touch me," she said in a raspy whisper. "I told you what I would do."

He chuckled and touched her cheek with the tip of a finger. "There. I did it. What are you going to do to me?"

Her eyes crackled with green fire. "Kill you . . .''

Alfred shivered in mock terror, then touched her again, the blunt edge of the knife sliding along the line of her jaw. "Oh, horrors, I did it again."

Rayna's face turned cold and distant, shuttered against any trace of human feeling save hatred and icy contempt. "I warned you," she said furiously. Her lips moving in a soundless chant, she closed her eyes and concentrated, willing her mind to focus, to gather and mold the thin wisps of energy flowing around her and pull them into herself. She could feel the familiar currents of energy threading around her, the wisps building to a crescendo, but there was something unnatural about them. Artificial. As if they were emanating from a well-spring of power she had never encountered before. A startled cry slipped from her throat as a tidal wave of energy suddenly swept through her body, so fierce and powerful that she screamed aloud.

Alfred stumbled backward, his mouth sliding open in disbelief. Eyes that had been human green a split second before had metamorphosed to a gleaming, predatory yellow. Beyond her, the sky began to shimmer and move in an unprogrammed change. His illusory moons dimmed, winked out of existence, then reappeared, far larger than their customary size. He gaped at his fantasy world in horror. Jagged fingers of lightning were crackling across the counterfeit night. Stars began raining downward, plunging into the virtual sea, only to rise once more and careen through the darkness like a covey of fiery birds.

"This is not possible!" Alfred screamed, ducking as a star wheeled past his head. The limbs shackling the girl to the base of the tree cracked, split, then fell away.

Terror spiraled down his spine. He groped at his forehead desperately, fingers clawing at his face in search of the off switch, but it was no longer there. "No . . ." he whimpered, eyes wide and frantic as she moved toward him. Alfred wheeled around and fled, running toward the water with all the speed he could muster. There were sounds close behind him, almost on his heels: huffy animal pants, the quick padding of paws in the muddy sand. The virtual knife slid from bloodless fingers as he clawed at his forehead again, searching for the escape switch. The sounds were closer now. Something grabbed the back of his robe, spinning him in a half circle. Alfred screamed.

"Blow them!" Dax shouted, and laid down covering fire as two of his soldiers placed a charge against the doors to

Alfred's cabin. There was a cry of pain around a juncture in the passageway, the boneless thud of a body colliding with the metal deck. Dax's mouth compressed. The ship was theirs now except for this level, the only holdouts Alfred's personal bodyguards.

The bulkheads trembled, and a dense fog of smoke boiled down the corridor as the doors blew inward. Dax jumped to his feet and zigzagged through the haze, crouching low as he eased through the charred hole that had once been a set of armored doors.

A thick pall of gray smoke hung over the Dunstan warlord's private lair, narrowing Dax's view to a few feet in any direction. Dax tightened his grip on the hand laser and felt his way toward the center of the cabin. "Rayna?" he called softly. A rush of fear climbed up his throat. She had to be here.

A squad of Vahnti soldiers moved into the cabin behind him, Carlo following close behind them. Dax blinked to clear his vision and took another step, breathing a curse as the toe of his boot bumped something soft and mushy and wet. He glanced downward and drew in a startled breath.

Carlo crept up beside him, his eyes widening when he spotted the corpse sprawled at Dax's feet. Alfred Dunstan was splayed on his back in a pool of blood, his corpulent face frozen in a grimace of terror, a scorched headset of some kind clutched in an outstretched hand. "It's Alfred," Carlo whispered, paling at the sight. The Dunstan warlord's left arm was flung off to the side, as if death had claimed him as he tried to claw toward a silver dagger on the floor nearby, only inches from his stiffening fingers.

A muscle spasmed along Dax's jaw. "What's left of him." Alfred's robe and body were ripped and bloodied, as if he'd been mauled by some . . . Comprehension flared in his eyes. "Rayna?" he called more loudly. "Where are you?"

He dropped the laser and stumbled deeper into the cabin, searching frantically. A huge bed loomed in front of him, a pale, motionless figure lying at its center. "Oh, gods . . ." His chest constricted, and his heart gave a painful thud of fear. She was so pale, so utterly still.

His hand shook as he reached out to touch her, fingertips

303

gently grazing the line of her cheek, then edging downward, searching along the hollow of her throat. A tremor passed through his body. Her pulse was faint and thready, but she was alive.

Dax sighed raggedly and smoothed a tangle of curls from her brow, his eyes darkening when he saw the neural stimulators attached to her temples. Bile climbed his throat as he examined the device more closely. It was a virtual headset, one rigged to play continuously, repeating the same sequence over and over again. He clenched his teeth and ripped the pads from her temples.

Rayna moaned softly when the pads were removed, a small, anguished whimper that made Dax wish Alfred were still alive, just so he could die again. He stared into her face worriedly. What sort of twisted game had Alfred subjected her to?

Carlo touched his elbow. "A med team is on the way, Dax." His eyes stilled on the neural stimulators Dax had tossed onto the bed. "What happened to her?"

"I'm not sure." His hands bunched into fists. He'd heard rumors that Alfred was obsessed with virtual reality, but never dreamed he was so depraved that he'd force anyone to take part in his fantasies. "They were both wearing headsets. I think he had her mind trapped inside some sort of virtual prison." He took several deep breaths, fighting to control his rage. What had Alfred done to her in there? "The filthy bastard got what he deserved," Dax said hoarsely. "I just wish I could have killed him myself."

Carlo frowned and glanced at Dunstan's body curiously. Vahnti soldiers had clustered around the mangled corpse, whispering speculatively among themselves. Who—or what—had killed Alfred Dunstan? The doors had been sealed with a security lock, and the only other person in the cabin was obviously unconscious. "I don't understand how he died in the first place," Carlo said, puzzled by the wounds on Alfred's body. "It almost looks like he was mauled by an animal."

Dax threw his cousin a piercing look but didn't respond. The Dominion would be rife with rumors and speculation about Alfred's strange demise and Rayna's involvement for years to come, but beyond himself, no one would ever discover the real truth—whatever that truth actually was. He'd make sure of it.

"He must have fallen on his knife," Dax said finally. His stony gaze swept around the room, daring anyone to challenge his pronouncement.

Carlo lifted a brow, glanced at Rayna's slack features suspiciously, then looked at his cousin again. "Yes, that must have been how it happened," he said slowly. "Alfred stumbled and fell on his knife." Quite a few times, he added to himself.

Dax released the tense breath he'd been holding and turned back to Rayna. He stroked her silky hair and watched her still face carefully, waiting for a twitch of movement, a sign that she might be regaining consciousness. But so far there was nothing. Had her mind been damaged by what Alfred had done? He shook off the thought, refusing to think along those lines.

"Wake up, Rayna," he whispered against her hair. "You have to come back to me. Whatever Alfred did, it's over now. You have to fight your way back to reality." He lifted her limp hand to his lips and pressed a kiss against her cool flesh. "Please . . . I can't bear the thought of losing you again." His voice broke, and he tried to swallow the lump of terror clotting his throat. What if she never awakened? What if Alfred *had* injured her mind in some way? He pulled her still form into his arms and laid his head atop her chest, sighing in relief when he felt the ragged rise and fall of her lungs against his soot-stained cheek. "I love you, Rayna Syn," he murmured in a voice thick with emotion. "I just never knew how much until I lost you."

A tiny frown passed across Rayna's forehead, a ripple of movement barely perceptible to the naked eye. The nightmare had begun to fade, drifting and curling along the edges of her mind like a half-remembered dream. If she concentrated very hard, she could hear Dax's urgent whispering, almost smell the clean, leathery scent that seemed to shadow him wherever he went. He loved her . . . needed her back . . . wanted a life with her as much as she did with him. Her brows pulled downward a fraction of an inch. Was it real or imagination?

His lips slid along the back of her hand, caressing, gently exploring her skin with feathery kisses. She remembered the feel, the warm touch of his flesh against her own. A contented smile touched the corners of her mouth. *Real, then.* "Love you . . ." she whispered to him. "Always will."

Dax's heart lurched, and his gaze stilled on her exotic face. He made a strangled sound, a small sob of relief mingled with joy. Her gold-flecked eyes were wide and fever-bright, boring into him with preternatural intensity. He saw the truth in those guileless eyes. She loved him, heart and soul. A tremor ran through his body as he pulled her to his chest, wrapping her inside the circle of his arms. He'd never let go this time. "I thought I'd lost you."

"Not possible," she said softly against him. He'd found her again, and always would, no matter how far or fast she tried to run from him. "I belong to you, remember?" Her fingers threaded through his hair, twining gently about the ebony strands. "And I quit running a long time ago."

Chapter Twenty-three

The beat of the drums thundered across the valley floor, the hollow sound swelling in the morning air like the dull throb of Dunstan laser cannons. A flock of squealing children darted past the drummers and raced toward a row of thatched huts, faces wreathed in excited smiles as they barreled through a knot of Vahnti soldiers waiting for the ceremony to begin. The mood in the village was festive, joyous, a happy contagion that had spread to Vahnti and Lakotan alike.

Long lines of villagers weaved around dozens of ceremonial fires, their bodies shifting and swaying in perfect sync with the haunting rhythm of the drums. On a dare from his comrades, a Vahnti soldier stripped off his armor and joined in, his writhings clumsy and awkward compared to the graceful Lakotans.

Shaking his head in silent wonder, Dax watched the dancers for a minute, then resumed his restless pacing, prowling back and forth in front of the wooden dais. How much longer would he have to wait? It felt like an eternity already. In the three days since he'd carried Rayna from Alfred's ship he had been permitted to see her only once. She was in seclusion, Javan had said, undergoing a Lakotan ritual to prepare herself. Three long, lonely days he'd spent in grueling negotiations with the wily Javan, or sitting in a steamy hut while his body was leached of moisture, all in preparation for this single moment in time.

But it was over now. He patted a pocket in his jacket, just to be sure the parchment was still safely tucked away. The negotiations had concluded near dawn, when Javan had finally agreed to the terms of the treaty and accepted the document as the customary offering required under Nirvannan law. The crafty old shaman was a gifted negotiator, winning major concessions that Dax had never dreamed he would make to anyone. All mining activities on the planet's surface were permanently forbidden, and the Nirvannans who'd been relocated would be returned to the plains within the month, with ample compensation for the inconvenience they'd suffered. The treaty also insured Vahnti-Nirvannan cooperation for decades to come. In a matter of weeks, the colonists were set to begin seeding the entire planet with the precious grass, as well as to aid Vahnti agriculturalists in the harvest itself. In future years, ten million square miles of grass would be harvested annually, but under strict ecological guidelines compiled by the Nirvannans to safeguard the planet's ecosystem. And though Nirvanna would always remain a Vahnti holding, the colonists had been granted the permanent right of self-rule, a concession Dax hoped didn't turn into a trend on his other worlds.

It had been a hard-fought battle of wills and words, but in the end Javan had gotten everything he wanted. The Vahnti count blew out an amused breath. But then, so had he.

He smoothed the front of his uniform nervously, adjusted

307

the dark peaked cap he wore only for state occasions, and paced some more, peering every now and again at his chronometer to check the time. Where was she? The ceremony was set to begin in half an hour, but Rayna had yet to make an appearance.

"I guess it's true," a gravelly voice said.

Dax glanced up and grinned in relief. He'd begun to think that Haywood wouldn't make it back in time from his mysterious errand. "What's true?"

Haywood grinned back. "That all bridegrooms are nervous on their wedding day."

He snorted and tugged at his cap again. "This one certainly is." Taking a deep breath to calm himself, he cast a worried glance at Javan's small hut. Still no sign of activity. "Especially since my bride has yet to arrive. No one has even seen her in two days."

"Quit worrying. She'll be here." Haywood gazed at his friend for long seconds, a pensive smile creasing his rugged face. "It was meant to be, Dax," he said more quietly. "Even I can see that now."

Dax clasped Haywood's hand and gave it a fierce squeeze. "Thanks, old friend. I'm glad you made it back for the ceremony." A curious frown swept across his sharp-planed features. "That reminds me, what was this mysterious errand you had to go on so suddenly?"

Haywood gave him an inscrutable smile. "I had to pick up my wedding present." He motioned to a squad of security guards waiting nearby. "They're delivering it now."

The squad moved toward the dais, the poorly dressed guard in the forefront propelled into motion by a kick in the rear from Leftenant Robichau.

Dax lifted a jet brow, the cant rising higher when he recognized the target of Robichau's ire. He flashed Haywood a startled look, then turned back to the man clad in the black-and-gold garb of a Vahnti soldier. "Well, isn't this a pleasant surprise." An ice-cold grin lit the Vahnti count's face. "You do seem to turn up in the oddest places, Petwitt." His gaze flicked over Petwitt's ill-fitting disguise. "And in the most unusual attire." He was dirt-streaked and bedraggled, flecks of dust and grass seed clinging to his unkempt beard, as if he'd been on the run for several sleepless days.

"We caught him a few hours ago," Haywood explained. "He was skulking around a Vahnti cargo ship about twenty miles south of here. Probably planned to sneak aboard and try to make his way back to Dunstan space."

Dax's chilly grin froze in place. "What do you have to say for yourself, Petwitt?"

Petwitt Dunstan sniffed and straightened. "I demand access to legal counsel, as well as the removal of these distasteful things." He lifted his hands a fraction, straining against the repulsor cuffs. "I also demand an immediate apology for the cavalier treatment I've received at the hands of your soldiers." His bearded chin rose to a haughty angle. "I am the heir to Clan Dunstan, after all."

"Not anymore." Dax's grin faded, and his pale eyes turned cold and flint-hard. "Your brother Marcus has already been installed as your clan's new warlord. He assumed the title yesterday."

A crimson flush crawled up Petwitt's cheeks. "Marcus!" he sputtered. "You can't do that! You have no right!"

"I'm afraid I do. Archduke Davies granted me full legal authority to mete out your clan's punishment, and since you were a coconspirator in your father's scheme, I decided that your title would be the first thing to go. Besides, Marcus will make a far better warlord than anyone else in your family." Dax lifted one shoulder in a half shrug. Marcus might be a spy, but in the end he had given information that helped save Rayna's life, which proved that he might not be cut completely from the same treacherous cloth as his siblings.

Petwitt glared at him sullenly.

"As for yourself," Dax went on, "I've decided to grant you your fondest wish." He smiled thinly. "You'll be a married man within the week, Petwitt. Then you and your precocious bride can go anywhere you want in the universe, as long as it's outside Vahnti borders. Flavian Modalbeau has agreed to provide the two of you with a generous stipend—with a bit of prodding, of course. She'll even allow you and Caccia to live on one of her worlds if you want." His eyes glittered dangerously, and the threat of violence clung to his low voice. "Just remember, if you so much as harm a hair on Caccia's head, you'll have to contend with me."

Petwitt's mouth fell. "You're going to allow me to marry her?" he said in astonishment.

"Yes, strangely enough." Dax grimaced. They truly would devour their young. "I think that will be punishment enough—for both of you."

Petwitt's mind raced, churning over the possibilities. Sanctuary, a generous stipend . . . and Caccia. He bit back a gleeful little smile. The future appeared far brighter than it had a few minutes ago.

At a nod from Dax, the security guards trundled their prisoner away.

Haywood frowned dubiously. "I'm not so sure that was a good idea, Dax."

He sighed and shrugged. "Neither am I." With Caccia at his side, there was no telling what sort of webs Petwitt would begin to weave. "We'll just have to keep a sharp eye on them."

The beat of the drums stopped abruptly, and Dax threw an expectant glance in the direction of Javan's hut. Rayna's aged grandfather was walking toward the dais, an attentive Carlo at his elbow. Dax's brows disappeared beneath the visor of his cap. His young cousin was shirtless, and his slender torso had been painted with bands of black similar to the ones he'd seen on Rayna the night he'd found her in the grass.

"Carlo?" Dax said curiously, eyeing the beads and feathers tied in his dark hair. He gestured to the boy's attire, or lack of it. "What's this all about?"

Carlo grinned happily. "I've decided to stay on Nirvanna, Dax." His gaze angled toward the ancient shaman. "Javan has offered to be my teacher. He's going to instruct me in the Nirvannan way of life." His smile broadened. "I'm to be his new apprentice."

Dax nodded slowly. The boy looked happier than he had in years. "If that's what you want."

"More than anything."

"No harm will come to him," Javan reassured Dax quietly.

"The Inner World is very strong within him, but his mind lacks training and discipline. I shall teach him those things . . . and more."

Haywood nudged Dax's arm. "Don't worry, Dax. I'll be on Nirvanna for a while longer myself. There's still a thousand or so Dunstan troops that are unaccounted for. Someone has to round them up out of the grass, and then I'll stay on to supervise the harvest." His gaze drifted beyond Dax, to the dark-haired Lakotan woman waiting for him nearby. They had met and shared a meal two nights before, an event that had led to a few blissful hours of passion beneath a mound of snowbear hides. Haywood heaved a contented sigh. The fierce-eyed Dovina was tall and powerfully built, her formidable body rippling with well-used muscles. A warrior through and through. "I'll be here another few months . . . at least."

Dax followed the direction of Haywood's heated gaze and smiled knowingly. "I see why." Everyone's future was set but his. He cleared his throat anxiously and shifted from foot to foot. "Now that all that's settled, would someone please tell me where I can find Rayna?"

Javan lifted a gnarled finger and pointed toward the endless sea of golden grass. "Just follow your heart." A slow, cryptic smile touched the edges of his mouth. "You'll find her."

The towering grass rippled and sighed in the morning breeze, the gentle movements like the slow rhythm of quiet breathing. Rayna stood on the crest of a hill and stretched her arms wide, allowing Nirvanna's whispery voice to curl around her, a soft wave of sound that told her all was right and well with her beloved world.

"Good-bye," she whispered back. A sudden gust of wind breathed through her hair, whipping the silky strands around her upturned face. She savored the beauty of the moment, the feel of her surroundings, memorizing the sights and smells of her past in exquisite detail. Though she would often return to Nirvanna in the coming years, her destiny lay on another world, in the arms of the man who had claimed her that fateful night so long ago.

The wolfens sitting beside her howled suddenly, and the gi

wound itself tighter around her neck, as if the animals knew she was leaving soon and already mourned her loss. "Don't worry," she told the creatures. "I'll be back to see you soon. I promise." She stroked the gi absently and scratched the wolfens' upright ears.

"Rayna?" Dax pushed his way through the dense grass and climbed the crest of the hill, nonplussed that he'd actually been able to find her so easily. *Just follow your heart,* Javan had said, and that was exactly what he had done. He glanced at the watching wolfens and the tiny gi perched on her shoulder, glad that he had decided to have the creatures brought home to Nirvanna. They belonged on this world. "What have you been doing out here?" The gi seemed to glare at him for a moment, then leaped from her shoulder and scurried into the swaying grass. "We're supposed to be getting married this morning."

"I was just saying good-bye." She smiled slowly and curled her arms around his neck. "To the animals . . . and Nirvanna."

Dax inhaled sharply, a sudden rush of desire smoldering in his eyes. Her copper hair was blowing around her slender frame, coiling about her face with each breath of wind. "You won't be gone forever," he said in a husky voice.

"I know, but we won't be able to come back as often as we wish."

He frowned curiously. "Why not?"

"You and I are going to be very busy in the future."

"Busy?" Running an empire that spanned dozens of worlds was no mean feat. His life had always moved at a frenetic pace. "In what way?"

Rayna smiled and pulled his hand downward, pressing his palm against her stomach. "With our son, first of all."

"Oh?" He grinned and cupped her abdomen protectively. "Are you sure about that? The child could be a daughter just as easily."

She shook her head vehemently. "The first four will be sons. Our daughters won't arrive for some years to come." His startled expression caused the corners of her mouth to tilt mischievously. "Strong, spirited children with destinies of their own. One will even rule the Dominion someday. Another will be born with the ability to shift, and you know what sort of havoc that will cause." She crushed his hand tight against her and sighed. "You and I are going to lead very busy lives, Dax Vahnti."

"I see." He wound his arms around her hips, a glint of amusement lighting his cerulean eyes. "And just how many children are we talking about?"

"Seven in all," Rayna said matter-of-factly.

Dax arched a single brow. She sounded so calm, so utterly certain. Still . . . "And just how would you know all that?"

Their eyes locked in a timeless embrace, one that spanned the future, and swept away the past.

Her mouth curved in an enigmatic smile. "Javan told me so."

Janice Tarantino

AUTHOR OF *THE CYRSTAL PROPHECY*

Zenobia—a secret metropolis nestled safely in the fertile crescent of the western desert of Glendarra— lay like its ruler's only daughter Chrysana, untouched by foreign hands.

One thrust is all it would take....

Torn between conscience and craving, duty and desire, peace-loving Chrysana d'Morne hardens herself to plunge her blade into the heart of Drew Richards—the sensual earthman her dreams warned will destroy her father's city. Haunted yet aroused by visions of the future, and by the allure of Drew's exotic eyes, the ravishing Seer struggles to choose between her homeland and her heart. For one stroke can mean release—from the mounting threat of Drew's enigmatic presence and the mysterious seduction he promises. But one caress could mean ecstasy—and a lifetime of love beyond the stars.

__52145-8 $4.99 US/$5.99 CAN

Dorchester Publishing Co., Inc.
P.O. Box 6640
Wayne, PA 19087-8640

Please add $1.75 for shipping and handling for the first book and $.50 for each book thereafter. NY, NYC, and PA residents, please add appropriate sales tax. No cash, stamps, or C.O.D.s. All orders shipped within 6 weeks via postal service book rate. Canadian orders require $2.00 extra postage and must be paid in U.S. dollars through a U.S. banking facility.

Name_____
Address_____
City_____ State_____ Zip_____
I have enclosed $_____ in payment for the checked book(s).
Payment <u>must</u> accompany all orders. ❏ Please send a free catalog.

Futuristic Romance

Star-Crossed

Saranne Dawson

Bestselling Author Of *Crystal Enchantment*

Rowena is a master artisan, a weaver of enchanted tapestries that whisper of past glories. Yet not even magic can help her foresee that she will be sent to assassinate an enemy leader. Her duty is clear—until the seductive beauty falls under the spell of the man she must kill.

His reputation says that he is a warmongering barbarian. But Zachary MacTavesh prefers conquering damsels' hearts over pillaging fallen cities. One look at Rowena tells him to gird his loins and prepare for the battle of his life. And if he has his way, his stunningly passionate rival will reign victorious as the mistress of his heart.

_51982-8 $4.99 US/$5.99 CAN

Futuristic Romance

Love in another time, another place.

Don't miss these tantalizing futuristic romances set on faraway worlds where passion is the lifeblood of every man and woman.

Warrior Moon by Marilyn Jordan. Dedicated to upholding the ancient ways of her race, Phada is loath to mix with the men of her world—but the young Keeper can't understand her burning attraction for virile and courageous Sarak. On a perilous quest to save her people from utter destruction, Phada must trust her very life to Sarak. And if she isn't careful, she'll find love, devotion, and ecstasy without end beneath a warrior moon.

_52083-4 $5.50 US/$7.50 CAN

Keeper Of The Rings by Nancy Cane. With a commanding presence and an impressive temper, Taurin is the obvious choice to be Leena's protector on her quest for a stolen sacred artifact. Curious about his mysterious background, and increasingly tempted by his tantalizing touch, Leena can only pray that their dangerous journey will be a success. If not, explosive secrets will be revealed and a passion unleashed that will forever change their world.

_52077-X $5.50 US/$7.50 CAN

Dorchester Publishing Co., Inc.
P.O. Box 6640
Wayne, PA 19087-8640

Please add $1.75 for shipping and handling for the first book and $.50 for each book thereafter. NY, NYC, and PA residents, please add appropriate sales tax. No cash, stamps, or C.O.D.s. All orders shipped within 6 weeks via postal service book rate. Canadian orders require $2.00 extra postage and must be paid in U.S. dollars through a U.S. banking facility.

Name_____
Address_____
City_____State_____Zip_____
I have enclosed $_____ in payment for the checked book(s).
Payment <u>must</u> accompany all orders. ❑ Please send a free catalog.

ALL'S FAIR

ANNE AVERY

For five long years, Rhys Fairdane has roamed the universe, trying to forget Calista York, who seared his soul with white-hot longing, then cast him into space. Yet by a twist of fate, he and Calista are both named trade representatives of the planet Karta. It will take all his strength to resist her voluptuous curves, all his cunning to subdue her feminine wiles. But if in war, as in love, all truly is fair, Calista has concealed weapons that will bring Rhys to his knees before the battle has even begun.

___52257-8 $5.50 US/$6.50 CAN